# Colin Dexter

**Death is Now My Neighbour**
'Dexter . . . has created a giant among fictional
detectives and has never short-changed his readers.'
*The Times*

**The Daughters of Cain**
'This is Colin Dexter at his most excitingly devious.'
*Daily Telegraph*

**The Way Through the Woods**
'Morse and his faithful Watson, Sergeant Lewis,
in supreme form . . . Hallelujah.'
*Observer*

**The Jewel That Was Ours**
'Traditional crime writing at its best; the kind
of book without which no armchair is complete.'
*Sunday Times*

**The Wench is Dead**
'Dextrously ingenious.'
*Guardian*

**The Secret of Annexe 3**
'A plot of classical cunning and intricacy.'
*Times Literary Supplement*

**The Riddle of the Third Mile**
'Runs the gamut of brain-racking unputdownability.'
*Observer*

**The Dead of Jericho**
'The writing is highly intelligent, the atmosphere
melancholy, the effect haunting.'
*Daily Telegraph*

**Service of All the Dead**
'A brilliantly plotted detective story.'
*Evening Standard*

**The Silent World of Nicholas Quinn**
'Morse's superman status is reinforced by an
ending which no ordinary mortal could have
possibly unravelled.'
*Financial Times*

**Last Seen Wearing**
'Brilliant characterisation in original whodunnit.'
*Sunday Telegraph*

**Last Bus to Woodstock**
'Let those who lament the decline of the English
detective story reach for Colin Dexter.'
*Guardian*

# THE DAUGHTERS OF CAIN

Colin Dexter graduated from Cambridge University in 1953 and has lived in Oxford since 1966. His first novel, *Last Bus to Woodstock*, was published in 1975. There are now thirteen novels in the series, of which *The Remorseful Day* is, sadly, the last.

Colin Dexter has won many awards for his novels, including the CWA Silver Dagger twice, and the CWA Gold Dagger for *The Wench is Dead* and *The Way Through the Woods*. In 1997 he was presented with the CWA Diamond Dagger for outstanding services to crime literature, and in 2000 was awarded the OBE in the Queen's Birthday Honours List.

The Inspector Morse novels have, of course, been adapted for the small screen with huge success by Carlton/Central Television, starring John Thaw and Kevin Whately.

*The Inspector Morse Novels*

LAST BUS TO WOODSTOCK
LAST SEEN WEARING
THE SILENT WORLD OF NICHOLAS QUINN
SERVICE OF ALL THE DEAD
THE DEAD OF JERICHO
THE RIDDLE OF THE THIRD MILE
THE SECRET OF ANNEXE 3
THE WENCH IS DEAD
THE JEWEL THAT WAS OURS
THE WAY THROUGH THE WOODS
THE DAUGHTERS OF CAIN
DEATH IS NOW MY NEIGHBOUR
THE REMORSEFUL DAY

*Also available in Pan Books*

MORSE'S GREATEST MYSTERY AND OTHER STORIES
THE FIRST INSPECTOR MORSE OMNIBUS
THE SECOND INSPECTOR MORSE OMNIBUS
THE THIRD INSPECTOR MORSE OMNIBUS
THE FOURTH INSPECTOR MORSE OMNIBUS

COLIN DEXTER

# THE DAUGHTERS OF CAIN

PAN BOOKS

First published 1994 by Macmillan

First published in paperback 1995 by Pan Books

This edition published 2011 by Pan Books
an imprint of Pan Macmillan, a division of Macmillan Publishers Limited
Pan Macmillan, 20 New Wharf Road, London N1 9RR
Basingstoke and Oxford
Associated companies throughout the world
www.panmacmillan.com

ISBN 978-0-330-47965-3

1 3 5 7 9 8 6 4 2

A CIP catalogue record for this book is available from
the British Library.

Typeset by SetSystems Ltd, Saffron Walden, Essex
Printed and bound by CPI Group (UK) Ltd, Croydon, CR0 4YY

For the staff of the Pitt Rivers Museum,
Oxford, with my gratitude to them for
their patient help.

# ACKNOWLEDGEMENTS

The author and publishers wish to thank the following who have kindly given permission for use of copyright materials:

Extract from *A Cornishman at Oxford* © A. L. Rowse;

Extract from *The Lesson* by Roger McGough, reprinted by permission of Peters Fraser & Dunlop Group Ltd;

Extracts by Cyril Connolly reproduced by kind permission of the Estate of Cyril Connolly c/o Rogers, Coleridge & White Ltd, 20 Powis Mews, London W11 1JN, © 1944 Cyril Connolly;

Extract from *The Observer* © by Oliver Sacks, 9 January 1994;

Faber & Faber Ltd for the extract from *New Year Letter* by W. H. Auden;

Extract from *Oxford* by Jan Morris, published by permission of Oxford University Press;

Extract from *Back to Methuselah* granted by The Society of Authors on behalf of the Bernard Shaw Estate;

Extract from *The Pitt Rivers Museum, A Souvenir Guide to the Collections* © Pitt Rivers Museum 1993;

Extract from *The Pitt Rivers Museum* taken from *The Memory of War and Children in Exile: Poems 1968–1983*, James Fenton, published by Penguin © 1982;

Kate Champkin for the extracts from *The Sleeping Life of Aspern Williams* by Peter Champkin;

N. F. Simpson for the extract from *One-Way Pendulum*;

Extract from *Berlioz, Romantic and Classic* by Ernest Newman published by Dover Publications;

Extract from *The Times* by Matthew Parris, published 7 March 1994;

Extract from *Marriage and Morals* by Bertrand Russell, published by permission of Routledge (Unwin Hyman);

Extracts from *The New Shorter Oxford English Dictionary*, published by permission of Oxford University Press;

Faber & Faber Ltd for the extract from 'La Figlia Che Piange' in *Collected Poems 1909–1962* by T. S. Eliot.

Oxford is the Latin quarter of Cowley
(Anon)

# PROLEGOMENA

## Wednesday, 25 May 1994

### (i)

*Natales grate numeras?*
(Do you count your birthdays with gratitude?)
(HORACE, *Epistles II*)

ON MONDAYS to Fridays it was fifty-fifty whether the postman called before Julia Stevens left for school.

So, at 8.15 a.m. on 25 May she lingered awhile at the dark blue front door of her two-bedroomed terraced house in East Oxford. No sign of her postman yet; but he'd be bringing something a bit later.

Occasionally she wondered whether she still felt just a little love for the ex-husband she'd sued for divorce eight years previously for reasons of manifold infidelity. Especially had she so wondered when, exactly a year ago now, he'd sent her that card – a large, tasteless, red-rosed affair – which in a sad sort of way had pleased her more than she'd wanted to admit. Particularly those few words he'd written inside: 'Don't forget we had some good times too!'

If anyone, perhaps, shouldn't she tell *him*?

Then there was Brenda: dear, precious, indispensable Brenda. So there would certainly be *one* envelope lying on the 'Welcome' doormat when she returned from school that afternoon.

Aged forty-six (today) the Titian-haired Julia Stevens would have been happier with life (though only a little) had she been able to tell herself that after nearly twenty-three years she was still enjoying her chosen profession. But she wasn't; and she knew that she would soon have packed it all in anyway, even if . . .

Even if . . .

But she put that thought to the back of her mind.

It wasn't so much the *pupils* – her thirteen- to eighteen-year-olds – though some of them would surely have ruffled the calm of a Mother Teresa. No. It wasn't that. It was the way the *system* was going: curriculum development, aims and objectives (whatever the difference between those was supposed to be!), assessment criteria, pastoral care, parent consultation, profiling, testing . . . God! When was there any time for *teaching* these days?

She'd made her own views clear, quite bravely so, at one of the staff meetings earlier that year. But the Head had paid little attention. Why should he? After all, he'd been appointed precisely *because* of his cocky conversance with curriculum development, aims and objectives and the rest . . . A young, shining ideas-man, who during his brief spell of teaching (as rumour had it) would have experienced considerable difficulty in maintaining discipline even amongst the glorious company of the angels.

There was a sad little smile on Julia's pale face as she fished her Freedom Ticket from her handbag and stepped on to the red Oxford City double-decker.

Still, there was one good thing. No one at school knew of her birthday. Certainly, she trusted, none of the pupils did, although she sensed a slight reddening under her high cheekbones as just for a few seconds she contemplated her embarrassment if one of her classes broke out into 'Happy Birthday, Mrs Stevens!' She no longer had much confidence in the powers of the Almighty; but she almost felt herself praying.

But if she were going to target any prayer, she could surely so easily find a better aim (or was it an 'objective'?) than averting a cacophonic chorus from 5C, for example. And in any case, 5C weren't all that bad, really; and she, Julia Stevens, *mirabile dictu*, was one of the few members of staff who could handle that motley and unruly crowd. No. If she were going to pray for anything, it would be for something that was of far greater importance.

Of far greater importance for herself . . .

As things turned out, her anxieties proved wholly groundless. She received no birthday greetings from a single soul, either in the staff-room or in any of the six classes she taught that day.

Yet there was, in 5C, just the one pupil who knew Mrs Stevens' birthday. Knew it well, for it was the same as his own: the twenty-fifth of May. Was it that strange coincidence that had caused them all the trouble?

Trouble? Oh, yes!

In the previous *Sunday Mirror*'s horoscope column, Kevin Costyn had scanned his personal 'Key to Destiny' with considerable interest:

> GEMINI
>
> Now that the lone planet voyages across your
> next romance chart, you swop false hope for
> thrilling fact. Maximum mental energy helps
> you through to a hard-to-reach person who
> is always close to your heart. Play it cool.

'Maximum mental energy' had never been Kevin's strong point. But if such mighty exertion were required to win his way through to such a person, well, for once he'd put his mind to things. At the very least, it would be an improvement on the 'brute-force-and-ignorance' approach he'd employed on that earlier occasion – when he'd tried to make amorous advances to one of his school-mistresses.

When he'd tried to rape Mrs Julia Stevens.

## (ii)

> Chaos ruled OK in the classroom
> as bravely the teacher walked in
> the havocwreakers ignored him
> his voice was lost in the din
> (ROGER MCGOUGH, *The Lesson*)

AT THE AGE of seventeen (today) Kevin Costyn was the dominant personality amongst the twenty-four pupils, of both sexes, comprising Form 5C at the

Proctor Memorial School in East Oxford. He was fourteen months or so above the average age of his class because he was significantly below the average Intelligence Quotient for his year, as measured by orthodox psychometric criteria.

In earlier years, Kevin's end-of-term reports had semi-optimistically suggested a possible capacity for improvement, should he ever begin to activate his dormant brain. But any realistic hopes of academic achievement had been abandoned many terms ago.

In spite of – or was it because of? – such intellectual shortcomings, Kevin was an individual of considerable menace and power; and if any pupil was likely to drive his teacher to retirement, to resignation, even to suicide, that pupil was Kevin Costyn. Both inside and outside school, this young man could be described only as crude and vicious; and during the current summer term his sole interest in class activities had focused upon his candidature for the British National Party in the school's annual mock-elections.

Teachers were fearful of his presence in the classroom, and blessed their good fortune whenever he was (allegedly) ill or playing hookey or appearing before the courts or cautioned (again!) by the police or being interviewed by probation officers, social workers, or psychiatrists. Only rarely was his conduct less than positively disruptive; and that when some overnight dissipation had sapped his wonted enthusiasm for selective subversion.

Always he sat in the front row, immediately to the right of the central gangway. This for three reasons. First, because he was thus enabled to turn round and thereby the more easily to orchestrate whatever disruption he had in mind. Second, because (without ever admitting it) he was slightly deaf; and although he had little wish to listen to his teachers' lessons, his talent for verbal repartee was always going to be diminished by any slight mis-hearing. Third, because Eloise Dring, the sexiest girl in the Fifth Year, was so very short-sighted that she was compelled (refusing spectacles) to take a ring-side view of each day's proceedings. And Kevin wanted to sit next to Eloise Dring.

So there he sat, his long legs sticking way out beneath his undersized desk; his feet shod in a scuffed, cracked, decrepit pair of winkle-pickers, two pairs of which had been bequeathed by some erstwhile lover to his mother – the latter a blowsy, frowsy single parent who had casually conceived her only son (as far as she could recall the occasion) in a lay-by just off the Cowley Ring Road, and who now lived in one of a string of council properties known to the largely unsympathetic locals as Prostitutes Row.

Kevin was a lankily built, gangly-boned youth, with long, dark, unwashed hair, and a less than virile sprouting on upper lip and chin, dressed that day in a gaudily floral T-shirt and tattered jeans. His sullen, dolichocephalic face could have been designed by some dyspeptic El Greco, and on his left forearm – covered this slightly chilly day by the sleeve of an off-white sweatshirt – was a tattoo. This tattoo was known to everyone of any status in the school, including the Head; and indeed the latter, in a rare moment of comparative courage, had called Costyn into his study the previous term and demanded to know exactly what the epidermal epigram might signify. And Kevin had been happy to tell him: to tell him how the fairly unequivocal slogan ('Fuck 'em All') would normally be interpreted by anyone; even by someone with the benefit of a university education.

Anyway, that was how Kevin reported the interview.

Whatever the truth of the matter though, his reputation was now approaching its apogee. And with two sentences in a young offenders' unit behind him, how could it have been otherwise? At the same time, his influence, both within the circle of his immediate contemporaries and within the wider confines of the whole school, was significantly increased by two further factors. First, he even managed in some curious manner to exude a crude yet apparently irresistible sexuality, which drew many a girl into his magnetic field. Second, he was – had been since the age of twelve – a devotee of the Martial Arts; and under the tutelage of a diminutive Chinaman who (rumour had it) had once single-handedly left a gang of street-muggers lying pleading for mercy on the pavement, Kevin could appear, often *did* appear, an intimidating figure.

'KC.' That was what was written in red capital letters in the girls' loo: Kevin Costyn; Karate Champion; King of the Condoms; or whatever.


Tradition at the Proctor Memorial School was for pupils to rise to their feet whenever any teacher entered the classroom. And this tradition perpetuated itself still, albeit in a dishonoured, desultory sort of way. Yet when Mrs Stevens walked into 5C, for the first period on the afternoon of her birthday, the whole class, following a cue from Kevin Costyn, rose to its feet in synchronized smartness, the hum of conversation cut immediately . . . as if some maestro had tapped his baton on the podium.

And there was a great calm.

## (iii)

> As I heard the tread of pupils coming up my ancient creaking stairs, I felt like a tired tart awaiting her clients
>
> (A. L. Rowse, *On Life as an Oxford Don*)

'It's only me,' he'd spoken into the rusted, serrated Entryphone beside the front door.

He'd heard a brief, distant whirring; then a click; then her voice: 'It's open.'

He walked up the three flights of shabbily carpeted stairs, his mind wholly on the young woman who lived on the top floor. The bone structure of her face looked gaunt below the pallid cheeks; her eyes (for all McClure knew) might once have sparkled like those of glaucopis Athene, but now were dull – a sludgy shade of green, like the waters of the Oxford canal; her nose – tip-tilted in slightly concave fashion, like the contour of a nursery ski-slope – was disfigured (as he saw things) by two cheap-looking silver rings, one drilled through either nostril; her lips, marginally on the thin side of the Aristotelian mean, were ever thickly daubed with a shade of bright orange – a shade that would have been permanently banned from her mouth by any mildly competent beautician, a shade which clashed horribly with the amateurishly applied deep-scarlet dye that streaked her longish, dark-brown hair.

But why such details of her face? Her hair? The mind of this young woman's second client that day, Wednesday, May 25, was firmly fixed on other things as a little breathlessly he ascended the last few narrow, squeaking stairs that led to the top of the Victorian property.

The young woman turned back the grubby top-sheet on the narrow bed, kicked a pair of knickers out of sight behind the shabby settee, poured out two glasses of red wine (£2.99 from Oddbins), and was sitting on the bed, swallowing the last mouthful of a Mars bar, when the first knock sounded softly on the door.

She was wearing a creased lime-green blouse, buttoned up completely down the front, black nylon stockings – whose tops came only to mid-thigh, held by a white suspender-belt – and red high-heeled shoes. Nothing more. That's how he wanted her; that's how she was. Beggars were proverbially precluded from overmuch choice and (perforce) 'beggar' she had become, with a triple burden of liabilities: negative equity on her 'studio flat', bought five years earlier at the height of the property boom; redundancy (*in*voluntary) from the sales office of a local engineering firm; and a steadily increasing consumption of alcohol. So she had soon taken on a ... well, a new 'job' really.

To say that in the course of her new employment she was experiencing any degree of what her previous employer called 'job satisfaction' would be an exaggeration. On the other hand, it was certainly the easiest work she'd ever undertaken, as well as being by far the best paid – and (as she knew) she was quite good at it. As soon as she'd settled her bigger debts, though, she'd pack it all in. She was quite definite about that. The sooner the quicker.

The only thing that sometimes worried her was the possibility of her mother finding out that she was earning her living as a cheap tart. Well, no, that wasn't true. An expensive tart, as her current client would soon be discovering yet again. Yes, fairly expensive; but that didn't stop her feeling very cheap.

At the second knock, she rose from the bed, straightened her left stocking, and was now opening the door. Within only a couple of minutes opening her legs, too, as she lay back on the constricted width of the bed, her mascara'ed eyes focusing on a discoloured patch of damp almost immediately above her head.

Almost immediately above *his* head, too.

It was all pretty simple, really. The trouble was it had never been satisfying, for she had rarely felt more than a minimal physical attraction towards any of her clients. In a curious way she wished she *could* so feel. But no. Not so far. There was occasionally a sort of wayward fondness, yes. And in fact she was fonder of this particular fellow than any of the others. Indeed, she had once surprised herself by wondering if when he died – well, he *was* nearly sixty-seven – she might manage to squeeze out a dutiful tear.

It had not occurred to her at the time that there are other ways of departing this earthly life; had not occurred to her, for example, that her present client,

THE DAUGHTERS OF CAIN

Dr Felix McClure, former Ancient History don of Wolsey College, Oxford, might fairly soon be murdered.

## (iv)

A highly geological home-made cake
(CHARLES DICKENS, *Martin Chuzzlewit*)

ONLY ONE communication, it appeared, was awaiting Julia Stevens that same day when she returned home just after 5 p.m.: a brown envelope (containing a gas bill) propped up against the table-lamp just inside her small entrance-hall.

The *white* envelope, unsealed, lay on the table in the living-room; and beside it was a glacé-iced cake, the legend 'Happy Birthday, Mrs Stevens' piped in purple on a white background, with an iced floral arrangement in violet and green, the leaves intricately, painstakingly crafted, and clearly the work of an expert in the skill.

Although Brenda Brooks had been Julia's cleaning-lady for almost four years now, she had never addressed her employer as anything but 'Mrs Stevens'; addressed her so again now, just as on the cake, in the letter folded inside the (NSPCC) birthday card.

Dear Mrs S,
Just a short note to wish you a very happy
birthday & I hope you will enjoy your surprise.

Don't look at it too closely as I had a little
'accident' & the icing isn't perfect. When I'd
made the flowers & when they were drying a
basin fell out of the cupboard & smashed the lot.
After saying something like 'oh bother' I had to
start again. Never mind I got there in the end.

Regarding my 'accident' I will tell you what
really happened. My husband decided to pick a
fight a few weeks ago & my doctor thinks he
could have broken a bone in my hand & so I
can't squeeze the bag very well. I was due to start
another icing course next week but he has saved
me £38.00!

Have a lovely day & I will see you in the
morning – can't wait.

Love & best wishes,<br>Brenda (Brooks)

After re-reading the letter, Julia looked down lovingly at the cake again, and suddenly felt very moved –
and very angry. Brenda (she knew) had hugely enjoyed
the cake-decorating classes at the Tech. and had
become proudly proficient in the icer's art. All right,
the injury was hardly of cosmic proportions, Julia
realized that; yet in its own little-world way the whole
thing was so terribly sad. And as she looked at the cake
again, Julia could now see what Brenda had meant. On
closer inspection, the 'Mrs' was really a bit of a mess;
and the loops in each of the 'y's in 'Happy Birthday'
were rather uncertain – decidedly wobbly, in fact – as if
formulated with tremulous fingers. 'Lacks her usual
Daedalian deftness' was Julia the Pedagogue's cool

appraisal; yet something warmer, something deeper inside herself, prompted her to immediate action. She fetched her broadest, sharpest kitchen knife and carefully cut a substantial segment of the cake, in such a way as to include most of the mis-handled 'Mrs'; and ate it all, straightaway.

The sponge-cake was in four layers, striated with cream, strawberry jam, and lemon-butter icing. Absolutely delicious; and she found herself wishing she could share it with someone.

Ten minutes later, the phone rang.

'I didn't say nuffin' in class, Miss, but I want to say 'appy birfday.'

'Where are you phoning from, Kevin?'

'Jus' down the road – near the bus-shelter.'

'Would you like to come along and have a piece of birthday cake with me? I mean, it's *your* birthday too, isn't it?'

'Jus' try stoppin' me, Miss!'

The phone went dead. And thoughtfully, a slight smile around her full lips, Julia retraced her steps to the living-room, where she cut two more segments of cake, the second of which sliced through the middle of the more obviously malformed 'y'; cut them with the same knife – the broadest, sharpest knife she had in all her kitchen armoury.

COLIN DEXTER

## (v)

After working for two weeks on a hard crossword
puzzle, Lumberjack Hafey, a teacher in Mandan,
became a raving maniac when unable to fill in
the last word. When found, he was in the alcove
of the old homestead sitting on the floor, pulling
his hair and shrieking unintelligible things
(*Illinois Chronicle*, 3 October 1993)

MUCH EARLIER that same day, Detective Sergeant
Lewis had found his chief sitting well forward in the
black-leather chair, shaking his head sadly over *The
Times* crossword puzzle.

'Not finished it yet, sir?'

Morse looked up briefly with ill-disguised disdain.
'There is, as doubtless you observe, Lewis, one clue and
one clue only remaining to be entered in the grid. The
rest I finished in six minutes flat; and, if you must know,
without your untimely interruption—'

'Sorry!'

Morse shook his head slowly. 'No. I've been sitting
here looking at the bloody thing for ten minutes.'

'Can I help?'

'Extremely improbable!'

'Don't you want to try me?'

Reluctantly Morse handed over the crossword, and
Lewis contemplated the troublesome clue: 'Kick in the
pants?' (3–5). Three of the eight letters were entered:
– I – – L – S –.

A short while later Lewis handed the crossword back

across the desk. He'd tried so hard, so very hard, to make some intelligent suggestion; to score some Brownie points. But nothing had come to mind.

'If it's OK with you, sir, I'd like to spend some time down at St Aldate's this morning – see if we can find some link between all these burglaries in North Oxford.'

'Why not? And good luck. Don't give 'em *my* address though, will you?'

After Lewis had gone, Morse stared down at the cross-word again. Seldom was it that he failed to finish things off, and that within a pretty smartish time, too. All he needed was a large Scotch ... and the answer (he knew) would hit him straight between the eyes. But it was only 8.35 a.m. and—

It hit him.

Scotch!

As he swiftly filled in the five remaining blank squares, he was smiling beatifically, wishing only that Lewis had been there to appreciate the *coup de grâce*.

But Lewis wasn't.

And it was only many months later that Lewis was to learn – and then purely by accident – the answer to that clue in *The Times* crossword for 25 May 1994, a day (as would appear in retrospect) on which so many things of fateful consequence were destined to occur.

# PART ONE

PART ONE

# CHAPTER ONE

**Pension:** generally understood to mean monies grudgingly bestowed on aging hirelings after a lifetime of occasional devotion to duty
(*Small's Enlarged English Dictionary*, 12th Edition)

JUST AFTER noon on Wednesday, 31 August 1994, Chief Inspector Morse was seated at his desk in the Thames Valley Police HQ building at Kidlington, Oxon – when the phone rang.

'Morse? You're there, are you? I thought you'd probably be in the pub by now.'

Morse forbore the sarcasm, and assured Chief Superintendent Strange – he had recognized the voice – that indeed he was there.

'Two things, Morse – but I'll come along to your office.'

'You wouldn't prefer me—?'

'I need the exercise, so the wife says.'

Not only the wife, mumbled Morse, as he cradled the phone, beginning now to clear the cluttered papers from the immediate desk-space in front of him.

Strange lumbered in five minutes later and sat down heavily on the chair opposite the desk.

'You may have to get that name-plate changed.'

Strange and Morse had never really been friends, but never really been enemies either; and some good-natured bantering had been the order of the day following the recommendation of the Sheehy Report six months earlier that the rank of Chief Inspector should be abolished. *Mutual* bantering, since Chief Superintendents too were also likely to descend a rung on the ladder.

It was a disgruntled Strange who now sat wheezing methodically and shaking his head slowly. 'It's like losing your stripes in the Army, isn't it? It's ... it's ...'

'Belittling,' suggested Morse.

Strange looked up keenly. '"Demeaning" – that's what I was going to say. Much better word, eh? So don't start trying to teach *me* the bloody English language.'

Fair point, thought Morse, as he reminded himself (as he'd often done before) that he and his fellow police-officers should never underestimate the formidable Chief Superintendent Strange.

'How can I help, sir? Two things, you said.'

'Ah! Well, yes. That's *one*, isn't it? What we've just been talking about. You see, I'm jacking the job in next year, as you've probably heard?'

Morse nodded cautiously.

'Well, that's it. It's the, er, pension I'm thinking about.'

'It won't affect the pension.'

'You think not?'

'Sure it won't. It's just a question of getting all the paperwork right. That's why they're sending all these forms around—'

'How do you know?' Strange's eyes shot up again, sharply focused, and it was Morse's turn to hesitate.

'I – I'm thinking of, er, jacking in the job myself, sir.'

4

'Don't be so bloody stupid, man! This place can't afford to lose me *and* you.'

'I shall only be going on for a couple of years, whatever happens.'

'And . . . and you've had the forms, you say?'

Morse nodded.

'And . . . and you've actually filled 'em *in*?' Strange's voice sounded incredulous.

'Not yet, no. Forms always give me a terrible headache. I've got a phobia about form-filling.'

No words from Morse could have been more pleasing, and Strange's moon-face positively beamed. 'You know, that's exactly what I said to the wife – about headaches and all that.'

'Why doesn't *she* help you?'

'Says it gives her a headache, too.'

The two men chuckled amiably.

'You'd like me to help?' asked Morse tentatively.

'Would you? Be a huge relief all round, I can tell you. We could go for a pint together next week, couldn't we? And if I go and buy a bottle of aspirin—'

'Make it *two* pints.'

'I'll make it two bottles, then.'

'You're on, sir.'

'Good. That's settled then.'

Strange was silent awhile, as if considering some matter of great moment. Then he spoke.

'Now, let's come to the second thing I want to talk about – far more important.'

Morse raised his eyebrows. 'Far more important than *pensions*?'

'Well, a bit more important perhaps.'

'Murder?'

'Murder.'

'Not *another* one?'

'Same one. The one near you. The McClure murder.'

'Phillotson's on it.'

'Phillotson's *off* it.'

'But—'

'His wife's ill. Very ill. I want you to take over.'

'But—'

'You see, you haven't got a wife who's very ill, have you? You haven't got a wife at all.'

'No,' replied Morse quietly. No good arguing with that.

'Happy to take over?'

'Is Lewis—?'

'I've just had a quick word with him in the canteen. Once he's finished his egg and chips . . .'

'Oh!'

'*And*' – Strange lifted his large frame laboriously from the chair – 'I've got this gut-feeling that Phillotson wouldn't have got very far with it anyway.'

'*Gut*-feeling?'

'What's wrong with that?' snapped Strange. 'Don't *you* ever get a gut-feeling?'

'Occasionally . . .'

'After too much booze!'

'Or mixing things, sir. You know what I mean: few pints of beer and a bottle of wine.'

'Yes . . .' Strange nodded. 'We'll probably both have a gut-feeling soon, eh? After a few pints of beer and a bottle of aspirin.'

He opened the door and looked at the name-plate again. 'Perhaps we shan't need to change them after all, Morse.'

# CHAPTER TWO

Like the sweet apple which reddens upon the
   topmost bough,
A-top on the topmost twig – which the pluckers
   forgot somehow –
Forgot it not, nay, but got it not, for none could
   get it till now
          (D. G. ROSSETTI, *Translations from Sappho*)

IT WAS to be only the second time that Morse had ever
taken over a murder enquiry after the preliminary –
invariably dramatic – trappings were done with: the
discovery of the deed, the importunate attention of the
media, the immediate scene-of-crime investigation, and
the final removal of the body.

Lewis, perceptively, had commented that it was all a
bit like getting into a football match twenty-five minutes
late, and asking a fellow spectator what the score was.
But Morse had been unimpressed by the simile, since
his life would not have been significantly impoverished
had the game of football never been invented.

Indeed, there was a sense in which Morse was
happier to have avoided any *in situ* inspection of the
corpse, since the liquid contents of his stomach almost
inevitably curdled at the sight of violent death. And he
knew that the death there *had* been violent – very
violent indeed. Much blood had been spilt, albeit now
caked and dirty-brown – blood that would still (he

supposed) be much in evidence around the chalk-lined contours of the spot on the saturated beige carpet where a man had been found with an horrific knife-wound in his lower belly.

'What's wrong with Phillotson?' Lewis had asked as they'd driven down to North Oxford.

'Nothing wrong with him – except incompetence. It's his wife. She's had something go wrong with an operation, so they say. Some, you know, some internal trouble . . . woman's trouble.'

'The womb, you mean, sir?'

'I don't *know*, do I, Lewis? I didn't ask. I'm not even quite sure exactly where the womb is. And, come to think of it, I don't even *like* the word.'

'I only asked.'

'And I only answered! His wife'll be fine, you'll see. It's him. He's just chickening out.'

'And the Super . . . didn't think he could cope with the case?'

'Well, he couldn't, could he? He's not exactly perched on the topmost twig of the Thames Valley intelligentsia, now is he?'

Lewis had glanced across at the man seated beside him in the passenger seat, noting the supercilious, almost arrogant, cast of the harsh blue eyes, and the complacent-looking smile about the lips. It was the sort of conceit which Lewis found the least endearing quality of his chief: worse even than his meanness with money and his almost total lack of gratitude. And suddenly he felt a shudder of distaste.

Yet only briefly. For Morse's face had become serious again as he'd pointed to the right; pointed to Daventry

Avenue; and amplified his answer as the car braked to a halt outside a block of flats:

'You see, we take a bit of beating, don't we, Lewis? Don't you reckon? Me and you? Morse and Lewis? Not *too* many twigs up there above us, are there?'

But as Morse unfastened his safety-belt, there now appeared a hint of diffidence upon his face.

'*Nous vieillissons, n'est-ce pas?*'

'Pardon, sir?'

'We're all getting older – that's what I said. And that's the only thing that's worrying me about this case, old friend.'

But then the smile again.

And Lewis saw the smile, and smiled himself; for at that moment he felt quite preternaturally content with life.

The constable designated to oversee the murder-premises volunteered to lead the way upstairs; but Morse shook his head, his response needlessly brusque:

'Just give me the key, lad.'

Only two short flights, of eight steps each, led up to the first floor; yet Morse was a little out of breath as Lewis opened the main door of the maisonette.

'Yes' – Morse's mind was still on Phillotson – 'I reckon he'd've been about as competent in this case as a dyslexic proofreader.'

'I like that, sir. That's good. Original, is it?'

Morse grunted. In fact it had been Strange's own appraisal of Phillotson's potential; but, as ever, Morse was perfectly happy to take full credit for the *bons mots* of others. Anyway, Strange himself had probably read it somewhere, hadn't he? Shrewd enough, was Strange: but hardly perched up there on the roof of Canary Wharf.

Smoothly the door swung open ... The door swung open on another case.

And as Lewis stepped through the small entrance-hall, and thence into the murder room, he found himself wondering how things would turn out here.

Certainly it hadn't sounded all that extraordinary a case when, two hours earlier, Detective Chief Inspector Phillotson had given them an hour-long briefing on the murder of Dr Felix McClure, former Student – late Student – of Wolsey College, Oxford ...

Bizarre and bewildering – that's what so many cases in the past had proved to be; and despite Phillotson's briefing the present case would probably be no different.

In this respect, at least, Lewis was correct in his thinking. What he could not have known – what, in fact, he never really came to know – was what unprecedented anguish the present case would cause to Morse's soul.

# CHAPTER THREE

Myself when young did eagerly frequent
  Doctor and Saint, and heard great Argument
  About it and about: but evermore
Came out by the same Door as in I went
  (EDWARD FITZGERALD, *The Rubaiyat of Omar
                                    Khayyam*)

DAVENTRY COURT (Phillotson had begun), comprising eight 'luxurious apartments' built in Daventry Avenue in 1989, had been difficult to sell. House prices had tumbled during the ever-deepening recession of the early nineties, and McClure had bought in the spring of 1993 when he'd convinced himself (rightly) that even in the continuing buyers' market Flat 6 was a bit of a snip at £99,500.

McClure himself was almost sixty-seven years old at the time of his murder, knifed (as Morse would be able to see for himself) in quite horrendous fashion. The knife, according to pathological findings, was unusually broad-bladed, and at least five inches in length. Of such a weapon, however, no trace whatsoever had been found. Blood, though? Oh, yes. Blood almost everywhere. Blood on almost everything. Blood on the murderer too? Surely so.

Blood certainly on his shoes (trainers?), with footprints – especially of the right foot – clearly traceable from the murder scene to the staircase, to the main entrance; but thence virtually lost, soon completely lost, on the gravelled forecourt outside. Successive scufflings by other residents had obviously obliterated all further traces of blood. Or had the murderer left by a car parked close to the main door? Or left on a bicycle chained to the nearest drainpipe? (Or taken his shoes off, Lewis thought.) But intensive search of the fore-court area had revealed nothing. No clues from the sides of the block either. No clues from the rear. No clues at all outside. (Or perhaps just the one clue, Morse had thought: the clue that there *were* no clues at all?)

Inside? Well, again, Morse would be able to see for himself. Evidence of extraneous fingerprints? Virtually none. Hopeless. And certainly no indication that the assailant – murderer – had entered the premises through any first-floor window.

'Very rare means of ingress, Morse, as you know. Pretty certainly came in the same way as he went out.'

'Reminds me a bit of Omar Khayyam,' Morse had muttered.

But Phillotson had merely looked puzzled, his own words clearly not reminding himself of anyone. Or anything.

No. Entry from the main door, surely, via the Entry-phone system, with McClure himself admitting whom-soever (not Phillotson's word) – be it man or woman. Someone known to McClure then? Most likely.

Time? Well, certainly after 8.30 a.m. on the Sunday he was murdered, since McClure had purchased two newspapers at about 8 a.m. that morning from the newsagent's in Summertown, where he was at least a

13

well-known face if not a well-known name; and where he (like Morse, as it happened) usually catered for both the coarse and the cultured sides of his nature with the *News of the World* and *The Sunday Times*. No doubts here. No hypothesis required. Each of the two news-sheets was found, unbloodied, on the work-top in the 'all-mod-con kitchen'.

After 8.30 a.m. then. But before when? Preliminary findings – well, *not* so preliminary – from the pathologist firmly suggested that McClure had been dead for about twenty hours or so before being found, at 7.45 a.m. the following morning, by his cleaning-lady.

Hypothesis here, then, for the time of the murder? Between 10 a.m., say, and noon the previous day. Roughly. But then everything was 'roughly' with these wretched pathologists, wasn't it? (And Morse had smiled sadly, and thought of Max; and nodded slowly, for Phillotson was preaching to the converted.)

One other circumstance most probably corroborating a pre-noon time for the murder was the readily observable, and duly observed, fact that there was no apparent sign, such as the preparation of meat and vegetables, for any potential Sunday lunch in Flat 6. Not that that was conclusive in itself, since it had already become clear, from sensibly orientated enquiries, that it had not been unusual for McClure to walk down the Banbury Road and order a Sunday lunch – 8oz Steak, French Fries, Salad – only £3.99 – at the King's Arms, washed down with a couple of pints of Best Bitter; no sweet; no coffee. But there had been no sign of steak or chips or lettuce or anything much else when the pathologist had split open the white-skinned belly of Dr

14

Felix McClure. No sign of any lunchtime sustenance at all.

The body had been found in a hunched-up, foetal posture, with both hands clutching the lower abdomen and the eyes screwed tightly closed as if McClure had died in the throes of some excruciating pain. He was dressed in a short-sleeved shirt, vertically striped in maroon and blue, a black Jaeger cardigan, and a pair of dark-grey flannels – the lower part of the shirt and the upper regions of the trousers stiff and steeped in the blood that had oozed so abundantly.

McClure had been one of those 'perpetual students in life' (Phillotson's words). After winning a Major Scholarship to Oxford in 1946, he had gained a First in Mods, a First in Greats – thereafter spending forty-plus years of his life as Ancient History Tutor in Wolsey College. In 1956 he had married one of his own pupils, an undergraduette from Somerville – the latter, after attaining exactly similar distinction, duly appointed to a Junior Fellowship in Merton, and in 1966 (life jumping forward in decades) running off with one of her own pupils, a bearded undergraduate from Trinity. No children, though; no legal problems. Just a whole lot of heartache, perhaps.

Few major publications to his name – mostly a series of articles written over the years for various classical journals. But at least he had lived long enough to see the publication of his *magnum opus*: *The Great Plague at Athens: Its Effect on the Course and Conduct of the Peloponnesian War*. A long title. A long work.

Witnesses?

Of the eight 'luxurious apartments' only four had

been sold, with two of the others being let, and the other two still empty, the 'For Sale' notices standing outside the respective properties – one of them the apartment immediately below McClure's, Number 5; the other Number 2. Questioning of the tenants had produced no information of any value: the newly-weds in Number 1 had spent most of the Sunday morning a-bed – sans breakfast, sans newspapers, sans everything except themselves; the blue-rinsed old lady in Number 3, extremely deaf, had insisted on making a very full statement to the effect that she had heard nothing on that fateful morn; the couple in Number 4 had been out all morning on a Charity 'Save the Whales' Walk in Wytham Woods; the temporary tenants of Number 7 were away in Tunisia; and the affectionate couple who had bought Number 8 had been uninterruptedly employed in redecorating their bathroom, with the radio on most of the morning as they caught up with *The Archers* omnibus. (For the first time in several minutes, Morse's interest had been activated.)

'Not *all* that much to go on,' Phillotson had admitted; yet all the same, not without some degree of pride, laying a hand on two green box-files filled with reports and statements and notes and documents and a plan showing the full specification of McClure's apartment, with arcs and rulings and arrows and dotted lines and measurements. Morse himself had never been able to follow such house-plans; and now glanced only cursorily through the stapled sheets supplied by Adkinsons, Surveyors, Valuers, and Estate Agents – as Phillotson came to the end of his briefing.

'By the way,' asked Morse, rising to his feet, 'how's the wife? I meant to ask earlier . . .'

'Very poorly, I'm afraid,' said Phillotson, miserably.

'Cheerful sod, isn't he, Lewis?'

The two men had been back in Morse's office then, Lewis seeking to find a place on the desk for the bulging box-files.

'Well, he must be pretty worried about his wife if—'

'Pah! He just didn't know where to go next – that was his trouble.'

'And we *do*?'

'Well, for a start, I wouldn't mind knowing which of those newspapers McClure read first.'

'If either.'

Morse nodded. 'And I wouldn't mind finding out if he made any phone-calls that morning.'

'Can't we get British Telecom to itemize things?'

'Can we?' asked Morse vaguely.

'You'll want to see the body?'

'Why on earth should I want to do that?'

'I just thought—'

'I wouldn't mind seeing that shirt, though. Maroon and blue vertical stripes, didn't Phillotson say?' Morse passed the index finger of his left hand round the inside of his slightly tight, slightly frayed shirt-collar. 'I'm thinking of, er, expanding my wardrobe a bit.'

But the intended humour was lost on Lewis, to whom it seemed exceeding strange that Morse should at the same time apparently show more interest in the dead man's shirt than in his colleague's wife. 'Apparently' though . . . that was always the thing about Morse: no one could ever really plot a graph of the thoughts that ran through that extraordinary mind.

'Did we learn anything – from Phillotson, sir?'

'You may have done: I didn't. I knew just as much about things when I went into his office as when I came out.'

'Reminds you a bit of Omar Khayyam, doesn't it?' suggested Lewis, innocently.

# CHAPTER FOUR

Krook chalked the letter upon the wall – in a very curious manner, beginning with the end of the letter, and shaping it backward. It was a capital letter, not a printed one.

'Can you read it?' he asked me with a keen glance

(CHARLES DICKENS, *Bleak House*)

THE sitting-cum-dining-room – the murder room – 12′ × 17′2″ as stated in Adkinsons' (doubtless accurate) specifications, was very much the kind of room one might expect as the main living-area of a retired Oxford don: an oak table with four chairs around it; a brown leather settee; a matching armchair; TV; CD and cassette player; books almost everywhere on floor-to-ceiling shelves; busts of Homer, Thucydides, Milton, and Beethoven; not enough space really for the many pictures – including the head, in the Pittura Pompeiana series, of Theseus, Slayer of the Minotaur. Those were the main things. Morse recognized three of the busts readily and easily, though he had to guess at the bronze head of Thucydides. As for Lewis, he recognized all four immediately, since his eyesight was now keener than Morse's, and the name of each of those immortals was inscribed in tiny capitals upon its plinth.

For a while Morse stood by the armchair, looking all round him, saying nothing. Through the open door of the kitchen – 6'10" × 9'6" – he could see the Oxford Almanack hanging from the wall facing him, and finally went through to admire 'St Hilda's College' from a watercolour by Sir Hugh Casson, RA. Pity, perhaps, it was the previous year's, for Morse now read its date, 'MDCCCCLXXXXIII'; and for a few moments he found himself considering whether any other year in the twentieth century – in *any* century – could command any lengthier designation. Fourteen characters required for '1993'.

Still, the Romans never knew much about numbers.

'Do you know how many walking-sticks plus umbrellas we've got in the hall-stand here?' shouted Lewis from the tiny entrance area.

'Fourteen!' shouted Morse in return.

'How the – how on earth—?'

'For me, Lewis, coincidence in life is wholly unexceptional; the readily predictable norm in life. You know that by now, surely?'

Lewis said nothing. He knew well where his duties lay in circumstances such as these: to do the donkey-work; to look through everything, without much purpose, and often without much hope. But Morse was a stickler for sifting the evidence; always had been. The only trouble was that he never wanted to waste his own time in helping to sift it, for such work was excessively tedious; and frequently fruitless, to boot.

So Lewis did it all. And as Morse sat back in the settee and looked through McClure's *magnum opus*, Lewis started to go through all the drawers and all the letters and all the piles of papers and the detritus of the litter-bins – just as earlier Phillotson and his team had done. Lewis didn't mind, though. Occasionally in the past he'd found some item unusual enough (well, unusual enough to Morse) that had set the great mind scurrying off into some subtly sign-posted avenue, or cul-de-sac; that had set the keenest-nosed hound in the pack on to some previously unsuspected scent.

Two things only of interest here, Lewis finally informed Morse. And Phillotson himself had pointed out the potential importance of the first of these, anyway: a black plastic W. H. Smith Telephone Index, with eighteen alphabetical divisions, the collocation of the less common letters, such as 'WX' and 'YZ', counting as one. The brief introductory instructions (under 'A') suggested that the user might find it valuable to record therein, for speed of reference, the telephone numbers of such indispensable personages as Decorator, Dentist, Doctor, Electrician, Plumber, Police . . .

Lewis opened the index at random: at the letter 'M'. Six names on the card there. Three of the telephone numbers were prefixed with the Inner London code, '071'; the other three were Oxford numbers, five digits each, all beginning with '5'.

Lewis sighed audibly. Eighteen times six? That was a hundred and eight . . . Still it might be worthwhile ringing round (had Phillotson thought the same?) provided there were no more than half a dozen or so per page. He pressed the index to a couple of other letters. 'P': eight names and numbers. 'C': just four. What about the twinned letters? He pressed 'KL': seven, with six of them 'L'; and just the one 'K' – and that (interestingly enough?) entered as the single capital letter 'K'. Who was K when he was at home?

Or she?

'What does "K" stand for, sir?'

Morse, a crossword fanatic from his early teens, knew some of the answers immediately: '"King"; "Kelvin" – unit of temperature, Lewis; er, "thousand"; "kilometre", of course; "Köchel", the man who catalogued Mozart, as you know; er . . .'

'Not much help.'

'Initial of someone's name?'

'Why just the initial?'

'Girl's name? Perhaps he's trying to disguise his simmering passion for a married woman – what about that? Or perhaps all the girls at the local knocking-shop are known by a letter of the alphabet?'

'Didn't know you had one up here, sir.'

'Lewis, we have everything in North Oxford. It's just a question of knowing where it is, that's the secret.'

Lewis mused aloud. 'Karen . . . or Kirsty . . .'

'Kylie?'

'You've heard of *her*, sir?'

'Only just.'

'Kathy . . .'

'Well, there's one pretty simple way of finding out, isn't there? Can't you just ring the number? Isn't that what you're supposed to be doing? That sort of thing?'

Lewis picked up the phone and dialled the five-digit number – and was answered immediately.

'Yeah? Wha' d'ya wan'?' a woman's voice bawled at him.

'Hullo. Er – have I got the right number for "K"?'

'Yeah. You 'ave. Bu' she's no' 'ere, is she?'

'No, obviously not. I'll try again later.'

'You a dur'y ol' man, or sump'n?'

Lewis quickly replaced the receiver, the colour rising in his pale cheeks.

Morse, who had heard the brief exchange clearly, grinned at his discomfited sergeant. 'You can't win 'em all.'

'Waste of time, if that's anything to go by.'

'You think so?'

'Don't *you?*'

'Lewis! You were only on the phone for about ten seconds but you learned she was a "she", probably a she with the name of "Kay".'

'I didn't!'

'A she of easy virtue who old Felix here spent a few happy hours with. Or, as you'd prefer it, with whom old Felix regularly spent a few felicitous hours.'

'You can't just say that—'

'Furthermore she's a local lass, judging by her curly Oxfordshire accent and her typical habit of omitting all her "t"s.'

'But I didn't even *get* the woman!'

Morse was silent for a few seconds; then he looked up, his face more serious. 'Are you sure, Lewis? Are you quite sure you haven't just been speaking to the cryptic "K" herself?'

Lewis shook his head, grinned ruefully, and said nothing. He knew – knew again now – why he'd never rise to any great heights in life himself. Morse had got it wrong, of course. Morse nearly always got things hopelessly, ridiculously wrong at the start of every case. But he always seemed to have thoughts that no one else was capable of thinking. Like now.

'Anyway, what's this other thing you've found?'

But before Lewis could answer, there was a quiet tap on the door and PC Roberts stuck a reverential, unhelmeted head into the room.

'There's a Mrs Wynne-Wilson here, sir, from one of the other flats. Says she wants a word, like.'

Morse looked up from his Thucydides. 'Haven't we already got a statement from her, Lewis?'

But it was Roberts who answered. 'She says she made a statement, sir, but when she heard someone else was in charge – well, she said Inspector Phillotson didn't really want to know, like.'

'Really?'

'And she's, well, she's a bit deaf, like.'

'Like what?' asked Morse.

'Pardon?'

'Forget it.'

'Shall I show her in, sir?'

'What? In here? You know what happened here, don't you? She'd probably faint, man.'

'Doubt it, sir. She says she was sort of in charge of nurses at some London hospital.'

'Ah, a matron,' said Morse.

'They don't call them "matrons" any longer,' interposed Lewis.

'Thank you very much, Lewis! Send her in.'

# CHAPTER FIVE

*O quid solutis est beatius curis,*
*Cum mens onus reponit, ac peregrino*
*Labore fessi venimus larem ad nostrum,*
*Desideratoque acquiescimus lecto?*

(What bliss! First spot the house – and then
Flop down – on one's old bed again)

(CATULLUS, *31*)

JULIA STEVENS had returned home that same
afternoon.

The flight had been on time (early, in fact); Customs
had been swift and uncomplicated; the Gatwick–
Heathrow–Oxford coach had been standing there, just
waiting for her, it seemed, welcoming her back to
England. From the bus station at Gloucester Green she
had taken a taxi (no queue) out to East Oxford, the
driver duly helping her with two heavyweight cases right
up to the front door of her house – a house which, as
the taxi turned into the street, she'd immediately
observed to be still standing there, unburned, unvan-
dalized; and, as she could see as she stood inside her
own living-room – at long last! – blessedly unburgled.

How glad she was to be back. Almost always, on the
first two nights of any holiday away from home, she
experienced a weepy nostalgia. But usually this proved
to be only a re-adjustment. Usually, too, at least for the

last two days of her statutory annual fortnight abroad, she felt a similar wrench on leaving her summer surroundings; on bidding farewell to her newly made holiday friends. One or two friends in particular.

One or two men, as often as not.

But such had not been the case this time on her package tour round the Swiss and Italian lakes. She couldn't explain why: the coach-driver had been very competent; the guide good; the scenery spectacular; the fellow-tourists pleasantly friendly. But she'd not enjoyed it at all. My god! What was happening to her?

(But she knew exactly what was happening to her.)

Not that she'd said anything, of course. And Brenda Brooks had received a cheerful postcard from a multi-starred hotel on Lake Lucerne:

> Wed.
> Having a splendid time here with a nice lot of people. My room looks right across the lake. Tomorrow we go over to Triebschen (hope I've spelt that right) where Richard Wagner spent some of his life. There was a firework display last night – tho' nobody told us why. Off to Lugano Friday.
> Love Julia
> PS Give St Giles a big hug for me.

As Julia walked through her front door that afternoon, her house smelt clean and fragrant; smelt of pine and polish and Windolene. Bless her – bless Brenda Brooks!

Then, on the kitchen table, there was a note – the sort of note that she, Julia, had ever come to expect:

> Dear Mrs S,
> I got your card thankyou & I'm glad you had a good time. St Giles has been fine, there are two more tins of Whiskas in the fridge. See you Monday. There's something I want to tell you about & perhaps you can help – I hope so. Welcome home!!
> Brenda (Brooks)

Julia smiled to herself. Brenda invariably appended her (bracketed) surname as though the household boasted a whole bevy of charladies. And always that deferential 'Mrs S'. Brenda had worked for her for four years now, and at fifty-two was nearly seven years her senior. Again Julia smiled to herself. Then, as she re-read the penultimate sentence, for a moment she found herself frowning slightly.

It was a pleasant sunny day, with September heralding a golden finale to what had been a hot and humid summer. Indeed, the temperature was well above the average for an autumn day. Yet Julia felt herself shivering slightly as she unlocked and unbolted the rear door. And if a few moments earlier she may have looked a little sad, a little strained – behold now a metamorphosis! A ginger cat parted the ground-cover greenery at the bottom of the small garden and peered up at his mistress; and suddenly Julia Stevens looked very happy once again.

And very beautiful.

# CHAPTER SIX

Envy and idleness married together beget curiosity
(THOMAS FULLER, *Gnomologia*)

MORSE DECIDED to interview Laura Wynne-Wilson, should that good lady allow it, in her own ground-floor apartment. And the good lady did so allow.

She was, she admitted, very doubtful about whether that previous policeman had attended to her evidence with sufficient seriousness. Indeed, she had formed the distinct impression that he had listened, albeit politely, in a wholly perfunctory way to what she had to say. Which was? Which was to do with Dr McClure – a nice gentleman; and a *very* good neighbour, who had acted as Secretary of the Residents' Action Committee and written such a *splendid* letter to that cowboy outfit supposedly responsible for the upkeep of the exterior of the properties.

She spoke primly and quietly, a thin smile upon thin lips.

'And what exactly have you got to tell us?' bawled Morse.

'Please don't *shout* at me, Inspector! Deaf people do *not* require excessive volume – they require only clarity of speech and appropriate lip-movement.'

Lewis smiled sweetly to himself as the small, white-haired octogenarian continued:

'What I have to tell you is this. Dr McClure had a fairly regular visitor here. A . . . a lady-friend.'

'Not all that unusual, is it?' suggested Morse, with what he hoped was adequate clarity and appropriate lip-movement.

'Oh, no. After all, it might well have been some female relative.'

Morse nodded. Already he knew that McClure had no living relatives apart from a niece in New Zealand; but still he nodded.

'And then again, Inspector, it might *not*. You see, he had no living relatives in the United Kingdom.'

'Oh.' Morse decided that, unlike Phillotson, he at least would treat the old girl with a modicum of respect.

'No. It was his "fancy woman", as we used to call it. By the way, I quite like that term myself, don't you?'

'Plenty of worse words, madam,' interposed Lewis, though apparently with less than adequate clarity.

'Pardon?' Laura W-W turned herself in the approximate direction of the man taking notes, as if he were merely some supernumerary presence.

And now it was Morse's turn to smile sweetly to himself.

'As I was saying, this . . . this woman came to see him several times – certainly three or four times during the last month.'

'What time of day was that?'

'Always at about half-past seven.'

'And you, er, you actually saw her?'

'"Actually" is a ridiculous word, isn't it? It's a weasel word, Inspector. It means nothing whatsoever. It's a space-filler. Whether I *actually* saw her, I don't know. What I *do* know is that I *saw* her. All right?'

Touché.

Morse's eyes wandered over to the wooden-frame casement, where the thin white lace curtains were pulled back in tight arcs at each side, with potted geraniums at either end of the window ledge, and three tasteful pieces of dark-blue and white porcelain positioned between them. But nothing there to clutter the clear view, from where Morse was sitting, over the whole front area of the apartments, especially of the two square, yellow-brick pillars which stood at either side of the entrance drive; and through which, per-force, everyone coming into Daventry Court must surely pass. Everyone except a burglar, perhaps. Or a murderer . . . And this nosey old woman would delight in observing the visitors who called upon her fellow residents, Morse felt confident of that.

'This could be very helpful to our enquiries, you realize that, don't you? If you saw her clearly . . . ?'

'My eyesight is not what it was, Inspector. But I had a good view of her, yes.' She glanced keenly at Morse. 'You see, I'm a nosey old woman with very little else to do – that's what you're thinking, anyway.'

'Well, I – we all like to know what's going on. It's only human nature.'

'Oh, no. I know several people who aren't in the *slightest* bit interested in "what's going on", as you put it. But I'm glad *you're* nosey, like me. That's good.'

Lewis was enjoying the interview immensely.

'Can you tell us something about this woman? Anything?'

'Let's say I found her interesting.'

'Why was that?'

'Well, for a start, I envied her. She was less than half his age, you see – good deal less, I shouldn't doubt.'

'And he,' mused Morse, 'was sixty-six . . .'

'Sixty-seven, Inspector, if he'd lived to the end of the month.'

'How—?'

'I looked him up in *Distinguished People of Today*. He's a Libra.'

Like me, thought Morse. And I wonder how old you are, you old biddy.

'And I'm eighty-three in December,' she continued, 'just in case you're wondering.'

'I was, yes,' said Morse, smiling at her, and himself now beginning to enjoy the interview.

'The other thing that struck me was that she wasn't at *all* nice-looking. Quite the opposite, in fact. Very shabbily dressed – darkish sort of clothes. Sloppy loose blouse, mini-skirt right up to . . .'

'The top of her tibia,' supplied Morse, enunciating the 't' of the last word with exaggerated exactitude.

'Absolutely! And she had a big old shoulder-bag, too.'

I wonder what was in that, thought Morse.

'Anything else you can remember?'

'Long – longish – dark hair. Earrings – great brassy-looking things about the size of hula-hoops. And she had a ring in her nose. I could see that. For all I know, she could have had *two* rings in her nose.'

God helps us all, thought Morse.

'But I'm not sure about that. As I say, my eyesight isn't what it used to be.'

I wonder what it used to be like, thought Lewis.

'Did she come by car?' asked Morse.

'No. If she did, she left it somewhere else.'

'Did she come in from . . . ?' Morse gestured vaguely to his left, towards the Banbury Road.

'Yes. She came from the Banbury Road – not the Woodstock Road.'

'Would you recognize her again?'

For the first time the old lady hesitated, rubbing the thin ringless fingers of her left hand with her right.

'Oh dear. Do you think she may have *murdered* him? I only—'

'No, no. I'm sure she didn't.' Morse spoke with the bogus confidence of a man who was beginning to wonder if she had.

'I only wanted to help. And I'm not at *all* sure if I would recognize her. Perhaps if she dolled herself up in some decent outfit and . . .'

Took that bull-ring out of her nose, thought Morse.

'. . . and took that ring out of her nose.'

Phew!

But some of the bounce had gone out of the old girl, Morse could see that. It was time to wind things up.

'Do you think they went to bed when she came?'

'I expect so, don't you?'

'Things must have changed a good deal since your day, Miss Wynne-Wilson.'

'Don't be silly, Inspector! I could teach some of these young flibbertigibbets a few things about going to bed

33

with men. After all, I spent most of my life looking after men in bed, now didn't I? And, by the way, it's *Mrs* Wynne-Wilson. I don't wear a wedding ring any longer . . .'

Phew!

Morse got to his feet. He had only one more question: 'Were you looking out of the window on Sunday morning – you know, about the time perhaps when Dr McClure was murdered?'

'No. On Sunday mornings I always hear the omnibus edition of *The Archers* on the wireless, that's from ten to eleven. Lovely. I have a really good long soak – and hear everything again.'

Dangerous thing that – having a radio in the bathroom, thought Lewis.

'It's dangerous they tell me – having a wireless propped up on the bath-rail. But I do so enjoy doing silly things, now that I'm so old.'

Phew!

It had not been much of a contest, Lewis appreciated that; but from his scorecard he had little hesitation in declaring Mrs W-W the winner, way ahead of Morse on points.

Quite mistakenly, of course.

# CHAPTER SEVEN

For 'tis in vain to think or guess
At women by appearances
(SAMUEL BUTLER, *Hudibras*)

'WHAT DID you make of that, then?' asked Lewis, when the two detectives had returned to McClure's apartment.

Morse appeared disappointed. 'I'd begun to think he was a civilized sort of fellow – you know . . .' Morse gestured vaguely around the bookshelves.

'But he wasn't?'

'We-ell.'

'You mean . . . this woman he was seeing?'

Morse's features reflected disapproval. 'Rings in her *nose*, Lewis? Pretty tasteless, isn't it? Like drinking lager with roast beef.'

'For all you know she may be a lovely girl, sir. You shouldn't really judge people just by appearances.'

'Oh?' Morse's eyes shot up swiftly. 'And why the hell not?'

'Well . . .' But Lewis wasn't sure why. He did have a point, though; he knew he did. Morse was always making snap judgements. All right, one or two would occasionally turn out to be accurate; but most of them were woefully wide of the mark – as, to be fair, Morse himself readily acknowledged.

Lewis thought of events earlier in the day; thought

of Phillotson's withdrawal from the present case; thought of Morse's almost contemptuous dismissal of the man's excuses. Almost automatically, it seemed, Morse had assumed him to be parading a few phoney pretexts about his wife's hospitalization in order to avoid the humiliation of failure in a murder case. Agreed, Phillotson wasn't exactly Sherlock Holmes, Lewis knew that. Yet Morse could be needlessly cruel about some of his colleagues. And why did he have to be so *sharp*? As he had been just now?

Still, Lewis knew exactly what to do about his own temporary irritation. Count to ten! – that's what Morse had once told him – before getting on to any high horse; and then, if necessary, count to twenty. Not that there was much sign that Morse ever heeded his own advice. *He* usually only counted to two or three. If that.

Deciding, therefore, the time to be as yet inopportune for any consideration of the old lady's testimony, Lewis reverted to his earlier task. There was still a great deal of material to look through, and he was glad to get down to something whose purpose he could readily grasp. The papers there, all the papers in the drawers and those stacked along the shelves, had already been examined – clearly that was the case. Not radically disturbed, though; not taken away to be documented in some dubious filing-system until sooner or later, as with almost everything in life, being duly labelled 'OBE'.

Overtaken By Events.

Glancing across at Morse, Lewis saw the chief abstracting another book from a set of volumes beautifully bound in golden leather; a slim volume this time;

a volume of verse by the look of it. And even as he watched, he saw Morse turning the book through ninety degrees and apparently reading some marginalia beside one of the poems there. For the present, however, the Do Not Disturb sign was prominently displayed, and with his usual competence Lewis resumed his own considerable task.

Thus it was that for the next half-hour or so the two men sat reading their different texts; preparing (as it were) for their different examinations; each conscious of the other's presence; yet each, for the moment, and for different reasons, unwilling to speak his own immediate thoughts.

Especially Morse.

Yet it was the latter who finally broke the silence.

'What did you make of her, then? Our Mrs Wynne-Wilson?'

'"*Mrs*", sir?' asked Lewis slowly.

Morse threw an interested, inquisitive look at his sergeant. 'Go on!'

'Well, I'd noticed from the start she wasn't wearing a wedding ring. As you did, of course.'

'Of course.'

'But I couldn't see any, you know, any mark of any ring like you'd normally have, wouldn't you? A sort of, you know, pale ring of skin, sort of thing, where the ring had been – before she took it off.'

'Not a particularly fluent sentence that, Lewis, if I may say so.'

'But you noticed that too?'

'Me? Your eyesight's far better than mine.'

'Makes you wonder, though.'

'You reckon she was making it up – about her marriage?'

'Wouldn't surprise me, sir.'

'And apart from that?'

'She seemed a pretty good witness. Her mind's pretty sharp. She got you weighed up all right.'

'Ye-es ... So you don't think she was making anything else up?'

'No. Do you?'

'Lew-is! When will you learn. She's a phoney. She's a phoney from A to Z.'

Lewis's look now was one of semi-exasperation. 'There you go again! I think you're far too quick—'

'Let me tell you something. She just about takes the biscuit, that woman – give or take one or two congenitally compulsive liars we've had in the past.'

Lewis shook his head sadly as Morse continued:

'Wedding ring? You're right. Odds strongly against her having worn one recently. Not necessarily the same as *not* being married though, is it? Suggestive, though, yes. Suggestive that she might be telling a few other fibs as well.'

'Such as?'

'Well, it was obvious she wasn't deaf at all. She heard everything I said. Easy. *Kein Problem.*'

'She didn't hear *me.*'

'She didn't want to hear you, Lewis.'

'If you say so, sir.'

'What about her eyesight? Kept telling us, didn't she, that she couldn't see half as well as she used to? But that didn't stop her giving us a detailed description of the woman who came to visit McClure. She knew she'd got a ring in one of her nostrils – at twenty-odd yards, Lewis! And the only reason she couldn't tell us if she'd got *two* rings in her nose was because she saw her in profile – like she sees everyone in profile coming in through that entrance.'

'Why don't you think she was making all *that* up too, sir – that description she gave?'

'Good point.' Morse looked down at the carpet briefly. 'But I don't think so; that bit rang true to me. In fact, I reckon it was the only thing of any value she did come up with.'

'What about—?'

'Lewis! She's a phoney. She's not even been a *nurse* – let alone a matron or whatever you call 'em.'

'How can you say that?'

'You heard her – we both heard her. Mini-skirt up to mid-tibia – remember me saying that? Mid-*tibia*? Your tibia's *below* your knee, Lewis. You know that. But *she* doesn't.'

'Unless she's deaf, and misheard—'

'She's not deaf, I told you that. She just doesn't know her tibia from her fibula, that's all. Never been near a nursing manual in her life.'

'And you deliberately tricked her about that?'

'*And*, Lewis – most important of all – she claims she's an *Archers* addict, but she doesn't even know when the omnibus edition comes on on a Sunday morning. Huh!'

'I wouldn't know—'

'She's a Walter Mitty sort of woman. She lives in a world of fantasy. She tells herself things so many times – tells other people things so many times – that she thinks they're true. And for her they *are* true.'

'But not for us.'

'Not for us, no.'

'Not even the time she was in the bath?'

'If she was in the bath.'

'Oh.'

'Anyway, I don't somehow think it's going to be of much importance to us, what time the murderer made his entrance . . .'

Morse was whining on a little wearily now; and like Miss (or Mrs) W-W he seemed to be running out of steam.

Both men became silent again.

And soon Lewis was feeling pleased with himself, for he was beginning to realize that the 'second thing' he'd found for Morse was looking far more promising.

And Morse himself, with melancholy mien, sat ever motionless, his eyes staring intently at the page before him: that selfsame page in the book of Latin poetry.

# CHAPTER EIGHT

*Caeli, Lesbia nostra, Lesbia illa,*
*Illa Lesbia, quam Catullus unam*
*Plus quam se atque suos amavit omnes,*
*Nunc in quadriviis et angiportis*
*Glubit magnanimi Remi nepotes*
(CATULLUS, *Poems LVIII*)

WHEN HE was a boy – well, when he was fifteen –
Morse had fallen deeply in love with a girl, a year his
junior, who like him had won a scholarship to one of
the two local grammar schools: one for boys, one for
girls. The long relationship between the pair of them
had been so formative, so crucial, so wonderful overall,
that when, three years later, he had been called up for
National Service in the Army, he had written (for the
first twelve weeks) a daily letter to his girl; only to learn
on his first weekend furlough, to learn quite accidentally, that one of his friends (friends!) had been openly
boasting about the sensually responsive lips of his
beloved.

Morse told himself that he had finally grown up that
weekend: and that was good. But he'd realized too, at
the same time, that his capacity for jealousy was pretty
nearly boundless.

It was only many years later that he'd seen those
deeply wise words, embroidered in multi-coloured silks,
in a B&B establishment in Maidstone:

– If you love her, set her free
– If she loves you, she will gladly return to you
– If she doesn't she never really loved you anyway

Such thoughts monopolized Morse's mind now as he looked again at Poem LVIII – a poem which his Classics master at school had exhorted the class to ignore, as being totally devoid of artistic merit. Such condemnation was almost invariably in direct proportion to the sexual content of the poem in question; and immediately after the lesson was over, Morse and his classmates had sought to find the meaning of that extraordinary word which Catullus had stuck at the beginning of the last line.

*Glubit.*

In the smaller Latin dictionary, *glubo, -ere* was given only as 'libidinously to excite emotions'. But in the larger dictionary there was a more cryptic, potentially more interesting definition . . . And here, in the margin of the book he was holding, McClure had translated the same poem.

To totters and toffs – in a levelish ratio –
My darling K offers her five-quid fellatio.
Near Carfax, perhaps, or at Cowley-Road Palais,
Or just by the Turf, up any old alley:
Preferring (just slightly) some kerb-crawling gent
High in the ranks of Her Majesty's Government.

Morse gave a mental tick to 'Carfax' for *quadriviis*; but thought 'Palais' a bit adolescent perhaps. Had his own translation been as good? Better? He couldn't remember. He doubted it. And it didn't matter anyway.

Or did it?

In the actual text of the poem, McClure had underlined in red Biro the words *Lesbia nostra, Lesbia illa, Illa Lesbia*: my Lesbia, that Lesbia of mine, that selfsame Lesbia.

Jealousy.

That most corrosive of all the emotions, gnawing away at the heart with a greater pain than failure or hatred – or even despair. But it seemed that McClure, like Catullus, had known his full share of it, with an ever-flirting, ever-hurting woman with whom he'd fallen in love; a woman who appeared willing to prostitute, at the appropriate price, whatever she possessed.

And suddenly, unexpectedly, Morse found himself thinking he'd rather like to meet the mysterious 'K'. Then, just as suddenly, he knew he wouldn't; unless, of course, that ambivalent lady held the key to the murder of Felix McClure – a circumstance which (at the time) he suspected was extremely improbable.

# CHAPTER NINE

And like a skylit water stood
The bluebells in the azured wood
(A. E. HOUSMAN, *A Shropshire Lad, XLI*)

MORSE SNAPPED Catullus to.

'You didn't hear what I just said, did you, sir?'

'Pardon? Sorry. Just pondering – just pondering.'

'Is it leading us anywhere, this, er, pondering?'

'We're learning quite a bit about this girl of his, aren't we? Building up quite an interesting—'

'The answer's "no" then, is it?'

Morse smiled weakly. 'Probably.'

'Not like you, that, sir – giving up so quickly.'

'No. You're right. We shall have to check up on her.'

'Find out where she lives.'

'What? Not much of a problem there,' said Morse.

'Really?'

'She came on foot, we know that. From the Banbury Road side.'

'I thought you said Mrs Thingummy was making everything up?'

But Morse ignored the interjection. 'Where do *you* think she lives?'

'Just round the corner, perhaps?'

'Doubt it. Doubt he'd meet any local girl locally, if you see what I mean.'

'Well, if she did have a car, she couldn't park it in the Banbury Road, that's for certain.'

'So she hasn't got a car?'

'Well, if she has, she doesn't use it.'

'She probably came by bus then.'

'If you say so, sir.'

'Number twenty-something: down the Cowley Road, through the High to Carfax, along Cornmarket and St Giles', then up the Banbury Road.'

'Has she got a season-ticket, sir?'

'Such flippancy ill becomes you, Lewis.'

'I'm not being flippant. I'm just confused. You'll be telling me next what colour her eyes are.'

'Give me a chance.'

'Which street she lives in . . .'

'Oh, I think I know that.'

Lewis grinned and shook his head. 'Come on, sir, tell me!'

'Pater Street, Lewis – that's where she lives. Named after Walter Pater, you know, the fellow who described the Mona Lisa as a woman who'd learned the secrets of the grave.'

'Pater Street? That's out in Cowley, isn't it?'

Morse nodded. 'McClure mentions Cowley in something he wrote here.' Morse tapped Catullus. 'And then there's this.'

He handed across the postcard he'd found marking the relevant page of notes at the back of the volume – notes including a chicken-hearted comment on *Glubit*: '*sensus obscenus*'.

Lewis took the card; and after glancing at the

coloured photograph, 'Bluebells in Wytham Woods', turned to the back where, to the left of McClure's address, he read the brief message, written boldly in black Biro:

---

> **P St out this Sat –**
> **either DC or wherever**　　　　　　　**K**

---

The unsmudged postmark gave the date as 10 August 1994.

'Ye-es. I see what you mean, sir. They'd arranged to meet at her place, perhaps, P-something Street, on the Saturday; then on the Wednesday something cropped up . . .'

'She may have had the decorators in.'

'. . . so it had to be "DC", Daventry Court, or "wherever".'

'Probably some hotel room.'

'Cost him, though. Double room'd be – what? – £70, £80, £90?'

'Or a B&B.'

'Even so. Still about £40, £50.'

'Then he's got to pay her for her services, don't forget that.'

'How much do you think, sir?'

'How the hell should *I* know?'

'Maybe she was worth every penny of it,' Lewis suggested quietly.

'Do you know, I very much doubt that,' asserted Morse with surprising vehemence, now walking over to the phone, consulting the black index, and dialling a number.

'Could be *Princess* Street, sir? That's just off the Cowley Road.'

Morse put his palm over the receiver and shook his head. 'No, Lewis. It's *Pater* Street. Hullo?'

'Yeah? Wha' d'ya wan'?'

'Have I got the right number for "K", please?'

'You 'ave. Bu' she ain't 'ere, is she?'

'That's what I hoped you'd be able to tell me.'

'You another dur'y ol' man or somethin'?'

'If I am, I'm a dirty old police inspector,' replied Morse, in what he trusted was a cultured, authoritative tone.

'Oh, sorry.'

'You say she's not there?'

'She's bin away for a week in Spain. Sent me a topless photo of 'erself from Torremolinos, didn't she? Only this mornin'.'

'A week, you say?'

'Yeah. Went las' Sa'dy – back this Sa'dy.'

'Does she have a . . . a client in North Oxford?'

'An' if she does?'

'You know his name?'

'Nah.'

'What about *her* name?'

'She in some sort of trouble?' Suddenly the voice sounded anxious, softer now – with a final 't' voiced upon that 'sort'.

'I could get all this information from Kidlington Police HQ – you know that, surely? I just thought it would save a bit of time and trouble if you answered me over the phone. Then when we've finished I can thank you for your kind co-operation with the police in their enquiries.'

Hesitation now at the other end of the line.

Then an answer: 'Kay Blaxendale. That's "Kay", K-A-Y. She jus' signs herself "K" – the letter "K".'

'Is that her real name? It sounds a bit posh?'

'It's her professional name. Her real name's Ellie Smith.'

'What about your name?'

'Do you have to know?'

'Yes.'

'Friday Banks – that's me.'

'Have *you* got another name?'

'No.'

'You've got another accent though, haven't you?'

'Pardon?'

'When you want to, you can speak very nicely. You've got a pleasant voice. I just wonder why you try to sound so cheap and common, that's all.'

'Heh! Come off it. I may be common, mista, but I ain't cheap – I can tell yer tha'.'

'All right.'

'Tha' all?'

'Er, do you like bluebells, Miss Banks?'

'Bluebells, you say? Bloody *blue*bells?' She snorted her derision. 'She does, though – Kay does. But me, I'm a red-rose girl, Inspector – if you're thinkin' of sendin' me a bunch of flowers.'

'You never know,' said Morse, as he winked across at Lewis.

'Tha' all?' she repeated.

'Just your address, please.'

'Do you have to know?' (An aspirated 'have'.)

'Yes.'

'It's 35 Princess Street.'

And now it was Lewis's turn, as he winked across at Morse.

# CHAPTER TEN

A long time passed – minutes or years – while the
two of us sat there in silence. Then I said something, asked something, but he didn't respond. I
looked up and I saw the moisture running down
his face

(EDUARDO GALEANO, *The Book of Embraces*)

MORSE'S FACE, after he had cradled the phone,
betrayed a suggestion of satisfaction; but after a short
while a stronger suggestion of *dis*satisfaction.

'Ever heard of a girl called Friday, Lewis?'

'I've heard of that story – *The Man Who Was
Thursday.*'

'It's a diminutive of Frideswide.'

'Right. Yes. We learnt about her at school – St
Frideswide. Patron saint of Oxford. She cured somebody who was blind, I think.'

'Somebody, Lewis, she'd already herself struck blind
in the first place.'

'Not a very nice girl, then.'

'Just like our girl.'

'Anyway, you can cross her off the list of suspects.'

'How do you make that out, Lewis?'

'Unless you still think that girl on the phone's a
phoney too.'

'No. I don't think that. Not now.'

'Well, she said McClure's girlfriend was in Spain when he was murdered, didn't she?'

'It's impolite to eavesdrop on telephone conversations.'

Lewis nodded. 'Interesting, too. I felt sure you were going to ask her to send you the photo – you know, the topless photo from Torremolinos.'

'Do you know,' said Morse quietly, 'I think, looking back on it, I should have done exactly that. I must be getting senile.'

'You can still cross her off your list,' maintained an unsympathetic Lewis.

'Perhaps she was never on it in the first place. You see, I don't think it was a woman who murdered McClure.'

'We shall still have to see her, though.'

'Oh yes. But the big thing we've got to do is learn more about McClure. The more we learn about the murdered man, the more we learn about the murderer.'

Music to Lewis's ears. 'But no firm ideas yet, sir?'

'What?' Morse walked over to the front window, but his eyes seemed not so much to be looking out as looking in. 'I once went to hear a panel of writers, Lewis, and I remember they had to answer an interesting question about titles – you know, how important a title is for a book.'

'*The Wind in the Willows* – that's my favourite.'

'Anyway, the other panellists said it was the most difficult thing of the lot, finding a good title. Then this last woman, she said it was no problem for her at all. Said she'd got half a dozen absolutely dazzling titles – but she just hadn't got any books to go with them. And it's the same with me, Lewis, that's all. I've got plenty of ideas already, but nothing to pin 'em to.'

'Not yet.'

'Not yet,' echoed Morse.

'Do you think Phillotson had any ideas – ideas he didn't tell us about?'

'For Christ's sake, forget Phillotson! He wouldn't know what to do if some fellow walked into his nearest nick with a knife dripping with blood and said he'd just murdered his missus.'

At least that's something you're never likely to do, thought Lewis. But the thought was not translated into words.

'Now,' continued Morse, 'just tell me about this second great discovery of yours.'

'Just give me ten more minutes – nearly ready.'

Morse ambled somewhat aimlessly around the rooms so splendidly cited by Messrs Adkinson: Sitting/Dining-Room; Fully Fitted Modern Kitchen; Cloaks/Shower Room; Guest Bedroom; Master Bedroom Suite; Luxury Bathroom. But nothing, it appeared, was able to hold his attention for long; and soon he returned to the murder room.

For Lewis, this brief period of time was profitable. His little dossier – well, three items held together by a paper-clip – was now, he thought, complete. Interesting. He was pleased with himself; trusted that Morse would be pleased with him, too.

Not that Morse had looked particularly pleased with anything these last few minutes; and Lewis watched him taking a few more books from the shelves, seemingly in random manner, opening each briefly at the title page, then shaking it quite vigorously from the spine as if expecting something to fall out. And even as Lewis watched, something did fall out from one of them – nothing less than the whole of its pages. But Lewis's cautious amusement was immediately stifled by a vicious scowl from Morse; and nothing was said.

In fact, over only one of the title pages had Morse lingered for more than a few moments:

# THE GREAT PLAGUE AT ATHENS

*Its Effect on the Course and Conduct
of the Peloponnesian War*

BY

FELIX FULLERTON McCLURE M.A., D.PHIL.
Student of Wolsey College, Oxford

Correction.
*Late* Student of Wolsey College, Oxford . . .


At 5.45 p.m. PC Roberts knocked, and entered in response to Morse's gruff behest.

'Super just rung through, sir—'

'"Rang" through,' muttered Morse.

'—and wanted me to tell you straightaway. It's Mrs Phillotson, sir. She died earlier this afternoon. Seems she had another emergency op . . . and well, she didn't pull through. He didn't tell me any more. He just wanted you to know, he said.'

Roberts left, and Lewis looked on as Morse slowly sat down in the brown leather armchair, staring, it seemed, at the design on the carpet – the eyes, usually so fierce and piercing, now dull and defeated; a look of such self-loathing on his face as Lewis had never seen before.

It was five minutes later that Lewis made an offer which (as he knew) could hardly be refused.

'Fancy a beer, sir? The King's Arms down the road's open – Open All Day, it says outside.'

But Morse shook his head, and sat there in continued silence.

So for a while Lewis pretended to complete an already completed task. Perhaps he should have felt puzzled? But no. He wasn't puzzled at all.

Tomorrow was Thursday . . .

And the next day was Friday . . .

Strange how they'd both cropped up already that day: the Man Who Was Thursday and the Girl Who Was Friday. Yet at this stage of the case, as they sat together in Daventry Court, neither Morse nor Lewis had the vaguest notion of how crucial one of the two was soon to become.

# CHAPTER ELEVEN

You; my Lady, certainly don't dye your hair to
deceive the others, nor even yourself; but only to
cheat your own image a little before the looking-
glass

(LUIGI PIRANDELLO, *Henry IV*)

WHEN FOR a second time she had put down the phone,
Eleanor Smith stared at her own carpet, in this case
a threadbare, tastelessly floral affair that stopped, at
each wall, about eighteen inches short of the chipped
skirting-boards.

The calls hadn't been unexpected. No. Ever since
she'd read of McClure's murder in the *Oxford Mail*
she'd half expected, half feared that the police would
be in touch. Twice, at least twice, she remembered
sending him a postcard; and once a letter – a rambling,
adolescent letter written just after they'd first met when
she'd felt particularly lonely on a dark and cloudy day.
And knowing Felix, even a bit, she thought he'd
probably have kept anything she might have sent him.

Their first meeting for a drink together had been in
the Chapters Bar of The Randolph. Good, that had
been. No pretences then, on either side. But he'd
gently refused to consider her a 'courtesan' if only for
the reason (as he'd smilingly informed her) that ana-
grammatically, and appropriately, the word gave rise to
'a sore——'.

Yes, quite good really, that first evening – that first night, in fact – together. Above all perhaps, from her point of view, it had marked a nascent interest in crossword puzzles, which Felix had later encouraged and patiently fostered . . .

They'd found her telephone number in his flat – of course they had. Not that it was any great secret. Not exactly an ex-directory, exclusive series of digits. A number, rather, that in the early days had been slipped into half the BT phone-boxes in East Oxford, on a card with an amateurishly drawn outline of a curvaceous brunette with bouncy boobs. Her! But it was there; there in that telephone-thing of his on the desk. She knew that, for she'd seen it there. Odd, really. She'd have expected someone with such a fine brain as Felix to have committed her five-figure number to a permanent place in his memory. Seemingly not, though.

Poor old Felix.

She'd never loved anyone in life really – except her mum. But amongst her clients, that rather endearing, kindly, caring sort of idiot, Felix, had perhaps come nearer than anyone.

He'd never mentioned any enemies. But he must have had at least one – that much was certain. Not that she could help. She knew nothing. If she *had* known something, she'd have volunteered the information before now.

Or would she?

The very last thing she wanted was to get involved with the police. With *her* job? Come off it! And in any case there was no point in it. The last time she'd been round to Felix's apartment had been three weeks ago, when he'd cooked steak for the two of them, with a bottle of vintage claret to wash it down; *and* two bottles of expensive champagne, one before . . . things; and one after.

Poor old Felix.

A very nice person in the very nasty world in which she'd lived these last few years.

Easy enough fooling the fuzz! Just said she wasn't there, hadn't she? Just said she was in Spain. Just said there'd been this photo of a bare-breasted tourist in Torremolinos. Been a bit of a problem if that second copper'd asked for the photo, though. But he'd sounded all right – they'd both sounded all right. Just not very bright, that's all. Would they check up on her? But what if they did? They'd soon understand why she'd told a few fibs. It was a joke. Bit of fun. No one wanted to get involved in a murder enquiry.

And whatever happened she *couldn't* be a suspect. Felix had been murdered on Sunday 28th August, hadn't he? And on that same Sunday she'd left Oxford at 6.30 a.m. (yes!) on a coach-trip to Bournemouth. Hadn't got back, either, until 9.45 p.m. So there! And thirty-four witnesses could testify to that. Thirty-five, if you included the driver.

Nothing to worry about, then – nothing at all.

And yet she couldn't *help* worrying: worrying about who, in his senses, would want to murder such an inoffensive fellow as Felix.

Or in *her* senses . . .

Was there some history, some incident, some background in Felix's life about which she knew nothing? Sure to be, really. Not that he'd ever hinted—

Then it struck her.

There *was* that one thing. Just over a year ago, late May (or was it early June?) when that undergraduate living on Felix's staircase had jumped out of his third-floor window – and broken his neck.

'That undergraduate'? Who was she fooling?

Poor Matthew!

Not that she'd had anything to do with that, either. Well, she'd fervently prayed that she hadn't. After all, she'd only met him once, when Felix had become so furiously jealous.

Jealousy!

At *his* age – forty-one years older than she was. A grandfather, almost. A father, certainly. Yet one of the very few clients who meant anything to her in that continuum of carnality which passed for some sort of purpose in her present life.

Yes, a father-figure.

A foster-father, perhaps.

Not a bloody *step*-father, though! Christ, no.

She looked at herself in the mirror of the old-fashioned dressing-table. The pallor of her skin looked ghastly; and her dark hair, streaked with a reddish-orange henna dye, looked lustreless – and cheap. But she felt cheap all over. And as she rested her oval face on her palms, the index finger of each hand stroking the silver rings at either side of her nostrils, her sludgy-green eyes stared back at her with an expression of dullness and dishonesty.

Dishonesty?

Yes. The truth was that she probably hadn't given a sod for McClure, not really. Come to think of it, he'd been getting something of a nuisance: wanting to monopolize her; pressurizing her; phoning at inconvenient moments – once at a *very* inconvenient moment. He'd become far too obsessive, far too possessive. And what was worse, he'd lost much of his former gaiety and humour in the process. Some men were like that.

Well, hard luck!

Yes, if she were honest with herself, she was glad it was all over. And as she continued to stare at herself, she was suddenly aware that the streaks of crimson in her hair were only perhaps a physical manifestation of the incipient streaks of cruelty in her heart.

# CHAPTER TWELVE

To run away from trouble is a form of cowardice
and, while it is true that the suicide braves death,
he does it not for some noble object but to escape
some ill

(ARISTOTLE, *Nicomachean Ethics*)

MORSE HAD finished the previous evening with four
pints of Best Bitter (under an ever-tightening waist-
belt) at the King's Arms in Banbury Road; and had
followed this with half a bottle of his dearly beloved
Glenfiddich (in his pyjamas) at his bachelor flat in the
same North Oxford.

Unsurprisingly, therefore, he had not exactly felt as
fit as a Stradivarius when Lewis had called the following
morning; and it was Lewis who now drove out to
Leicester.

It was Lewis who *had* to drive out to Leicester.

As the Jaguar reached the outskirts of that city,
Morse was looking again through the items (four of
them now, not three) which Lewis had seen fit to
salvage from McClure's apartment, and which – glory
be! – Morse had instantly agreed could well be of
importance to the case. Certainly they threw light upon
that murky drink-drugs-sex scene which had established
itself in some few parts of Oxford University. First was a
cutting from the *Oxford Mail* dated Tuesday, 8 June
1993 (fourteen months earlier):

# DRUG LINK WITH
# DREAM SON'S SUICIDE

At an inquest held yesterday, the Coroner, Mr Arnold Hoskins, recorded a verdict of suicide on the death of Mr Matthew Rodway, a third-year undergraduate reading English at Oxford.

Rodway's body had been discovered by one of the college scouts in the early hours of Friday, 21 May, at the foot of his third-floor window in the Drinkwater Quad of Wolsey College.

There was some discrepancy in the statements read out at the inquest, with suggestions made that Mr Rodway may perhaps have fallen accidentally after a fairly heavy drinking-party in his rooms on Staircase G.

There was also clear evidence, however, that Mr Rodway had been deeply depressed during the previous weeks, apparently about his prospects in his forthcoming Finals examination.

What was not disputed was that Rodway had taken refuge amongst one or two groups where drugs were regularly taken in various forms.

Dr Felix McClure, one of Rodway's former tutors, was questioned about an obviously genuine but unfinished letter found in Rodway's rooms, containing the sentence 'I've had enough of all this'.

Whilst he stoutly maintained that the words themselves were ambivalent in their implication, Dr McClure agreed with the Coroner that the most likely explanation of events was that Rodway had been driven to take his own life.

Pathological evidence substantiated the fact that Rodway had taken drugs, on a regular basis, yet there appeared no evidence to suggest that he was a suicidal type with some obsessive death-wish.

In his summing up, the Coroner stressed the evil nature of trafficking in drugs, and pointed to the ready availability of such drugs as a major contributory factor in Rodway's death.

Taken in the first place to alleviate anxiety, they had in all probability merely served to aggravate it, with the tragic consequences of which the court had heard.

Matthew's mother is reluctant to accept the Coroner's verdict. Speaking from her home in Leicester, Mrs Mary Rodway wished only to recall a bright, caring son who had every prospect of success before him.

'He was so talented in many ways. He was very good at hockey and tennis. He had a great love of music, and played the viola in the National Youth Orchestra.

'I know I'm making him sound like a dream son. Well, that's what he was.' (See Leader, p.8)

Morse turned to the second cutting, taken from the same issue:

## A DEGREE TOO FAR

A recently commissioned study highlights the increasing percentage of Oxford graduates who fail to find suitable employment. Dr Clive Hornsby, Senior Reader in Social Sciences at Lonsdale College, has endorsed the implications of these findings, and suggests that many students, fully aware of employment prospects, strive for higher-class degrees than they are competent to achieve. Others, as yet mercifully few, adopt the alternative course of abandoning hope, of seeking consolation in drink and drugs, and sometimes of concluding that life is not worth the living of it. It may well be that Oxford University, through its various advisory agencies and helplines, is fully aware of these and related problems, although we are not wholly convinced of this. The latest suicide in an Oxford college (see p.1) prompts renewed concern about the pressures on our undergraduate community here, and the ways in which additional advice and help can be provided.

Morse now turned again to the third cutting, taken from the *Oxford Times* of Friday, 18 June 1993: a shorter article, flanked by a photograph of 'Dr F. F. Maclure', a clean-shaven, rather mournful-looking man, pictured in full academic dress.

# PASTORAL CARE DEFENDED

Following the latest in a disturbing sequence of suicides, considerable criticism has been levelled against the University's counselling arrangements. But Dr Felix McLure, former Senior Lecturer in Ancient History at Wolsey College, has expressed his disappointment that so many have rushed into the arena with allegations of indifference and neglect. In fact, according to Dr Mac-Clure, the University has been instrumental over the past year in promoting several initiatives, including the formation of Oxford University Counselling and Help (OUCH) of which he was a founder-member. 'More should be done,' he told our reporter. 'We all agree on that score. But there should also be some recognition of the University's present concern and commitment.'

'You'll soon know those things off by heart,' ventured a well-pleased Lewis as he stopped in a leafy lane on the eastern side of the London Road and briefly consulted his street-map, before setting off again.

'It's not that. It's just that I'm a slow reader.'

'What if you'd been a quick reader, sir? Where would you be now?'

'Probably been a proofreader in a newspaper office. They could certainly do with one,' mumbled Morse as he considered 'Maclure' and 'McLure' and 'MacClure' in the last cutting, with still no sign of the genuine article, 'former Senior Lecturer . . .'

Interesting, that extra little piece of the jigsaw – that 'former' . . .

Lewis braked gently outside Number 14 Evington Road South; then decided to continue into the drive, where the low-profile tyres of the Jaguar crunched into the deep gravel.

# CHAPTER THIRTEEN

> Whatever crazy sorrow saith,
> No life that breathes with human breath
> Has ever truly longed for death
> (ALFRED, LORD TENNYSON, *The Two Voices*)

MRS MARY RODWAY, a smartly dressed, slim-figured, pleasantly featured woman in her late forties, seemed quite willing to talk about herself – at least for a start.

Four years previously (she told the detectives) her husband, a highly-salaried constructional engineer, had run off with his Personal Assistant. The only contact between herself and her former marriage-partner was now effected via the agency of solicitors and banks. She lived on her own happily enough, she supposed – if anyone could ever live happily again after the death of an only child, especially a child who had died in such dubious circumstances.

She had seen McClure's murder reported in *The Independent*; and Morse wasted no time in telling her of the specific reason for his visit: the cuttings discovered among the murdered man's papers which appeared firmly to underline his keen interest in her son, Matthew, and perhaps in the reasons for his suicide.

'He was quite wrong – the Coroner. You do realize that?' Mary Rodway lit another cigarette and inhaled deeply.

'You don't believe it was suicide?'

'I didn't say that. What I do say is that the Coroner was wrong in making such a big thing about those hard drugs. That's what they call them: "hard" as opposed to "soft". It's just the same with pornography, I believe, Inspector.'

Whilst Morse nodded his head innocently, Mrs Rodway shook her own in vague exasperation. 'Life's a far more *complicated* thing than that – Matthew's was – and that Coroner, he made it all sound so ... *un*complicated.'

'Don't be too, er, hard on him, Mrs Rodway. A Coroner's main job isn't dealing with right and wrong, and making moral judgements, and all that sort of thing. He's just there to put the bits and pieces into some sort of pattern, and then to stick some verdict, as best he can, in one of the few slots he's got available to him.'

If Mrs Rodway was at all impressed by this amalgam of metaphors, she gave no indication of it. Perhaps she hadn't even been listening, for she continued in her former vein: 'There were two things – two quite separate things – and they ought to have been *considered* separately. It's difficult to put it into words, Inspector, but you see there are causes of things, and symptoms of things. And in Matthew's case this drugs business was a symptom of something – it wasn't a cause. I *knew* Matthew – I knew him better than anyone.'

'So you think ... ?'

'I've stopped thinking. What on earth's the good of churning things over and over again in your mind for the umpteenth time?'

She stubbed out a half-smoked cigarette savagely, and immediately lit another.

'You don't mind me smoking?'

'No, no.'

'Can I offer you gentlemen one?' She held out a packet of King-Size Dunhill International, first to Lewis who shook his head with a smile; then to Morse who shook his head with stoical resolve, since only that same morning, when he'd woken up just before six with parched mouth and pounding head, he had decided to forgo – for evermore – the spurious gratification not only of alcohol but of nicotine also.

Perhaps his decision could wait until tomorrow for its full implementation, though; and he relented. 'Most kind, Mrs Rodway. Thank you . . . And it's very valuable, what you're saying. Please do go on.'

'There's nothing more to say.'

'But if you felt – feel – so strongly, why didn't you agree to give evidence at the Inquest?'

'How could I? I couldn't even bear to switch on the TV or the radio in case there might be something about it. *You* couldn't bear that, could you, Inspector? If it had been your child?'

'I – I take your point,' admitted Morse awkwardly.

'You know usually, when things like that happen, you get all the rumour and all the gossip as well. But we didn't have any of that – at the Inquest.'

Three times now Mary Rodway inhaled on her cigarette with such ferocity that she seemed to Lewis hell-bent on inflicting some irreparable damage to her respiratory tract.

But Morse's mind for a few seconds was far away, a glimmer of light at last appearing at the far end of a long, black tunnel.

'So . . .' he picked his slow words carefully, 'you'd hoped that there might be some other evidence given at the Inquest, but you didn't want to provide any of it yourself?'

'Perhaps it wasn't all that important anyway.'

'Please tell me.'

'No.'

Morse looked around the large lounge. The day was warm already, yet he suspected (rightly) that the two long radiators were turned up to full capacity. Much space on the walls was devoted to pictures: prints of still-life paintings by Braque, Matisse, Picasso; photographs and watercolours of great buildings and palaces, including Versailles and Blenheim – and Wolsey College, Oxford. But virtually no people were photographed or represented there. It was as if those 'things' so frequently resorted to by Mrs Rodway in her conversation were now figuring more prominently than people.

'You knew Dr McClure, I think,' said Morse.

'I met him first when Matthew went up to Oxford. He was Matthew's tutor.'

'Didn't he have rooms on the same staircase as Matthew?' (Lewis had spent most of the previous evening doing his homework; *and* Morse's homework.)

'The first year, and the third year, yes. He was out of college his second year.'

'Where was that, do you remember?'

Did Lewis observe a flicker of unease in Mary Rodway's eyes? Did Morse?

'I'm not sure.'

'Oh, it doesn't matter. Sergeant Lewis here can check up on that easily enough.'

But she had her answer now. 'It was in East Oxford somewhere. Cowley Road, was it?'

Morse continued his questioning, poker-faced, as if he had failed to hear the tintinnabulation of a bell: 'What did you think of Dr McClure?'

'Very nice man. Kindly – genuine sort of person. And, as you say, he took a real interest in Matthew.'

Morse produced a letter, and passed it across to Mrs Rodway: a single handwritten sheet, on the pre-printed stationery of 14 Evington Road South, Leicester, dated 2 June, the day after the Coroner's verdict on Matthew Rodway's death.

> Dear Felix
> I was glad to talk to you on the phone however briefly. I was so choked I could hardly speak to you. Please do as we agreed. If you find anything else among M's things which would be upsetting please get rid of them. This includes any of my letters he may have kept. He had two family photos in his room, one a framed one of the two of us. I'd like both of them back. But all clothes and personal effects and papers – get rid of them all for me.
>
> I must thank you for all you tried to do for Matthew. He often spoke of your kindness, as you know. I'm so sorry, I can't go on with this letter any more.
> Sincerely yours
> Mary

Morse now accepted a second cigarette; and as Mrs Rodway read through the letter Lewis turned his head away from the exhalation of smoke. He was not over-much concerned about the health risks supposedly linked with passive smoking, but it must have some effect; had already *had* its effect on the room here, where a thin patina of nicotine could be seen on the emulsioned walls. In fact the whole room could surely do with a good wash-down and redecoration? The corners of the high ceiling were deeply stained, and just above one of the radiators an oblong of pristinely bright magnolia served to emphasize a slight neglect of household renovation.

'Did you write that?' asked Morse.

'Yes.'

'Is there anything you want to tell us about it?'

'Pretty clear, isn't it?'

'Did Dr McClure find anything in Matthew's rooms?'

'I don't know.'

'Would he have told you if, let's say, he'd found some drugs?'

'I doubt it.'

'Did he think Matthew was taking drugs?'

It was hard for her to say it. But she said it: 'Yes.'

'Did you ever find out where he got his drugs from?'

'No.'

'Did he ever say anything about his friends being on drugs?'

'No.'

'Do you think they may have been?'

'I only met one or two of them – on the same staircase.'

'Do you think drugs were available inside the college?'

'I don't know.'

'Would Dr McClure have known, if they were?'

'I suppose he would, yes.'

'Was Matthew fairly easily influenced by his friends, would you say?'

'No, I wouldn't.'

The answers elicited from Mrs Rodway hardly appeared to Lewis exciting; or even informative, for that matter. But Morse appeared content to keep his interlocution at low key.

'Do you blame anyone? About the drugs?'

'I'm in no position to blame anyone.'

'Do you blame yourself?'

'Don't we all blame ourselves?'

'What about Dr McClure – where did he put the blame?'

'He did say once . . . I remember . . .' But the voice trailed off as she lit another cigarette. 'It was very odd really. He was talking about all the pressures on young people these days – you know, about youth culture and all that sort of thing, about whether standards were declining in . . . well, in everything, I suppose.'

'What exactly did he say?' prompted Morse gently.

But Mary Rodway was not listening. 'You know, if only Matthew hadn't . . . killed himself that night, whatever the reason was – reason or reasons – he'd probably have been perfectly happy with life a few days later, a week later . . . That's what I can't . . . I can't get over.'

Tears were dropping now.

And Lewis looked away.

But not Morse.

'What exactly did he say?' he repeated.

Mrs Rodway wiped her tears and blew her nose noisily. 'He said it was always difficult to apportion blame in life. But he said . . . he said if he had to blame anybody it would be the students.'

'Is that all?'

'Yes.'

'Why was that an "odd" thing to say, though?'

'Because, you see, he was always on the students' side. Always. So it was a bit like hearing a trade-union boss suddenly siding with the Conservative Party.'

'Thank you. You've been very kind, Mrs Rodway.'

Clearly (as Lewis could see) it was time to depart; and he closed his notebook with what might have passed for a slight flourish – had anyone been interested enough to observe the gesture.

But equally clearly (as Lewis could also see) Morse was momentarily transfixed, the blue eyes gleaming with that strangely distanced, almost ethereal gaze, which Lewis had observed so often before – a gaze which usually betokened a breakthrough in a major case.

As now?

The three of them rose to their feet.

'Did you get to university yourself?' asked Morse.

'No. I left school at sixteen – went to a posh secretarial college – did well – got a good job – met a nice boss – became his PA – and he married me . . . As I told you, Inspector, he's got a weakness for his PAs.'

Morse nodded. 'Just one last question. *When* did your husband leave you?'

'I told you, don't you remember? Four years ago.'
Suddenly her voice sounded sharp.

'When *exactly*, Mrs Rodway?' Suddenly Morse's voice, too, sounded sharp.

'November the fifth – Bonfire Night. Not likely to forget the date, am I?'

'Not *quite* four years ago then?'

Mrs Rodway made no further reply.

# CHAPTER FOURTEEN

Everyone can master a grief but he that has it
(SHAKESPEARE, *Much Ado About Nothing*)

'BIG THING you've got to remember is that it's a great healer – time. Just give it a while, you'll see.'

It was just before lunchtime that same day, in his office at Kidlington Police HQ, that Chief Superintendent Strange thus sought to convey his commiserations to Detective Chief Inspector Phillotson – going on to suggest that an extended period of furlough might well be a good thing after ... well, after things were over. And if anyone could help in any way, Phillotson only had to mention it.

'Trouble with things like this,' continued Strange, as he rose from behind his desk and walked round to place a kindly hand on his colleague's shoulder, 'is that nothing really helps much at all, does it?'

'I don't know about that, sir. People are being very kind.'

'I know, yes. I know.' And Strange resumed his seat, contemplating his own kindliness with some gratification.

'You know, sir, I've heard from people I never expected to show much sympathy.'

'You have?'

'People like Morse, for instance.'

'Morse? When did you see Morse? He told me he was off to Leicester this morning.'

'No. He put a note through the letter-box, that's all. Must have been latish last night – it wasn't there when I put the milk-tokens out . . .'

'I'd say he probably wrote it in a pub, knowing Morse.'

'Does it matter where he wrote it, sir?'

'Course not. But I can't imagine *him* being much comfort to anybody. He's a pagan, you know that. Got no time for the Church and . . . Hope and Faith and all that stuff. Doesn't even believe in God, let alone in any sort of life after death.'

'Bit like some of our Bishops,' said Phillotson sadly.

'Like some Theology dons in Oxford, too.'

'I was still glad to get his letter.'

'What did he say?'

'Said what you just said really, sir; said he'd got no faith in the Almighty; said I just ought to forget all this mumbo-jumbo about meeting . . . meeting up again in some future life; told me just to accept the truth of it all – that she's gone for good and I'll never see her again; told me I'd probably never get over it, and not to take any notice of people who gave you all this stuff about time healing—' Phillotson suddenly checked himself, realizing what he'd just said.

'Doesn't sound much help to me.'

'Do you know, though, in an odd sort of way it was. It was sort of *honest*. He just said that he was sad, when he heard, and he was thinking of me . . . At the end, he said it was always a jolly sight easier in life to face up to the truths than the half-truths. I'm not quite sure what he meant ... but, well, somehow it helps, when I remember what he said.'

Phillotson could trust himself to say no more, and he rose to leave.

At the door he turned back. 'Did you say Morse went to Leicester this morning?'

'That's where he said he was going.'

'Funny! Odds are I'd have been in Leicester myself. I bet he's gone to see the parents of that lad who killed himself in Wolsey a year or so ago.'

'What's that got to do with things?'

'There were a few newspaper articles, that's all, about the lad, among McClure's papers. *And* a letter from the mother. She started it off "Dear Felix" – as if they'd known each other pretty well, if you see what I mean.'

Strange grunted.

'Do you think I should mention it to Morse, sir?'

'No. For Christ's sake don't do that. He's got far too many ideas already, you can be sure of that.'

# CHAPTER FIFTEEN

Say, for what were hop-yards meant
Or why was Burton built on Trent?
Oh many a peer of England brews
Livelier liquor than the Muse,
And malt does more than Milton can
To justify God's ways to man
    (A. E. HOUSMAN, *A Shropshire Lad, LXII*)

THE TURF TAVERN, nestling beneath the old walls of New College, Oxford, may be approached from Holywell Street, immediately opposite Holywell Music Room, via a narrow, irregularly cobbled lane of mediaeval aspect.

A notice above the entrance advises all patrons (although Morse is not a particularly tall man) to mind their heads (DUCK OR GROUSE) and inside the rough-stoned, black-beamed rooms the true connoisseur of beers can seat himself at one of the small wooden tables and enjoy a finely cask-conditioned pint; and it is in order to drink and to talk and to think that patrons frequent this elusively situated tavern in a blessedly music – Muzak – free environment.

The landlord of this splendid hostelry, a stoutly compact, middle-aged ex-Royal Navy man, with a grizzled beard and a gold ring in his left ear, was anticipatorily pulling a pint of real ale on seeing Morse enter, followed by the dutiful Lewis, at 1.50 p.m.

The latter, in fact, was feeling quite pleased with himself. Only sixty-five minutes from Leicester. A bit over the speed-limit all the way along (agreed); but fast-driving was one of his very few vices, and the jazzy-looking maroon Jaguar had been in a wonderfully slick and silky mood as it sped down the M40 on the last stretch of the journey from Banbury to Oxford.

Morse had resisted several pubs which, *en route*, had paraded their credentials – at Lutterworth, Rugby, Banbury. But, as Lewis knew, the time of drinking, and of thinking, was surely soon at hand.

In North Oxford, Morse had asked to be dropped off briefly at his flat: 'I ought to call in at the bank, Lewis.' And this news had further cheered Lewis, since (on half the salary) it was invariably *he* who bought about three-quarters of the drinks consumed between the pair of them. Only temporarily cheered, however, since he had wholly misunderstood the mission: five minutes later it was he himself who was pushing a variety of old soldiers through their appropriate holes (White, Green, Brown) in the Summertown Bottle Bank.

Thence, straight down the Banbury Road to the Martyrs' Memorial, where turning left (as instructed) he had driven to the far end of Broad Street. Here, as ever, there appeared no immediate prospect of leaving a car legitimately, and Morse had insisted that he parked the Jaguar on the cobblestone area outside the Old Clarendon building, just opposite Blackwell's.

'Don't worry, Lewis. All the traffic wardens know my car. They'll think I'm on duty.'

'Which you are, sir.'

'Which I am.'

'How are we, Chief Inspector?'

'Less of the "Chief". Sheehy's going to demote me. I'll soon be just an insignificant Inspector.'

'The usual?'

Morse nodded.

'And you, Sergeant?'

'An orange juice,' said Morse.

'Where've you parked?' asked Biff. It was a question which had become of paramount importance in Central Oxford over the past decade. 'I only ask because they're having a blitz this week, so Pam says.'

'Ah! How *is* that beautiful lady of yours?'

'I'll tell her you're here. She should be down soon anyway.' Morse stood at the bar searching through his pockets in unconvincing manner. 'And a packet of – do you still sell cigarettes?'

Biff pointed to the machine. 'You'll need the right change.'

'Ah! Have you got any change on you by any chance, Lewis . . . ?'

When, at a table in the inner bar, Morse was finally settled behind his pint, his second pint, he took from his inside jacket-pocket the used envelope on which Lewis had seen him scribbling certain headings on their return to Oxford.

'Did you know that Wolsey College is frequently referred to, especially by those who are in it, as "The House"?'

'Can't say I did, no.'

'Do you know why?'

'Let me concentrate on the orange juice, sir.'

'It's because of its Latin name, *Aedes Archiepiscopi*, the House of the Bishop.'

'Well, that explains it, doesn't it?'

'Another peculiarity is that in all the other colleges they call the dons and the readers and the tutors and so on – they call them "Fellows". You with me? But at Wolsey they call them "Students".'

'What do they call the students then?'

'Doesn't *matter* what they call 'em, does it? Look! Let's just consider where we are. We've discovered a couple of possible links in this case so far: McClure's fancy woman; and the Rodway woman, the mother of one of his former pupils. Now neither of 'em comes within a million miles of being a murderer, I know that; but they're both adding to what we know of McClure himself, agreed? He's a respected scholar; a conscientious don—'

'"Student", sir.'

'A conscientious Student; a man who's got every sympathy with his stu—'

Lewis looked across.

' – with the young people he comes into contact with; a founder member of a society to help dedicated druggies; a man who met Matthew's mum, and probably slipped in between the sheets with her—'

Lewis shook his head vigorously. 'You *can't* just say that sort of thing.'

'And why not? How the hell do you think we're going to get to the bottom of this case unless we make the odd hypothesis here and there? You don't know?

Well, let me tell you. We think of anything that's unlikely. That's how. Any bloody idiot can tell you what's *likely*.'

'If you say so, sir.'

'I *do* say so,' snapped Morse. 'Except that what I say is *not* particularly unlikely, is it? They obviously got on pretty well, didn't they? Take that salutation and vale-diction, for instance.'

Lewis lifted his eyebrows.

'All Christian-name, palsy-walsy stuff, wasn't it? Then there's this business of her husband leaving her – you'll recall I pressed her on that point? And for a very good reason. It was November, a month or so after her precious Matthew had first gone up to Oxford. And it occurred to me, Lewis – and I'm surprised it didn't occur to you – that things may well have been the other way round, eh? She may have left *him*, and it was only then that he started playing around with his new PA.'

'We could always look at a copy of the divorce proceedings.'

'What makes you think they're divorced?'

Lewis surrendered, sipped his orange juice, and was silent.

'But it doesn't matter, does it? It's got bugger-all to do with McClure's murder. You can make a heap of all the money you've got and wager it on *that*. No risk there!'

Lewis fingered the only money he had left in his pockets – three pound coins – and decided that he was hardly going to become a rich man, however long the odds that Morse was offering. But it was time to mention something. Had Morse, he wondered, seen that oblong patch of pristine magnolia . . . ?

'There was,' Lewis began slowly, 'a light-coloured patch on the wall in Mrs Rodway's lounge, sir—'

'Ah! Glad you noticed that. Fiver to a cracked piss-pot that was a picture of *him*, Lewis – of McClure! That's why she took it down. She didn't want us to see it, but something like that's always going to leave its mark, agreed?'

'Unless she put something else up there to cover it.'

Morse scorned the objection. 'She wouldn't have taken a photo of her *son* down, would she? Where's the point of that? Very unlikely.'

'You just said that's exactly what we're looking for, sir – something "unlikely".'

Morse was spared any possible answer to this astute question by the arrival of the landlady, a slimly attractive brunette, with small, neat features, and an extra sparkle in her eyes as she greeted Morse with a kiss on his cheek.

'Not seen you for a little while, Inspector.'

'How's things, beautiful?'

'Another beer?'

'Well, if you insist.'

'I'm not really insisting—'

'Pint of the best bitter for me.'

'You, Sergeant?'

'He's driving,' said Morse.

Biff, the landlord, came over to join them, and the four sat together for the next ten minutes. Morse, after explaining that the word 'Turf' had appeared in the margin of one of McClure's books, asked whether they, either landlord or landlady, would have known the murdered man if they had seen him in the pub ('No');

whether they'd ever seen the young man from Wolsey who'd committed suicide ('Don't think so'); whether they'd ever seen a young woman with rings in her nose and red streaks in her hair ('Hundreds of 'em').

Yet the landlady had one piece of information.

'There's one of the chaps comes in here sometimes who was a scout on that staircase . . . when, you know . . . I heard him talking to somebody about it.'

'That's right.' The landlord was remembering too. 'Said he used to go to the Bulldog – or was it the Old Tom, Pam?'

'Can't remember.'

'He was a scout, you say?' asked Morse.

'Yeah. Only started coming in here after he moved – moved to the Pitt Rivers, I think it was. Well, only just up the road, isn't it?'

'He still comes?'

Biff considered. 'Haven't seen him for a little while now you come to mention it. Have you, love?'

Pam shook her pretty head.

'Know his name?' asked Lewis.

'Brooks – Ted Brooks.'


'Just let me get this clear,' said Lewis, as he and Morse left the Turf Tavern, this time via St Helen's Passage, just off New College Lane. 'You're saying that Mrs Rodway misunderstood what McClure said to her – about the "students"?'

'You've got it. What he meant was that he blamed the dons, the set-up there, the authorities. He wasn't saying they were a load of crooks – just that they should have known what was going on there, and should have done something about it.'

'*If* anything was going on, sir.'

'Which'll be one of our next jobs, Lewis – to find out exactly that.'

It was Lewis who spotted it first: the traffic-warden's notice stuck beneath the near-side windscreen-wiper of the unmarked Jaguar.

By three o'clock that afternoon, Mary Rodway had assembled the new passe-partout for the picture-frame. Like most things in the room (she agreed) it had been getting very dingy. But it looked splendid now, as she carefully replaced the re-mounted photograph, standing back repeatedly and adjusting it, to the millimetre – that photograph of herself and her son which Felix had sent to her as she'd requested.

Nothing further of any great moment occurred that day, except for one thing – something which for Lewis was the most extraordinary, the most 'unlikely' event of the past six months.

'Come in a minute and let me pay you for those cigarettes,' Morse had said, as the Jaguar came to a stop outside the bachelor flat in North Oxford.

# CHAPTER SIXTEEN

And sidelong glanced, as to explore,
In meditated flight, the door
(SIR WALTER SCOTT, *Rokeby*)

WHAT MORSE had vaguely referred to as the 'authorities' at Wolsey were immediately co-operative; and at 10 a.m. the following day he and Lewis were soon learning many things about the place: specifically, in due course, about Staircase G in Drinkwater Quad, on which Dr McClure had spent nine years of his university life, from 1984 until his retirement from academe at the end of the Trinity Term, 1993.

From his rooms overlooking the expansive quad ('Largest in Oxford, gentlemen – 264 by 261 feet') the Deputy Bursar had explained, rather too slowly and too pedantically for Morse's taste, the way things, er, worked in the, er, House, it clearly seeming to this former Air-Vice Marshal ('Often mis-spelt, you know – and more often mis-hyphenated') that these non-University people needed some elementary explanations.

Scouts?

Interested in *scouts*, were they?

Well, each scout ('Interesting word – origin obscure') looked after one staircase, and one staircase only – with that area guarded as jealously as any blackbird's territory in a garden, and considered almost as a sort of mediaeval fiefdom ('If you know what I mean?'). Several of the scouts had been with them, what, twenty, thirty years? Forty-nine years, one of them! What exactly did they do? Well, it would be sensible to go and hear things from the horse's mouth, as it were. What?

Escorted therefore through Great Quad, and away to the left of it into what seemed to Morse the unhappily named 'Drinkwater Quad', the policemen thanked their cicerone, the Air-hyphen-Vice Marshal ('One "l"') and made their way to Staircase G.

Where a surprise was in store for them.

Not really a scout at all – more a girl-guide.

Susan Ewers, too, was friendly and helpful – a married woman (no children yet) who was very happy to have the opportunity of supplementing the family income; very happy, too, with the work itself. The majority of scouts were women now, she explained: only three or four men still doing the job at Wolsey. In fact, she'd taken over from a man – a man who'd left to work at the Pitt Rivers Museum.

'Mr Brooks, was that?' asked Morse.

'Yes. Do you know him?'

'Heard of him, er . . . please go on.'

Her duties? Well, everything really. The immediate area outside; the entrance; the porchway; the stairs; the eight sets of rooms, all of them occupied during term-time, of course; and some of them during the vacs, like now, by delegates and visitors to various do's and conferences. Her first job each morning was to empty all the rubbish-baskets into black bags; then to clean

the three WCs, one on each floor (no *en suite* facilities
as yet); same with the wash-basins. Then, only twice a
week, though, to Hoover all the floors, and generally to
dust around, polish any brasswork, that sort of thing;
and in general to see that the living quarters of her
charges were kept as neat and tidy as could be expected
with young men and young women who would (she
felt) probably prefer to live in – well, to live in a bit of
a mess, really. No bed-making, though. Thank
goodness!

Willingly she showed the detectives the rooms at G4,
on the second floor of her staircase, where until
fourteen months previously the name 'Dr F. F.
McClure' had been printed in black Gothic capitals
beside the Oxford-blue double doors.

But if Morse had expected to find anything of
significance in these rooms, he was disappointed. All
fixtures befitting the status of a respected scholar had
been replaced by the furniture of standard undergraduate accommodation: a three-seater settee; two armchairs; two desks; two bookcases . . . It reminded Morse
of his own unhappy, unsuccessful days at Oxford; but
made no other impact.

It might have been helpful to move quietly around
the lounge and the spacious bedroom there, and seek
to detect any vibrations, any reverberations, left behind
by a cultured and (it seemed) a fairly kindly soul.

But clearly Morse could see little point in such
divination.

'Is G8 free?' he asked.

'There *is* a gentleman there. But he's not in at the
minute. If you want just a quick look inside?'

'It's where Matthew Rodway, the man who . . .'

'I know,' said Susan Ewers quietly.

But G8 proved to be equally disappointing: a three-seater settee, two (faded fabric) armchairs . . . cloned and cleaned of every reminder of the young man who had thrown himself down on to the paved area below the window there – the window at which Morse and Lewis now stood for a little while. Silently.

'You didn't know Mr Rodway, either?' asked Morse.

'No. As I say, I didn't come till September last year.'

'Do people on the staircase still take drugs?'

Mrs Ewers was taken aback by the abruptness of Morse's question.

'Well, they still have parties, like, you know. Drink and . . . and so on.'

'But you've never seen any evidence of drugs – any packets of drugs? Crack? Speed? Ecstasy? Anything? Anything at all?'

Had she?

'No,' she said. Almost truthfully.

'You've never smelt anything suspicious?'

'I wouldn't know what they smell like, drugs,' she said. Truthfully.

As they walked down the stairs, Lewis pointed to a door marked with a little floral plaque: 'Susan's Pantry'.

'That where you keep all your things, madam?'

She nodded. 'Every scout has a pantry.'

'Can we take a look inside?'

She unlocked the door and led the way into a fairly

small, high-ceilinged room, cluttered – yet so neatly cluttered – with buckets, mops, bin-liners, black plastic bags, transparent polythene bags, light bulbs, toilet rolls, towels, sheets, two Hoovers. And inside the white-painted cupboards rows of cleaners and detergents: Jif, Flash, Ajax, Windolene ... And everything so clean – so meticulously, antiseptically clean.

Morse had little doubt that Susan Ewers was the sort of housewife to polish her bath-taps daily; the sort to feel aggrieved at finding a stray trace of toothpaste in the wash-basin. If cleanliness were next to saint-liness, then this lady was probably on the verge of beatification.

So what?

Apart from mentally extending his lively sympathies to *Mr* Ewers, Morse was aware that his thought-processes were hardly operating *vivamente* that morning; and he stood in the slightly claustrophobic pantry, feeling somewhat feckless.

It was Lewis who, as so frequently, was the catalyst.

'What's your husband do, Mrs Ewers?'

'He's – well, at the minute he's unemployed, actually. He did work at the old RAC offices in Summertown, but they made him redundant.'

'When was that?'

'Last year.'

'When exactly?' (If Morse could ask such questions, why not Lewis?)

'Last, er, August.'

'Good thing you getting the job then. Help tide things over a bit, like.'

Lewis smiled sympathetically.

And Morse smiled gratefully.

Bless you, Lewis – bless you!

*Gestalt* – that's what the Germans call it. That flash of unified perception, that synoptic totality which is more than the sum of the parts into which it may be logically analysable; parts, in this case, like drugs and scouts and a suicide and a murder and a staircase and changing jobs and not having a job and retirement and money and times and dates ... Yes, especially times and dates ...

Most probably, in the circumstances, Matthew Rodway's rooms would not have been re-occupied for the few remaining weeks at the end of Trinity Term the previous year; and if (as now) only *some* of the rooms were in use during the Long Vac, it might well be that Mrs Ewers had been the very first person to look closely around the suicide's chambers. But no; that was wrong. McClure had already gone through things, hadn't he? Mrs Rodway had asked him to. But would he have been half as thorough as this newly appointed woman?

He'd questioned her on the point already, he knew that. But he hadn't asked the right questions, perhaps? Not quite.

'Just going back a minute, Mrs Ewers ... When you got Mr Rodway's old rooms ready for the beginning of the Michaelmas term, had anyone else been in there – during the summer?'

'I don't think so, no.'

'But you still didn't find anything?'

'No, like I just said—'

'Oh, I believe you. If there'd been anything to find, you'd have found it.'

She looked relieved.

'In his rooms, that is,' added Morse slowly.

'Pardon?'

'All I'm saying is that you've got a very tidy mind, haven't you? Let's put it this way. I bet I know the first thing you did when you took over here. I bet you gave this room the best spring-clean – best autumn-clean – it's ever had – last September – when *you* moved in – and the previous scout moved out.'

Susan Ewers looked puzzled. 'Well, I scrubbed and cleaned the place from top to bottom, yes – filthy, it was. Two whole days it took me. But I never found anything – any drugs – honest to God, I didn't!'

Morse, who had been seated on the only chair the room could offer, got to his feet, moved over to the door, and put his penultimate question:

'Do you have a mortgage?'

'Yes.'

'Big one?'

She nodded miserably.

As they stood there, the three of them, outside Susan's Pantry, Morse's eyes glanced back at the door, now closed again, fitting flush enough with the jambs on either side, but with a two-centimetre gap of parallel regularity showing between the bottom of the turquoise-blue door and the linoed floor of the landing.

Morse asked his last question simply and quietly: 'When did the envelopes first start coming, Susan?'

And Susan's eyes jumped up to his, suddenly flashing the unmistakable sign of fear.

# CHAPTER SEVENTEEN

**Examination:** trial; test of knowledge and, as also may be hoped, capacity; close inspection (especially med.)

(*Small's Enlarged English Dictionary*, 1812 Edition)

ON FRIDAY, 2 September, two days after Julia Stevens' return to Oxford, there were already three items of importance on her day's agenda.

First, school.

Not as yet the dreaded restart (three whole days away, praise be!) but a visit to the Secretary's Office to look through the GCSE and A-level results, both lists having been published during her fortnight's absence abroad. Like every self-respecting teacher, she wanted to discover the relative success of the pupils she herself had taught.

In former days it had often been difficult enough for some pupils to *sit* examinations, let alone pass them. And even in the comparatively recent years of Julia's girlhood several of her own classmates had been deemed not to possess the requisite acumen even to attempt the 11 Plus. It was a question of the sheep and the goats – just like the division between those who were lost and those who were saved in the New Testament – a work with which the young Julia had become increasingly familiar, through the crusading fervour of a local curate with whom (aged ten and a half) she had fallen passionately in love.

How things had changed.

Now, in 1994, it was an occasion for considerable surprise if anyone somehow managed to *fail* an examination. Indeed, to be recorded in the Unclassified ranks of the GCSE was, in Julia's view, a feat of quite astonishing incompetence, which carried with it a sort of bravura badge of monumental under-achievement. And as far as Christian doctrine was concerned, it was becoming far easier to cope with sin, now that Hell was (semi-officially) abolished.

She looked through 5C's English results. Very much as she'd expected. Then looked a little more closely at the results of the only pupil in the class whose name had begun with 'C'. Costyn, K: Religious Education, 'Unclassified'; English, 'D'; Maths, 'Unclassified'; Geography, 'Unclassified'; Metalwork, 'Unclassified'. Well, at least he'd got something – after twelve years of schooling ... thirty-six terms. But it was difficult to imagine him getting much further than the Job Centre. Nowhere else for him to go, was there – except to jail, perhaps?

How she wished that 'D' had been a 'C', though.

At 10.30 a.m. she hurried fairly quickly away from the school premises and made her way on foot to the Churchill Hospital where her appointment at the clinic was for 11 a.m.; and where a few minutes ahead of schedule she was seated in the upstairs waiting-room, no longer thinking of Kevin Costyn and his former classmates – but of herself.

'How are you feeling?' asked Basil Shepstone, a large, balding, slightly stooping South African.

'You want me to undress?'

'I'd love you to undrress,' he said with that characteristic rolling of the 'r'. 'No need today, though. Next time, I'll insist.'

His friendly brown eyes were suddenly sad, and he reached across to place his right hand on her shoulder.

'You want the good news first? Or the bad news?' he asked quietly.

'The good news.'

'Well, your condition's fairly stable. And that's good – that's very good news.'

Julia found herself swallowing hard. 'And the bad news?'

'Well, it's not exactly bad news. Shall I read it?'

Julia could see the Oxfordshire Health Authority heading on the letter, but no more. She closed her eyes.

'It says . . . blah, blah, blah . . . "In the event of any deterioration, however, we regret to have to inform Mrs Stevens that her condition is inoperable."'

'They can't operate if it gets worse, they mean?'

Shepstone put down the letter. 'I prrefer your English to theirs.'

She sighed deeply; then opened her eyes and looked at him, knowing that she loved him for everything he'd tried to do for her. He had always been so gentle, so kindly, so professional; and now, watching him, she could understand why his eyes remained downcast as his Biro hatched the 'O' of 'Oxfordshire'.

'How long?' she asked simply.

He shook his head. 'Anyone who prredicts something like that – he's a fool.'

'A year?'

'Could be.'

'Six months?'

He looked defeated as he shrugged his broad shoulders.

'Less?'

'As I say—'

'Would you give up work if you were me?'

'Fairly soon, I think, yes.'

'Would you tell anyone?'

He hesitated. 'Only if it were someone you loved.'

She smiled, and got to her feet. 'There are not many people I love. You, of course – and my cleaning-lady – with whom incidentally' – she consulted her wristwatch – 'in exactly one hour's time, I have a slap-up lunch engagement at the Old Parsonage.'

'You're not inviting me?'

She shook her head. 'We've got some very private things to discuss, I'm afraid.'


After Mrs Stevens had left, the consultant took a handkerchief from his pocket and quickly wiped his eyes. What the dickens was he supposed to say? Because it never really did much good to lie. Or so he believed.

He blamed himself, for example, for lying so blatantly to the woman who'd died only two days previously – lying to Mrs Phillotson.

Not much difference in the case-histories.

No hope in either.

# CHAPTER EIGHTEEN

Dead flies cause the ointment of the apothecary
to send forth a stinking savour: so doth a little
folly him that is in reputation for wisdom and
honour

(*Ecclesiastes*, ch. 10, v. 1)

MORSE NOW realized that he would have few, if any,
further cases of murder to solve during his career
with Thames Valley CID. All right, orchestral con-
ductors and High Court judges could pursue their
professions into their twilight years, regardless – indeed
sometimes completely oblivious – of their inevitably
deteriorating talents. But more often than not policemen finished long before any incipient senility; and
Morse himself was now within a couple of years of
normal retirement.

For many persons it was difficult to tell where the
dividing line came between latish middle-age and
advisable pensionability. Perhaps it had something to
do with the point at which nostalgia took over from
hope; or perhaps with a sad realization that it was no
longer possible to fall in love again; or, certainly in
Morse's case, the time when, as now, he had to sit
down on the side of the bed in order to pull his trousers
on.

Such and similar thoughts were circulating in
Morse's mind as on Saturday, 3 September, the morn-

ing after his visit with Lewis to Wolsey (and the statement made, immediately thereafter, by Mrs Ewers), he sat in the Summertown Health Centre.

A mild cold had, as usual with Morse, developed into a fit of intermittently barking bronchitis; but he comforted himself with the thought that very shortly, after a sermon on the stupidity of cigarette-smoking, he would emerge from the Centre with a slip of paper happily prescribing a dose of powerful antibiotics.

Clutching his prescription, Morse was about to leave when he remembered *The Times*, left in his erstwhile seat in the waiting-room. Returning, he found that his earlier companions – the anorexic girl and the spotty-faced, overweight youth – had now been joined by a slatternly looking, slackly dressed young woman, with rings in her nostrils; a woman to whom Morse took an immediate and intense dislike.

Predictably so.

From the chair next to the newcomer he picked up his newspaper, without a word; though not without a hurried glance into the woman's dull-green eyes, the colour of the Oxford Canal along by Wolvercote. And if Morse had waited there only a few seconds longer, he would have heard someone call her name: 'Eleanor Smith?'

But Morse had gone.


She'd already got the address of an abortion clinic; but one of her friends, an authority in the field, had informed her that it was now closed. So! So she'd have to find some other place. And the quack ought to be able to point her somewhere not too far away, surely? That's exactly the sort of thing quacks were there for.

In a marked police car, standing on a Strictly Doctors Only lot in the Centre's very restricted parking-area, Lewis sat thinking and waiting; waiting in fact, quite patiently, since the case appeared to be developing in a reasonably satisfactory way.

When, the previous afternoon, Susan Ewers had made (and signed) her statement, many things already adumbrated by Morse had dawned at last on Lewis's understanding.

Suspicion, prima facie, could and should now be levelled against Mr Edward Brooks, the man who had been Mrs Ewers' immediate predecessor as scout on Staircase G in Drinkwater Quad. Why? Morse's unusually simple and unspectacular hypothesis had been stated as follows:

It should be assumed, in all probability, that Brooks had played a key role, albeit an intermediary one, in supplying a substantial quantity of drugs to the young people living on his staircase – including Matthew Rodway; that Rodway's suicide had necessarily resulted in some thorough investigation by the college authorities into the goings-on on the staircase; that McClure, already living on the same staircase anyway, had become deeply involved – indeed had probably been the prime mover in seeing that Brooks was 'removed' from his post (coincidentally at the same time as McClure's retirement); that, as Mrs Ewers had now testified, the former scout had continued his trafficking in drugs, and that this information had somehow reached McClure's ears; that McClure had threatened Brooks with exposure, disgrace, criminal prosecution, and almost certain imprisonment; that finally, at a showdown in Daventry Court, Brooks had murdered McClure.

Such a hypothesis had the merit of fitting all the known facts; and if it could be corroborated by the new facts which would doubtless emerge from the meeting arranged for that afternoon at the Pitt Rivers Museum . . .

Yes.

But there was the 'one potential fly in the ointment', as Lewis had expressed himself half an hour earlier.

And Morse had winced at the phrase. 'The cliché's bad enough in itself, Lewis – but what's a "potential fly" look like when it's on the window-pane?'

'Dunno, sir. But if Brooks *was* ambulanced off that Sunday with a heart attack—'

'Wouldn't *you* be likely to have a heart attack if you'd just killed somebody?'

'We can check up straightaway at the hospital.'

'All in good time,' Morse had said. 'You'll have *me* in hospital if you don't get me down to the Health Centre . . .'

Still thinking and still waiting, Lewis looked again at the brief supplementary report from the police pathologist, which had been left on Morse's desk that morning.

Attn. Det. C.I. Morse.

No more re time of McClure's death – but confirmation re probable 'within which':
8 a.m.–12 a.m. 28 Aug. Little more on knife/knife-thrust: blade unusually (?) broad, 4–5 cms and about 14–15 cms in length/penetration. Straight through everything with massive internal and external bleeding (as reported). Blade not really sharp, judging by ugly lacerations round immediate entry-area. Forceful thrust. Man rather than woman? Perhaps woman with good wrist/arm (or angry heart?). Certainly one or two of our weaker (!) sex I met a year ago on a martial arts course.
Full details available if required.
All very technical – but possibly helpful?

Laura Hobson

'At least she understands the full-stop,' Morse had said.

Never having really mastered the full-stop himself, Lewis had refrained from any comment.

Yet they both realized the importance of finding the knife. Few murder prosecutions were likely to get off on the right foot without the finding of a weapon. But they hadn't found a weapon. A fairly perfunctory search had earlier been made by Phillotson and his team; and Lewis himself had instigated a very detailed search of the area surrounding Daventry Court and the gardens of the adjacent properties. But still without success.

Anyway, Morse was never the man to hunt through a haystack for a needle. Much rather he'd always seek to intensify (as he saw it) the magnetic field of his mind and trust that the missing needle would suddenly appear under his nose. Not much intensification as yet, though; the only thing under Morse's nose lately – and that under a towel – had been a bowl of steaming Friar's Balsam.

But here came Morse at last (10.40 a.m.), cum prescription. And Lewis could predict the imminent conversation:

'Chemist just around the corner, Lewis. If you'd just nip along and . . . I'd be grateful. Only problem' – searching pockets – 'I seem . . .'

Lewis was half right anyway.

'There's a chemist's just round the corner. If you'd be so good? I don't know how much these wretched Tories charge these days but' – searching pockets – 'here's a tenner.'

Lewis left him there on the reserved parking lot, just starting *The Times* crossword; and walked happily up to Boots in Lower Summertown.

What was happening to Morse?

The third item appearing on Julia Stevens' agenda the previous day had been postponed. On her arrival at the Old Parsonage Hotel, a telephone message was handed to her: Mrs Brooks would not be able to make the lunch; she was sorry; she would ring later if she could, and explain; please not to ring her.

Understandably, perhaps, Julia had not felt unduly

disappointed, for her mind was full of other thoughts, especially of herself. And she enjoyed the solitude of her glass of Bruno Paillard Brut Premier Cru (daring!) seated on a high stool at the Parsonage Bar, before walking down to the taxi-rank by the Martyrs' Memorial and thence being driven home in style and in a taxi gaudily advertising the Old Orleans Restaurant and Cocktail Bar.

It was not until later that evening that her brain began to weave its curious fancies about what exactly could have caused the problem . . .

Brenda Brooks rang (in a hurry, she'd said) just before the *Nine O'Clock News* on BBC1. Could they make it the next day, Saturday? A bit earlier? Twelve – twelve noon, say?

After she had put down the phone, Julia sat silently for a while, staring at nothing. A little bit odd, that – Brenda ringing (almost certainly) from a telephone-box when she had a phone of her own in the house. It would be something – everything – to do with that utterly despicable husband of hers. For from the very earliest days of their marriage, Ted Brooks had been a repulsive fly in the nuptial ointment; an ointment which had, over the thirteen increasingly unhappy and some-times desperate years (as Julia had learned), regularly sent forth its stinking savour.

# CHAPTER NINETEEN

The true index of a man's character is the health
of his wife

(CYRIL CONNOLLY)

As BRENDA BROOKS waited at the bus-stop that Saturday morning, then again as she made her bus journey down to Carfax, a series of videos, as it were, flashed in a nightmare of repeats across her mind; and her mood was an amalgam of anticipation and anxiety.

It had been three days earlier, Wednesday, 31 August, that she'd been seen at the Orthopaedic Clinic . . .

'At least it's not made your fracture.'

'Pardon, doctor?' So nervous had she been that so many of his words made little or no sense to her.

'I said, it's not a major fracture, Mrs Brooks. But it *is* a fracture.'

'Oh deary me.'

But she'd finally realized it was something more than a sprain – that's why she'd eventually gone to her GP, who in turn had referred her to a specialist. And now she was hearing all about it: about the meta-something between the wrist and the fingers. She'd try to look it up in that big dark-blue *Gray's Anatomy* she'd often dusted on one of Mrs Stevens' bookshelves. Not too difficult to remember: she'd just have to think of 'met a couple' – that's what it sounded like.

'And you'll be very sensible, if you can, to stop using your right hand completely. No housework. Rest! That's what it needs. The big thing for the time being is to give it a bit of support. So before you leave, the nurse here'll let you have one of those "Tubigrips" – fits over your hand like a glove. And, as I say, we'll get you in just as soon as, er ... are you a member of BUPA, by the way?'

'Pardon?'

'Doesn't matter. We'll get you in just as soon as we can. Only twenty-four hours, with a bit of luck. Just a little op to set the bone and plaster you up for a week or two.'

'It's not quite so easy as that, Doctor. My husband's been in hospital for a few days. He's had a bit of a heart attack, and he's only just home this morning, so ...'

'We can put you in touch with a home-help.'

'I can do a *little* bit of housework, can't I?'

'Not if you're sensible. Can't you get a cleaning-lady in for a couple of days a week?'

'I *am* a cleaning-lady,' she replied, at last feeling that she'd rediscovered her bearings; re-established her identity in life.

She'd hurried home that morning, inserting and turning the Yale key with her left hand, since it was becoming too painful to perform such an operation with her right.

'I'm back, Ted!'

Walking straight through into the living-room, she

found her husband, fully dressed, lounging in front of the TV, his fingers on the black control-panel.

'Christ! Where the 'ell a' you bin, woman?'

Brenda bit her lip. 'There was an emergency – just before my turn. It held everything up.'

'I thought *you* were the bloody emergency from all the fuss you've bin making.'

'Baked beans all right for lunch?'

'*Baked beans?*'

'I've got something nice in for tea.'

A few minutes later she took a tin of baked beans from a pantry shelf; and holding it in her right hand beneath a tin-opener fixed beside the kitchen door, she slowly turned the handle with her left. Slowly – yes, very slowly, like the worm that was finally turning . . .

And why?

If ever Brenda Brooks could begin to contemplate the murder of her husband, she would surely acknowledge as her primary, her abiding motive, the ways in which mentally and verbally he had so cruelly abused her for so long.

But no!

Belittlement had been her regular lot in life; and on that score he was, in reality, robbing her at most of a dignity that she had never known.

Would the underlying motive then be found in the knowledge of her husband's sexual abuse of an adolescent and increasingly attractive step-daughter?

Perhaps.

But it was all so much simpler than that. One thing there had been in her life – just the one thing – in which she could rejoice, in which until so very recently she *had* rejoiced: the skills she had acquired with her hands. And Edward Brooks had robbed her of them; had robbed her even of the little that she had, which was her all.

*And for that she could never forgive him.*


Brenda decided she needn't replay *all* that last bit to Mrs Stevens; but she did need to explain what had gone wrong the day before. Not that there was much to say, really. What was it *he*'d said when she'd told him she'd been invited out to lunch with Mrs S?

'Well if you think you're going to leave me this lunchtime, you bloody ain't, see? Not while I'm feeling groggy like this.'

Why had she ever married the man?

She'd known it was a mistake even before that ghastly wedding – as she'd prayed for God to boom down some unanswerable objection from the hammer-beam roof when the vicar had invited any just cause or impediment. But the Voice had been silent; and the invited guests were seated quietly on each side of the nave; and the son of Brenda's only sister (a sub-postmistress in Inverness), a spotty but mellifluous young soprano, was all rehearsed to render the 'Pie Jesu' from the Fauré *Requiem*.

Often in life it was difficult enough to gird up one's loins and go through with one's commitments. On this occasion, though, it had been far more difficult *not* to do so . . .

\*

But at least Ted Brooks had relented somewhat, that previous evening – *and she knew why*. He'd decided he was feeling a whole lot better. He thought he might venture out – *would* venture out – into the big wide world again: the big wide world in this case being the East Oxford Conservative Club, well within gentle walking distance, where (he said) he'd be glad to meet the lads again, have a pint – even try a frame of snooker, perhaps. *And* he'd have a bite to eat in the club there; so she needn't bother 'erself about any more bloody baked beans.

Brenda had almost been smiling to herself that evening, when on the pretext of getting another pint of milk from the corner-shop she'd given Mrs S a quick ring from the nearby BT kiosk, just before nine o'clock.

But what . . . what about those other two things?


She was a good ten minutes early; and in leisurely, but tremulous, fashion, she crossed the Broad and walked up St Giles'; past Balliol College; past St John's College; past the Lamb and Flag; and then, waiting for the traffic lights just before Keble Road, she'd quickly checked (yet again) that the letter was there in her handbag.

For a few moments this letter almost assumed as much importance as that second thing – the event which had caught her up in such distress, such fear, since the previous Sunday, when her husband had returned home, the stains on the lower front of his shirt and the top of his grey flannel trousers *almost* adequately concealed by a beige summer cardigan (new from M&S); but only by the *back* of this cardigan, since the front of it was saturated with much blood. And it was only later that she'd noticed the soles of his trainers . . .

Opposite her, the Green Man flashed, and the bleeper bleeped; and Mrs Brenda Brooks walked quickly over to the Old Parsonage Hotel, at Number 1, Banbury Road.

# CHAPTER TWENTY

When you live next to the cemetery, you cannot
weep for everyone

(Russian proverb)

THE OLD PARSONAGE HOTEL, dating back to 1660,
and situated between Keble College to the east and
Somerville College to the west, stands just north of the
point where the broad plane-tree'd avenue of St Giles'
forks into the Woodstock Road to the left and the
Banbury Road to the right. Completely refurbished a
few years since, and now incorporating such splendid
twentieth-century features as *en suite*, centrally-heated
bedrooms, the stone-built hotel has sought to preserve
the intimacy and charm of former times.

With success, in Julia Stevens' judgement.

In the judgement, too, of Brenda Brooks, as she
seated herself in a wall-settee, in front of a small, highly
polished mahogany table in the Parsonage Bar, lushly
carpeted in avocado green with a tiny pink-and-peach
motif.

'Lordy me!' Brenda managed to say in her soft
Oxfordshire burr, gently shaking her tightly curled grey
hair.

Whether, etymologically speaking, such an expression of obvious approval was a conflation of 'Lord'
and 'Lumme', Julia could not know. But she was
gratified with the reaction, and watched as Brenda's

eyes surveyed the walls around her, the lower half painted in gentle gardenia; the upper half in pale magnolia, almost totally covered with paintings, prints, cartoons.

'Lordy me!' repeated Brenda in a hushed voice, her vocabulary clearly inadequate to elaborate upon her earlier expression of delight.

'What would you like to drink?'

'Oh, coffee, please – that'll be fine.'

'No it won't. I insist on something stronger than coffee. Please!'

Minutes later, as they sipped their gins and slimline tonics, they read through the menu: Julia with the conviction that this was an imaginative selection of goodies; Brenda with more than a little puzzlement, since many of the imported words therein – Bagel, Couscous, Hummus, Linguini, Mozzarella – had never figured in her own cuisine. Indeed, the sight of such exotic fare might well, a decade or so back, have prompted within her a stab of some sympathy with a husband constantly complaining about baked beans, about sardines, about spaghetti . . .

In the past, yes.

But no longer.

'What's it to be, then?'

Brenda shook her head. 'I'm sorry, but I just can't eat anything. I'm all – I'm all full up, Mrs Stevens, if you know what I mean.'

Julia was too sensible to argue; and in any case she understood only too well, for she'd experienced exactly the same the day before when she'd sat on a bar-stool there, alone, feeling ... well, feeling 'all full up', as Brenda had so economically phrased it.

Half an hour later, as she was finishing her Poached Salmon with Lemon Butter, Salad, and New Potatoes, Julia Stevens had been put in the (latest) picture about Ted Brooks. She'd known all about the verbal abuse which had led to a broken heart; and now she learned of the physical abuse which had led to a broken hand.

'I'm so wicked – did you know that? You know why? I wished' (she whispered closely in Julia's ear) 'I wished him dead! Can you believe that?'

Most people in your position would have *murdered* him, you dear old thing, said Julia, but only to herself. And suddenly the realization that such a viciously cruel man should have ruined the life of such a sweet and lovable woman made her so very angry. Yet, at the same time, so very much in control.

Was it perhaps that the simultaneous keeping of her *own* secret with the hearing of *another's* was an unsuspected source of strength? But Julia had no opportunity of pursuing this interesting line of thought, for Brenda now opened her handbag and passed over the letter she'd received the previous Tuesday – not through the post, but pushed by hand through her letter-box.

'Just read it, please! No need to say anything.'

As Julia put on her school-ma'amish spectacles, she was aware that the woman seated beside her was now in tears.

\*

The silent weeping had subsided into intermittent snuffling as Julia finished reading the agonized and agonizing pages.

'My God,' she whispered.

'But that's not all. There's something else – something even worse. I shall just have to tell somebody, Mrs Stevens – if you can bear it.'

# Chapter Twenty-One

Hate is the consequence of fear; we fear something before we hate it. A child who fears becomes
an adult who hates
     (Cyril Connolly, *The Unquiet Grave*)

Dear mum – dearest mum!
Its been a long time hasn't it and I didn't really
want to write but I can't talk about it, I just can't.
I was never much good with words but I'm going
to try. Its about why I left home and how I
couldn't really ever tell you about it. I'm writing
now because my friend at the hospital told me
about <u>him</u> and she said he's a lot better and
going home soon – and all I want you to do is let
him get very much worse again and don't look
after him – just let him die that's what I want
because he bloody deserves it! You thought I left
because I hated school and dreamt of boys and
sex and got mixed up with drugs and all the
punk scene and all that, and you were right in a
way because I did. But you got upset about the
wrong things, that's what I'm saying. Why did I
leave <u>you</u> mum – tell me that. You can't think it
was much fun for me with sod all to pay for
anything and nowhere to bloody go, I'd just got
one thing going for me and that was what you
and dear old dad gave me, a good pair of thighs

and a good pair of tits all the randy buggers
wanted to get their hands on and believe me they
paid good money for it. All I'm saying mum is I
never really had to slum it after those first few
weeks in London anyway. I never had the guts to
tell you why but I've got to tell you now so here
goes. Don't get too upset about it all, well not
about me anyway, just about that horny bastard
you married thirteen years ago.

I was thirteen when it started and we had the
flu together him and me and so you remember
we were both in bed when you went off cleaning
one Thursday morning, you see I even remember
the day of the week, and he came into my
bedroom about eleven and brought me a cup of
bovril and he said how nice looking I was getting
and what a nice little figure I was getting and all
that bullshit and how proud he was to have a
daughter like me, well a step-daughter. Then he
put his arm round me and started rubbing my
neck and back a bit through my pajamas and told
me to relax because that would do me good and
soon I was lying down again with my back to him,
and then I'm not sure how it happened but <u>he</u>
was lying down and I could feel his hand inside
my pajama top and he was feeling me, and I
didn't know what to do because for a start I just
thought he was being affectionate and I didn't
want to upset him because we'd both be
embarassed if I tried to push him away. Please
mum try to understand! Perhaps its difficult to
know where the line comes between affection

and sex but I knew because I felt something hard
against me and I knew what it was. I just felt
scared then like that first day in school when I
was in a room I shouldn't have been in and when
I just got kept in for what wasn't my fault at all,
but I thought it was my fault. Oh mum I'm not
explaining things very well. And then he grabbed
my hand and pulled it back behind him and
pushed it inside his pajamas and told me to rub
him, and I just didn't know what I was doing. It
was the first time I'd ever felt a man like that and
he was sort of silky and warm and I felt afraid
and fascinated at the same time. All I know is I'd
done what he wanted before I had the chance of
thinking about what I was doing and suddenly
there was all that sticky stuff all over my pajama
bottoms, and you won't remember but when you
came home I told you I'd put them in the
washing machine because I'd been sweating.
Afterwards he kept on saying that it was me
who'd agreed to do it, me who'd started it all not
him. Mum! He was a wicked liar, but even if it
was just one per cent me you've got to forgive
me. He made the most of everything, my God he
did. He said if I told you about what he'd done
he'd tell you about what I done, and I got scared
stiff you'd find out, and it was like blackmail all
the time those next three awful years when he
made me do everything he wanted. You could
never believe how I loathed him, even the sight
of him, I hated him more than I've ever hated
anybody since. Well that's it mum, I wonder what

117

your thinking. He's a shit and I never never never want to see him again unless its to stick a bloody great big knife in his great fat gut and watch him squirm and hear him squeal like the great fat pig he is. And if you want any help with sticking the fucking pig you just let me know because I'll only be too glad to help. There's only one other thing to tell you and perhaps its why I've written to you now. I've always kept in touch with Auntie Beryl, its been a secret but she's always let me know how you are and she wrote a fortnight ago and told me how he's been treating you mum – you must have let her know. Your mad to stick it, your a matyr that's what you are. I've just read through all this and I know one thing I said you can do but you can't – not yet – and that's get in touch with me, but its better that way though don't be surprised if you see me. Not just yet though, its been such a long long time and I can't quite face it, not yet. I love you mum, I shall always love you better than anybody. One last thing and its odd really but I read in the Oxford—

Julia turned over the page but that was the finish: the last part of the letter was missing.

# CHAPTER TWENTY-TWO

We all wish to be of importance in one way or
another

(RALPH WALDO EMERSON, *Journals*)

LEWIS, on his way for an appointment with the House
Matron of Wolsey, had dropped Morse in the Broad,
where the Chief Inspector had swilled down a double
dosage of penicillin pills with a pint of Hook Norton in
the White Horse, before making his way to the Pitt
Rivers Museum of Ethnology and Pre-History – for his
own appointment.

Sooner or later, inevitably, a golden afternoon will
captivate the visitor to Oxford; and as he walked
leisurely up Parks Road, past the front of Wadham on
his right, past the blue wrought-iron gates at the back
of Trinity on his left, Morse felt deeply grateful that he
had been privileged to spend so much of his lifetime
there.

And one of those captivated visitors might have
noticed a smile of quiet satisfaction around Morse's lips
that early afternoon as he turned right, just opposite
Keble, into the grounds of the Oxford University
Museum – that monument to the nineteenth-century
Gothic Revival, and the home of the Dodo and the Dino-
saur. Some clouds there were in the pale blue sky that
September day: some white, some grey; but not many.

No, not many, Morse.

Oddly, he'd enjoyed the short walk, although he
believed that the delights of walking were often ludi-
crously exaggerated. *Solvitur ambulando*, though, as the
Romans used to say; and even if the 'ambulando' was
meant to be a figurative rather than a physical bit of
'walking' – well, so much the better. Not that there was
anything intrinsically wrong with the occasional bit of
physical walking; after all, Housman had composed
some of his loveliest lyrics while walking around the
Backs at Cambridge, after a couple of lunchtime beers.

*Solvitur ambulando,* yes.

Walk along then, Morse, since perhaps you are now
walking towards the solution.

On the stone steps leading up to the entrance porch,
he read the notice:

> THIS MUSEUM IS OPEN
> TO THE PUBLIC
> 12 a.m.–4.30 p.m. Mon–Sat.

It was already past noon, and on the grass a large party
of visiting schoolchildren were unharnessing ruck-sacks
and extracting packed lunches as Morse walked hurriedly by. It wasn't that he positively disliked schoolchildren; just that he didn't want to meet any of them.

Inside the glass-roofed, galleried building, Morse
continued on his course, quickly past a huge recon-
struction of a dinosaur ('Bipedal, but capable of quad-
ripedal locomotion'); quickly past some assembled
skeletons of African and Asian elephants. Nor was he

long (if at all) detained by the tall show-cases displaying their specimens of the birds and insects of Australasia. Finally, after making his way between a statue of the Prince Consort and a well-stuffed ostrich, Morse emerged from the University Museum into the Pitt Rivers Museum; where he turned right, and knocked on the door of the Administrator.

Capital 'A'.


'Coffee?' she invited.

'No thanks. I've just had some.'

'Some beer, you mean.'

'Is it that obvious?'

'Yes.'

She was a tall, slim woman in her mid-forties, with prematurely white hair, and an attractively diffident smile about her lips.

'Some women,' began Morse, 'have an extraordinarily well-developed sense of smell—' But then he stopped. For a second or two he'd anticipated a little mild flirtation with Jane Cotterell. Clearly it was not to be, though, for he felt her clear, intelligent eyes upon him, and the tone of her voice was unambiguously no-nonsense:

'How can I help you?'

For the next ten minutes she answered his questions. Brooks had joined the eight-strong team of attendants at the Pitt Rivers Museum – quite separate from the University Museum – almost exactly a year ago. He worked a fairly regular thirty-five-hour week, 8.30 a.m. to 4.30 p.m., with an hour off for lunch. The attendants had the job of cleaning and maintaining the premises; of keeping a watchful eye on all visitors, in particular on the many school-parties regularly arriving by coach from near and far; sometimes of performing specific tasks, like manning the museum shop; of being helpful and courteous to the public at all times – 'more friendly than fierce'; and above all, of course, of safeguarding the unrivalled collection of anthropological and ethnographic items housed in the museum . . .

'A unique museum, Inspector.'

'Do you ever get anybody trying to steal things?'

'*Very* rarely. Last summer we had someone trying to get into the case with the shrunken heads in it, but—'

'Hope you caught him.'

'*Her*, actually.'

'I'd rather rob a bank, myself.'

'I'd rather not rob at all.'

Morse was losing out, he realized that; and reverted to his questioning about Brooks.

The man was, in the Administrator's view, competent in his job, not frightened of work, punctual, reasonably pleasant with the public; private sort of person, though, something of a loner. There were certainly some of his colleagues with slightly more endearing qualities.

'If you'd known what you know now, would you have appointed him?'

'No.'

'Mind if I smoke?' asked Morse.

'I'd rather you didn't.'

'Did *he* smoke?'

'Not in the museum. No one smokes in the museum.'

'In the Common Room, or whatever you have?'

'I don't know.'

'You don't associate him with drugs at all?'

She glanced at him keenly before replying. 'There are no drugs here – not on my staff.'

'You'd know – if there were?'

'As you say, some women have a particularly well-developed sense of smell, Inspector.'

Morse let it go. 'Have you still got his references?'

The Administrator unlocked a filing-cabinet beside her and produced a green folder marked 'BROOKS, E'; and Morse looked through the half-dozen sheets it contained: Brooks's CV; a carbon of the letter appointing him wef 1 September 1993; a photocopied page giving details of Salary, National Insurance, Job Specification, Shift-Patterns; two open, blandly worded testimonials; and one hand-written reference, equally bland.

Morse read this last item a second time, slowly.

---

To the Administrator, Pitt Rivers Museum
Dear Madam,

I understand that Mr Edward Brooks has applied to you for the post (as advertised in the University Gazette, June '93) of Assistant Attendant at the Museum.

Brooks has worked as a scout at Wolsey College for almost ten years and I recommend to you his experience and diligence.

Yours sincerely,
Felix McClure (Dr)

---

Well, well.

'Did you know Dr McClure?' asked Morse.

'No. And I shan't have a chance of knowing him now, shall I?'

'You heard . . . ?'

'I read it in the *Oxford Mail*. I know all about Mr Brooks's illness too: his wife rang through early on Monday morning. But from what they say he's on the mend.'

Morse changed tack once more. 'I know a lot of the exhibits here are invaluable; but . . . but are there things here that are just plain *valuable*, if you know what I mean? Commercially valuable, saleable . . . ?'

'My goodness, yes. I wouldn't mind getting my fingers on some of the precious stones and rings here. Or do I mean *in* some of them?'

But Morse appeared to miss the Administrator's gentle humour.

'Does Mr Brooks have access to, well, to almost everything here really?'

'Yes, he does. Each of the attendants has a key to the wall-safe where we keep the keys to all the cabinets and drawers and so on.'

'So, if he took a fancy to one of your shrunken heads?'

'No problem. He wouldn't have to use a crow-bar.'

'I see.'

Jane Cotterell smiled, and thereby melted a little more of Morse's heart.

'Do I gather you want me to show you a bit about the security system here?'

'Not really,' protested Morse.

She rose to her feet. 'I'd better show you then.'

Twenty minutes later they returned to her office.

'Thank you,' said Morse. 'Thank you for your patience and your time. You're a very important person, I can see that.'

'Really? How—?'

'Well, you've got a capital "A" for a start; then you've got a wall-to-wall carpet; and for all I know you've not only got a parking space, you've probably got one with your name on it.'

'No name on it, I'm afraid.'

'Still . . .'

'What about you?'

'I've got my name on the door, at least for the present. But I've only got a little carpet, with a great big threadbare patch where my megapodic sergeant stands.'

'Is there such a word – "megapodic"?'

'I'll look it up when I get home. I've just treated myself to the *Shorter Oxford*.'

'Where is your home?'

'Top of the Banbury Road . . . Anywhere near you?'

'No. That's quite a way from where I live.' For a few seconds her eyes looked down at the carpet – that old carpet of hers, whose virtues had so suddenly, so unexpectedly expanded.

Only semi-reluctantly, a few minutes earlier, had Brenda Brooks been persuaded to hand over the last sheet of her daughter's letter. Its content, as Julia saw things, was very much as before. But, yes, it *was* a bit self-incriminating; especially that rather fine passage just before the end:

> He's undermined everything for me mum,
> including sex! But the very worst thing he ever
> did was to make me feel it could all have been
> my fault. Mum! Mum! He's bloody fucked up my
> life, and if he ever turns up murdered
> somewhere you'll know it was *me*, alright?

Strangely, however, Julia had experienced little sense of shock. A hardening of heart, rather; and a growing conviction that if Brooks *were* to turn up murdered somewhere his step-daughter would not be figuring alone on any list of possible suspects.

# CHAPTER TWENTY-THREE

One night I contrived to stay in the Natural
History Museum, hiding myself at closing time in
the Fossil Invertebrate Gallery, and spending an
enchanted night alone in the museum, wandering
from gallery to gallery with a flashlight

(OLIVER SACKS, *The Observer*, 9 January 1994)

MORSE SPENT a while wandering vaguely around the
galleries. On the ground floor he gave as much of his
attention as he could muster to the tall, glass show-cases
illustrating the evolution of fire-arms, Japanese Noh
masks, the history of Looms and Weaving, old musical
instruments, shields, pots, models of boats, bull-roarers,
North American dress, and a myriad precious and semi-
precious stones . . .

Then, feeling like a man who in some great picture
gallery has had his fill of fourteenth-century crucifix-
ions, he walked up a flight of stone steps to see what
the Upper Gallery had to offer; and duly experienced
a similar sense of satiety as he ambled aimlessly along a
series of black-wood, glass-topped display-cases, sev-
erally containing scores of axes, adzes, tongs, scissors,
keys, coins, animal-traps, specialized tools . . . Burmese,
Siamese, Japanese, Indonesian . . .

In one display-case he counted sixty-four Early Medical Instruments, each item labelled in a neat manu-
script, in black ink on a white card, with documentation

of provenance and purpose (where known). Among these many items, all laid out flat on biscuit-coloured backing-material (clearly recently renovated), his attention was drawn to a pair of primitive tooth-extractors from Tonga; and not for the first time he thanked the gods that he had been born after the general availability of anaesthetics.

But he had seen quite enough, he thought, wholly unaware, at this point, that he had made one extraordinarily interesting observation. So he decided it was time to leave. Very soon Lewis would be at the front waiting for him. Lewis would be on time. Lewis was always on time.

For the moment, however, he was conscious that there was no one else around in the Upper Gallery. And suddenly the place had grown a little forbidding, a little uncanny; and he felt a quick shiver down his spine as he made his way back into the main University Museum.

But even here it was quieter now, more sombre, beneath the glass-roofed atrium, as if perhaps a cloud had passed across the sun outside. And Morse found himself wondering what it would be like to be in this place, be locked in this place, when everyone else had gone; when the schoolchildren were back on their coaches; when the rest of the public, when the attendants, when the Administrator had all left ... Then perhaps, in the silent, eerie atmosphere, might not the spirits of the Dodo and the Dinosaur, never suspecting their curious extinction, be calling for their mates again on some primeval shore?

*

Jane Cotterell sat at her desk for several minutes after the door had closed behind Morse. She shouldn't really have said that about the beer. Silly of her! Why, she could just do with a drink herself, and it would have been nice if he'd asked her out for a lunchtime gin. She felt herself wishing that he'd forgotten something: a folding umbrella or a notebook or something. But as she'd observed, the Inspector had taken no notes at all; and outside, the sun now seemed to be shining gloriously once more.

# CHAPTER TWENTY-FOUR

Cruelty is, perhaps, the worst kind of sin. Intellectual cruelty is certainly the worst kind of cruelty
(G. K. CHESTERTON, *All Things Considered*)

AFTER READING the (now complete) letter, Julia Stevens re-arranged the pages and read them again; whilst beside her, in a semi-distraught state, sat the original addressee; for whom, strangely enough, one of the most disturbing aspects of the letter was the revelation that her sister Beryl had told her niece the events of that terrible night. Had she (Brenda) made too much of everything when Ted had handled her so roughly? Had it been as much an accident as an incident? But no. No, it hadn't. And whether her account of it had been exaggerated or whether it had been understated – either to her sister over the phone or to her employer in person – certain it was that the recollection of that night in May would remain ever vivid in Brenda's memory . . .

'You're ever so late, Ted. What time is it?'
    'Twelve, is it?'
    'It's far later than that.'
    'If you know what the bloody time is, why the 'ell do you ask me in the first place?'

'It's just that I can't get off to sleep when I know you're still out. I feel worried—'

'Christ! You want to worry when I start gettin' in 'alf-past bloody three, woman.'

'Come to bed now, anyway.'

'I bloody shan't – no!'

'Well, go and sleep in the spare room, then – I've got to get some sleep.'

'All the bloody same to me, innit – if I go in there, or if I stay in 'ere. Might just as well a' bin in different rooms all the bloody time, you know that. Frigid as a fuckin' ice-box! That's what you are. Always 'ave bin.'

'That's just not fair – that's not fair, what you just said!'

'If the bloody cap fits—'

'It can't go on like this, Ted – it just *can't*. I can't stick it any more.'

'Well, bloody *don't* then! Sling your 'ook and go, if you can't stick it! But just stop moanin' at me, d'you hear? Stop fuckin' *moanin*'! All right?'

She was folding her candlewick dressing-gown round her small figure and edging past him at the foot of the double bed, when he stopped her, grabbing hold of her fiercely by the shoulders and glaring furiously into her face before pushing her back.

'You stay where you are!'

Twice previously he had physically maltreated her in a similar way, but on neither occasion had she suffered physical hurt. That night, though, she had stumbled – *had* to stumble – against the iron fireplace in the bedroom; and as she'd put out her right hand to

131

cushion the fall, something had happened; something had snapped. Not that it had been too painful. Not then.

As a young girl Brenda had been alongside when her mother had slipped in the snow one February morning and landed on her wrist; broken her wrist. And passers-by had been so concerned, so helpful, that as she'd sat in the Casualty Department at the old Radcliffe Infirmary, she'd told her daughter that it had almost been worthwhile, the accident – to discover such unsuspected kindness.

But that night Ted had just told her to get up; told her not to be such a bloody ninny. And she'd started to weep then – to weep not so much from pain or shock but from the humiliation of being treated in such a way by the man she had married . . .

Julia handed back the letter.

'I think she hates him even more than you do.'

Brenda nodded miserably. 'I must have loved him once, though, mustn't I? I suppose he was – well, after Sid died – he was just *there* really. I suppose I needed something – somebody – and Ted was there, and he made a bit of a fuss of me – and I was lonely. After that . . . but it doesn't matter any more.'

For a while there was a silence between the two women.

'Mrs Stevens?'

'Yes?'

'What about this other thing? What am I going to do about it? Please help me! Please!'

It was with anger that Julia had listened to Brenda's earlier confidences; with anger, too, that she had read the letter. The man was an animal – she might have known it; had known it. But the possibility that he was a *murderer*? Could Brenda have got it all wrong? Ridiculously wrong?

Julia had never really got to know Ted Brooks. In the early days of Brenda working for her, she'd met him a few times – three or four, no more. And once, only once, had she gone round to the Brooks's house, when Brenda had been stricken with some stomach bug; and when, as she had left, Ted Brooks's hand had moved, non-accidentally, against her breasts as he was supposedly helping her on with her mackintosh.

Take your horny hands off me, you lecherous sod, she'd thought then; and she had never seen him since that day. Never would, if she could help it. Yet he was not an ill-looking fellow, she conceded that.

The contents of the letter, therefore, had come as something less of a shock than may have been expected, since she had long known that Brenda had fairly regularly been on the receiving end of her husband's tongue and temper, and had suspected other things, perhaps . . .

But Brooks a *murderer*?

She looked across with a sort of loving distress at the busy, faithful little lady who had been such a godsend to her; a little lady dressed now in a navy-blue, two-piece suit; an oldish suit certainly, yet beautifully clean, with the pleats in the skirt most meticulously pressed for this special occasion. She felt an overwhelming surge of compassion for her, and she was going to do everything she could to help. Of course she was.

What about 'this other thing', though? My god, what could she do about that?

'Brenda? Brenda? You know what you said about . . . about the blood? Are you sure? Are you *sure*?'

'Mrs Stevens?' Brenda whispered. 'I wasn't going to tell you – I wasn't even going to tell *you*. But yes, I *am* sure. And shall I tell you why I'm sure?'


It was twenty-past two when Julia's taxi dropped Brenda – not immediately outside her house, but very close, just beside the Pakistani grocer's shop on the corner.

'Don't forget, Brenda! Make sure you run out of milk again tonight. Just before nine. And don't say or do anything before then. Agreed? Bye.'

On her way home, Julia spotted the *Oxford Mail* placard outside a newsagent's in the Cowley Road:

POLICE
HUNT
MURDER
WEAPON

and she asked the taxi-driver to stop.


Just before 3 p.m., Ted Brooks was lining up the shot, his eyes coolly assessing the angle between the white cue-ball and the last colour. Smoothly his cue drove through the line of his aim, and the black swiftly disappeared into the bottom right-hand pocket.

His opponent, an older man, slapped a pound coin down on the side of the table.

'Not done your snooker much harm, Ted.'

'No. Back at work in a fortnight, so the doc says. With a bit o' luck.'

# CHAPTER TWENTY-FIVE

The older I grow, the more I distrust the familiar
doctrine that age brings wisdom
                                        (H. L. MENCKEN)

As MORSE had expected, Lewis was already sitting
waiting for him outside the museum.

'How did things go, sir?'

'All right.'

'Learn anything new?'

'Wouldn't go quite so far as that. What about you?'

'Interesting. That woman, well – she's a sort of major-
domo – Amazonian type, sir. I wouldn't like her as
Chief Constable.'

'Give it five years, Lewis.'

'Anyway, it's about Matthew Rodway. In the autumn
term—'

'We call it the Michaelmas Term here, Lewis.'

'In the Michaelmas Term, in his third year, when he
was back in college again—'

'In the House.'

'In the House again, he was sharing rooms with
another fellow—'

'Another undergraduate.'

'Another undergraduate called Ashley Davies. But
not for long, it seems. Davies got himself temporarily
booted out of college—'

'Rusticated.'

'Rusticated that term. Some sort of personal trouble, she said, but didn't want to go into it. Said we should see Davies for ourselves, really.'

'Like me, then, you didn't learn very much.'

'Ah! Just a minute, sir,' smiled Lewis. 'Mr Ashley Davies, our undergraduate, in the Michaelmas Term 1993, was rusticated from the House on the say-so of one Dr Felix McClure, former Student – capital "S", sir – of Wolsey College.'

'The plot thickens.'

'Bad blood, perhaps, sir? Ruined his chances, certainly – Davies was expected to get a First, she'd heard. And he didn't return this year, either. Murky circumstances . . . Drugs, do you think?'

'Or booze.'

'Or love.'

'Well?'

'I've got his address. Living with his parents in Bedford.'

'Did any good thing ever come out of Bedford?'

'John Bunyan, sir?'

'You go and see him, then. I can't do everything myself.'

'What's wrong?' asked Lewis quietly.

'I dunno. My chest's sore. My legs ache. My head's throbbing. I feel sick. I feel sweaty. It's the wrong question, isn't it? You mean, what's *right?*'

'Have you had your pills?'

'Course I have. Somebody's got to keep fit.'

'When were you last fit, sir?'

Morse pulled the safety-belt across him and fumbled for a few seconds to fix the tongue into the buckle.

'I don't ever remember feeling really fit.'

# COLIN DEXTER

'I'm sure you'll blast my head off, sir, but—'

'I ought not to drink so much.'

'I wouldn't be surprised if you'd just washed your pills down with a pint.'

'Would you be surprised if you were quite wrong about that?'

'Washed 'em down with *two* pints, you mean?'

Morse smiled and wiped his forehead with a once-white handkerchief.

'You know the difference between us, sir – between you and me?'

'Tell me.'

'I got married, and so I've got a missus who's always tried to look after me.'

'You're lucky, though. Most people your age are divorced by now.'

'You never – never met a woman – you know, the right woman?'

Morse's eyes seemed focused far away. 'Nearly. Nearly, once.'

'Plenty of time.'

'Nonsense! You don't start things at my age. You pack 'em up. Like the job, Lewis.' Morse hesitated. 'Look, I've not told anybody yet – well, only Strange. I'm packing in the job next autumn.'

Lewis smiled sadly. 'Next Michaelmas, isn't it?'

'I could stay on another couple of years after that but . . .'

'Won't you miss things?'

'Course I bloody won't. I've been very lucky – at least in that respect. But I don't want to push the luck too far. I mean, we might get put on to a case we can't crack.'

138

'Not this one, I hope?'

'Oh no, Lewis, not this one.'

'What's the programme—?'

But Morse interrupted him: 'You just asked me if I'll miss things and I shan't, no. Only one thing, I suppose. I shall miss you, old friend, that's all.'

He had spoken simply, almost awkwardly, and for a little while Lewis hardly trusted himself to look up. Somewhere behind his eyes he felt a slight prickling; and somewhere – in his heart, perhaps – he felt a sadness he could barely comprehend.

'Not getting very far sitting here, Lewis, are we? What's the programme?'

'That's what I just asked you.'

'Well, there's this fellow from Bedford, you say?'

'Former undergraduate, sir.'

'Yes, well – is he at home?'

'Dunno. I can soon find out.'

'Do that, then. See him.'

'When—?'

'What's wrong with now? The way you drive you'll be back by teatime.'

'Don't *you* want to see him?'

Morse hesitated. 'No. There's something much more important for me to do this afternoon.'

'Go to bed, you mean?'

Slowly, resignedly, Morse nodded. 'And try to fix something up with Brooks. Time we paid him a little visit, isn't it?'

'Monday?'

'What's wrong with tomorrow? That'll be exactly a week after he murdered McClure, won't it?'

# CHAPTER TWENTY-SIX

Three may keep a secret if two of them are dead
(BENJAMIN FRANKLIN)

BRENDA BROOKS was in a state of considerable agitation when she went through into the kitchen to put the kettle on. But at least she was relieved to be home before *him*; to have time for a cup of tea; to try to stop shaking. The anguish, the sheer misery of it all, were as strong as ever; with only her growing fear a new element in the tragedy...

After the first inevitable bewilderment – after the uncomprehending questions and the incomprehensible answers – her immediate reaction had been to wash the bloodstained clothing – shirt, trousers, cardigan; but instead, she had followed the fierce instructions given from the invalid's bed that the clothes be carted off to the rubbish dump, and that the affair never be referred to again.

Yet there the event stood – whatever had happened, whatever it all meant – forming that terrible and terrifying secret between them, between husband and wife. No longer a proper secret, though, for she had shared that secret ... those secrets; or would it not be more honest to say that she had betrayed them? Particularly, therefore, did her fear centre on his return now: the fear that when he came in he would only have to look at her – *to know*. And as she squeezed the tea-bag with the tongs, she could do nothing to stop the constant trembling in her hands.

Automatically almost, between sips of tea, she wiped the tongs clean of any tannin stain and replaced them in the drawer to the right of the sink, in the compartment next to the set of beautifully crafted knives which her sister Beryl had given her for her first wedding – knives of many shapes and sizes, some small and slim, some with much longer and broader blades, which lay there before her in shining and sharpened array.

The phone rang at 2.45 p.m.: the Pitt Rivers Museum.

The phone rang again just before 3 p.m.: Mrs Stevens.
  'Is he home yet?'
  'No.'
  'Good. Now listen!'

The front door slammed at 3.20 p.m., when, miraculously as it seemed to Brenda, the shaking in her hands had ceased.

Almost invariably, whenever he came in, she would use those same three words: 'That you, Ted?' That afternoon, however, there was a change, subconscious perhaps, yet still significant.

'That you?' she asked in a firm voice. Just the two words now – as if the query had become depersonalized, as if she could be asking the information of any-one; dehumanized, as if she could be speaking to a dog.

As yet, still holding out on the battle-field, was a small fortress. It was likely to collapse very soon, of course; but there was the possibility that it might hold out for some little time, since it had been recently reinforced. And when the door had slammed shut she had been suddenly conscious – yes! – of just a little power.

'That you?' she repeated.

'Who do you think it is?'

'Cup o' tea?'

'You can get me a can o' beer.'

'The museum just rang. The lady wanted to know how you were. Kind of her, wasn't it?'

'Kind? Was it fuck! Only wanted to know when I'd be back, that's all. Must be short-staffed – that's the only reason she rung.'

'You'd have thought people would be glad of a job like that, with all this unemployment—'

'Would be, wouldn't they, if they paid you decent bloody rates?'

'They pay you reasonably well, surely?'

He glared at her viciously. 'How do you know that? You bin lookin' at my things when I was in 'ospital? Christ, you better not 'a bin, woman!'

'I don't know what they pay you. You've never told me.'

'Exackly! So you know fuck-all about it, right? Look at *you*! You go out for that bloody teacher and what's 'er rates, eh? Bloody slave-labour, that's what you are.

Four quid an hour? Less? Christ, if you add up what *she* gets an hour – all those 'olidays and everything.'

Brenda made no answer, but the flag was still flying on the small fortress. And, oddly enough, he was right. Mrs Stevens *did* pay her less than £4 an hour: £10 for three hours – two mornings a week. But Brenda knew why that was, for unlike her husband her employer had told her exactly where she stood on the financial ladder: one rung from the bottom. In fact, Mrs Stevens had even been talking that lunchtime of having to get rid of her B-registration Volvo, which stood in one of the rundown garages at the end of her road, rented at £15 per calendar month.

As Brenda knew, the protection which that rusting, corrugated shack could afford to any vehicle was minimal; but it did mean that the car had a space – which was more than could be said for the length of road immediately outside Julia's own front door, where so often some other car or van was parked, with just as much right to do so as she had (so the Council had informed her). It wasn't that the sale of the old Volvo ('£340, madam – no, let's make it £350') would materially boost her current account at Lloyds; but it would mean a huge saving on all those other wretched expenses: insurance, road tax, servicing, repairs, MOT, garaging . . . what, about £800 a year?

'So why keep it?' that's what Julia had asked Brenda.

She would have been more honest if she had told Brenda why she was going to sell it. But that lunchtime, at least, the telling of secrets had been all one-way traffic.

*

After dropping off the drooping Morse, Lewis returned to Kidlington HQ, where before doing anything else he looked at the copy of the *Oxford Mail* that had been left on Morse's desk. He was glad they'd managed to get the item in – at the bottom of page 1:

# MURDERED DON

The police are appealing for help in their enquiries into the brutal murder of Dr Felix McClure, discovered knifed to death in his apartment in Daventry Court, North Oxford, last Sunday.

Det. Sergeant Lewis, of Thames Valley C.I.D., informed our reporter that in spite of an extensive search the murder weapon has not been discovered.

Police are asking residents in Daventry Avenue to help by searching their own properties, since it is believed the murderer may have thrown the knife away as he left the scene.

The knife may be of the sort used in the kitchen for cutting meat, probably with a blade about 2″ broad and 5–6″ in length. If found it should be left untouched, and the police informed immediately.

# CHAPTER TWENTY-SEVEN

Men will pay large sums to whores
For telling them they are not bores
(W. H. AUDEN, *New Year Letter*)

LATER THAT afternoon it was to be the B–B–B route: Bicester–Buckingham–Bedford. Fortunately for Lewis the detached Davies' residence was on the western outskirts of Bedford; and the door of 248 Northampton Road was answered immediately – by Ashley Davies himself.

After only a little skirmishing Davies had come up with his own version of the events which had preceded the showdown between himself and Matthew Rodway ... and Dr Felix McClure: an old carcass whose bones Lewis had been commissioned to pick over yet again.

Davies had known Matthew Rodway in their first year together. They'd met in the University Conservative Association (Lewis felt glad that Morse was abed); but apart from such political sympathy, the two young men had also found themselves fellow members of the East Oxford Martial Arts Club.

'Judo, karate – that sort of thing?' Lewis, himself a former boxer, was interested.

'Not so much the physical side of things – that was part of it, of course. But it's a sort of two-way process, physical and mental; mind and body. Both of us were more interested in the yoga side than anything. You know, "union" – that's what yoga means, isn't it?'

Lewis nodded sagely.

'Then you get into TM, of course.'

'TM, sir?'

'Transcendental Meditation. You know, towards spiritual well-being. You sit and repeat this word to yourself – this "mantra" – and you find yourself feeling good, content ... happy. Everything was OK, between Matthew and me, until this girl, this woman, joined. I just couldn't take my eyes off her. I just couldn't think of anything else.'

'The TM wasn't working properly?' suggested Lewis helpfully.

'Huh! It wasn't even as if she was attractive, really. Well, no. She *was* attractive, that's the whole point. Not beautiful or good-looking, or anything like that. But, well, she just had to look at you really, just look into your eyes, and your heart started melting away.'

'Sounds a bit of a dangerous woman.'

'You can say that again. I took her out twice – once to the Mitre, once to The Randolph – and she was quite open about things. Said she'd be willing to have sex and so on: fifty quid a time; hundred quid for a night together. No emotional involvement, though – she was very definite about that.'

'You agreed?'

'Well, I couldn't afford that sort of money. Hundred? Plus a B&B somewhere? But I did ask her about coming up to my room one evening – that was just after I'd started sharing with Matthew – when he had to go home for a family funeral. But it was a Tuesday, I remember, and she said she had to be very careful which day of the week it was. She could only do Saturday or perhaps Sunday because she knew somebody on the staircase and she wasn't prepared to take any risks.'

'What risks?'

'I don't know.'

'One of the other students – undergraduates there?'

For the first time the casually dressed, easy-mannered Davies hesitated. 'She didn't say.'

'Who else could it have been?'

Davies shrugged, but made no reply.

'There were two dons on the staircase, I understand – "Students" don't you call them?'

'Only a bloody pedant would call 'em Students these days.'

'I see. And, er, Dr McClure was one of those dons.'

'You've done your homework.'

'Go on please, sir.'

'Well, I had to go up for a Civil Service Selection thing on November the fifth, Bonfire Night, in Whitehall. Whole weekend of it – Friday, Saturday, Sunday. Anyway, I got so pissed off with all the palaver that I didn't stay for the Sunday session. I caught the ten-something from Paddington back to Oxford on Saturday night and when I got back to the staircase – well, there they were. We had two single beds in the one room, you see; and she was in his bed, and he was in mine. I don't quite know why, but it just made me see red and . . .'

'You'd tried to do the same yourself, though, so you said?'

'I know, yes.'

'You were just jealous, I suppose?'

'It was more than that. It's difficult to explain.'

'You mean, perhaps, if she'd been in *your* bed . . . ?'

'I don't know. You'd have to ask Freud. Anyway, I went berserk. I just went for him, that's all. He'd got nothing on – neither of 'em had – and soon we were wrestling and punching each other and knocking everything all over the bloody place, and there must have been one helluva racket because there was this great banging on the door and, well, we quietened down and I opened the door and there – there he was: that stuffed prick McClure. Well, that's about it, really. Matthew'd got a cut on his mouth and one of his eyes was badly bruised; I'd got a gash on my left arm but . . . no great damage, not considering. McClure wanted to know all about it, of course: who the girl was—'

'Who was she?'

'She called herself Ellie – Ellie Smith.'

'Then?'

'Well, they put me in one of the guest rooms in Great Quad, and Ellie went off – I think McClure put her in a taxi – and that was that. The Senior Tutor sent for me the next morning, and you know the rest.'

'Why didn't Mr Rodway get rusticated too?'

'Well, I'd started it. My fault, wasn't it?'

'Wasn't he disciplined at all?'

'Warned, yes. You get a warning in things like that. Then, if it happens again . . .'

Lewis thought he was beginning to get the picture. 'And perhaps you'd already had a warning yourself, sir?' he asked quietly.

Unblinking, the thickset Davies looked for several seconds into Lewis's eyes before nodding. 'I'd had a fight in a pub in my first year.'

'Much damage done then?'

'He broke his jaw.'

'Don't you mean *you* broke his jaw, sir?'

It was a pleasant little rejoinder, and perhaps Davies should have smiled. But Lewis saw no humour, only what he thought may have been a hint of cruelty, in the young man's eyes.

'You've got it, Sergeant.'

'Was that over a woman as well?'

'Yeah, 'fraid so. There was this other guy and he kept, you know, messing around a bit with this girl of mine.'

'Which pub was that?'

'The Grapes – in George Street. I think this guy thought it was called The Gropes.'

'And you hit him.'

'Yeah. I'd told him to fuck off.'

'And he hadn't.'

'Not straightaway, no.'

'But later he wished he had.'

'You could say that.'

'How did it get reported?'

'The landlord called the police. Bit unlucky, really. Wasn't all that much of a fight at all.'

Lewis consulted his notes. 'You wouldn't say you "went berserk" on that occasion?'

'No.'

'Why do you reckon you got so violent with Mr Rodway, then?'

149

Davies stared awhile at the carpet, then answered, though without looking up. 'It's simple, really. I was in love with her.'

'And so was Mr Rodway?'

Davies nodded. 'Yeah.'

'Have you seen her since?'

'A few times.'

'Recently?'

'No.'

'Can you tell me why you didn't go back to Oxford – to finish your degree? You were only rusticated for a term, weren't you?'

'Rest of the Michaelmas *and* all the Hilary. And by the time I was back, what with Finals and everything . . . I just couldn't face it.'

'How did your parents feel about that?'

'Disappointed, naturally.'

'Have you told them why I'm here today?'

'They're on a cruise in the Aegean.'

'I see.' Lewis stood up and closed his notebook and walked over to the window, enviously admiring the white Porsche that stood in the drive. 'They've left you the car, I see?'

'No, that's mine.'

Lewis turned. 'I thought you – well, you gave me the impression, sir, that fifty pounds might be a bit on the expensive side . . .'

'I came into some money. That's perhaps another reason I didn't go back to Oxford. Rich aunt, bless her! She left me . . . well, more than enough, let's say.'

Lewis asked a final question as the two men stood

in the front porch: 'Where were you last Sunday, sir?'

'Last *Sunday*?'

'Yes. The day Dr McClure was murdered.'

'Oh dear! You're not going to tell me ...? What possible reason could I have—'

'I suppose you could say it was because of Dr McClure that...'

'That they kicked me out? Yes.'

'You must have hated him for that.'

'No. You couldn't really hate him. He was just an officious bloody bore, that's all.'

'Did you know that he fell in love with Ellie Smith too?'

Davies sighed deeply. 'Yes.'

'Last Sunday, then?' repeated Lewis.

'I went bird-watching.'

'On your own?'

'Yes. I went out – must've been about nine, half-nine? Got back about three.'

'Whereabouts did you go?'

Davies mentioned a few names – woods or lakes, as Lewis assumed.

'Meet anyone you knew?'

'No.'

'Pub? Did you call at a pub? Hotel? Snackbar? Shop? Garage?'

'No, don't think so.'

'Must have been quite a lot of other bird-watchers around?'

'No. It's not the best time of year for bird-watching. Too many leaves still on the trees in late summer.

Unless you know a bit about flight, song, habitat – well, you're not going to spot much, are you? Do you know anything about bird-watching, Sergeant?'

'No.'

As Lewis left, he noticed the RSPB sticker on the rear window of a car he would have given quite a lot to drive. Perhaps not so much as fifty pounds, though.

# CHAPTER TWENTY-EIGHT

I do not love thee, Doctor Fell,
The reason why I cannot tell,
But this one thing I know full well:
I do not love thee, Doctor Fell
(THOMAS BROWN, *I Do Not Love Thee, Doctor Fell*)

STANDING QUITE still behind the curtained window of the first-floor front bedroom, she looked down across the drive at the departing policeman. She had a very good idea of what the interview had been about. Of course she had.

She was completely naked except for the dressing-gown (his) draped around a figure which was beginning to wobble dangerously between the voluptuous and the overblown – the beginnings of a pot-belly quite certainly calling for some fairly regular visits to the Temple Cowley pool in East Oxford, to plough through some thirty or forty lengths a time (for she was an excellent swimmer).

The smell of her was seductive though, she knew that. How else, with that posh eau-de-toilette just squirted everywhere about her person? 'Mimosa Pour Moi' – the last thing Felix had bought her.

Felix . . .

Always (above all perhaps?) he'd adored the sight and the smell of her when she'd just finished drying herself after one of her frequent baths. And how she treasured that letter – well, sort of letter – he'd written that morning in a posh London hotel as he'd sat waiting (and waiting and waiting) to go down to breakfast whilst she reclined luxuriously, reluctant to make any decisive move from the bath-tub.

How she loved a long, hot bath.

Yummy!

And how she loved what he'd written – one of the very few things she carried around in that scuffed shoulder-bag of hers:

> I ask my darling if she is ready for breakfast; and
> she stands in front of me; and with a
> synchronized circular swish of her deodorant-
> can, she sprays first her left armpit, then her
> right.
> But she gives no answer.
> I ask my darling if she has been thinking of me
> during our night together; and she forms her lips
> into a moue and rocks her right hand to and fro,
> as if she was stretching it forward to steady a
> rickety table on the stone-flagged floor at The
> Trout.
> But she gives no answer.
> I ask my darling why she can't occasionally be
> more punctual for any rendezvous with me; and I
> would be so glad if she could speak and dip into
> a pool of unconvincing excuses.
> But she gives no answer.
> I ask my darling what she loves most of all in her
> life; and she smiles (at last, a smile!) and she
> points behind her to the deep, scented water in

which she has just been soaking and poaching,
her full breasts seemingly floating on the surface.
    It is, I must suppose, the nearest I shall ever
come to an answer.

She'd read it many, many times. Above all she
enjoyed reading about herself in the third person. It
was as if she were a key character in some *roman-à-clef*
(Felix had told her about that sort of book – told her
how to pronounce it): a character far more important
on the page than in reality. Oh, yes. Because in real life
she wasn't important at all; nor ever would be. After all,
she wouldn't exactly be riding up to the abortion clinic
that Wednesday in a Roller, now would she? God, no.
Just standing on that perishing Platform Number 2,
waiting for the early bloody train up to bloody
Birmingham.

Ashley Davies opened the bedroom door and walked
up behind her, unloosening the belt of her (his)
dressing-gown.
    'God, am I ready—'
But she slipped away from him – and slipped out of
the dressing-gown, fixing first her black suspender-belt,
then her black bra; then pulling a thin dark blue dress
over her ridiculously colourful head before hooking a
pair of laddered black stockings up her legs.
    Davies had watched her, silently. He felt almost as
sexually aroused by watching her dress as watching her
undress.
    At last he spoke:

'What's the matter? What have I done wrong?'

She made no reply, but stood tip-tilting her chin towards the dressing-table mirror as she applied some transparent substance to her pouting lips.

'Ellie!'

'I'm off.'

'What d'you mean, you're off? I'm taking you out to lunch, remember?'

'I'm off.'

'You can't do this to me!'

'Just watch me!'

'Is it the police?'

'Could be.'

'But he's gone – it's over – it's all right.'

She picked up a small, overnight grip of faded pink canvas, inscribed with the names of pop groups and punk stars.

'I'm off.'

'When do I see you again?'

'You don't.'

'Ellie!'

'I don't want to see you any more.' (It seemed a long sentence.)

Davies sat down miserably on the side of the double bed in which he and Ellie had slept – half slept – the previous night.

'You don't love me at all, do you?'

'No.'

'Have you ever loved me?'

'No.'

'Did you love Matthew?'

'No.'

'Don't tell me you loved McClure? Don't tell me you loved *that* prick?'

'About the only thing about him I did love.'

'Christ! You shouldn't *say* things like that.'

'Why ask, then?'

'Have you ever loved anybody?'

'Me mum, yeah.'

'Nobody else?'

'Me dad – me real dad, I suppose. Can't remember.'

With a series of upward brushes she applied some black colouration to her eyelashes.

'Where d'you think you're going now?'

'Oxford.'

Davies sighed miserably, stood up, and reached inside his trouser-pocket for his car-keys.

'Come on, then.'

'I'm not going with *you*.'

'What's that supposed to mean?'

'I'll hitch a lift.'

'You can't do that.'

'Course I bloody can. That's all they're lookin' for, most of these lecherous sods. All I gotta do—'

'*Ellie!*'

'First car, like as not. You see.'

In fact, Ellie Smith's prediction was unduly optimistic, since the first car drove past her with little observable sign of interest, no detectable sign of deceleration.

The second car did exactly the same.

But not the third.

# CHAPTER TWENTY-NINE

My predestinated lot in life, alas, has amounted to
this: a mens not particularly sana in a corpore not
particularly sano
(VISCOUNT MUMBLES, *Reflections on My Life*)

ON THE following day, Sunday 4 September, Ted
Brooks was sitting up in bed, two pillows behind his
back, reading the more salacious offerings in the *News
of the World*. It was exactly 11.30 a.m., he knew that,
since he had been looking at his wristwatch every
minute or so since 11.15.

Now, for some reason, he began to feel slightly less
agitated as the minute-hand moved slowly up in the
climb towards the twelve – the 'prick of noon', as
Shakespeare has it. His mind, similarly, was moving
slowly; perhaps it had never moved all that quickly
anyway.

Whatever happened, though, he was going to make
the most of his heart attack – his 'mild' heart attack, as
they'd assured him in the Coronary Care Unit. Well, he
hoped it was mild. He didn't want to die. Course he
bloody didn't. Paradoxically, however, he found himself wishing it wasn't *all that* mild. A heart attack
– whatever its measurement on the Richter Scale – was
still a heart attack; and the maximum sympathy and
attention should be extracted from such an affliction,
so Brenda'd better bloody understand *that*.

He shouted downstairs for a cup of Bovril. But before the beverage could arrive, he heard the double-burred ring of the telephone: an unusual occurrence in the Brooks's household at any time; and virtually unprecedented on a Sunday.

He got out of bed, and stood listening beside the bedroom door as Brenda answered the call in the narrow entrance-hall at the bottom of the stairs.

'Oh, I see . . .'

'I do understand, yes . . .'

'Look, let me try to put him on . . .'

She found him sitting on the side of the bed, pulling on his socks.

'Thames Valley Police, Ted. They want to come and talk to you.'

'Christ!' he hissed. 'Don't they know I've only just got out of 'ospital?'

Brenda's upper lip was trembling slightly, but her voice sounded strangely calm. 'Would you like to speak to him yourself? Or tell me what to say? I don't care – but don't let's keep him waiting.'

'What's 'is name, this feller?'

'Lewis. Detective Sergeant Lewis.'


Lewis put down the phone.

Like Brooks a few minutes earlier, he was sitting on the side of the bed – Morse's bed.

'That's fixed that up, then, sir. I still feel you'd be better off staying in bed, though.'

'Nonsense!'

Lewis looked with some concern across at his chief,

lying back against three pillows, in pyjamas striped in maroon, pale blue, and white, with an array of bottles and medicaments on the bedside table: aspirin, Alka Seltzer, indigestion tablets, penicillin, paracetamol – and a bottle of The Macallan, almost empty.

He looked blotchy.

He looked ghastly.

'No rush, is there, sir?' he asked in a kindly manner.

'Not much danger of me rushing today.' He put down the book he'd been reading, and Lewis saw its title: *The Anatomy of Melancholy*.

'Trying to cheer yourself up, sir?'

'Oddly enough, I am. Listen to this: "There is no greater cause of melancholy than idleness; no better cure than busyness" – that's what old Burton says. So tell me all about Bedford.'

So Lewis told him, trying so very hard to miss nothing out; and conscious, as always, that Morse would probably consider of vital importance those things he himself had assumed to be obviously trivial.

And vice versa, of course.

Morse listened, with only the occasional interruption.

'So you can see, sir, he's not got much of an alibi, has he?'

'Lew-is! We won't *want* another suspect. We know who killed McClure: the fellow we're off to see this afternoon. All we're looking for is a bit more background, a slightly different angle on things. We can't take Brooks in yet – well, we *can*; but he's not going to run away. We ought to wait for a bit more evidence to accumulate.'

'We certainly haven't got much, to be truthful, have we?'

'You've still got people looking for the knife?'

Lewis nodded. 'Eight men on that, sir. Doing the houses Phillotson's lads didn't – along most of the road, both sides.'

Morse grunted. 'I don't like this fellow Brooks.'

'You've not even *seen* him yet.'

'I just don't like this drugs business.'

'I doubt if Davies had any part in that. Didn't seem the type at all.'

'Just in on the sex.'

'He fell for that woman in a pretty big way, no doubt about that.'

'Mm. And you say there may have been somebody in the house while you were there?'

'As I say, I heard the loo flushing.'

'Well, a trained detective like you would, wouldn't he?'

'When the cat's away . . .'

'Looks like it.'

'I think he's the sort of fellow who just welcomes all the floozies with open arms—'

'And open flies.'

'You don't think . . .' The thought struck Lewis for the first time. 'You don't think . . . ?'

'The loo-flusher was one and the same as our stair-case Lulu? No. Not a chance. Forget it! The really interesting thing is what Davies told you about her – about Ellie Smith, or whatever her name is.'

Morse broke off, wearily, wiping the glistering perspiration from his forehead with a grubby white handkerchief taken from his pyjama top – top number three, in fact, for he had already sweated his way through two pairs of pyjamas since taking to his bed the previous afternoon.

'Did you take your dose this morning, sir?'

Morse nodded. 'Double dose, Lewis. That's always been the secret for me.'

'I meant the medicine, not the Malt.'

Morse grinned weakly, his forehead immediately prickling with moisture once more, like a windscreen in persistent drizzle.

He lit a cigarette; and coughed revoltingly, his chest feeling like a chunk of excoriated flesh. Then spoke:

''She said she couldn't see him on a weekday, right? Saturday OK, though, and perhaps Sunday. Why? Pretty clearly because she knew somebody there on the staircase; and you thought – be honest, now! – you thought it must be somebody who buggered off to his cottage in the Cotswolds somewhere every weekend, and left the coast clear. You thought it was one of the two Students, didn't you? You thought it was McClure.'

'To be honest with you, I didn't, no. I thought it was somebody who didn't work after Saturday lunchtime until starting up again on Monday morning. I thought it was the scout. I thought it was Brooks.'

'Oh!'

'Wasn't I supposed to think that?'

Morse wiped his brow yet again. 'I'm not really up to things at the minute, am I?'

'No, I don't think you are.'

'Oh!'

'I think Brooks wasn't just a pusher; I think he was a

pimp as well. And it was probably too risky for him to let any of his girls get into the college – into the *House*, sir. So, if this particular girl *was* going to get in, it was going to be at weekends, when he wasn't there, when she could make her own arrangements, take her own risks, and set her own fee – without cutting him in at all.'

Morse was coughing again. 'Why don't I put you in charge of this case, Lewis?'

'Because I couldn't handle it.'

'Don't you think you can handle Brooks?'

'No.'

'You think we ought to wait a couple of days, don't you – before we see him?'

'Yes.'

'And you think I'll agree to that?'

'No.'

Morse closed Burton's immortal work, and folded the duvet aside.

'Will you do me a quick favour, Lewis, while I get dressed?'

'Course.'

'Just nip out and get me the *News of the World*, will you?'

# CHAPTER THIRTY

Randolph, you're not going to like this, but I was
in bed with your wife
(*Murder Ink: Alibis we never want to hear again*)

AT 1.15 P.M., on the way to the Brooks's residence in
East Oxford, they had called briefly at Daventry
Avenue. Still no sign of any murder weapon.

'Give 'em a chance,' Lewis had said.

Morse had insisted on taking the Jaguar, with Lewis
driving: he thought the finale of *Die Walküre* might well
refresh his drooping spirits, and the tape (he said) was
already in position there. But strangely enough he
hadn't turned it on; even more strangely he appeared
ready to engage in conversation in a car.

Most unusual.

'You ought to invest in a bit of Wagner, Lewis. Do
you far more good than all that rubbish you play.'

'Not when you're there, I don't.'

'Thank God!'

'I don't get on to you, for what you like.'

'What do *you* like best?'

Lewis came up to the roundabout at the Plain, and
took the second exit, the one after St Clements, into
the Cowley Road.

'I'll tell you what I can't stand, sir – the bagpipes.'

Morse smiled. 'Somebody once said that was his

164

favourite music – the sound of bagpipes slowly fading away into the distance.'

It was a quarter-to two when Ted and Brenda Brooks, side by side on the living-room settee, sat facing the two detectives: Morse in the only armchair there, Lewis on an upright chair imported for the occasion from the kitchen.

Brooks himself, in his late forties, dressed in a white, short-sleeved shirt and well-pressed grey slacks, looked pale and strained. But soon he appeared to relax a little, and was confirming, with an occasional nod of his greying head, the background details which Morse now briefly rehearsed: his years as a scout at Wolsey, where he had got to know Matthew Rodway ('Yup'); and Dr McClure ('Yup'); his present employment at the Pitt Rivers Museum ('Yup').

The skirmishing had been very civilized, and Mrs Brooks asked them all if they'd like a cup of tea.

But Morse declined, speaking, as it appeared, for all three of them, and turning back to Brooks and to the trickier part of the examination paper.

'Do you want your wife to be here, sir, while I ask you – I'm sorry – some rather awkward questions?'

'She stays. You stay, don't you, Bren? Nothing she shouldn't know about, Inspector.'

Lewis watched the man carefully, but could see no greater signs of nervousness than was normal among witnesses being interviewed by the police. Wasn't *she*, Mrs Brooks, the more obviously nervous of the two?

'Mr Brooks,' Morse began. 'I know you've been in

hospital, but please bear with me. We have evidence that there was some trading in drugs on your old staircase over the last three or four years.'

'Nothin' to do wi' me if there was.'

'You knew nothing of it?'

'No.'

'It's difficult for us, you see, because we have a statement to the effect that you did know something about it.'

'Christ! I'd like to know who it was as told you that. Load o' bloody lies!'

'You'd have no objections to coming along to HQ and going through that statement with us?'

'I can't – not just now, I can't – but I will – I'll be 'appy to – when I'm better. You don't want to give me another bloody 'eart attack, do you?'

Brooks's manner of speaking, which had begun in a gentle Oxfordshire burr, had suddenly switched into the coarse articulation with which he was wont to address his wife.

'Would you have known, Mr Brooks, if there had been drugs?'

'No job o' mine to interfere. Everybody's got their own lives to live.'

'There were parties there, on the staircase?'

'You try an' stop 'em!'

'Did *you* try?'

'If you talk to people they'll all tell you I were a good scout. That's all that worried me.'

'I'm afraid we shan't be able to talk to Dr McClure, shall we?'

'There's others.'

'Did you like Dr McClure?'

'OK, yeah.'

'You both left at the same time, I believe.'

'So wha'?'

'I just wondered if you had a farewell drink together, that's all.'

'Don't know much about Town and Gown, do you?'

Morse turned to Lewis. 'Sergeant?'

'We've obviously got to interview anyone, sir, who had a link with Dr McClure. That's why we're here, as I told you on the phone. So I shall have to ask you where you were last Sunday – Sunday the twenty-eighth of August.'

'Huh! Last Sunday?' He turned to his wife. 'Hear that, Bren? Not bloody difficult, that one, is it? You tell 'em. You remember better 'an I do. Bloody 'ell! If you reckon I 'ad anything to do wi' *that* – last *Sunday*? Christ!'

Brenda Brooks folded her hands nervously in her lap, and for the first time Morse noticed that the right hand, beneath an elastic support, might be slightly deformed. Perhaps she held them to stop them shaking? But there was nothing she could do about her trembling upper-lip.

'Well ... Ted woke me about three o'clock that Sunday morning—'

'More like 'alf-two.'

'—with this awful pain in his chest, and I got up to find the indigestion tablets and I made a cup o' tea and you seemed better, didn't you, Ted? Well, a bit better anyway and I slept a bit and he did, just a bit, but it was a bad night.'

'Terrible!'

'I got up at six and made some more tea and asked Ted if he wanted any breakfast but he didn't and the pain was still there, and I said we ought to ring the doctor but Ted said not yet, well, you know, it was Sunday and he'd have to come out special, like. Anyway he got up about ten because I remember we sat in the kitchen listening to *The Archers* at quarter-past while I got the meat ready – lamb and mint sauce – but Ted couldn't face it. Then about half-past one, quarter-to two, it got so bad, well, it was no good hanging on any longer and I rang the ambulance and they came in about . . . well, it was only about ten minutes – ever so quick. He was on a machine at half-past two – about then, weren't you, Ted?'

'Intensive Care,' said the ex-scout, not without a touch of pride. 'The pain 'ad got t'rific – I knew it were summat serious. Told you so at the time, didn't I, Bren?'

Brenda nodded dutifully.

It had immediately become clear to Morse that there was now a very considerable obstacle between him and any decision to arrest Edward Brooks on suspicion of murder; a considerable objection even to leaving his name on the list of suspects – which indeed would be a dramatic set-back for the whole case, since Brooks's name was the *only* one appearing on Morse's list.

He looked across now at the faithful little lady sitting there in her skirt and summer blouse next to her husband. If she persisted in her present lies (for Morse was convinced that such they were) it was going to be extremely difficult to discredit her testimony, appearing, as she did, to possess that formidable combination of nervousness and innocence. Any jury would strongly sympathize.

Morse changed tack completely.

'Do you know, I'm beginning to feel a bit thirsty, Mrs Brooks. Does that offer of a cuppa still stand?'

After Mrs Brooks had put the kettle on and taken the china cups from the dresser, she stood close to the kitchen door. Her hearing was still good. It was the white-haired one who was speaking . . .

'Have you got a car, sir?'

'Not 'ad one for ten year or more.'

'How do you get to work?'

'Still go on the bus, mostly.'

'You don't bike?'

'Why d'you ask that?'

'I saw your cycling helmet in the hall, that's all.'

'So?'

'Didn't mind me asking, did you?'

'Why the 'ell should I?'

'Well, Dr McClure was knifed to death, as you know, and there was an awful lot of blood all over the place – and all over the murderer, like as not. So if he'd driven off in a car, well . . . these clever lads in the labs, they can trace the tiniest speck of blood . . .'

'As I said, though, I 'aven't got a car.'

'I still think we'd quite like to have a look at your bike. What do you think, Sergeant Lewis?'

'Not a question of "liking", sir. I'm afraid we shall *have* to take it away.'

'Well, that's where you're wrong, 'cos I 'aven't got no bike no longer, 'ave I? Bloody stolen, wasn't it?

Sat'day lunchtime, that were – week yesterday. Just went to the Club for a pint and when I got out – there it was, gone! Lock 'n' all on the back wheel. Ten bloody quid, that fancy lock cost me.'

'Did you report the theft, sir?'

'Wha'? Report a stolen bike? In Oxford? You must be jokin'.'

Mrs Brooks came in with a tray.

'I must ask you to report the theft of your bike, sir,' said Lewis quietly. 'To St Aldate's.'

'Milk and sugar, Inspector?'

For the first time her eyes looked unflinchingly straight into his, and suddenly Morse knew that behind the nervousness, behind the fear, there lay a look of good companionship. He smiled at her; and she, fleetingly, smiled back at him.

And he felt touched.

And he felt poorly again.

And he felt convinced that he was sitting opposite the man who had murdered Felix McClure; felt it in his bones and in his brains; would have felt it in his soul, had he known what such a thing was and where it was located.

When ten minutes later Mrs Brooks was about to show them out, Morse asked about the two photographs hanging on the wall of the entrance-hall.

'Well, that one' – she pointed to a dark, broody-looking girl in her mid-teens or so – 'that's my daughter. That's Ellie. Her first name was Kay, really, but she likes to be called Ellie.'

Phew!

With an effort, Lewis managed not to exchange glances with Morse.

'That one' – she pointed to a photograph of herself arm-in-arm, in front of a coach, with a younger, taller, strikingly attractive woman – 'that's me and Mrs Stevens, when we went on a school-party to Stratford last year. Lovely, it was. And with a bit of luck I'll be going with her again this next week. She teaches at the Proctor Memorial School. I clean for her ... Well, as I say ... I clean for her.'

It seemed for a few seconds that she was going to add a gloss to that last repeated statement. But her husband had shouted from within, and Morse managed not to look down at that disfigured palm again as Brenda Brooks's hands indulged in a further spasm of floccillation.

# CHAPTER THIRTY-ONE

There is nothing which has yet been contrived by
man by which so much happiness is produced as
by a good tavern

(SAMUEL JOHNSON, *Obiter Dictum*,
21 March 1776)

'WELL, *well*! What do you make of all that?'

The Jaguar was gently negotiating half a dozen
traffic-calming humps, before reaching the T-junction
at the Cowley Road.

'Not now, Lewis!'

'How're you feeling, sir?'

'Just change the first letter of my name from "M" to
"W".'

'You should be in bed.'

Morse looked at his wristwatch. 'Nearest pub, Lewis.
We need to think a little.'

Morse was comparatively unfamiliar with the part of
Oxford in which he now found himself. In his own
undergraduate days, it had seemed a long way out,
being dubbed a 'Bridge Too Far' – on the farther side,
the eastern side, the *wrong* side, of Magdalen Bridge –
beyond the pale, as it were. Yet even then, three
decades earlier, it had been (as it still was) a cosmopol-
itan, commercial area of fascinating contrasts: of the
drab and the delightful; of boarded-up premises and
thriving small businesses; of decay and regeneration –

a Private Sex Shop at the city-centre end, and a police station at the far Ring Road end, with almost everything between, including (and particularly) a string of highly starred Indian restaurants. Including too (as Morse now trusted) a local pub selling real ale.

Lewis himself knew the area well; and after turning right at the T-junction, he almost immediately turned left into Marsh Road, pulling up there beside the Marsh Harrier.

Ashley Davies, he thought, would almost certainly have approved.

The *Good Pubs of Oxford* guide always reserved its highest praise for those hostelries where conversation was not impeded (let alone wholly precluded) by stentorian juke-boxes. And certainly Morse was gratified to find no music here. Yet he appeared to Lewis clearly ill-at-ease as he started – well, almost finished really – his first swift pint of Fuller's 'London Pride'.

'What's worrying you, sir?'

'I dunno. I've just got a sort of premonition—'

'Didn't know you believed in them.'

'—about this copy-cat-crime business. You know, you get a crime reported in the press – somebody pinching a baby from outside a supermarket, say – and before you can say "Ann Robinson" somebody else's having a go at the same thing.'

Lewis followed the drift of Morse's thought. 'The article we placed in the *Oxford Mail*?'

'Perhaps.'

'You mean, we shouldn't perhaps . . . ?'

'Oh, no! It was our duty to print that. And for all we know it could still produce something. Though I doubt it.'

Morse drained his beer before continuing: 'You know, that knife's somewhere, isn't it? The knife that someone stuck into McClure. The knife that *Brooks* stuck into McClure. That's the infuriating thing for me. Knowing that the bloody thing's *somewhere*, even if it's at the bottom of the canal.'

'Or the Cherwell.'

'Or the Isis.'

'Or the gravel-pits . . .'

But the conversation was briefly interrupted whilst Lewis, on the landlord's announcement of Last Orders, was now despatched to the bar for the second round.

Perhaps it was Morse's bronchial affliction which was affecting his short-term memory, since he appeared to be suffering under the misapprehension that it was he who had purchased the first.

Whatever the case, however, Morse quite certainly looked happier as he picked up his second pint, and picked up the earlier conversation.

'Brooks wouldn't have been too near any water, would he?'

'Not that far off, surely. And he'd have to go over Magdalen Bridge on his way home, anyway.'

'On his blood-saddled bike . . .'

'All he'd need to do was drop his knife over the bridge there – probably be safe till Kingdom Come.'

Morse shook his head. 'He'd have been worried about being seen.'

Lewis shrugged. 'He could have waited till it was dark.'

'It was bloody *morning*, Lewis!'

'He could've ditched it earlier. In a garden or somewhere.'

'No! We'd have found it by now, surely.'

'We're still trying,' said Lewis, quietly.

'You know' – Morse sounded weary – 'it's not quite so easy as you think – getting rid of things. You get a guilt-complex about being seen. I remember a few weeks ago trying to get rid of an old soldier in a rubbish-bin in Banbury Road. And just after I'd dropped it in, somebody I knew drove past in a car, and waved . . .'

'He'd seen you?'

'What makes you think it was a "he"?'

'You felt a bit guilty?'

Morse nodded. 'So it's vitally important that we find the knife. I just can't see how we're going to make a case out against Brooks unless we can find the murder weapon.'

'Have you thought of the other possibility, sir?'

'What's that?' Morse looked up with the air of a Professor of Mathematics being challenged by an innumerate pupil.

'He took the knife home with him.'

'No chance. We're talking about instinctive behaviour here. You don't stab somebody – and then just go back home and wash your knife up in Co-op detergent with the rest of the cutlery – and put it back in the kitchen drawer.'

'There'd be a knife missing, though – from a set, perhaps.'

'So what? Knives get lost, broken . . .'

'So *Mrs* Brooks would probably know?'

'But she's not going to tell us, is she?'

Morse seemed to relax as he leaned back against the wall-seat, and looked around him.

'You sure it *was* Brooks?' asked Lewis quietly.

'Too many coincidences, Lewis. All right, they play a far bigger part in life than most of us are prepared to admit. But not in this case. Just think! Brooks left Wolsey, for good, on exactly the same day as the man who was murdered – McClure. Not only that, the pair of them had been on the same staircase together – exactly the same staircase – for several years. Then, a year later, Brooks has a heart attack on exactly the same day as McClure gets murdered. Just add all that up – go on, Lewis!'

'Like I say, though, you've always believed in coincidences.'

'Look! I could stomach two, perhaps – but not *three*.'

Lewis, who'd believed that Morse could easily stomach at least four, was not particularly impressed; and now, looking around him, he saw that he and Morse were the only clients left in the Marsh Harrier.

It was 3.10 p.m.

'We'd better be off, sir.'

'Nonsense! My turn, isn't it?'

'It's way past closing time.'

'Nonsense!'

But the landlord, after explaining that serving further drinks after 3 p.m. on Sundays was wholly against the law, was distinctly unimpressed by Morse's assertion that he, the latter, *was* the law. And a minute or so later it was a slightly embarrassed Lewis who was unlocking the passenger door of the Jaguar – before making his way back to North Oxford.

# Chapter Thirty-Two

These are, as I began, cumbersome ways
to kill a man. Simpler, direct and much more neat
is to see he is living somewhere in the middle
of the twentieth century, and leave him there
          (EDWIN BROCK, *Five Ways to Kill a Man*)

PERPETUALLY, on the drive back to North Oxford, Morse had been wiping the perspiration from his forehead; and Lewis was growing increasingly worried, especially when, once back home, Morse immediately poured himself a can of beer.

'Just to replace the moisture,' Morse had averred.

'You ought to get the doc in, you know that. And you ought not to be drinking any more, with all those pills.'

'Lewis!' Morse's voice was vicious. 'I appreciate your concern for my health. But never again – never! – lecture me about what I drink. Or if I drink. Or when I drink. *Is – that – clear?*'

In a flush of anger, Lewis rose to his feet. 'I'll be getting back—'

'Siddown!'

Morse took out a cigarette, and then looked up at the still-standing Lewis. 'You don't think I ought to smoke, either?'

'It's your life, sir. If you're determined to dig yourself an early grave . . .'

'I don't want to die, not just yet,' said Morse quietly.

And suddenly, as if by some strange alchemy, Lewis felt his anger evaporating; and, as bidden, he sat down.

Morse put the cigarette back in its packet. 'I'm sorry – sorry I got so cross. Forgive me. It's just that I've always valued my independence so much – too much, perhaps. I just don't like being told what to do, all right?'

'All right.'

'Well, talk to me. Tell me what you thought about Brooks.'

'No, sir. You're the thinker – that's why you get a bigger pay-packet than me. You tell *me*.'

'Well, I think exactly the same as I did before. After young Rodway's suicide, McClure found out about the availability of drugs on the staircase there – cannabis, amphetamines, cocaine, crack, ecstasy, LSD, heroin, whatever – and he also found out that it was Brooks who was supplying them, and making a pretty penny for himself in the process. Then, at some point, McClure told Brooks he'd got two options: either he packed up his job as a scout and left; or else he'd be reported to the University authorities – and probably the police – and faced with criminal proceedings. So Brooks had just about enough nous to read the writing on the wall: he resigned, and got another job, with a reluctant McClure providing a luke-warm testimonial to the Pitt Rivers Museum. But there were too many links with his former clients – and not just on the old staircase; and he kept up his lucrative little sideline *after* he'd left Wolsey – until McClure somehow got wind of the situation – and confronted him – and told him that this time it wasn't just an empty threat. I suspect Brooks must have had some sort of hold on McClure, I don't know. But Brooks said he was ready to step into line, and do whatever McClure wanted. *And he arranged a meeting with McClure* – at McClure's place in Daventry Court, a week ago today. That's the way I see it.'

'So you don't believe a word of his alibi?'

'No. And it isn't *his* alibi at all – it's hers. Mrs Brooks's alibi for him.'

'And you think he biked up to see McClure?'

'He biked, yes. Whether he'd already decided to murder McClure then, I don't know. But he took a murder weapon with him, a knife from his wife's kitchen drawer; and I've not the slightest doubt he took as many precautions as he could to keep himself from being recognized – probably wrapped a scarf round his face as if he'd got the toothache. And with his cycling helmet—'

'You're making it all up, sir.'

Morse wiped his brow once more. 'Of *course* I am! In a case like this you've got to put up some ... some scaffolding. You've got to sort of take a few leaps in the dark, Lewis. You've got to hypothesize . . .'

'Hypothesize about the knife then, sir.'

'He threw it in the canal.'

'So we're not going to find it?'

'I'm sure we're not. We'd have found it by now.'

'Unless, as I say, he took it home with him – and washed it up and wiped it dry and then put it back in the kitchen drawer.'

'Ye-es.'

'Probably he *did* mean to throw it in the canal, or

somewhere. But something could have stopped him, couldn't it?'

'Such as?'

'Such as a heart attack,' suggested Lewis gently.

Morse nodded. 'If he suddenly realized he hadn't got any time to . . . if he suddenly felt a terrible pain . . .'

'"T'rific", that's what he said.'

'Mm.'

'What about the bike, though? He must have ridden it up to Daventry Court, mustn't he? So if he'd felt the pain starting, you'd have thought he'd get back home as fast as he could.'

Morse shook his head. 'It doesn't add up, does it? He must have ditched his bike somewhere on the way back.'

'Where, though?'

Morse pondered the problem awhile. Then, remembering Brooks's contempt for anyone taking the trouble to report a bicycle-theft in Oxford, he suddenly saw that it had ceased to be a problem at all.

'Do you know a poem called "Five Ways to Kill a Man"?'

'No.'

Wearily Morse rose to his feet, fetched an anthology of modern verse from his shelves, looked up Brock in the index, turned to the poem – and read the last stanza aloud.

But Lewis, though not unaccustomed to hearing Morse make some apposite quotation from the poets between draughts of real ale, could see no possible connexion in logic here.

'I'm not with you.'

Morse looked down at the stanza again; then slowly recited his own parody of the lines:

'There are several cumbersome ways
of losing a bike – like pushing it in the canal.
Neater and simpler, though, is to take it somewhere
like Cornmarket in Oxford – and just leave it there.'

'You ought to have been a poet, sir.'

'I am a poet, Lewis.'

Morse now coughed violently, expectorating into a tissue a disgusting gobbet of yellowish-green phlegm streaked with bright blood.

Lewis, although he saw it, said nothing.

And Morse continued:

'First thing is to get Brooks in, and go through Susan Ewers' statement with him. She's a good witness, that one – and he'll have to come up with something better than he gave us this afternoon.'

'When shall we bring him in, though? He's got a point, hasn't he? We don't want to give him another heart attack.'

'Don't we?'

'Day or two?'

'Day or three.'

Morse finished his beer. It had taken that swift drinker an inordinately long time to do so; and if Morse had experienced a premonition earlier, Lewis himself now sensed that his chief was seriously ill.

'What about the photograph, sir? Mrs Brooks's daughter?'

'Interesting question. I wonder. I wonder where that young lady fits into the picture.'

'Pretty well everywhere, wouldn't you say?'

'Ye-es. "Kay" – "K" – "Eleanor" – "Ellie" – we've got to assume she's the same girl, I suppose: Mrs B's daughter – Mr B's step-daughter – staircase-tart for Messrs Rodway and Davies – mistress for Dr McClure . . .'

'She must be quite a girl.'

'But what about that other photograph, Lewis? The school-mistress? D'you know, I've got a feeling she might be able to shed a little light—'

But Morse was coughing uncontrollably now, finally disappearing into the bathroom, whence was heard a series of revolting retches.

Lewis walked out into the entrance hall, where he flicked open Morse's black plastic telephone-index to the letter 'S'. He was lucky. Under 'Summertown Health Centre' he found an 'Appointments' number; and an 'Emergency' number.

He rang the latter.


That same afternoon, just after four o'clock, Dr Richard Rayson, Chaucerian scholar, and fellow of Trinity College, Oxford, strolled round his garden in Daventry Avenue. For almost three weeks he had been away with his family in the Dolomites. Gardening, in truth, had never been the greatest passion of his life; and as he stood surveying the state of his neglected front lawn, the epithet which sprang most readily to his literate mind was 'agrestal': somewhat overgrown; run to seed; wild, as the *Shorter Oxford* might define it.

Yet strangely, for such an unobservant man, he'd spotted the knife almost immediately – a couple of feet or so inside the property, between an untrimmed laurel bush and the vertical slats of a front fence sorely in need of some re-creosoting. There it was, lying next to a semi-squashed tin of Coca Cola.

Nina Rayson, a compensatingly practical sort of partner, had welcomed her husband's discovery, promptly washing it in Sainsbury's 'Economy' washing-up liquid, and forthwith adding it to her own canteen of cutlery. A good knife, it was: a fairly new, sturdy, unusually broad-bladed instrument, in no immediate need of any further sharpening.

That same evening, at nine-thirty, Brenda Brooks was aware that her jangled nerves could stand very little more that day. Paradoxically, though, she felt almost competent about coping with the loathsome man she'd just seen to bed, with a cup of tea, two digestive biscuits, and one sleeping tablet. At least she knew him: knew the *worst* about him – for there was nothing but the worst to know. It was now the *unknown* that was worrying her the more deeply: that strange technical jargon of the doctors and nurses at the hospital; the brusque yet not wholly unsympathetic questions of the two policemen who had earlier called there.

She found herself neurotically dreading any phone-call; any ringing of the door-bell. Anything.

What was that?

What was *that*?

Was she imagining things – imagining noises?

There it was again: a muffled, insistent, insidious, tapping . . .

Fearfully, she edged towards the front door.

And there, behind the frosted glass, she saw a vaguely human silhouette; and she turned the Yale lock, and opened the door, her heart fluttering nervously.

'You!' she whispered.

# CHAPTER THIRTY-THREE

It is an inexorable sort of festivity – in September 1914 they tried to cancel it, but the Home Secretary himself admitted that he was powerless to do so

(JAN MORRIS, *Oxford*)

OXFORD'S St Giles' Fair is held annually on the first Monday and Tuesday after the first Sunday every September, with the whole area of St Giles' brought into use, from the Martyrs' Memorial up to (and beyond) St Giles' Church at the northern end, where the broad, tree-lined avenue bifurcates to form the Woodstock Road to the left and the Banbury Road to the right.

In mid-afternoon on Tuesday, 6 September (two days after Lewis had telephoned the Summertown Health Centre), Kevin Costyn was sauntering under the plane trees there, along the various rides and amusements and candy-floss stalls. Nothing could really kindle his imagination or interest, for the Naked Lady of earlier years, in her rat-infested cage, no longer figured in the fair's attractions. And as Kevin considered the jazzy, jolty, vertiginous cars and carriages, he felt no real wish to part with any of his limited money.

That day the children in the state schools in Oxfordshire had returned to their classrooms; and for the first time in twelve years Costyn himself was not one of them. No more school. But no job yet, either. He'd

186

signed on at the Job Centre. Even taken away some literature on *Youth Employment Schemes and Opportunities.* Not that he was going to read that bumf. He wasn't interested in jobs. Just money. Well, not *just* money, no.

Smugly he grinned to himself as he stood outside the Bird and Baby and watched the gigantic, gyrating structure of the Big Wheel.

The previous month he'd been part of a three-man ram-raid at a Summertown supermarket, but it hadn't proved the windfall they'd expected. Shop windows – *replaced* shop windows – were being made of tougher glass; and several regular, and formerly profitable, targets were now protected by concrete frontal pillars. That wasn't the real trouble, though. It was getting rid of the stuff that was getting trickier all the time. Cigarettes had usually been the best bet: lightweight, handy to stack, easy to sell. But booze was becoming one helluva job to sell; and the cases of whisky, gin, and vodka they'd got away with then had changed hands for a miserly £850, though according to Costyn's (admittedly less than competent) calculation their street-value would have been four times that amount. It was the police – becoming far cannier at tracking down the wholesale-market contacts – they were the real trouble.

There must be easier ways of being able to afford the life of Riley, surely?

Yes, occasionally there were . . .

It had been Kevin Costyn himself who had answered the door the previous afternoon, to find Mrs Stevens standing there – a subtly scented Mrs Stevens, with a moist, red beauty at her lips.

Could she come in? She'd come in.

Would he listen to what she had to say? He'd listened.

Would he be willing to do as she asked? He'd be willing.

Would he be able to do what she wanted? He'd be able.

Payment? What about payment? Did he understand she had very little money? He'd understood.

How would he like her to pay him, then?

Well . . .

'What time's your mother back?' she'd asked.

No one over the past few years had deemed it necessary, or deemed it wise, to challenge Costyn's minority; nor did the young barmaid now, as she pulled him a pint of Burton Ale in the Bird and Baby ('Open All Day').

Ten minutes later he made his way to the Gents, where he spat a globule of phlegm on to the tiled floor, and where his left hand was directing his urination whilst his right hand was seeking, wholly ineffectually, to spell out FUCK in red Biro on the corrugated surface of the wall in front of him.

'Fuck' was a key word in Costyn's limited vocabulary. Had already been so for many years, ever since, night after night, his mum and dad (*perhaps*, his dad) had bawled their mutual 'fuck-off's at each other. Until the day when his dad had apparently interpreted the injunction rather too literally – and just, well, 'fucked off'. Indeed, so significant had the word become to the sole son of that hapless, unhappy union, that he regularly inserted it, in its present-participial form, into any lengthy-ish word which seemed to invite some internal profanation. Such a process is known, in the Homeric epics, as 'tmesis' – although, in truth, Costyn knew of 'Homer' only as a breed of pigeon; for his father had once kept such a pigeon, trained (once released) to find its way home from the most improbable distances. Which is more than its owner had done, once he had left his home, and his wife, and his son . . . and his pigeon.

Before leaving the Gents, Costyn made a purchase. The condom machine looked, even to him, pretty theft-proof; and he decided for once to pay for his potential pleasures. For a few seconds he mentally debated the respective merits of 'lubrication', 'sensitivity', and 'silk-iness'; finally plumping for the latter as he thought – yet again! – of the blouse that he'd slowly eased down over the suntanned shoulders of Mrs Julia Stevens.

At 4 p.m., standing waiting for a Cowley Road bus outside Marks and Spencer in Queen's Street, Costyn recognized an ex-pupil of the Proctor Memorial immediately in front of him; and he put a hand on her untanned shoulder.

'Bin 'avin' a ride, darlin'?'

She turned round. 'Wha' d'you want?'

'What about a little ride with *me*, darlin'? I got the necessaries.'

'Fuck off!'

Few girls ever spoke to him in such a fashion. But Costyn felt little resentment as he fingered the two packets of Silken Dalliance in his pocket . . .

Payment for his services?

'Half now; half later,' that's what Mrs Stevens had promised. And as he sat upstairs on the Cowley Road bus, Costyn savoured yet again that intoxicating cocktail of excitement and sensuality.

Half later . . . when the job was done; when the jobs (plural, perhaps), were done.

Was it terribly risky, what he'd so willingly agreed to do? Especially since she wasn't exactly sure of when she'd be calling on him. So what? Much riskier for her than for him. Not that she'd ever need to worry about *him*: he'd never breathe a word of it to any living soul.

Never.

And anyone who thought he would was suffering under a misapprefuckinhension.

# CHAPTER THIRTY-FOUR

The gaudy, blabbing, and remorseful day
Is crept into the bosom of the sea
(SHAKESPEARE, *Henry IV, Part II*)

## (i)

ON WEDNESDAY, 7 September 1994, at 11.20 a.m., Ms Ellie Smith sat in a taxi, every half-minute or so nervously consulting her wristwatch and cursing herself for not having taken up Ashley Davies's offer.

Rightly or wrongly, before walking out on him the previous weekend, she'd informed him of her situation: she was twelve weeks' pregnant; she was determined to have another abortion; she had an appointment at a South Birmingham clinic for preliminary consultation and advice. But when Davies had rung her the previous afternoon, she'd turned down his offer of a lift – once again. He'd been quite insistent really, saying that he'd got to be in Oxford later the next day, anyway; and it was so quick to Brum now – M40, M42 – and in *his* car, well, they'd do it in an hour almost; save her no end of time and trouble – and the rail fare into the bargain.

But she'd refused.

She was going by train, catching the 9.11 a.m. from Oxford, due to arrive at Birmingham New Street at 10.30 a.m., which would give her a whole hour to get to the clinic, only five miles distant from the railway station.

That was the plan.

But with the combination of a 'signalling failure' just before Leamington Spa and a security scare at Coventry, the train had finally rumbled into New Street forty-eight minutes late – and she'd had no option but to take a taxi. Not that she need have bothered too much, for it was 11.55 a.m. before she was called into the consulting-room.

Looking back on things, Ms Smith knew that she had been strangely impressed by the small, white-coated Pakistani doctor – a kindly, compassionate man, with Spaniel eyes – who had gently encouraged her at least to consider the alternative: that of keeping the child she had conceived.

She felt glad that she had tried to present herself in rather more conventional guise, putting on bra and pants (both!) beneath her only presentable summer dress – *and* removing the rings from her nostrils. Admittedly that left her hair, still streaked with crimson like the horizon in an angry sunset; but she felt (dare she admit it to herself?) somehow . . . expiated!

She couldn't really think why.

No, she *could* think why.

It was something to do with being with her mum once more . . .

The 15.09 train from New Street, timetabled to arrive in Oxford at 16.31 p.m., arrived virtually on time. And half an hour later Ellie Smith was back at her flat, reading the brief note contained in the white envelope ('By Hand') which she'd found propped up at the foot of her white-painted door on the third floor:

> Hope things went OK. Any chance of you
> thinking again? If there's even a remote chance
> of its being mine, I'll marry you and make an
> honest woman of you yet. Don't be cross with me
> for badgering you.
>> Ashley, with lots and lots of kisses.

As she put her key into the lock, Ellie Smith wondered whether she'd sadly misjudged Mr Ashley Davies.

## (ii)

'THANKS for coming,' said a sombre Phillotson.

In vain Lewis sought to find some suitable rejoinder.

'Morse on the mend?'

'Out tomorrow, so they say.'

'Will he be fit enough to carry on – with the case?'

'Dunno, sir. I suppose he'll please himself whatever happens.'

'I suppose he will, yes.'

Lewis moved away, and briefly surveyed the wreaths laid out there, including a splendid display of white lilies from the Thames Valley Police HQ.

Phillotson's wife had lived a gently unspectacular life, and died at the age of forty-six. Not much of an innings, really; and not too much of a memorial either, although her husband, her next of kin, and all of her friends, would hope that the little rose-bush (*Rosa rubrifolia*), already happily stuck into a wodge of blackly-rich compost in the Garden of Remembrance, would thrive and prosper – and, metempsychotically, as it were, take over.

If Chief Inspector Morse had been present at the short service, he would have been impatient with what he saw as the pretentious prayers; and yet, almost certainly, he would have welcomed the hymn that was played there – 'O Love that wilt not let me go' – and his quiet unmusical baritone would probably have mingled with the singing.

But Morse was not one of the thirty-seven mourners Lewis counted at the Oxford Crematorium that Wednesday lunchtime.

## (iii)

'WHAT EXACTLY'S *wrong* with you, Morse?'

'I'm only here for observation.'

'Yes, I know that. But what exactly is it they're *observing*?'

Morse drew a deep breath. 'I'm suffering from bronchi-something beginning with "e"; my liver and kidneys are disintegrating; my blood pressure isn't quite off the top of the scale – not yet; I'm nursing another stomach ulcer; and as if that wasn't enough I'm on the verge of diabetes, because my pancreas, they tell me, isn't producing sufficient insulin to counteract my occasional intake of alcohol. Oh yes, and my cholesterol's dangerously high.'

'I see. Perhaps I should have asked what exactly's *right* with you, Morse.'

Strange shifted his great bulk awkwardly on the small wooden chair beside Morse's bed in Ward 7 of the John Radcliffe Two Hospital out at Headington, whither, in spite of his every protestation of being in excellent health, Morse had been conveyed by ambulance, half an hour after the doctor had been summoned the previous Sunday afternoon.

'I had an endoscopy yesterday,' continued Morse.

'Sounds painful. Where do they stick that?'

'In the *mouth*, sir.'

'Ah. No more dramatic finds?'

'No more corpses under the floorboards.'

'Well, the wife'll be very pleased if you can last out till – fairly soon, isn't it? – when you've got a speaking engagement, I understand.'

'I *have?*'

'You know – the WI group-meeting in Kidlington. Likely to be a good crowd there, she says. So try to make it, old man. She's, er . . . you know, she's the President this year. Means a lot to her.'

'Tell her I'll be there, even if they have to wheel me in.'

'Good. Good. "The Grislier Aspects of Murder." Nice little title, that.'

With which Morse's mind reverted to the investigation. 'If you see Lewis, sir, tell him to call in tonight, will you? I'd like to know how things are going.'

'He was going to Mrs Phillotson's funeral this lunchtime.'

'What? Nobody told me about that.'

'No, well ... we didn't want to, er ... Not a nice subject, death, is it.'

The clock showed 2.45 p.m. when Strange made his way out of Ward 7; and for several minutes Morse lay back on his pillows and pondered. Perhaps a hospital was an appropriate place to meditate on death, for there was plenty of it going on all around. But most men or women preferred not to think or talk about it. Morse had known only one person who positively relished discussing the topic – Max the police pathologist, who in a macabre kind of way had almost made a friend of Death. But Death had made no reciprocal arrangement; and Max was police pathologist no longer.

## (iv)

ALTHOUGH THE autumn term had only begun the day before, clearly one or two of the local schools had been planning, well in advance, to despatch their pupils on some of the dreaded GCSE 'projects' at the earliest possible opportunity. Certainly, until about 4.05 p.m., twenty or so schoolchildren had still been studying a range of anthropological exhibits in the Upper Gallery of the Pitt Rivers Museum.

Which was rather worrying.

But by 4.15 p.m., the galleries were virtually – by 4.20 p.m., totally – deserted. And from where he stood, beside the collection made in the South Pacific by Captain Cook on his second visit there in 1772, the young man observed most carefully whilst a suntanned, balding attendant walked briskly round the Upper Gallery, doubtless checking that no bags or satchels or writing-pads had inadvertently been left behind; and in so doing, as was immediately apparent, giving a quick, upward 'lift' to each of the glass covers of the locked cabinets there, like a potential car-thief swiftly moving along a line of vehicles in a Park and Ride and testing the doors.

Two minutes later, the young man was following in the attendant's same pre-closure tracks; but stopping now, at a particular spot, where he looked down at a collection of knives – knives of all shapes and sizes, knives from many parts of the world – displayed in Cabinet Number 52.

Quickly, his heart pounding, he took a chisel from his summer sweatshirt and inserted its recently sharpened edge between the metal rim of the display-case top and the darkly stained wooden slat below it, into which the cabinet's lock was set.

Easy!

No great splintering of wood or moaning of metal. Just a single, quick 'click'. Yet it had been a bad moment; and the young man checked anxiously to his left, then to his right, before lifting the glass lid and putting a hand inside.

It was 4.29 p.m. when he walked through the museum shop. He might have bought a postcard of the forty-foot-high Haida Totem Pole (British Columbia), but an assistant was already totting up the takings, and he wished to cause no trouble. As the prominent notice had advised him as he'd entered, the Pitt Rivers Museum of Ethnology and Pre-History closed at 4.30 p.m. each day.

## (v)

AT THE Proctor Memorial School, the take-up for the *Twelfth Night* trip to the Shakespeare Theatre had been encouraging. Before the end of the summer term, Julia Stevens had made her usual block-booking of thirty-one seats; and with twenty-three pupils (mostly fifth- and sixth-formers), two other members of staff, plus two parents, only three tickets had been going begging. Only *two*, in fact – and those soon to be snapped up with alacrity at the box office – because Julia Stevens had invited Brenda Brooks (as she had done the previous year) to join the school-party.

At the Stratford Coach Park, the three teachers had distributed the brown-paper-wrapped rations: two rolls, one with mayonnaised-curried-chicken, the other with a soft-cheese filling; one packet of crisps; and one banana – with a plastic cup of orangeade.

On the way back, though not on the way out, Mrs Stevens and Mrs Brooks sat side by side in the front seats: the former semi-listening (with some gratification) to her pupils' pronouncements on the performances of Sirs Toby Belch and Andrew Aguecheek; the latter, until Woodstock, trying to read the latest instalment of a romantic serial in *Woman's Weekly*, before apparently falling into a deep slumber, and not awakening therefrom until, two minutes before midnight on

Wednesday, 7 September, the coach made its first stop at Carfax Tower, from where the streets of Oxford looked strangely beautiful; and slightly sinister.

# PART TWO

# CHAPTER THIRTY-FIVE

In me there dwells
No greatness, save it be some far-off touch
Of greatness to know well I am not great
(ALFRED, LORD TENNYSON, *Lancelot and Elaine*)

AFTER RINGING the emergency number the previous Sunday, it had been a sad sight that confronted Lewis in the bathroom: Morse standing creased over the pedestal basin, his cheeks wholly drained of colour, his vomit streaked with blood forming a chrysanthemum pattern, scarlet on white, across the porcelain.

Dr Paul Roblin had been adamant.

Ambulance!

Lewis had woken up to the truth an hour or so later: for a while at least, he was going to be left alone with a murder investigation.

Such a prospect would normally have daunted him; yet the present case was unusual in that it had already established itself into a pattern. In the past, the more spectacular cases on which he and Morse had worked together had often involved some bizarre, occasionally some almost incredible, twists of fate. But the murder of Dr Felix McClure appeared – surely *was* – a comparatively straightforward affair. There could be little doubt – none in Morse's mind – about the identity of the murderer. It was just a question of timing now, and patience: of the accumulation, the aggregation of evidence, against a man who'd had the means, the motive, and the opportunity, to murder McClure. Only concerning the actual commission of the crime was there lack of positive evidence. Lack of any evidence. And what a feather in his cap it would be if he, Lewis, could come up with something on *that*, during Morse's reluctant, yet enforced, immobility.

For the present, then, it was he who was sole arbiter of the course of further enquiries; of the most productive deployment of police resources. He had not been born great, Lewis was aware of that; nor did the rank of Detective Sergeant mark him out as a man who had achieved any significant greatness. Yet for a few days now, some measure of vicarious greatness was being thrust upon him; and he would have been encouraged by the Latin proverb (had he known it) that 'Greatness is but many small littles', since it was upon a series of 'small littles' that he embarked over the following three days – Monday, Tuesday, Wednesday, 5, 6, 7 September.

Over these few days many statements were taken from people, both Town and Gown, some fairly closely, some only peripherally, connected with the murdered man and with his putative murderer. And it was Lewis himself who had visited the JR2 on Tuesday afternoon for it to be confirmed, quite unequivocally, that Mr Edward Brooks had been admitted, via Casualty, to the Coronary Care Unit at 2.32 p.m. on Sunday, 28 August; that Brooks had spent twenty-four hours in Intensive Care before being transferred to Level 7, whence he had been discharged three days later.

Whilst in the hospital, Lewis had called in to see Morse (his second visit), but had refused to be drawn into any discussion of new developments in the enquiry. This for two reasons: first, that there were no new developments; and, second, that Superintendent Strange had strongly urged against such a course of action – 'Start talking about it, and he'll start thinking about it. And once he starts thinking, he'll start thinking about drinking, whatever the state of his innards . . .' So Lewis stayed only a few minutes that afternoon, taking a 'Get Well' card from Mrs Lewis, and a small bunch of seedless white grapes from himself, the latter immediately confiscated by the hawk-eyed ward-sister.

From the JR2, Lewis had gone on to interview the Brooks's family GP, Dr Philip Gregson, at the Cowley Road Health Centre.

The brief medical report on Edward Brooks which Lewis read there was quite optimistic: 'Mild heart attack – condition now stable – surprisingly swift recovery. GP appt 1 wk; JR2 out/p appt 2 wk.'

About Brenda Brooks, however, Gregson was more circumspect. She had, yes, suffered a very nasty little injury to her right hand; and, yes, he had referred her to a specialist. But he couldn't comment in any way upon his colleague's findings. If further information were considered necessary . . .

In such fashion was it that Lewis's queries were concluded late that Tuesday afternoon – with the telephone number of an orthopaedic surgeon, and with the knowledge that he was getting nowhere fairly slowly.

Yet only twenty-four hours were to elapse before the first major breakthrough in the case was destined to occur.

# CHAPTER THIRTY-SIX

Is this a dagger which I see before me,
The handle towards my hand?
(SHAKESPEARE, *Macbeth*)

IT TOOK a long time, an inordinately long time, for the penny to drop.

Dr Richard Rayson had been wholly unaware of the great excitement which had been witnessed by the residents of Daventry Avenue over the previous week. Yet his inability to establish any connection between the discovery of a knife and the death of a neighbour is readily explicable. In the first place, the physical police presence around Daventry Court had been withdrawn on the day prior to his return from abroad. Then, too, Rayson had not as yet re-instated his standing-order with the Summertown newsagent for the daily delivery of the *Oxford Mail*; he had therefore missed the brief item tucked away at the bottom of page 3 on Monday (would probably have missed it anyway). And finally, and most significantly, his communications with his neighbours, on either side, had been almost completely severed of late – this breakdown occasioned by a series of increasingly bitter differences of view over the maintenance of boundary fences, the planting of inter-property trees, an application for planning permission, and (most recently) the dangerous precedent of a teenage party.

Thus, after spending the whole of the Monday and Tuesday with his wife in regrooming their garden, it was only at lunchtime on Wednesday, 7 September, that Rayson was re-introduced into the mainstream of Oxford life and gossip – at a cocktail reception in Trinity College to meet a group of librarians from Oklahoma.

'Fine drop of claret, what, Richard?' one of his colleagues had affirmed.

'Beautifully balanced little wine, George.'

'By the way, you must have known old McClure, I suppose? Lives only a few doors from you, what? *Lived*, rather.'

Rayson had frowned. 'McClure?'

'You know, the poor sod who got himself knifed?'

McClure. Felix McClure. Knifed.

*The knife.*


Just after five o'clock that afternoon, Detective Sergeant Lewis stood looking down at the prime exhibit, laid out on the Formica-topped surface of the kitchen in Rayson's elegant detached house in Daventry Avenue – seven properties distant, on the Woodstock Road side, from the scene of McClure's murder. As Rayson had explained over the phone, the knife had been found just inside the front fence, had been picked up, washed, dried, put away, picked up again, used to cut a roll of boiled ham, re-washed, re-dried, put away again – and picked up yet again when Rayson had returned from Trinity in the late afternoon, and examined it with a sort of ghoulish fascination.

With no prospects, therefore, of the exhibit retaining any incriminating fingerprints or blood-stains, Lewis in turn now picked up the black-handled knife, its blade unusually broad at the base, but tapering to a sharp-looking point at the end. And concurrently several thoughts coursed through his mind – exciting thoughts. There was the description, for a start, of the murder weapon – so very similar to this knife – which had appeared in the *Oxford Mail*, the description which was perhaps worrying Morse somewhat when he'd mentioned his premonition about the possibility of a copy-cat killing. Then there was the firm likelihood that the second of Morse's necessary prerequisites had now been met – not only a body, but also a weapon; and this one surely seemed to fit the bill so very nicely. And then – by far the most exciting thought of all – the strong possibility that the knife had come from a set of such knives, *one of which Lewis had seen so very recently*: that slim, elegant, black-handled little knife with which Mrs Brenda Brooks had sliced the Madeira cake the previous Sunday afternoon.

# CHAPTER THIRTY-SEVEN

I enjoy convalescence; it is the part that makes the
illness worth while
                                (GEORGE BERNARD SHAW)

ON THURSDAY, 8 September, as on the previous day,
so many things were happening in close sequence that
it is difficult for the chronicler to decide upon the most
comprehensible way in which to record events, events
which were to some degree contemporaneous but
which also overlapped and which in their full implications stretched both before and beyond their strict
temporal occurrence.

Let the account begin at Morse's flat in North
Oxford.

Morse was due to be discharged at ten o'clock that
morning. Lewis had rung through to the ward-sister
half an hour earlier to save Morse any wait for an
ambulance and to chauffeur him home in style – only
to discover that his chief had already discharged himself, getting a lift from one of the consultants there who
was on his way out to Bicester.

Lewis rang the door-bell at 9.45 a.m., experiencing a
customary qualm of semi-apprehension as he waited
outside that lonely flat – until a fully dressed Morse, his

cheeks rosy-red, suddenly appeared on the threshold, panting like a breathless bulldog.

'I'm just starting a new regimen, Lewis. No more nicotine, limited – very limited – alcohol, plenty of fresh fruit and salad, and regular exercise. What about that? I've' – he paused awhile to get his breath – 'I've just done a dozen press-ups. You'd never have thought that possible a week ago, now, would you?'

'You must be feeling quite, er, elated, sir.'

'"Knackered" is the word I think you're looking for, Lewis. But come in! Good to see you. Have a drink.'

Almost as if he were trespassing, Lewis entered the lounge and sat down.

'Nothing for me, thanks.'

'I'll just . . .' Morse quickly drained a tumbler of some pale amber liquid that stood on one of the shelves of the book-lined room beside the Deutsche Grammophon cassettes of *Tristan und Isolde*. 'A small, celebratory libation, that, Lewis – in gratitude to whatever gods there be that temporarily I have survived the perils and dangers of this mortal life.'

Lewis managed a grin, half sad, half happy – and immediately told Morse about the knife.

'I don't believe it! We'd had those gardens searched.'

'Only up to six either side, sir. If only we'd gone a couple further.'

'But why didn't this fellow Rayson find it earlier? Is he blind or something?'

'He was in Italy.'

'Oh.'

'You don't sound all that pleased about it.'

'What? Course I am. Well done!'

'I know you were a bit worried about that *Oxford Mail* article . . .'

'I was?'

'You know, the premonition you had—'

'Nonsense! I don't even know what a premonition is.'

'Well, if that description's anywhere near accurate, sir, I think we've got the knife that was used to kill McClure. And I think I know where it came from. And I think you do, too.'

The small round-faced clock on the mantelpiece showed two minutes after ten, and for a while Morse sat in silence. Then, of a sudden, he jumped to his feet and, against all the medical advice he'd so meekly accepted over the previous few days, insisted on being driven immediately to police HQ, stopping (as it happened) only briefly along the journey, in a slip-road on the left, just opposite the Sainsbury supermarket in Kidlington, to buy a packet of Dunhill King-Size cigarettes.


Brenda Brooks had spent the previous night not in her own house in Addison Road but in the spare bedroom, the only other bedroom, of Julia Stevens' house in Baldwin Road. After Mrs Stevens had left for school at 8.15 a.m., Brenda had eaten a bowl of Corn Flakes and a round of toast and marmalade. Her appointment at the hairdresser's was for 9.15 a.m.; and fairly soon after her breakfast she was closing the Oxford-blue front door behind her, testing (as always) that the lock was firmly engaged, and walking down towards the Cowley Road for her Special Offer Wash-and-Perm.

On her way home, well over an hour and a half later, she bought two salmon fillets, a pack of butter, and a carton of ecologically friendly washing-up liquid.

The sun was shining.

As she turned into Addison Road she immediately spotted the marked police car, parked on the double-yellow lines across the road from her house; spotted a second car, too, the elegant-looking lovingly polished maroon-coloured Jaguar she'd seen the previous Sunday afternoon.

Even as she put her key into the Yale lock, she felt the hand on her shoulder, heard the man's voice, and heard, too, the ringing of the telephone just inside the hall.

'Get a move on,' said Morse quickly. 'You may just catch it.'

But the ringing stopped just before she could reach the phone; and taking off her lightweight summer coat, and gently patting the back of her blue-rinsed curls, she turned to the two men who stood just outside, the two men she'd seen the previous Sunday afternoon.

'If it's Ted you want, you'll have to come back later, I'm afraid. He's up at the JR2 – he's got an Outpatient appointment.'

'When do you expect him back?' asked Lewis.

'I don't know really. He'll be back for lunch, I should think, unless he calls in at the Club for a game of snooker.'

'How did he get to the hospital?'

Mrs Brooks hesitated. 'I ... I don't know.' The

fingers of her left hand were plucking their way along the invisible rosary she held in her right. 'You'd better come in, hadn't you?'

Haltingly, nervously, as they sat again in the lounge, in the same sedentary formation as before, Mrs Brooks sought to explain the situation. She had been to Stratford the previous evening with a friend and hadn't returned until late – about midnight – as she'd known she would, anyway. And she'd stayed with this person, this friend, at her house – overnight. Ted knew all about the arrangement. He was due at Outpatients the next morning, and she hadn't wanted to disturb his night's sleep – *hadn't* disturbed his night's sleep. He was getting along quite nicely and the doctors said how important it was to rest – to have regular rest and sleep. He hadn't shown her the little blue appointments card from the Oxfordshire Health Authority, but she thought he was due at the hospital somewhere between nine and ten.

'You haven't been here, in this house, since – since when?' asked Morse, rather brusquely.

'Four o'clock, yesterday afternoon. Or just before. The coach left at five.'

'You don't seem to have been too worried about Mr Brooks coping . . . with meals, that sort of thing?'

'Don't you think so, Inspector?' Her eyes, rather sad and weary now, looked into Morse's; and it was Morse who was the first to look away.

Lewis sounded a kindlier note. 'You've just come back from the hairdresser's?'

She nodded the tightly permed hair. 'The Golden Scissors, in Cowley Road.'

'Er . . . what was the play, by the way?'

'*Twelfth Night.*'

'Did you enjoy it?'

She half-smiled. 'Well, I couldn't quite follow all the – you know, what they were saying. But I loved it, yes, and I'd love to see it again.'

'And you went with . . . with a friend, you say?'

'Yes, with a school-party.'

'And this friend . . . ?'

Lewis was noting her name and address when the telephone rang once more; and this time Mrs Brooks reached the hall swiftly. As she did so, Morse immediately pointed in the opposite direction, and Lewis, equally swiftly, stepped quietly into the kitchen where he opened a drawer by the side of the sink.

Morse meanwhile listened keenly to one side of a telephone conversation.

'Yes?'

'Is he all right?'

'I don't understand.'

'What's happened, do you think?'

'No. I wasn't here, you see.'

'Of course I will.'

'Can you just give me the number again?'

'All right.'

Brenda Brooks put down the phone slowly, her face anxious as she walked back into the lounge – only a few seconds after Lewis, with a silent thumbs-up sign, had re-appeared from the kitchen and quickly resumed his seat.

'Anything important?' asked Morse.

'It was the hospital. Ted's not been there. Not yet. So the lady at Appointments says. He was due there at twenty-past nine, it seems.'

'What do you think's happened to him?' asked Morse quietly.

'That's what she asked me. I don't know.'

'I'm sure everything's fine,' continued Morse. 'He's probably just got the time wrong.'

'That's exactly what she said,' whispered Brenda Brooks.

'She'll ring you back – when he gets there.'

'That's . . . that's exactly . . .'

But the tears had started now.

She opened her handbag and took out a handkerchief, and said, 'Sorry'; said 'Sorry' five times. And then, 'Oh dear! Where's my purse? I must have . . .' She got up and went to the hall where she patted the pockets of her summer coat, and came back and looked rather fecklessly around. 'I must have . . .'

'You did some shopping, didn't you? You may have left it . . . ?' suggested Lewis.

A few minutes later, Mrs Brooks was seated in the back of the police car, impatient and worried; but so glad to be away from the two detectives – who now stood in her kitchen.

'What do you reckon, sir?'

'About Brooks? Buggered off, hasn't he – sensible chap! He must have guessed we were on his tail.'

'What about her? She seemed glad to get away.'

'She's worried about her purse – money, cards, keys . . .'

'More than that, I think.'

'Well, *you* made her feel a bit guilty, didn't you, checking up on her hairdresser – and Stratford.'

'What?'

'Quite right too, Lewis. She was telling us a load of lies, wasn't she? She knows exactly where he is! He may treat her like a skivvy, but she's still his missus.'

Lewis opened the drawer again, this time selecting four knives, of different sizes, but of the same basic pattern, of the same make – each with a black handle, one side of which, the side of the cutting-edge, was slightly sinuous, with an indented curve at the top to fit the joint of the index finger, and a similar curve at the lower end for the little finger.

Four knives.

Four from a set of five?

But if so, the fifth was missing . . . yet not really all that far away, neatly docketed and safely stored as it was in an Exhibits Locker at Thames Valley Police HQ.

Oh, yes!

Lewis nodded to himself, and to Morse.

And Morse nodded to himself, and to Lewis.

It seemed to Morse no great surprise that Mr Edward Brooks, ex-scout of Wolsey, and current assistant-custodian of the Pitt Rivers Collection, had decided to make a bolt for it – once news of the discovery of that fatal fifth knife had leaked out.

Which it hadn't . . .

Lewis had seen to that.

# CHAPTER THIRTY-EIGHT

The museum has retained much of its Victorian
character. Painstakingly hand-written labels can
still be found attached to some of the artefacts in
the crammed black cases there

> (*The Pitt Rivers Museum, A Souvenir Guide*)

THE DETAILS of what was to prove the key discovery
in the case – or, to be more accurate, the 'lack-of-key'
discovery in the case – were not communicated by the
City Police to Kidlington HQ until just after 1 p.m. that
same day, although the discovery had in fact been made
as early as 8.45 a.m.

Janis Lawrence, an unmarried young woman, lived
with her mother, an unmarried middle-aged woman,
on the Cutteslowe Estate in North Oxford. The household was completed by Janis's four-year-old son, Jason –
a name chosen not to commemorate the intrepid
leader of the Argonauts but the lead guitarist of a long-
forgotten pop group. Jason found it impossible to pass
by any stone or small brick without picking it up and
hurling it at anything which moved across his vision –
dogs, prams, pedestrians, motor-vehicles, and similar
obstructions. Thus it was that Janis Lawrence was ever
longing for the time when she could transfer complete
responsibility for the child to the hapless teachers of
the local Cutteslowe Primary School. And when she
had learned of a temporary (August to September)

cleaning job at the Pitt Rivers Museum, she had applied for it. And got it.

The Cutteslowe Estate in North Oxford, built in the 1930s, had achieved national notoriety because of the Cutteslowe Wall, a seven-foot high, spiked-topped, brick-built wall, which segregated the upper-middle-class residents of the Banbury Road from the working-class tenants of the Council Estate. But the wall had been demolished in 1959; and on the bright morning of Thursday, 8 September 1994, as on each weekday for the past month, Janis walked without hindrance up to the Banbury Road, where she caught a bus down to Keble Road, thence walking across to Parks Road, and into the museum itself, where from Mondays to Saturdays she began work at 8.30 a.m.

Her first job as always was to clear up any litter, such as the rings of zig-zag shavings often left behind by pupils who had sharpened their pencils the previous afternoon. And for a short while that morning, as she cleaned the floor and dusted the cabinets in the Upper Gallery, she paid little attention to the bright-yellow splinter of wood on the floor below one of the cabinets there – until she noticed that the glass-topped lid was not resting flush upon its base. Then, too, she became aware of the slight disarray of the cabinet's contents, since there appeared one unfilled space in the ranks of the exhibits there, with both the artefact to the left of this gap, and the artefact to the right of it, knocked somewhat askew on the light-beige hessian material which formed the backing for the display: 'Knives from Africa and South-East Asia'.

THE DAUGHTERS OF CAIN

Janis reported her discovery immediately. And just after 9 a.m. Mr Herbert Godwin, attendant with responsibility for the Upper Gallery, was staring down at Cabinet 52.

'Oh dear!'

'Somebody's pinched somethin', Bert?'

'I reckon you could say that again.'

'What's gone?'

'Good question.'

'When could it have been, though?'

'Dunno. *After* I checked last night. Must have been. I allus check on these cabinets.'

'Well, it couldn't have been this morning. Nobody else's been here, 'cept me.'

'Have you got summat hidden in your knicker-pocket, Janis?'

'I've told you *before*, Bert. I only wear knickers on a Sunday.'

Gently Herbert Godwin patted the not-unattractive Janis on her ample bottom: 'We'd better go and inform our superiors, my love.'

Paradoxically Jane Cotterell, Administrator of the Museum, was attending a meeting that morning at the Ashmolean on 'Museum Security'. But straightway she was summoned to the telephone and was soon issuing her orders: the University Marshal was to be informed immediately, as were the police; the lower steps to the Upper Gallery were to be roped across, with the 'Temporarily Closed' sign positioned there; Dr Cooper, the Assistant Curator (Documentation) – and *only* Dr Cooper – should go along and, without touching anything, seek to ascertain, from his inventory lists, which object(s) had been stolen. She herself would be back in the Pitt Rivers as soon as she could possibly manage it.

Which was three-quarters of an hour later, her return coinciding with the arrival of the police from St Aldate's; *and* with the production of a sheet of paper on which she found the following sketch:

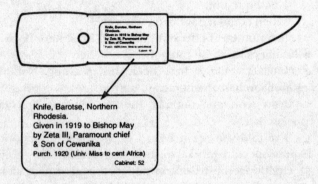

Knife, Barotse, Northern
Rhodesia.
Given in 1919 to Bishop May
by Zeta III, Paramount chief
& Son of Cewanika
Purch. 1920 (Univ. Miss to cent Africa)
Cabinet: 52

'That's it!' exclaimed a jubilant-looking Dr Cooper, as if the museum had suddenly acquired a valuable new exhibit, instead of losing one. 'Forty-seven knives – forty-seven! – there were in that cabinet. And you know how many there are now, Jane?'

'Forty-*six*, perhaps?' suggested the Administrator innocently.

# CHAPTER THIRTY-NINE

Yes
You have come upon the fabled lands where myths
Go when they die
(JAMES FENTON, 'The Pitt Rivers Museum')

AT FIVE minutes to two, parked in front of the Radcliffe Science Library, Morse switched off *The Archers* (repeat).

'Well, we'd better go and have a look at things, I suppose.'

In retrospect, the linkage (if there were one) appeared so very obvious. Yet someone had to make it first, that someone being Jane Cotterell: the linkage between the earlier visit of the police; the museum's employment of Edward Brooks; the murder by knifing of Dr McClure; and now the theft of another knife, from one of the museum's cabinets.

Thus, it was Jane Cotterell herself who had argued that the City Police should link their enquiry into the theft with the Kidlington HQ enquiry into the murder of McClure; and Jane Cotterell herself who greeted Morse and Lewis, in the Pitt Rivers' Upper Gallery, at 2 p.m.

'It's what I was afraid of, though God knows why,' mumbled Morse to himself as he looked down at

Cabinet 52, now dusted liberally with fine aluminium fingerprint-powder.

Ten minutes later, whilst Lewis was taking statements from Janis Lawrence and Herbert Godwin, Morse was seated opposite the Administrator, quickly realizing that he was unlikely to learn (at least from her) more than two fairly simple facts: first, that almost certainly the cabinet had been forced between 4.15 and 4.30 p.m. the previous afternoon; second, since the contents of the cabinet had been fully documented only six months earlier – when exhibits had been re-arranged and cabinets re-lined – it could be stated quite authoritatively that one artefact, *and one only*, the Northern Rhodesian Knife, had been abstracted.

Yet Morse seemed uneasy.

'Could one of your own staff have pinched it?'

'Good Lord, no. Why should any of them want to do that? Most of them have access to the key-cupboard anyway.'

'I see.' Morse nodded vaguely; and stood up. 'By the way, what do you line your cabinets with? What material?'

'It's some sort of new-style hessian – supposed to keep its colour for yonks, so the advert said.'

Morse smiled, suddenly feeling close to her. 'Can I say something? I'd never have expected you to say "yonks".'

She smiled back at him, shyly. 'You wouldn't?'

It seemed a good moment for one of them to say something more, to elaborate on this intimate turn of the conversation. But neither did so. And Morse reverted to his earlier line of enquiry.

'You don't think anyone could have hidden himself, after closing time, and spent the night here in the museum?'

'Or herself? No. No, I don't. Unless they stood pretty motionless all through the night. You see, the place is positively bristling with burglar alarms. And anyway, it would be far too spooky, surely? I couldn't do it. Could *you?*'

'No. I've always been frightened of the dark myself,' admitted Morse. 'It's a bit eerie, this place, even in broad daylight.'

'Yes,' she said softly. 'When you come in here you enter a place where all the lovely myths go when they die.'

Suddenly Morse felt very moved.

After he had left her office, Jane felt guilty about not telling Morse that the 'myths' bit was far from original. And indeed she'd looked around to try to find him, to tell him so.

But he had left.

# CHAPTER FORTY

Thursday is a bad day. Wednesday is quite a good day. Friday is an even better one. But Thursday, whatever the reason, is a day on which my spirit and my resolution, are at their lowest ebb. Yet even worse is any day of the week upon which, after a period of blessed idleness, I come face to face with the prospect of a premature return to my labours

(DIOGENES SMALL, *Autobiography*)

AN HOUR later, Morse was seated in the black leather chair in his office, still considering the sketch of the knife – when Lewis came back from the canteen carrying two polystyrene cups of steaming coffee.

'Northern Rhodesia, Lewis. Know where that is? Trouble is they keep changing all these place-names in Africa.'

'Zambia, sir. You know that.'

Morse looked up with genuine pain in his eyes. 'I never did any Geography at school.'

'You get a newspaper every day, though.'

'Yes, but I never look at the international news. Just the Crossword – and the Letters.'

'That's not true. I've often seen you reading the Obituaries.'

'Only to look at the years when they were born.'

Morse unwrapped the cellophane from his cigarettes, took one from the packet, and lit it, inhaling deeply.

'*You*'ll be in the obituary columns if you don't soon pack up smoking. Anyway, you said you *had* packed it up.'

'I have, Lewis. It's just that I need to make a sort of gesture – some sort of sacrifice. That's it! A sacrifice. All right? You see, I'm only going to smoke this one cigarette. Only one. And the rest of them?'

Morse appeared to have reached a fateful decision. He picked up the packet and flicked it, with surprising accuracy, into the metal waste-bin.

'Satisfied?'

Lewis reached for the phone and rang the JR2 Outpatients department: no news. Then he rang Brenda Brooks: no news.

Edward Brooks was still missing.

'You don't think somebody's murdered *him*, sir?'

But Morse, as he studied yet again the details of the stolen knife, appeared not to hear. 'Would you rather be a bishop – or a paramount chief?'

'I don't want to be either, really.'

'Mm. I wouldn't have minded if they'd made me a paramount chief.'

'I thought they had, sir.'

'Where would a paramount chief go from here, Lewis?'

'I just asked you, sir, whether—'

'I heard you. The answer's "no". Brooks is alive and well. No. He may not be well, of course – but he's alive. You can bet your Granny Bonds on that.'

'Where *do* we go from here, then?'

'Well, I'm going to spend the rest of the afternoon in bed. I want to feel fresh for this evening. I've got a date with a beautiful lady.'

'Who's she?'

'Mrs Stevens – Julia Stevens.'

'When did you fix that up?'

'While you were getting the coffee.'

'You want me to come along?'

'Lew-is! I just told you. It's a *date*.'

'Didn't you believe Mrs Brooks? About where she spent last night?'

'I believed *that* all right. It's just that I reckon she knows where her husband is, that's all. And it's on the cards that if she does know, she probably told her friend, Mrs Stevens.'

'What would you like me to do, sir?'

'I'd like you to go and see Mrs Brooks's daughter – Ellie Smith, or whatever she calls herself. She's a key character in this case, don't you reckon? McClure's mistress – and Brooks's step-daughter.'

'Shouldn't *you* be seeing her then?'

'All in good time. I'm only just out of hospital, remember?'

'You mean she's not so attractive as Mrs Stevens.'

'Purely incidental, that is.'

'Anything else?'

'Yes. You'd better get back to the museum for a while. I don't think we're going to get very far on the fingerprint front – but you never know.'

Lewis was frowning. 'I just don't see the link myself – between the McClure murder, and now this Pitt Rivers business.'

'*She* saw a link, though, didn't she? Jane Cotterell? Clever lass, that one.'

'But she said whoever else it was, it couldn't have been Brooks who took the knife.'

'Exactly.'

'So?'

'So what?'

'So where's the link?'

Morse's eyes remained unblinking for several seconds, staring at nothing it seemed, and yet perhaps staring at everything. 'I'm not at all sure now that there is a link,' he said quietly. 'To find some connection between one event and another ensuing event is often difficult; and especially difficult perhaps when they *appear* to have a connection . . .'

Morse was aware of feeling worried at the prospect – the actuality, really – of his return to work. For, in truth, he had little real idea of the correct answers to the questions Lewis had just asked. He needed some assistance from somewhere; and as he drove down to North Oxford he patted his jacket-pocket where he felt the reassurance of the square packet he had retrieved from the waste-bin immediately after Lewis had left for the Pitt Rivers Museum.

# CHAPTER FORTY-ONE

His failing powers disconcerted him, for what he
would do with women he was unsure to perform,
and he could rarely accept the appearance of
females who thought of topics other than *coitus*
(PETER CHAMPKIN, *The Sleeping Life of Aspern
Williams*)

NOW JULIA STEVENS was very fair to behold, for there
was a gentle beauty in the pallor of the skin beneath
that Titian hair, and the softest invitation in the redness
of her lips. And as he sat opposite her that evening,
Morse was immediately made aware of an animal
magnetism.

'Care for a drink, Inspector?'

'No – er, no thank you.'

'Does that mean "yes"?'

'Yes.'

'Scotch?'

'Why not?'

'Say when.'

'When.'

'Cheers!'

'Mind if I smoke?'

'Yes, I do.'

She left the room, and re-appeared with an ashtray.
Perhaps they were beginning to understand each other.

'Mrs Brooks stayed the night here?' began Morse.

'Yes.'

'You see, her husband's gone missing – he failed to keep an appointment at the hospital this morning.'

'I know. Brenda rang me.'

'You'd both been to Stratford, I understand.'

'Yes.'

'Enjoy the play?'

'No.'

'Why?'

'My life will not be significantly impoverished if I never see another Shakespearian comedy.'

'Mrs Brooks enjoyed it though, I believe?'

Julia nodded, with a slow reminiscence. 'Bless her! Yes. She's not had much to smile about recently.'

'Have *you*?'

'Not much, really, no. Why do you ask that?'

But Morse made no direct answer. 'Isn't it just a bit odd, perhaps, that Mrs Brooks didn't call in to see if her husband was all right?'

'Odd? It's the most natural thing in the world.'

'Is it?'

'She hates him.'

'And why's that?'

'He treats her in such a cruel way – that's why.'

'How do you know that?'

'Brenda's told me.'

'You've no first-hand evidence?'

'I've always tried to avoid him.'

'Aren't you being a bit unfair, then?'

'I don't think so.'

'Have you any idea where he might be?'

'No. But I hope somebody's stuck a knife into him somewhere.'

As he looked across at the school-mistress, Morse found himself wondering whether her pale complexion was due not so much to that inherited colouration so common with the auburn type, as to some illness, possibly; for he had observed, in a face almost completely devoid of any other cosmetic device, some skin-tinted application to the darkened rings beneath her eyes.

'Did Mrs Brooks go out last night, after you'd got back?'

Julia smiled tolerantly. 'You mean, did she just nip out for a few minutes and bump him off?'

'*Could* she have gone out? That's all I'm asking.'

'Technically, I suppose – yes. She'd have a key to get back in here with. I just wonder what you think she did with the body, that's all.'

'She *didn't* go out – is that what you're telling me?'

'Look! The only thing I know for certain is that she was fast asleep when I took her a cup of tea just before seven this morning.'

'So she'd been with you the whole time since yesterday afternoon?'

'Since about a quarter-to four, yes. I would have picked her up in the car, but the wretched thing wanted to stay at home in the garage. Suffering from electrical trouble.'

Morse, who didn't know the difference between brake fluid and anti-freeze, nodded wisely. 'You should get a car like mine. I've got a *pre*-electrics model.'

Julia smiled politely. 'We took a bus up to school and, well, that's about it, really.'

'Did you actually go into the Brooks's house?'

'Well, I suppose I did, yes – only into the hallway, though.'

'Was Mr Brooks there?'

'Only just. He was getting ready to go out, but he was still there when we left.'

'Did you speak to him?'

'You mean ... ask him politely if he was feeling better? You must be joking.'

'Did his wife speak to him?'

'Yes. She said "goodbye".'

'She didn't say "cheerio" or "see you soon"?'

'No. She said "goodbye".'

'What about you? Did *you* go out last night?'

'Do you suspect me as well?'

'Suspect you of what, Mrs Stevens?'

Julia's clear, grey eyes sparkled almost gleefully. 'Well, if somebody's bumped off old Brooks—'

'You look as if you hope someone has.'

'Didn't I make that clear from the start, Inspector?'

'Have you actually *seen* Mrs Brooks since you left home this morning?'

'No. I've been in school all day. Bad day, Thursday! No free periods. Then we had a staff-meeting after school to try to decide whether we're all satisfying the criteria for the National Curriculum.'

'Oh.'

It was a dampener; and for a little while each was silent, with Morse looking around the neatly cluttered room. He saw, on the settee beside Julia, a copy of Ernest Dowson's *Poems*. He pointed to it:

'You enjoy Dowson?'

'You've *heard* of him?'

'They are not long, the weeping and the laughter,
    Love and desire and hate . . .'

'I'm impressed. Can you go on?'

'Oh, yes,' said Morse quietly.

For some reason, and for the first time that evening, Julia Stevens betrayed some sign of discomfiture, and Morse saw, or perhaps he saw, a film of tears across her eyes.

'Anything else I can do for you, Inspector?'

Yes, you can take me to bed with you. I may feel no love for you, perhaps, but I perceive the beauty and the readiness of this moment, and soon there will be no beauty and no readiness.

'No, I think that's all,' he said.

The phone rang as they walked into the narrow hallway, and Julia quickly picked up the receiver.

'Hullo? Oh, hullo! Look, I'll ring you back in five minutes, all right? Just give me the number, will you?' She wrote down five digits on a small yellow pad beside the phone, and said 'Bye' – as did a male voice at the other end of the line (if Morse had heard aright).

As they took leave of each other at the doorway, it seemed for a moment that they might have embraced, however perfunctorily.

But they did not do so.

It might have been possible, too, for Morse to have spotted the true importance of what Julia Stevens had told him.

But he did not do so.

# CHAPTER FORTY-TWO

> You can lead a whore to culture
> but you can't make her think
> (Attributed to Dorothy Parker)

'HAVEN'T YOU got any *decent* music in this car?' she asked, as Lewis drove down the Iffley Road towards Magdalen Bridge.

'Don't you like it? That's your Mozart, that is. That's your slow movement of the Clarinet Concerto. I keep getting told I ought to educate my musical tastes a bit.'

'Bit miserable, innit?'

'Don't you go and say that to my boss.'

'Who's he when he's at home?'

'Chief Inspector Morse. Chap you're going to see. You're getting the VIP treatment this morning.'

'Don't you think I'm used to that, Sergeant?'

Lewis glanced across briefly at the young woman beside him in the front seat; but he made no reply.

'Don't believe me, do you?' she asked, a curious smile on her lips.

'Shall I ... ?' Lewis's left hand hovered over the cassette 'on-off' switch.

'Nah! Leave it.'

She leaned back languorously; and even to the staid

Lewis, as he made his way up to Kidlington, she seemed to exude a powerful sexuality.

When he had rung her late the previous afternoon, Lewis had been unable to get an answer; also been unable to get an answer in the early evening, when he had called at the house in Princess Street, off the Iffley Road, where she had her bed-sitter-cum-bathroom, and where he had left a note for her to call him back as soon as possible. Which was not very soon at all, in fact, since it had been only at 9.45 that morning when she'd rung, expressing the preference to be interviewed at Kidlington, and when Morse (sounding, from his home, in adequate fettle) had stated his intention to be present at the interview.

After Lewis had parked outside the HQ building, his passenger eased herself out of the car; and then, standing on the tarmac in full view of a good many interested eyes, stretched out her arms horizontally, slowly pressing them back behind her as far as the trapezius muscles would allow, her breasts straining forward against her thin blouse. Lewis, too, observed the brazen gesture with a gentle smile – and wondered what Morse would make of Ms Eleanor Smith.

In fact the answer would appear to be not very much, for the interview was strangely low-key, with Morse himself clearly deciding to leave everything to Lewis. First, Ms Smith gave what (as both detectives knew) was a heavily censored account of her lifestyle, appearing in no way surprised that for a variety of reasons she should be worthy of police attention – even police suspicion, perhaps. She'd had nothing to do with the murder of poor Dr McClure, of course; and she was confident that she could produce, if it proved necessary, some corroborative witnesses to account for most of her activities on that Sunday, 28 August: thirty-five of them, in fact, including the coach-driver. Yes, she'd known Matthew Rodway – and liked him. Yes, she'd known, still knew, Ashley Davies – and liked him as well; in fact it was with Davies she had been out the previous evening when the police had tried to contact her.

'You must have been with him a long time?' suggested Lewis.

Ms Smith made no reply, merely fingering her right (re-ringed) nostril with her right forefinger.

She was dismissive with the series of questions Lewis proceeded to put about drugs, and her knowledge of drugs. Surely the police didn't need *her* to tell them about what was going on? The easy availability of drugs. Their widespread use? What century were the police living in, for God's sake? And Morse found himself quietly amused as Lewis, just a little disconcerted now, persisted with this line of enquiry like some sheltered middle-aged father learning all about sex-parties and the like from some cruelly knowing little daughter of ten.

Last Wednesday? Where had she been then? Well, if they must know, she'd been in Birmingham for most of that day, on . . . well, on a personal matter. She'd got back to Oxford, back to Oxford station, at about half-past four. The train – surprise, surprise! – had been on time. And then? (Lewis had persisted.) Then she'd invited one of her friends – one of her girlfriends – up to her flat – her bed-sit! – where they'd drunk a bottle of far-from-vintage champers; and this muted celebration (the occasion for which Eleanor failed to specify) was followed by a somewhat louder merrymaking at the local pub; whence she had gone home, whence she'd been *escorted* home, at closing-time. And if they wanted to know whether she'd woken up with a bad head, the answer was 'yes' – a bloody *dreadful* head.

Why all this interest in Wednesday, though? Why Wednesday afternoon? Why Wednesday evening? That's what she wanted to know.

Morse and Lewis had exchanged glances then. If she were telling the truth, it was not this woman, not McClure's former mistress, not Brooks's step-daughter, who had stolen the knife from Cabinet 52 – or done anything with it afterwards. Not, at least, on the Wednesday evening, for Lewis had been making a careful note of times and places and names; and if Eleanor Smith had been fabricating so much detail, she was doing it at some considerable peril. And after another glance from Morse, and a nod, Lewis told her of the theft from the Pitt Rivers, which had now pretty certainly been pin-pointed to between 4.20 p.m. and 4.30 p.m. on Wednesday, the seventh; told her, too, of the disappearance of her step-father.

Ah, her step-father! Well, she could tell them something about him, all right. He was a pig. She'd buggered off from home because of him; and the miracle was that her mother hadn't buggered off from home because of him, too. She'd no idea (she claimed) that he was missing. But that wasn't going to cause her too much grief, was it? She just hoped that he'd remain missing, that's all; hoped they'd find him lying in a gutter somewhere with a knife – *that* knife – stuck firmly in his bloody guts.

The Chief Inspector had not spoken a single word to the woman he'd so recently heralded as his key-witness in the case; and the truth was that, like some maverick magnet, he had felt half repelled, half attracted by the strange creature seated there, with her off-hand (*deliberately* common, perhaps?) manner of speech; with her lack of any respect for the dignity of police procedure; with her contempt concerning the well-being of her step-father, Mr Edward Brooks.

A note had been brought into the room a few minutes earlier and handed to Morse. And now, with the interview apparently nearing its end, Morse jerked his head towards the door and led the way into the corridor. The press, he told Lewis, had got wind of the Pitt Rivers business, and questions were being asked about a possible linkage with the murder enquiry. Clearly some of the brighter news editors were putting two and two together and coming up with an aggregate considerably higher than the sum of the component parts. Lewis had better go and mollify the media, and not worry too much about concealing any confidential information – which shouldn't be terribly difficult since there *was* no confidential information. He himself, Morse, would see that Ms Smith was escorted safely home.

# CHAPTER FORTY-THREE

The scenery in the play was beautiful, but the
actors got in front of it
(ALEXANDER WOOLLCOTT)

SHE SPOKE as Morse came up to the first roundabout
on his way towards Oxford:

'Have you got *any* decent music in this car?'

'Such as what?'

'Well, your nice sergeant played me some Mozart.
Fellah playin' the clarinet.'

'Jack Brymer, was it?'

'Dunno. He was great, though. It'd pay him to join a
jazz group.'

'You think so?'

'If he's lookin' to the future.'

'He's about eighty.'

'Really? Ah well, you're no chicken yourself, are
you?'

Morse, unsmiling, kept his eyes on the road.

'Your sergeant said you was tryin' to educate his
musical tastes.'

'Did he?'

'You don't think *I* need a bit of educatin'?'

'I doubt it. I'd guess you're a whole lot better
educated than you pretend to be. For all I know, you're
probably quite a sensitive and appreciative lass –
underneath.'

'Yeah? Christ! What the 'ell's *that* s'posed to mean?'

Morse hesitated before answering her. 'I'll tell you what your trouble is, shall I? You're suffering from a form of inverted snobbery, that's all. Not unusual, you know, in girls – in young ladies of ... in young ladies like you.'

'If that's supposed to be a bloody insult, mister, you couldn't a' done much bleedin' better, could you?'

'I'm only guessing – don't be cross. I don't know you at all, do I? We've never even spoken—'

'Except on the phone. Remember?'

Morse almost managed a weak smile as he waited at the busy Cutteslowe roundabout.

'I remember.'

'Great, that was. You know, pretendin' to be somebody else. I sometimes think I should a' been an actress.'

'I think you are an actress – that's exactly what I was saying.'

'Well, I'll tell you somethin'. Right at this minute there's one thing I'd swap even for an Oscar.'

'What's that?'

'Plate of steak and chips. I'm starvin'.'

'Do you know how much steak costs these days?'

'Yeah. £3.99 at the King's Arms just down the road here: salad and chips chucked in. I saw it on the way up.'

'It says "French Fries", though, on the sign outside. You see, that's exactly what I meant about—'

'Yeah, you told me. I'm sufferin' summat chronic from inverted snobbery.'

\*

'Don't *you* ever eat?' demanded Ellie, wiping her mouth on the sleeve of her blouse, and draining her third glass of red wine.

'Not very often at meal-times, no.'

'A fellah needs his calories, though. Got to keep his strength up – if you know what I mean.'

'I usually take most of my calories in liquid form at lunchtimes.'

'Funny, isn't it? You bein' a copper and all that – and then drinkin' all the beer you do.'

'Don't worry. I'm the only person in Oxford who gets more sober the more he drinks.'

'How do you manage that?'

'Years of practice. I don't recommend it though.'

'Wouldn't help you much with a bleedin' breathalyser, would it?'

'No,' admitted Morse quietly.

'Do you know when you've had enough?'

'Not always.'

'You had enough now?'

'Nearly.'

'Can I buy *you* something?'

'You know, nineteen times out of twenty . . . But I've got to drive you home and then get back to give Sergeant Lewis his next music lesson.'

'What's all them weasel words s'posed to mean?'

'Pint of Best Bitter,' said Morse. 'If you insist.'


'Would you ever think of giving *me* a music lesson?' she asked, as after a wait at the lights in Longwall Street the Jaguar made its way over Magdalen Bridge.

'No.'

'Why not?'

'You want me to be honest?'

'Why not?'

'I just couldn't stick looking at those rings in your nose.'

She felt the insult like a slap across the face; and had the car still been queuing at the Longwall lights she would have jumped out of the Jaguar and left him. But they were travelling now quite quickly up the Iffley Road, and by the time they reached Princess Street she was feeling fractionally less furious.

'Look! Just tell your sergeant somethin' from me, will you?'

'*I'm* in charge of the case,' said Morse defensively, 'not Sergeant Lewis.'

'Well, you could a' fooled me. You never asked me nothin' – not at the station, did you? You hadn't said a single word till we got in the car.'

'Except on the phone. Remember?' said Morse quietly.

'Yeah, well, like I said, that was good fun . . .' But the wind had been taken from her sails, and she glanced across at Morse in a slightly new light. In the pub, as she'd noticed, he'd averted his gaze from her for much of the time. And now she knew why . . . He was a bit different – a lot different, really – from the rest of them; the rest of the men *his* age, anyway. Felix had once told her that she looked at people with eyes that were 'interested and interesting', and she would never forget that: it was the most wonderful compliment anyone had ever paid her. But this man, Morse, hadn't even looked at her eyes; just looked at his beer for most of the time.

What the hell, though.

Bloody police!

'Look, somethin' for you or your sergeant, OK? If he wants to check up about Wednesday, when I went to Brum, I went to an abortion clinic there. Sort o' consultation. But I decided I wasn't goin' to go through with it – not this time, OK? Then, about last night, I went out with Ashley – Ashley Davies – and he asked me to marry him. With or without me bloody nose-rings, mister, OK?'

With that she opened the near-side door and jumped out.

She slammed it so hard that for a moment Morse was worried that some damage might have been incurred by the Jaguar's (pre-electrics) locking mechanism.

'And you can stuff your fuckin' Mozart, OK?'

# CHAPTER FORTY-FOUR

No small art is it to sleep: it is necessary to keep
awake all day for that purpose
(FRIEDRICH NIETZSCHE)

IT IS sometimes maintained, and with some cause, that
insomnia does not exist. The argument, put most
briefly, is that anyone unable to fall asleep has no real
*need* to fall asleep. But there were several key players in
the present drama who would have readily challenged
such an argument that night – the night of Friday, 9
September.

Morse himself, who only infrequently had the slightest
trouble in falling asleep, often had the contrary problem of 'falling awake' during the small hours, either to
visit the loo, or to drink some water – the latter liquid
figuring quite prominently with him during the night,
though virtually never during the day. Yet sleep was as
important to Morse as to any other soul; and specifically
on the subject of sleep, the Greek poets and the Greek
prose-writers had left behind several pieces of their
literary baggage in the lumber-room of Morse's mind.
And if, for him, the whole of the classical corpus had to
be jettisoned except for one single passage, he would
probably have opted for the scene depicting the death
of Sarpedon, from Book XVI of the *Iliad*, where those

swift companions, the twin brothers Sleep and Death, bear the dead hero to the broad and pleasant land of Lycia. And so very close behind Homer's words would have been those of Socrates, as he prepared to drink the hemlock, that if death were just one long and dreamless sleep then mortals could have nought to fear.

That night, though, Morse had a vivid dream – a dream that he was playing the saxophone in a jazz ensemble, yet (even in his dream) ever wondering whence he had acquired such dazzling virtuosity, and ever worried that his skill would at any second desert him in front of his adulatory audience – amongst whom he had spotted a girl with two rings in her nose; a girl who could never be Eleanor Smith, though, since the girl in the dream was disfigured and ugly; and Eleanor Smith could never be that . . .

Julia Stevens tossed back and forth in her bed that night, repeatedly turning over the upper of her two pillows as she sought to cool her hot and aching head. At half-past midnight, she got up and made herself another cup of Ovaltine, swallowing with it two further Nurofen. A great block of pain had settled this last week at the back of her head, and there was a ceaseless surge of something (blood?) that broke in rhythmic waves inside her ears.

During the daytime, she had so little fear of dying; but recently, in the hours of darkness, Fear had been stalking her bedroom, reporting to her its terrifying tales, and bullying her into confessing (Oh, God!) that, no, she didn't want to die. In her dream that night, when finally she drifted off into a fitful sleep, she beheld an image of the Pale Horse; and knew that the name of the one who rode thereon was Death . . .

Covering the space over and alongside the single bed pushed up against the inside wall of the small bedroom, were three large posters, featuring Jimi Hendrix, Jim Morrison, and Kurt Cobain – rock idols who during their comparatively short lives had regularly diced with drugs and death. At 1 a.m., still dressed, Kevin Costyn was sitting on the bed, his back against the creaking headboard, listening on his Walkman to some ear-blasting fury of punk music. In a perverse sort of way, he found it quite soothing. *Eroticon IV*, a crudely pornographic paperback, lay open on the bed beside him; but for the moment Kevin's mind was not beset with sexual fantasies.

Surprisingly, in a week of virtually unparalleled excitement, his thoughts were now centred more soberly on the nature of his surroundings: the litter-strewn front gardens along the road, with derelict, disembowelled cars propped up in drives; the shoddy, undusted, threadbare house in which he lived with his feckless mother; above all the sordid state of his own bedroom, and particularly of the dingy, soiled, creased sheets in which he'd slept for the past seven weeks or more. It was the contrast that had caught his imagination – the contrast between all this and the tidy if unpretentious terrace in which Mrs Julia Stevens lived; the polished, clean, sweet-smelling rooms in her house; above all, the snow-white, crisply laundered sheets on her inviting bed.

He thought he'd always known what makes the difference in life.

Money.

And as he took off his socks and trousers and got into bed, he found himself wondering how much money Mrs Stevens might have saved in life.

In the past few weeks Mrs Rodway was beginning to sleep more soundly. Sleeping pills, therapy, exercise, holidays, diet – none of them had been all that much help. But she had discovered something very simple which did help: she *counted*. One thousand and one; one thousand and two ... and after a little while she would stop her counting, and whisper some few words aloud to herself: 'And – there – was – a – great – calm' ... Then she would begin counting again, backwards this time: one thousand and five; one thousand and four ...

Sometimes, as she counted, she almost managed not to think of Matthew. On a few nights recently, she didn't have to count at all. But this particular night was not one of them ...

The previous evening, Ashley Davies had taken Ellie Smith to a motel near Buckingham where he, flushed with the success of his marriage proposal, and she, much flushed with much champagne, had slept between pale green sheets – an idyllic introit, one might have thought, to their newly plighted state.

And perhaps it was.

But as Davies lay awake, alone, this following night, he began to doubt that it was so.

His own sexual enjoyment had been intense, for *in medio coitu* she had surrendered her body to his with a wondrous abandon. Yet before and after their love-making – both! – he had sensed a disturbing degree of reserve in her, of holding back. Twice had she turned her mouth away from him when his lips had craved some full commitment, some deeper tenderness. And in retrospect he knew that there must be some tiny corner in her heart which she'd not unlocked as yet to any man.

In the early hours, she had turned fully away from him, seeming to grow colder and colder, as if sleep and the night were best; as if, too, somewhere within her was a secret passion committed already to someone else . . .

Restless, too, that night was the scout now given responsibility for Staircase G in the Drinkwater Quad at Wolsey. At 2 a.m. she went downstairs to the kitchen to make herself a cup of tea, looking in the mirror there at a neatly featured face, with its auburn hair cut in a fringe across the forehead: getting just a little long now, and almost covering a pair of worried eyes.

Susan had agreed to check and sign (at 10 o'clock

the following morning, Saturday) the statement earlier made to Sergeant Lewis. And the prospect worried her. It was like reporting some local vandals to the police, when there was always the fear that those same vandals would return to wreak even greater havoc, precisely for having been reported. In her own case, though – as Susan was too intelligent not to appreciate – the risk was considerably greater. This was not a case of vandalism; but of murder. As such, she'd had little option but to make a full (if guarded) statement; yet she feared she would now be open to some sort of retaliation – to threats of physical violence, perhaps, from a man who, by an almost unanimous verdict, was seen as a very nasty piece of work indeed.

Back in bed, Susan tried a cure she'd once been told: to close one's eyes gently (yes, *gently*) and then to look (yes, *look*) at a point about four or five inches in front of one's nose. Such a strategy, it was claimed, would ensure that the eyeballs remained fairly still, being focused as they were upon some specific point, however notional that point might be; and since it had been demonstrated that the rapid revolving of the eyeballs in their sockets was a major cause of sleeplessness, insomniacs most certainly should experiment along such lines.

That night, therefore, Mrs Susan Ewers had so experimented, though with only limited success. As it happened, however, her apprehension was wholly groundless, since Edward Brooks was never destined to become a threat to Susan or to any other living person. One of those twins from Morse's schooldays, the one

# COLIN DEXTER

whose name was Death, had already claimed him for
his own; and together with his brother, Sleep, had
borne him off, though not perhaps to the broad and
pleasant land of Lycia, wherein Sarpedon lies.

# CHAPTER FORTY-FIVE

Keep careful watch too on the moral faults of your patients, which may cause them to tell untruths about things prescribed – and things proscribed

(*Corpus Hippocraticum*)

A WEEK in a murder enquiry, especially one in which there is virtually no development, can be a wearisome time. And so it was for Sergeant Lewis in the days between Friday 9 and Friday 16 September.

The whereabouts and movements of key characters in the Pitt Rivers enquiry, most particularly on the evening and night of Wednesday the seventh, immediately after the knife had been stolen, had been checked and in every case confirmed, with appropriate statements made and (with the more obvious mis-spellings corrected) duly signed and filed. Nothing else, though.

Nothing else, either, on the murder scene. House-to-house enquiries in Daventry Avenue had come to an end; and come to nothing. Three former undergraduates from Staircase G on Drinkwater Quad had been traced with no difficulty; but with no real consequence either, since apart from confirming the general availability of drugs during their years in Oxford they had each denied any specific knowledge of drug-trafficking on their own staircase.

What worried Lewis slightly was that Morse appeared

just as interested in the disappearance of a knife as in the death of a don, as though the connection between the two events (Morse had yet again reversed his views) was both logically necessary and self-evidently true.

But *was* it?

And on the morning of Thursday, 15 September, he had voiced his growing doubt.

'Brooks, sir – Brooks is the only real connection, isn't he? Brooks who's top of your murder-suspects; and Brooks who's got a job at the Pitt Rivers.'

'Have you ever thought, Lewis, that it could have been Brooks who stole the knife?'

'You can't be serious?'

'No. Brooks didn't steal the knife. Sorry. Go on!'

'Well, you said so yourself early on: we often get people who do copy-cat things, don't we? And whoever stole the knife – well, it might not have anything to do with the murder at all. Somebody just read that bit in the *Oxford Mail* and . . .'

'Ye-es. To tell you the truth, I've been thinking the same.'

'It could just be a coincidence.'

'Yes, it could. Perhaps it was.'

'I mean, you've often said coincidences happen all the time; just that some of us don't spot 'em.'

'Yes, I've often thought that.'

'So there may be no causal connection after all—?'

'Stop sounding like a philosopher, Lewis, and go and get us some coffee.'

Morse, too, was finding this period of inactivity frustrating. *And* a time of considerable stress, since for three whole days now he had not smoked a single cigarette, and had arrived at that crucial point where his self-mastery had already been demonstrated, his victory over nicotine finally won. So? So it was no longer a question of relapsing, of re-indulging. If he wished to re-*start*, though ... for, in truth, the fourth day was proving even harder than the third.

The earlier wave of euphoria was ebbing still further on the fifth day, when it was his own turn to have a medical check-up, and when ten minutes before his appointment time he checked in at the Outpatients reception at the JR2 and sat down in the appropriate area to await his call, scheduled for 9.20 a.m. By some minor coincidence (yes!) this was the same time that Mr Edward Brooks had been expected for his own designated brand of Outpatient care – an appointment which had not been kept eight days earlier ... and which was unkept still.

After undergoing a fairly thorough examination; after skilfully parrying the questions put to him about avoirdupois and alcohol; after politely declining a suggested consultation with a dietitian; after going along the corridor to have three further blood-samples taken – Morse was out again; out into the morning sunshine, with a new date (six whole weeks away!) written into his little blue card, and with the look of a man who feels fresh confidence in life. What was it that the doc had said?

'You know, I'm not quite sure why, but you're over things pretty well. You don't deserve to be, Mr Morse; but, well, you seem surprisingly fit to me.'

Walking along to the southern car park and savouring still the happy tidings, Morse caught sight of a young woman standing at the bus-stop there. By some minor coincidence (yes!) they had earlier been present together in the same waiting-room at the Summertown Health Centre, where neither had known the other. And now, here they were together again, on the same morning, at the same time, at the same hospital, both of them (as it appeared) on their way back home.

'Good morning, Miss Smith!' said the cheerful Chief Inspector, taking care to articulate a clear 'Miss', and not (as he always saw it) the ugly, pretentious, fuzzy 'Ms'.

Little that morning could have dampened Morse's spirits, for the gods were surely smiling on him. Even had she ignored his greeting, he would have walked serenely past, with little sense of personal slight. Yet perhaps he would have felt a touch of disappointment too; for he had seen the sadness in her face, and knew that for a little while he wanted to be with her.

# CHAPTER FORTY-SIX

I once knew a person who spoke in dialect
with an accent

(IRVIN COBB)

'THERE'S NO need really,' she said, manoeuvring herself into the passenger seat. 'I'm not short o' money, you know.'

'How long have you been waiting?'

'Long enough! Mind if I smoke?' she asked, as Morse turned left into Headley Way.

'Go ahead.'

'You want one?'

'Er, no thanks – not for me.'

'You *do* smoke, though. Else your wife does. Ashtray's full, innit? Think I'd make a good detective?'

'Which way's best?' asked Morse.

'Left at the White Horse.'

'Or *in* the White Horse, perhaps?'

'Er, no thanks – not for me,' she mimicked.

'Why's that?'

'They're not bloody open yet, that's why.' It was meant to be humorous, no doubt, but her voice was strained; and glancing sideways, Morse guessed that something was sorely wrong with her.

'Want to tell me about it?'

'Why the 'ell should I tell *you*?'

Morse breathed in deeply as she stubbed out her

cigarette with venom. 'I think you've been in hospital overnight. I could see a bit of a white nightie peeping out of the hold-all. The last time we met you told me you were expecting a baby, and the JR1 is where they look after babies, isn't it? They wouldn't normally take a mum who's had a miscarriage, though – that'd be the Churchill. But if you had a *threatened* miscarriage, with some internal bleeding, perhaps, then they might well get you into the JR1 for observation. That's the sort of thing a policeman gets to know, over the years. And please remember,' he added gently, 'I only asked if you wanted to tell me about it.'

Tears coursed down cheeks that were themselves wholly devoid of make-up; washing down with them, though, some of the heavy eye-shadow from around her dull-green eyes.

'I lost it,' she said, finally.

For a moment or two Morse considered placing his hand very gently, very lightly on hers, but he feared that his action would be misconstrued.

'I'm sorry,' he said simply, not speaking again until he reached Princess Street.

She got out of the car and picked up her hold-all from the back. 'Thank you.'

'I wasn't much help, I'm afraid. But if I *can* ever be of any help, you've only got to give me a ring.' He wrote down his ex-directory telephone number.

'Well, you could help now, actually. It's a lousy little place I live in – but I'd be quite glad if you'd come in and have a drink with me.'

'Not this morning.'

'Why the 'ell *not*, for Christ's sake? You just said to

give you a ring if I needed any help – and I bloody *do*, OK? *Now.*'

'All right. I'll come in and have one quick drink. On one condition, though.'

'What's that?'

'You don't slam the car-door. Agreed?'

'Doesn't seem *too* lousy a little place?' suggested Morse as, whisky in hand, he leaned back in the only armchair in the only room – the fairly large room, though – which was Eleanor Smith's bed-sitter-cum-bathroom.

'I can assure you it *is*. Crawling with all those microscopic creatures – you've seen photographs of them?'

Morse looked at her. Was he imagining things? Hadn't she just spoken to him with a degree of verbal and grammatical fluency that was puzzlingly at odds with her habitual mode of speech. 'Crawlin' wiv all them little bugs an' things' – wasn't *that* how she'd normally have expressed herself?

'I think I know why you're lookin' at me like that,' she said.

'Pardon?'

In answer, she placed an index finger on each nostril. On each ringless nostril.

And Morse nodded. 'Yes, I prefer you as you are now.'

'So you said.'

'You know that your step-father's still missing?'

'So what? You want me to break out into goose-pimples or something?'

'Why do you hate him so much?'

'Next question.'

'All right. You said you were going to get married. Does all this – the loss of your baby – does it make any difference?'

'Gettin' deep, ain't we? Cigarette?'

Ellie held out the packet; and stupidly, inevitably, Morse capitulated.

'You're still going ahead with getting married?'

'Why not? It's about time I settled down, don't you think?'

'I suppose so.'

'What else can I tell you?'

Well, if she was inviting questions (Morse decided) it was a good opportunity to probe a little more deeply into the heart of the mystery, since he was convinced that the key to the case – the key to *both* cases – lay somewhere in those late afternoon hours of Wednesday, 7 September, when someone had stolen the knife from the Pitt Rivers Museum.

'After your trip to Birmingham, you *could* have caught an earlier train back?'

She shrugged. 'Dunno. I didn't, though.'

'Do you remember exactly what time you asked your friend up here – when you got back that afternoon?'

'Exactly? Course, I can't. *She* might. Doubt it, though. We were both tight as ticks later that night.'

Was she lying? And if so, why?

'On that Wednesday—'

But she let him get no further. 'Christ! Give it a rest about Wednesday, will you? What's wrong with Tuesday? Or Monday? I 'aven't a bleedin' clue what I was doin' them days. So why *Wednesday*? Like I say, I know where I was all the bloody time that day.'

'It's just that there may be a connection between Dr McClure's murder and the theft of the knife.'

She seemed unimpressed, but mollified again. 'Drop more?'

'No, I must be off.'

'Please yourself.' She poured herself another Scotch, and lit another cigarette. 'Beginnin' to taste better. I hadn't smoked a fag for three days – three days! – before that one in your car. Tasted terrible, that first one.'

Morse rose to his feet and put his empty glass down on the cluttered mantelpiece, above which, on the white chimney-breast, four six-inch squares in different shades of yellow had been painted – with the name of each shade written in thick pencil inside each square: Wild Primrose, Sunbeam, Buttermilk, Daffodil White.

'Which d'you like best?' she asked. 'I'm considering some redecoration.'

There it was again, in that last sentence – the gear-shift from casual slang to elegance of speech. Interesting . . .

'But won't you be leaving here – after you're married?'

'Christ! You can't leave it alone, can you? All these bloody questions!'

Morse turned towards her now, looking down at her as she sat on the side of the bed.

'Why did you invite me here? I only ask because you're making me feel I'm unwelcome – an intruder – a Nosey Parker. Do you realize that?'

She looked down into her glass. 'I felt lonely, that's all. I wanted a bit of company.'

'Haven't you told Mr Davies – about your miscarriage?'

'No.'

'Don't you think—'

'Augh, shut up! You wouldn't know what it feels like, would you? To be on your own in life . . .'

'I'm on my own all the time,' said Morse.

'That's what they all say, did you know that? All them middle-aged fellows like you.'

Morse nodded and half-smiled; and as he walked to the door he looked at the chimney-breast again.

'Yellow's a difficult colour to live with; but I'd go for the Daffodil White, if I were you.'

Leaving her still seated on the bed, he trod down the narrow, squeaking stairs to the Jaguar, where for a few minutes he sat motionless, with the old familiar sensation tingling across his shoulders.

*Why hadn't he thought of it before?*

# CHAPTER FORTY-SEVEN

> Given a number which is a square, when can we
> write it as the sum of two other squares?
>
> (DIOPHANTUS, *Arithmetic*)

LEWIS WAS eager to pass on his news. Appeals on
Radio Oxford and Fox FM, an article in the *Oxford
Mail*, local enquiries into the purchase, description,
and condition of Brooks's comparatively new bicycle,
had proved, it appeared, successful. An anonymous
phone-call (woman's voice) had hurriedly informed St
Aldate's City Police that if they were interested there
was a 'green bike' chained to the railings outside St
Mary Mags in Cornmarket. No other details.

'Phone plonked down pronto,' the duty sergeant
had said.

'Sure it wasn't a "Green dyke" chained to the railings?' Lewis had asked, in a rare excursion into
humour.

Quite sure, since the City Police were now in possession of one bicycle, bright green – awaiting
instructions.

The call had come through just after midday, and
Lewis felt excitement, and gratification. Somebody –
some mother or wife or girlfriend – had clearly decided
to push the hot property back into public circulation.
Once in a while procedure and patience paid divi-
dends. Like now.

*If* it was Brooks's bike, of course.

Morse, however, on his rather late return from lunch, was to give Lewis no immediate opportunity of reporting his potentially glad tidings.

'Get on all right at the hospital, sir?'

'Fine. No problem.'

'I've got some news—'

'Just a minute. I saw Miss Smith this morning. She'd been in the JR1 overnight.'

'All right, is she?'

'Don't know about that. But she's a mixed-up young girl, is our Eleanor,' confided Morse.

'Not really a *girl*, sir.'

'Yes, she is. Half my age, Lewis. Makes me feel old.'

'Well, perhaps . . .'

'She gave me an idea, though. A beautiful idea.' Morse stripped the cellophane from a packet of cigarettes, took one out, and lit it from a box of matches, on which his eyes lingered as he inhaled deeply. 'You know the problem we're faced with in this case? We've got to square the first case – the murder of McClure.'

'No argument there.'

'Then we've got to square the second case – the theft of a Northern Rhodesian knife. And the connection between these two—'

'But you said perhaps there wasn't any connection.'

'Well, there is and now *I know what it is.*'

'I see,' said Lewis, unseeing.

'As I say, if we square the first case, and then we square the second case . . . all we've got to do is to work out the sum of the two squares.'

Lewis looked puzzled. 'I'm not quite following you, sir.'

'Have you heard of "Pythagorean Triplets"?'

'We did Pythagoras Theorem at school.'

'Exactly. The most famous of all the triplets, that is – "3, 4, 5": $3^2 + 4^2 = 5^2$. Agreed?'

'Agreed.'

'But there are more spectacular examples than that. The Egyptians, for example, knew all about "5961, 6480, 8161".'

'That's good news, sir. I didn't realize you were up in things like that.'

Morse looked down at the desk. 'I'm not. I was just reading from the back of this matchbox here.'

Lewis grinned as Morse continued.

'There was this fellow called Fermat, it seems – I called in at home and looked him up. He knew all about "things like that", as you put it: square-roots, and cube-roots, and all that sort of stuff.'

'Has he got much to do with *us*, though – this fellow?'

'Dunno, Lewis. But he was a marvellous man. In one of the books on arithmetic he was studying he wrote something like: "I've got a truly marvellous demonstration of this proposition which this margin is too narrow to contain." Isn't that a wonderful sentence?'

'If you say so, sir.'

'Well, I've worked out the square of three and the square of four and I've added them together and I've come up with – guess what, Lewis!'

'Twenty-five?'

'Much more! You see, this morning I suddenly realized where we've been going wrong in this case. We've been assuming what we were *meant* to assume . . . No. Let me start again. As you know, I felt pretty certain almost from the beginning that McClure was murdered by Brooks. And I think now, though I can't be certain of course, that Brooks himself was murdered last week. And I know – listen, Lewis! – I now know what Brooks's murderer *wanted* us to think.'

Lewis looked at the Chief Inspector, and saw that not uncommon, strangely distanced, almost mystical look in the gentian-blue eyes.

'You see, Brooks's body is somewhere where we'll never find it – I feel oddly sure about that. Pushed in a furnace, perhaps, or buried under concrete, or left in a rubbish-dump—'

'Waste Reception Area, sir.'

'Wherever, yes. But consider the *consequences* of the body never being found. We all jump to the same conclusion – the conclusion our very intelligent Administrator at the Pitt Rivers jumped to: that there was a direct link between the murder of Brooks and the theft of the knife. Now, there was a grand deception here. The person who murdered Brooks wanted us to take one fact for granted, and almost – almost! – he succeeded.'

'Or she.'

'Oh, yes. Or she . . . But as I say the key question is this: why was the knife stolen? So let me tell you. That theft was a great big bluff! For what purpose? To convince us that Brooks was murdered after 4.30 p.m. on that Wednesday the seventh. But he wasn't,' asserted

Morse slowly. '*He was murdered the day before* – he was murdered on Tuesday the sixth.'

'But he was seen alive on the Wednesday, sir. His wife saw him – Mrs Stevens saw him—'

'Liars!'

'Both of 'em?'

'Both of them.'

'You mean . . . you mean *they* murdered Brooks?'

'That's exactly what I do mean, yes. As I see things, it must have been Julia Stevens who supplied the brains, who somehow arranged the business with the knife. But what – *what*, Lewis – if Brooks was murdered by *another* knife – a household knife, let's say – a knife just like the one McClure was murdered with, the knife that was found in Daventry Avenue, the knife that was missing from the Brooks's kitchen.'

Lewis shook his head slowly. 'Why all this palaver, though?'

'Good question. So I'll give you a good answer. To give the murderer – murderers – watertight alibis for that *Wednesday*. I sensed something of the sort when I interviewed Julia Stevens; and I suddenly *knew* it this morning when I was interviewing our punk-wonder.'

'She's in it, too, you reckon?'

Morse nodded. 'All three of them have been telling us the same thing, really. In effect they've been saying: "Look! I don't mind being suspected of doing something on Tuesday – but *not on the Wednesday*." They're happy about not having an alibi for the day Brooks was murdered. It was for the day afterwards – the Wednesday – that for some reason they figured an alibi was vital. And – surprise, surprise! – they've each of 'em got

a beautiful alibi for then. It's been very clever of them
– this sort of casual indifference they've shown for the
*actual* day of the murder, the Tuesday. You see, they all
knew they'd be the likely suspects, and they've been
very gently, very cleverly, pushing us all along in the
direction they wanted.'

'All three of them, you think?'

'Yes. They'd *all* have gladly murdered Brooks, even
if they hadn't known he was a murderer himself: the
wife he'd treated so cruelly; the step-daughter he'd
probably abused; and Julia Stevens, who could see how
her little cleaner was being knocked about by the man
she'd married. So they hatch a plot. They arrange for
the knife to be stolen, having made sure that none of
*them* could have stolen it—'

'Ellie Smith could have stolen it,' interposed Lewis
quietly.

'Yes . . . perhaps she could, yes. But I don't think so.
Didn't the attendant think it was more likely to have
been a man? No. My guess is that they bribed someone
to steal it – someone they could trust . . . someone *one*
of them could trust.'

'Ashley Davies?'

'Why not? He's got his reward, hasn't he?'

'You think that's a reward, sir, marrying *her*?'

Morse was silent awhile. 'Do you know, Lewis, it
might be. It might be . . .'

'What did they do with the knife?'

'That's the whole point. That's what I'm telling you.
*They didn't use the stolen knife at all.* They just got rid of
it.'

'But you can't just get rid of things like that.'

'Why not? Stick it in a black bag and leave it for the dustmen. You could leave a dismembered corpse in one of those and get away with it. *Kein Problem*. The only thing the dustmen won't take is garden-refuse – that's a well-known fact, isn't it?'

'You seem to be assuming an awful lot of brains somewhere.'

'Look, Lewis! There seems to be a myth going round these days that criminals are a load of morons and that CID personnel are all members of Mensa.'

'Perhaps I should apply then,' said Lewis slowly.

'Pardon?'

'Well, I've been very clever, sir, while you were away. I think I've found Brooks's bike.'

'You have? Why the hell didn't you tell me before?'

# CHAPTER FORTY-EIGHT

It'll do him good to lie there unconscious for a
bit. Give his brain a rest

      (N. F. SIMPSON, *One-Way Pendulum*)

AT THE Proctor Memorial School that Friday afternoon the talk was predominantly of a ram-raid made
on an off-licence in the Blackbird Leys Estate the
previous evening, when by some happy chance a routine police patrol-car had been cruising round the
neighbourhood just as three youths were looting the
smashed shop in Verbena Avenue; when, too, a little
later, the same police car had been only fifty or so yards
behind when the stolen getaway car had crashed at full
speed into a juggernaut lorry near the Horspath roundabout on the Eastern Ring Road . . .

When the chase was over one of the three was seated
dead in the driving seat, his chest crushed by the
collapsed steering-wheel; another, the one in the front
passenger seat, had his right foot mangled and trapped
beneath the engine-mounting; the third, the one seated
in the back, had severe lacerations and contusions
around the head and face and was still unconscious
after the firemen had finally cut free his colleagues in
crime from the concertina'ed Escort.

The considerable interest in this incident – accident
– is readily explicable, since two of the youths, the two
who survived the crash, had spent five years at the

Proctor Memorial School; had spent fifteen terms mocking the attempts of their teachers to instil a little knowledge and a few of the more civilized values into their lives. Had they received their education at one of the nation's more prestigious establishments – an Eton, say, or a Harrow, or a Winchester – the youths would probably have been designated 'Old Boys' instead of the 'former pupils' printed in the late afternoon edition of the *Oxford Mail*. And the former pupil who had been seated in the back of the car had left his Alma Mater only the previous term.

His name was Kevin Costyn.


Julia Stevens walked round to her former pupil's house during the lunch-break that Friday, wishing, if she could, to speak to Kevin's mother. But the door-bell, like most of the other fixtures there by the look of things, was out of order; and no one answered her repeated knockings. As she slowly turned and walked back through the neglected, litter-strewn front garden, a young woman, with two small children in a push-chair, stopped for a moment by the broken gate, and spoke to her.

'The people in there are usually out.'

That was all.

Perhaps, thought Julia Stevens, as she made her way thoughtfully back to school – perhaps that brief, some-what enigmatic utterance could explain more about her former pupil than she herself had ever learned.

*

In the Major Trauma Ward, on Level 5 of the JR2 in Headington, she explained to the ward-sister that she had rung an hour earlier, at 6 p.m., and been told that it would be all right for her to visit Mr Kevin Costyn.

'How is he?'

'Probably not quite so bad as he looks. He's had a CT test – Computerized Tomography – and there doesn't *seem* to be any damage but we're a little bit worried about his brain, yes. And he looks an awful mess, I'm afraid. Please prepare yourself, Mrs Stevens.'

He was awake, and recognized her immediately.

'I'm sorry,' he whispered, speaking through a dreadfully lop-sided mouth, like one who has just received half a dozen injections of local anaesthetic into one half of the jaw.

'Sh! I've just come to see how you're getting on, that's all.'

'I'm sorry.'

'Listen! I'm the teacher, remember? Just let *me* do the talking.'

'That were the worst thing I ever done in my life.'

'Don't talk about it now! *You* weren't driving.'

He turned his face towards her, revealing the left cheek, so terribly bloodied and stitched and torn.

'It's not that, Mrs Stevens. It's when I asked you for the money.' His eyes pleaded with her. 'I should never a' done that. You're the only person that was ever good to me, really – and then I go and . . .'

His words were faltering further, and there was a film of tears across his eyes.

'Don't worry about that, Kevin!'

'Will you promise me something? *Please?*'

'If I can, of course I will.'

'*You* won't worry if I don't worry.'

'I promise.'

'There's no need, you see. I won't ever tell anybody what I done for you – honest to God, I won't.'

A few minutes later, Julia was aware of movement behind her, and she turned to see the nurse standing there with a uniformed policeman, the latter clutching his flat hat rather awkwardly to his rib-cage.

It was time to go; and laying her hand for a few seconds on Kevin's right arm, an arm swathed in bandages and ribbed with tubes, she took her leave.

As she waited for the lift down to the ground floor, she smiled sadly to herself as she recalled the nurse's words: 'But we're a little bit worried about his brain' . . . just like almost all the staff at the Proctor Memorial School had been, for five years . . . for fifteen terms.

And then, as she tried to remember exactly where she'd parked the Volvo, she found herself, for some reason, thinking of Chief Inspector Morse.

# CHAPTER FORTY-NINE

I sometimes wonder which would be nicer – an
opera without an interval, or an interval without
an opera
(ERNEST NEWMAN, *Berlioz, Romantic and Classic*)

OF THE four separate operas which comprise *Der Ring
des Nibelungen* (an achievement which in his view ranked
as one of the seven great wonders of the modern
world), *Siegfried* had always been Morse's least favourite.
And on the evening of Saturday, 17 September, he
decided he would seek again to discover whether the
fault lay with himself or with Wagner. But the evening
was destined not to pass without its interruptions.

At 7.35 p.m. Lewis had rung through with the
dramatic news that the handle-bars and the saddle on
the bicycle recovered from the railings outside the
parish church of St Mary Magdalene still bore traces of
blood, and that preliminary tests pointed strongly to its
being McClure's blood. Such findings, if confirmed,
would provide the police with their first physical link
between Felix McClure and Edward Brooks, since the
latter's wife, Brenda, had now identified the bike as her
husband's; as had one of the assistants at Halford Cycles
on the Cowley Road, where Brooks had purchased the
bike four months previously. A warrant, therefore,
should be made out asap for the arrest of Mr Edward
Brooks – with Morse's say-so.

And Morse now said so.

The fact that the person against whom the warrant would be issued was nowhere to be found had clearly taken some of the cream from Lewis's éclair. But Morse seemed oddly content: he maintained that Lewis was doing a wonderful job, but forbad him to disturb him again that evening, barring some quite prodigious event – such as the birth of another Richard Wagner.

So Morse sat back again, poured himself another Scotch, lit another cigarette, and turned *Siegfried* back on.

Paradise enow.

Very few people knew Morse's personal (ex-directory) telephone number, and in fact he had changed it yet again a few months earlier. When, therefore, forty minutes further into *Siegfried*, the telephone rang once more, Morse knew that it must be Lewis again; and thumping down his libretto with an ill grace, he answered tetchily.

'What do you want this time?'

'Hullo? Chief Inspector Morse?' It was a woman's voice, and Morse knew whose. Why had he been such a numbskull as to give his private number to the pink-haired punk-wonder?

'Yes?'

'Hi! You told me if ever I wanted any help, all I'd got to do was pick up the phone, remember?'

'How can I help?' asked Morse wearily, a hint of exasperation in his voice.

'You don't sound overjoyed to hear from me.'

273

'Just a bit tired, that's all.'

'Too tired for me to treat you to a pint?'

Morse wasn't quite sure at that moment whether his spirits were rising or falling. 'Sometime next week, perhaps?' he suggested.

'No. I want to see you tonight. Now. Right *now*.'

'I'm sorry, I can't see you tonight—'

'Why not?'

'Well, to tell you the truth, I'm in the bath.'

'Wiggle the water a bit so I can hear.'

'I can't do that – I'd get the phone wet.'

'So you didn't really mean what you said at all.'

'Yes, I did. I'll be only too glad to help. What's the trouble?'

'It's no good – not over the phone.'

'Why on earth not?'

'You'll see.'

'I don't follow you.'

'I'm just going out to catch a bus to the City Centre. With a bit of luck I'll be there in twenty minutes – outside Marks and Sparks – that's where it stops, and then I'm going to walk up St Giles', and I'm goin' in the Old Parsonage for a drink. I'll stay there half an hour. And if you've not turned up by then, I'll just take a taxi up to your place – OK with you?'

'No, it's not. You don't know where I live anyway—'

'Nice fellah, Sergeant Lewis. I could fall for 'im.'

'He's never told you my address!'

'Why don't you ring and ask 'im?'

Morse looked at his wristwatch: almost half-past eight.

'Give me half an hour.'

'Won't you need a bit longer?'

'Why's that?'

'Well, you've got to get yourself dried and then get dressed and then make sure you can find your wallet and then catch a bus—'

'Make it three-quarters of an hour, then,' said Morse, wondering, in fact, where his wallet was, for he seldom used it when Lewis was around.

Lewis himself rang again that evening, about ten minutes after Morse had left. The path lab had confirmed that the blood found on the recovered bicycle was McClure's; and on his way home (a little disappointed) he pushed a note to that effect through the front door of Morse's bachelor flat – together with the newspaper cutting from the previous week's *Oxford Times* received from one of his St Aldate's colleagues:

## THIEVES PUT SPOKE
## IN THINGS

An optimistic scheme to provide free bicycles was scrapped yesterday by the Billingdon Rural District Council.

The cycles, painted green, and repaired by young offenders on community service, were put into specially constructed stands outside the church for villagers to use and then return.

However within thirty-six hours of the scheme being launched, all twelve cycles, purchased at a cost of £1100, had disappeared.

The chair of the Council, Mrs Jean Ashton, strongly defended the initiative. 'The bikes are still somewhere on the road,' she maintained.

DC Watson of the Thames Valley Police agreed: 'Most of them probably in Oxford or Banbury, resprayed a bright red.'

Ashley Davies also had repeatedly rung an Oxford number that Saturday evening, but with similar lack of success; and he (like Sergeant Lewis) felt some disappointment. Ellie had told him that she would be out all day, but suggested that he gave her a ring in the evening. His news could wait – well, it wasn't really 'news', at all. He just wanted her to know how efficient he'd been.

He'd visited the plush, recently opened Register Office in New Road, where he'd been treated with courtesy and competence. In the circumstances 'Notice by Certificate' (he'd been informed) would be the best procedure – with Saturday, 15 October a possible, probable, marriage date, giving ample time for the requisite notices to be posted both at Bedford and at Oxford. He'd agreed to ring the Registrar the following Monday with final confirmation.

A few 'family' to witness the ceremony would have been nice. But, as Ashley was sadly aware, his own mother and father had long since distanced themselves from 'that tart'; and although Ellie's mum could definitely be counted upon, no invitation would ever be sent to her step-father – and that not just because he had left no forwarding address, but because Ellie would never allow even the mention of his name.

Only one wedding guest so far then. But it would be easy to find a few others; and anyway the legal requirement (Ellie, oddly enough, had known all about this) was only for two.

Ashley rang her number again at 10 p.m. Still no answer. And for more than a few minutes he felt a surge of jealousy as he wondered where she was, and with whom she was spending the evening.

# CHAPTER FIFTY

There is not so variable a thing in nature as a
lady's head-dress: within my own memory I have
known it rise and fall above thirty degrees

(JOSEPH ADDISON, *The Spectator*)

SHE WAS nowhere to be seen in the area known as the
Parsonage Bar, which (as we know) served as a combined bar and restaurant. There were, however, two
temporarily unescorted young women there, one
blonde, the other brunette. The former, immaculately
coiffured, and dressed in a white suit, would attract
interest wherever she went; the latter, her hair cut
stylishly short, and dressed in a fold-over Oxford-blue
creation, would perhaps attract her own fair share of
attention too, but her face was turned away from Morse,
and it was difficult for him to be certain.

With no real ale on offer, he ordered a glass of
claret, and stood at the bar for a couple of minutes
watching the main door; then sat on one of the green
bar-stools for a further few minutes, still watching the
main door.

But Miss Smith made no entrance.

'Are you on your own?'

The exaggeratedly seductive voice had come from
directly behind him, and Morse swivelled to find one of
the two women, the brunette, climbing somewhat in-
elegantly on to the adjoining stool.

'For the moment I am, yes. Er, can I buy – ?'

He had been looking at her hair, a rich dark brown, with bottled-auburn highlights. But it was not her hair that had caused the mid-sentence hiatus, for now he was looking into her eyes – eyes that were sludgy-green, like the waters of the Oxford Canal.

'Ye gods!' he exclaimed.

'Didn't recognize me, did you? I've been sittin' waitin'. Good job I've got a bit of initiative.'

'What will you have to drink?'

'Champagne. I fancy some champagne.'

'Oh.' Morse looked down at the selection of 'Wines available by the Glass'.

'Can't we stretch to a bottle?' she asked.

Morse turned over the price-list and surveyed 'A Selection of Vintage Champagnes', noting with at least partial relief that most of them were available in half-bottles. He pointed to the cheapest (cheapest!) of these, a Brut Premier Cru: £18.80.

'That should be all right, perhaps?'

She smiled at him slyly. 'You look a little shell-shocked, Inspector.'

In fact Morse was beginning to feel annoyed at the way she was mocking him, manipulating him. He'd show her!

'Bottle of Number 19, waiter.'

Her eyebrows lifted and the green eyes glowed as if the sun were shining on the waters. She had crossed her legs as she sat on the bar-stool, and Morse now contemplated a long expanse of thigh.

'"Barely Black" they're called – the stockings. Sort of sexy name, isn't it?'

Morse drained his wine, only newly aware of why Eleanor Smith could so easily have captivated (*inter alios*) Dr Felix McClure.

They sat opposite each other at one of the small circular-topped tables.

'Cheers, Inspector.'

'Cheers.'

He noticed how she held the champagne glass by the stem, and mentally awarded her plus-one for so doing; at the same time cancelling it with minus-one for the fingernails chewed down to the quicks.

'It's OK – I'm workin' on it.'

'Pardon?'

'Me fingernails – you were lookin' at 'em, weren't you? Felix used to tell me off about 'em.' She speared first a green, then a black olive.

'You can't blame me for not recognizing you. You look completely different – your hair . . .'

'Yeah. Got one o' me friends to cut it and then I washed it out – four times! – then I put some other stuff on, as near me own colour as I could get. Like it?'

She pushed her hair back from her temples and Morse noticed the amethyst earrings in the small, neat ears.

'Is your birthday in February?'

'I say! What a clever old stick you are.'

'Why this . . . this change of heart, though?'

She shook her head. 'Just change of appearance. You can't change your heart. Didn't you know that?'

'You know what I mean,' said Morse defensively.

'Well, like I told you, I'm gettin' spliced – got to be a respectable girl now – all that sort o' thing.'

Morse watched her as she spoke and recalled from the first time he'd seen her the glossy-lipsticked mouth in the powder-pale face. But everything had changed now. The rings had gone too, at least temporarily, from her nose; and from fingers, too, for previously she had worn a whole panoply of silverish rings. Now she wore just one, a slender, elegant-looking thing, with a single diamond, on the third finger of her left hand.

'How can I help you?' asked Morse.

'Well, I thought you might like to *see* me for starters – that wouldn't 'ave bin no good over the blower, would it?'

'Why do you have to keep talking in that sort of way? You've got a pleasant voice and you can speak very nicely. But sometimes you deliberately seem to try to sound like a . . .'

'A trollop?'

'Yes.'

Neither of them spoke for a while. Then it was Ellie:

'I wanted to ask you two things really.'

'I'm all ears.'

'Actually you've got quite nice ears, for a man. Has anyone ever told you that?'

'Not recently, no.'

'Look. You think my step-father's dead, don't you?'

'I'm not sure what I think.'

'If he is dead, though, *when* do you think . . . ?'

'As I say – I just don't know.'

'Can't you guess?'

'Not to you, Miss Smith, no.'

'Can't you call me "Ellie"?'

'All right.'

'What do I call you?'

'They just call me Morse.'

'Yes – but your Christian name?'

'Begins with "E", like yours.'

'No more information?'

'No more information.'

'OK. Let me tell you what's worrying me. You think Mum's had something to do with all this, don't you?'

'As I say—'

'I agree with you. She may well have had, for all I know – and good luck to her if she did. But *if* she did, it must have been before that Wednesday. You know why? Because – she doesn't know this – but I've been keeping an eye on her since then, and there's no way – *no way* – she could have done it after . . .'

'After what?' asked Morse quietly.

'Look, I've read about the Pitt Rivers business – everybody has. It's just that . . . I just wonder if something has occurred to you, Inspector.'

'Occasionally things occur to me,' said Morse.

'Have you got any cigarettes, by the way?'

'No, I've given up.'

'Well, as I was saying, what if the knife was stolen on the Wednesday afternoon to give everybody the impression that the murder – if there *is* a murder – was committed *after* that Wednesday afternoon? Do you see what I mean? OK, the knife was *stolen* then – but what if it wasn't *used*? What if the murder was committed with a *different* knife?'

'Go on.'

'That's it really. Isn't that enough?'

'You realize what you're saying, don't you? If your step-father *has* been murdered; if he was murdered *before* the theft of the knife, then your mother is under far more suspicion, not less. As you say, quite rightly, she's got a continuous alibi from the time she left for Stratford with Mrs Stevens on that Wednesday, but she hasn't got much of one for the day before. In fact she probably hasn't got one at all.'

Ellie looked down at the avocado-coloured carpet, and sipped the last of her champagne.

'Would you like me to go and get a packet of cigarettes, Inspector?'

Morse drained his own glass.

'Yes.'

Whilst she was gone (for he made no effort to carry out the errand himself) Morse sat back and wondered exactly what it was that Ellie Smith was trying to tell him ... or what it was that she was trying *not* to tell him. The point she had just made was exactly the one which he himself (rather proudly) had made to Sergeant Lewis, except that she had made it rather better.

'Now, second thing,' she said as each of them sat drinking again and (now) smoking. 'I want to ask you a favour. I said, didn't I, that me and Ashley—'

'Ashley and I.'

'Ashley and I are getting married, at the Registry Office—'

'Register Office,' corrected the pedantic Inspector.

'—and we wondered – *I* wondered – if you'd be willing to come along and be a witness.'

'Why me?'

'Because . . . well, no reason really, perhaps, except I'd like you to be there, with me mum. It'd make me . . . I'd be pleased, that's all.'

'When is it – the wedding?'

'"Wedding"? Sounds a bit posh, doesn't it? We're just getting married: no bridesmaids, no bouquets – and not too much bloody confetti, I hope.'

An avuncular Morse nodded, like an understanding senior citizen.

'Not like all the razzmatazz you probably had at your wedding,' she said.

Morse looked down at the carpet, as she had done earlier; then looked up again. For a second or two it was as though an electric current had shot across his forehead, and for some strange reason he found himself wanting to reach out across the table and just for a moment touch the hand of the young woman seated opposite.

'How are you getting home, Ellie?'


In the taxi ('Iffley Road – then the top of the Banbury Road,' Morse had instructed), Ellie had interlaced her fingers into his; and Morse felt moved and confused and more than a little loving.

'Did you see that watercolour?' she asked. 'The one just by our table? *Our* table?'

'No.'

'It was lovely – with fields and sheep and clouds. And the clouds . . .'

'What about them?' asked Morse quietly.

'Well, they were white at the top and then a sort of

middling, muddy grey, and then a darker grey at the bottom. Clouds are like that, aren't they?'

'Are they?' Morse, the non-Nephologist, had never consciously contemplated a cloud in his life, and he felt unable to comment further.

'It's just that – well, all I'm tryin' to say is that I enjoyed bein' with you, that's all. For a little while I felt I was on the top o' one o' them clouds, OK?'

After the taxi had dropped her off, and was making its way from East Oxford to North Oxford, Morse realized that he too had almost been on top of one of 'them clouds' that evening.

Back in his flat, he looked with some care at the only watercolour he had. The clouds there had been painted exactly as Ellie Smith had said. And he nodded to himself, just a little sadly.

# CHAPTER FIFTY-ONE

Needles and pins, needles and pins,
When a man marries his trouble begins
(Old nursery rhyme)

IN THE waiting area of the Churchill Hospital, immediately Mrs Stevens had been called in to see her specialist, at 10.35 a.m. on Tuesday, 20 September, Brenda Brooks picked up a surprisingly recent issue of *Good Housekeeping*, and flicked through its glossy pages. But she found it difficult to concentrate on any particular article.

Brenda was a person who took much pleasure in the simple things of life. Others, she knew, had their yearnings for power or wealth or knowledge, but two of her own greatest delights were cleanliness and tidiness. What a joy she felt each week, for example, when she watched the dustmen casually hurl her black bags into the back of the yellow rubbish-cart – then seeing them no more. It seemed like Pilgrim finally ridding himself of his burden of sin.

For her own part, she had seldom made any mess at all in her life. But there was always an accumulation of things to be thrown away: bits of cabbage-leaves, and empty tins, and cigarette stubs from her husband's ashtrays ... Yes. It was always good to see the black bags, well, *disappear* really. You could put almost anything in them: bloodstained items like shirts, shoes, trousers – anything.

There were the green bags, too – the bags labelled 'Garden Waste', issued by Oxford City Council, at 50p apiece. Householders were permitted to put out two such bags every week; but the Brooks's garden was small, and Brenda seldom made use of more than one a fortnight.

Then there were those strong, transparent bags which Ted had brought home a couple of years ago, a heavy stack of them piled in the garden shed, just to the left of the lawn-mower. Precisely what purpose her husband had envisaged for such receptacles had been unclear, but they had occasionally proved useful for twigs and small branches, because the material from which they were manufactured was stout, heavy-duty stuff, not easily torn.

But the real joy of Brenda's life had ever centred on the manual skills – knitting, needlework, embroidery – for her hands had always worked confidently and easily with needles and crochet-hooks and bodkins and such things. Of late, too, she had begun to extend the area of her manual competence by joining a cake-icing class, although (as we have seen) it had been only with considerable and increasing pain that she had been able to continue the course, before finally being compelled to pack it up altogether.

She was still able, however, to indulge in some of her former skills; had, in fact, so very recently indulged in them when, wearing a leather glove instead of the uncomfortable Tubigrip, she had stitched the 'body-bag' (a word she had heard on the radio) in which her late and unlamented husband was destined to be wrapped. Never could she have imagined, of course, that the disposal of a body would cause a problem in her gently undemanding life. But it had, and she had seen to it. Not that the task had been a labour of love. Far from it. It had been a labour of hate.

She had watched, a few months earlier, some men who had come along and cut down a branch overarching the road there, about twelve feet long and about nine inches across. (Wasn't a human head about nine inches across?) The men had got rid of that pretty easily: just put it in that quite extraordinary machine they had – from which, after a scream of whirring, the thick wood had come out the other end . . . sawdust.

Then there was the furnace up at the Proctor Memorial School – that would have left even less physical trace perhaps. But (as Mrs Stevens had said) there was a pretty big problem of 'logistics' associated with such waste-disposal. And so, although Brenda had not quite understood the objection, this method had been discounted.

The Redbridge Waste Reception Area had seemed to her a rather safer bet. It was close enough, and there was no one there to ask questions about what you'd brought in your bags – not like the time she and Ted had come through Customs and the man with the gold on his hat had discovered all those cigarettes . . . No, they didn't ask you anything at the rubbish dump. You just backed the car up to the skip, opened the boot, and threw the bags down on to the great heap already there, soon to be carted away, and dumped, and bulldozed into a pit, and buried there.

But none of these methods had found favour.

*Dis aliter visum.*

The stiffish transparent bags measured 28½ inches by 36 inches, and Brenda had taken three. After slitting open the bottoms of two of them, she had stitched the three together cunningly, with a bodkin and some green garden string. She had then repeated the process, and prepared a second envelope. Then a third.

It was later to be recorded that at the time of his murder Mr Edward Brooks was 5 feet 8 inches in height, and 10½ stones in weight. And although the insertion of the body into the first, the second, and the third of the winding-sheets had been a traumatic event, it had not involved too troublesome an effort physically. Not for her, anyway.

Edward Brooks had been almost ready for disposal.

Almost.

By some happy chance, the roll of old brown carpet which had stood for over two years just to the right of the lawn-mower, measured 6 feet by 6 feet.

Ideal.

With some difficulty the body had been manipulated into its container, and four lengths of stout cord were knotted – very neatly! – around the bundle. The outer tegument made the whole thing a bit heavier, of course – but neater, too. And neatness, as we have seen, was an important factor in life (and now in death) for Brenda Brooks. The parcel, now complete, was ready for carriage.

It might be expected perhaps – expected certainly? – that such an experience would permanently have traumatized the soul of such a delicate woman as Mrs Brenda Brooks. But, strangely enough, such was not the case; and as she thought back on these things, and flicked through another few pages of *Good Housekeeping*, and waited for Mrs Stevens to re-emerge, she found herself half-smiling – if not with cruelty at least with a grim satisfaction . . .

There was an empty Walkers crisp-packet on the floor, just two seats away; and unostentatiously Brenda rose and picked it up, and placed it in the nearest wastepaper basket.

Mrs Stevens did not come out of the consulting-room until 11.20 a.m. that morning; and when she finally did, Brenda saw that her dearest friend in life had been weeping . . .

It had been that last little bit really.

'You've got some friends coming over from California, you say?'

'Yes. Just after Christmas. I've not seen them for almost ten years. I went to school with her – with the wife.'

'Can I suggest something? Please?' He spoke quietly.

'Of course.' Julia had looked up into the brown eyes of Basil Shepstone, and seen a deep and helpless sadness there. And she'd known what he was going to say.

'If it's possible . . . if it's at all possible, can you get your friends to come over, shall we say, a month earlier? A month or two earlier?'

# CHAPTER FIFTY-TWO

I said this was fine utterance and sounded well
though it could have been polished and made to
mean less

(PETER CHAMPKIN, *The Sleeping Life of Aspern
Williams*)

THE CASE was not progressing speedily.

That, in his own words, is what Lewis felt embol-
dened to assert the following morning – the morning
of Wednesday, 21 September – as he sat in Morse's
office at HQ.

'Things are going a bit slow, sir.'

'That,' said Morse, 'is a figure of speech the literati
call "hyperbole", a rhetorical term for "exaggeration".
What I think you're trying to tell me is that we're
grinding to a dead halt. Right?'

Lewis nodded.

And Morse nodded.

They were both right . . .

Considerable activity had centred on the Brooks's
household following the finding of the bicycle, with
Brenda Brooks herself gladly co-operating. Yet there
seemed little about which she was able to co-operate,
apart from the retraction of her earlier statement that
her husband had been at home throughout the morn-

ing of Sunday, 28 August. In a nervous, gentle recantation, she was now willing (she'd said) to tell the police the whole truth. He had gone out on his bike, earlyish that morning; he had returned in a taxi, latish that morning – with a good deal of blood on his clothing. Her first thought, naturally enough, was that he'd been involved in a road accident. Somehow she'd got him into his pyjamas, into bed – and then, fairly soon afterwards, she'd called the ambulance, for she had suddenly realized that he was very ill. The bloodstained clothing she had put into a black bag and taken to the Redbridge Waste Reception Area the following morning, walking across the Iffley Road, then via Donnington Bridge Road to the Abingdon Road.

Not a very heavy load, she said.

Not so heavy as Pilgrim's, she thought.

That was almost all, though. The police could look round the house – of course, they could. There was nothing to hide, and they could take away whatever they liked. She fully understood: murder, after all, was a serious business. But no letters, no receipts, no addresses, had been found; few photographs, few mementos, few books; no drugs – certainly no drugs; nothing much at all apart from the pedestrian possessions of an undistinguished, unattractive man, whose only memorable achievement in life had been the murder of an Oxford don.

There had been just that one discovery, though, which had raised a few eyebrows, including (and particularly) the eyebrows of Brenda Brooks. Although only £217 was in Brooks's current account at Lloyds

Bank (Carfax branch), a building society book, found in a box beside Brooks's bed, showed a very healthy balance stashed away in the Halifax – a balance of £19,500. The box had been locked, but Brenda Brooks had not demurred when Lewis had asked her permission to force the lid – a task which he had accomplished with far more permanent damage than had been effected by the (still unidentified) thief at the Pitt Rivers Museum . . .

'You think he's dead?' asked Lewis.

'Every day that goes by makes it more likely.'

'We need a body, though.'

'We do. At least – with McClure – we had a body.'

'And a weapon.'

'And a weapon.'

'But with Brooks we've still not got a body.'

'And still not got a weapon,' added Morse rather miserably.

Ten minutes later, without knocking, Strange lumbered into the office. He had been on a week's furlough to the west coast of Scotland and had returned three days earlier. But this was his first day back at HQ, having attended a two-day Superintendents' Conference at Eastbourne.

He looked less than happy with life.

'How're things going, Morse?'

'Progressing, sir,' said Morse uneasily.

Strange looked at him sourly. 'You mean they're *not* progressing, is that it?'

'We're hoping for some developments—'

'Augh, don't give me that bullshit! Just tell me where we are – and don't take all bloody day over it.'

So Morse told him.

He knew (he said) – well, was ninety-nine per cent certain – that Brooks had murdered McClure: they'd got the knife from Brooks's kitchen, *without* any blood on it, agreed – but now they'd got his bike, *with* blood on it – McClure's blood on it. The only thing missing was Brooks himself. No news of him. No trace of him. Not yet. He'd last been seen by his wife, Brenda Brooks, and by Mrs Stevens – by the two of them together – on the afternoon of Wednesday, 7 September, the afternoon that the knife was stolen from the Pitt Rivers.

'Where does that leave us then?' asked Strange. 'Sounds as if you might just as well have taken a week's holiday yourself.'

'For what it's worth, sir, I think the two women are lying to us. I don't think they *did* see him that Wednesday afternoon. I think that one of them – or both of them – murdered Brooks. But not on that Wednesday – and not on the Thursday, either. I think that Brooks was murdered the day *before*, on the Tuesday; and I think that all this Pitt Rivers thingummy is a blind, arranged so that we should think there *was* a link-up between the two things. I think that they got somebody, some accomplice, to pinch the African knife – well, *any* knife from one of the cabinets there—'

'All right. You think – and you seem to be doing one helluva lot of "thinking", Morse – that the knife was stolen *the day after* Brooks was murdered.'

'Yes, sir.'

'Go on.'

Morse was very conscious that he had scarcely thought through his conclusions with any definitive clarity, but he ploughed on:

'It's all to do with their alibis. They couldn't have stolen the knife themselves – they were on a school bus going to Stratford. And so if we all make the obvious link, which we *do*, between the murder of Brooks and the theft, then they're in the clear, pretty well. You see, if Brooks's body is ever found, which I very strongly doubt—'

'What makes you say that?'

'Because if he's found, he won't have the Pitt Rivers knife stuck in him at all. It'll be *another* knife – like as not another kitchen knife. But they're certainly never going to let us find the body. That would mean the alibis they've fixed up for themselves have gone for a Burton.'

'What's the origin of that phrase?'

Morse shook his head. 'Something to do with beer, is it?'

Strange looked at his watch: just after midday. 'You know I was a bit surprised to find you here, Morse. I thought you'd probably gone for a Burton yourself.'

Morse smiled dutifully, and Lewis grinned hugely, as Strange continued: 'It's all too fanciful, mate. Stop thinking so much – and *do* something. Let's have a bit of action.'

'There's one other thing, sir. Lewis here got on to it . . .'

Morse gestured to his sergeant, the latter now taking up the narrative.

'Fellow called Davies, Ashley Davies. He's got quite a few connections with things, sir. He was on Staircase G in Drinkwater Quad when Matthew Rodway was there – had a fight with him, in fact, and got himself kicked out' – he looked at Morse – 'rusticated. The fight was about a girl, a girl called Eleanor Smith; and *she* was the girl who was Dr McClure's mistress. And now, Davies has got himself engaged to be married to her – *and* she's Brooks's step-daughter.'

'That's good, Lewis. That's just the sort of cumulative evidence I like to hear. Did *he* murder Brooks?'

'It's not that so much, sir. It's just that the Chief Inspector here . . .'

Lewis tailed off, and Morse took over.

'It's just that I'd been wondering why Miss Smith had agreed to marry him, that's all. And I thought that perhaps he might have done some favour for her. Lewis here found that he was in Oxford that Wednesday afternoon, and if it *was* Davies who went to the Pitt Rivers—'

'What! You're bringing *her* into it now? The daughter?'

'Step-daughter, sir.'

Strange shook his head. 'That's bad, Morse. You're in Disneyland again.'

Morse sighed, and sat back in the old black leather chair. He knew that his brief résumé of the case had been less than well presented; and, worse than that, realized that even if he'd polished it all up a bit, it still wouldn't have amounted to much. Might even have amounted to less.

Strange struggled to his feet.

'Hope you had a good holiday, sir,' remarked Lewis.

'No, I didn't. If you really want to know it was a bloody awful holiday. I got pissed off with it – rained all the bloody time.'

Strange waddled over to the door and stood there, offering a final piece of advice to his senior chief inspector: 'Just let's get cracking, mate. Find that body – or get Lewis here to find it for you. And when you do – you mark my words, Morse! – you'll find that thing-ummy knife o' yours stuck right up his rectum.'

After he was gone, Lewis looked across at a subdued and silent Morse.

'You know that "all the bloody time", sir? That's what they call – what the literati call – "hyperbole".'

Morse nodded, grinning weakly.

'And he wasn't just pissed off on his holiday, was he?'

'He wasn't?'

'No, sir. He was pissed *on* as well!'

Morse nodded again, grinning happily now, and looking at his watch.

'What about going for a Burton, Lewis?'

# CHAPTER FIFTY-THREE

'Jo, my poor fellow!'

'I hear you, sir, in the dark, but I'm a-gropin –
a-gropin – let me catch hold of your hand.'

'Jo, can you say what I say?'

'I'll say anythink as you say, sir, for I knows it's
good.'

'OUR FATHER.'

'Our Father! – yes, that's wery good, sir.'

(CHARLES DICKENS, *Bleak House*)

WE MUST now briefly record several apparently disparate events which occurred between 21 and 24
September.

On Wednesday, 21, Julia Stevens was one of four people
who rang the JR2 to ask for the latest bulletin on Kevin
Costyn, who the previous day had been transferred to
the Intensive Care Unit. His doctors had become
increasingly concerned about a blood-clot in the brain,
and a decision would very shortly be taken about
possible surgery. For each of the four (including Kevin's mother) the message, couched in its conventionally
cautious terms, was the same: 'Critical but stable'.

Not very promising, Julia realized that. Considerably
better, though, than the prognosis on her own
condition.

As she lay in bed that night, she would gladly have prayed for herself, as well as for Kevin, had she managed to retain any residual faith in a personal deity. But she had not so managed. And as she lay staring up at the ceiling, knowing that she could never again look forward to any good nights, quite certainly not to any cheerful awakenings, she pondered how very much more easy such things must be for people with some comfortable belief in a future life. And for just a little while her resolution wavered sufficiently for her to find herself kneeling on the Golden Floor and quietly reciting the opening lines of the Lord's Prayer.

Photographs of the three young men involved in the Eastern Ring Road accident had appeared on page 2 of *The Star* (22 September), a free newspaper distributed throughout Oxford each Thursday. Below these photographs, a brief article had made no mention whatsoever of the concomitant circumstances of the 'accident'. But it was the dolichocephalic face of Kevin Costyn, appropriately positioned between his dead partner-in-crime, to the left, and his amputee partner-in-crime, to the right, that had caught the attention of one of the attendants at the Pitt Rivers Museum. In particular it had been the sight of the small crucifix earring that had jerked his jaded memory into sudden overdrive. Earlier the police had questioned all of them about whether they could remember anything unusual, or *anyone* unusual, on that Wednesday afternoon when Cabinet 52 had been forced. Like each of his colleagues, he'd had to admit that he couldn't.

But now he could.

Just before the museum closed, on Thursday, 22 September, he walked along the passage, up the stone steps, and diffidently knocked on the door of the Administrator (capital 'A').

Late that same afternoon Morse asked Lewis an unusual question.

'If you had to get a wedding present, what sort of thing would you have in mind – for the bride?'

'You don't do it that way, sir. You buy a present for both of them. They'll have a list, like as not – you know, dinner-service, saucepans, set of knives—'

'Very funny!'

'Well, if you don't want to lash out too much you can always get her a tin-opener or an orange-squeezer.'

'Not exactly much help in times of trouble, are you?'

'Ellie Smith, is it?'

'Yes.' Morse hesitated. 'It's just that I'd like to buy her something . . . for herself.'

'Well, there's nothing to stop you giving her a personal present – just forget the wedding bit. Perfume, say? Scarf? Gloves? Jewellery, perhaps? Brooch? Pendant?'

'Ye-es. A nice little pendant, perhaps . . .'

'So long as her husband's not going to mind somebody else's present hanging round her neck all the time.'

'Do people still get jealous these days, Lewis?'

'I don't think the world'll get rid of jealousy in a hurry, sir.'

'No. I suppose not,' said Morse slowly.

Five minutes later the phone rang.

It was the Administrator.


In the Vaults Bar at The Randolph at lunchtime on Friday, 23 September, Ellie Smith pushed her half-finished plate of lasagne away from her and lit a cigarette.

'Like I say, though, it's nice of him to agree, isn't it?'

'Oh, give it a rest, Ellie! Don't start talking about *him* again.'

'You jealous or something?'

Ashley Davies smiled sadly.

'Yeah, I suppose I am.'

She leaned towards him, put her hand on his arm, and gently kissed his left cheek.

'You silly noodle!'

'Perhaps everybody feels a bit jealous sometimes.'

'Yeah.'

'You mean *you* do?'

Ellie nodded. 'Awful thing – sort of corrosive. Yuk!'

There was a silence between them.

'What are you thinking about?' he asked.

Ellie stubbed out her cigarette, and pushed her chair back from the table. 'Do you really want to know?'

'Please tell me.'

'I was just wondering what *she*'s like that's all.'

'Who are you talking about?'

'*Mrs* Morse.'

The sun had drifted behind the clouds, and Ashley got up and paid the bill.

A few minutes later, her arm through his, they walked along Cornmarket, over Carfax, and then through St Aldate's to Folly Bridge, where they stood and looked down at the waters of the Thames.

'Would you like to go on a boat trip?' he asked.

'What, this afternoon?'

'Why not? Up to Iffley Lock and back? Won't take long.'

'No. Not for me.'

'What would you like to do?'

She felt a sudden tenderness towards him, and wished to make him happy.

'Would you like to come along to my place?'

The sun had slipped out from behind the clouds, and was shining brightly once more.

# CHAPTER FIFTY-FOUR

Cambridge has espoused the river, has opened its
arms to the river, has built some of its finest
Houses alongside the river. Oxford has turned its
back on the river, for only at some points down-
stream from Folly Bridge does the Isis glitter so
gloriously as does the Cam

(J. J. SMITHFIELD-WATERSTONE,
*Oxford and Cambridge: A Comparison*)

THE TWO rivers, the Thames (or Isis) and the Cherwell, making their confluence just to the south of the
City Centre, have long provided enjoyable amenities
for Oxford folk, both Town and Gown: punting,
rowing, sculling, canoeing, and pleasure-boating. For
the less athletic, and for the more arthritic, the river-
cruise down from Folly Bridge via the Iffley and Sand-
ford locks to Abingdon, has always been a favourite.

For such a trip, Mr Anthony Hughes, a prosperous
accountant now living out on Boar's Hill, had booked
two tickets on a fifty-passenger steamer, the *Iffley Princess*, timetabled to sail from Folly Bridge at 9.15 a.m. on
Sunday, 25 September.

The previous evening he had slowly traced the
course of the river on the Ordnance Survey Map,
pointing out to his son such landmarks as the Green
Bank, the Gut, the concrete bridge at Donnington,

Haystacks Corner, and the rest, which they would pass before arriving at Iffley Lock.

For young James, the morrow's prospects were magical. He was in several ways an attractive little chap – earnest, bespectacled, bright – with his name down for the Dragon School in North Oxford, a preparatory school geared (indeed, fifth-geared) to high academic and athletic excellence. The lad was already exhibiting an intelligent and apparently insatiable interest both in his own locality and in the Universe in general. Such Aristotelian curiosity was quite naturally a great delight to his parents; and the four-and-a-half year old young James was picking up, and mentally hoarding, bits of knowledge with much the same sort of regularity that young Jason was picking up, and physically hurling, bits of brick and stone around the Cutteslowe Estate.

Spanning the fifty-yard-wide Isis, and thus linking the Iffley Road with Abingdon Road, Donnington Bridge was a flattish arc of concrete, surmounted by railings painted, slightly incongruously, a light Cambridge-blue. And as the *Iffley Princess* rounded the Gut, young James pointed to the large-lettered SOMERVILLE, followed by two crossed oars, painted in black on a red background, across the upper part of the bridge, just below the parapet railings.

'What's that, Dad?'

But before the proud father could respond, this question was followed by another:

'What's *that*, Dad?'

Young James pointed to an in-cut, on the left, where a concrete slipway had been constructed to allow owners of cars to back the boats they were towing directly down into the river. There, trapped at the side of the slipway, was what appeared to be an elongated bundle, a foot or so below the surface of the nacre-green water. And several of the passengers on the port side now spotted the same thing: something potentially sinister; something wrapped up; but something no longer wholly concealed.

Fred Andrews, skipper of the *Iffley Princess*, pulled over into Salters' Boat Yard, only some twenty yards below the bridge. He was an experienced waterman, and decided to dial 999 immediately. It was only after he had briefly explained his purpose to his passengers that an extraordinarily ancient man, seated in the bow of the boat, and dressed in a faded striped blazer, off-white flannels, and a straw boater, produced a mobile telephone from somewhere about his person, and volunteered to dial the three nines himself.

# CHAPTER FIFTY-FIVE

It's a strong stomach that has no turning
(OLIVER HERFORD)

FROM Donnington Bridge Road, Lewis turned right into Meadow Lane, then almost immediately left, along a broad track, where wooden structures on the right housed the Sea Cadet Corps and the Riverside Centre. Ahead of him, painted in alternate bands of red and white, was a barrier, open now and upright; and beyond the barrier, four cars, one Land-Rover, and one black van; and a group of some fifteen persons standing round something – something covered with greyish canvas.

Forty or fifty other persons were standing on the bridge, just to the left, leaning over the railings and surveying the scene some fifty feet below them, like members of the public watching the Boat Race on one of the bridges between Mortlake and Putney. And seated silently beside Lewis, Morse himself would willingly have allowed any one of these ghoulish gawpers to look in his stead beneath the canvas, at the body just taken from the Thames.

Events had moved swiftly after the first emergency call to St Aldate's. PC Carter had arrived within ten minutes in a white police car and had been more than grateful for the advice of the Warden of the Riverside Centre, a dark, thick-set man, who had dealt with many a body during his twenty-five years' service there. The Underwater Search Unit had been summoned from Sulhamstead; and in due course a doctor. The body, that of a man, still sheeted in plastic, but now in danger of slithering out of its wrapping of carpet, had been taken from the water, placed at the top of the slipway – and promptly covered up, untouched. St Aldate's CID had been contacted immediately, and Inspector Morrison had arrived to join a scene-of-crimes officer, and a police photographer. With the arrival of a cheerful young undertaker, just before noon, the cast was almost complete.

Apart from Morse and Lewis.


The reasons for such a sequence of events was clear enough to those directly and closely involved; clear even to a few of the twitchers, with their powerful binoculars, who had swelled the ranks of the bridge spectators. For this was clearly not a run-of-the-mill drowning. Even through the triple layers of plastic sheeting in which the body was wrapped, one thing stood out clearly (*literally* stood out clearly): the broad handle of a knife which appeared to be wedged firmly into the dead man's back. And when, under Morrison's careful directions – after many photographic flashings, from many angles – the stitching at the top of the improvised body-bag had been painstakingly unpicked, and one pocket of the corpse had been painstakingly picked (as it were), the identity of the man was quickly established.

On the noticeboard in the foyer of St Aldate's station was pinned a photograph of a 'Missing Person' whom the police were most anxious to trace; and beneath the photograph there appeared a name, together with a few physical details. But it was not the corpse's blackened features which Morrison had recognized; it was the name he found in the sodden wallet.

The name of Edward Brooks.

Thus was a further relay of telephone-calls initiated. Thus was Morse himself now summoned to the scene.

Sometimes procedures worked well; and sometimes (as now) there was every reason for the police to be congratulated on the way situations were handled. On this occasion one thing only (perhaps two?) had marred police professionalism.

PC Carter, newly recruited to the Force, had been reasonably well prepared for the sight of a body, particularly one so comparatively well preserved as this one. What he had been totally unprepared for was the indescribable stench which had emanated from the body even before the Inspector had authorized the opening of the envelope: a stench which was the accumulation, it seemed, of the dank depths of the river, of blocked drains, of incipient decomposition – of death itself. And PC Carter had turned away, and vomited rather noisily into the Thames, trusting that few had observed the incident.

But inevitably almost everyone, including the audience in the gods, had noticed the brief, embarrassing incident.

It was Morse's turn now.

Phobias are common enough. Some persons suffer from arachnophobia, or hypsophobia, or myophobia, or pterophobia ... Well-nigh everyone suffers occasionally from thanatophobia; many from necrophobia – although Morse was not really afraid of dead bodies at all, or so he told himself. What he really suffered from was a completely new phobia, one that was all his own: *the fear of being sick* at the sight of bodies which had met their deaths in strange or terrible circumstances. Even Morse, for all his classical education, was unable to coin an appropriately descriptive, or etymologically accurate, term for such a phobia: and even had he been so able, the word would certainly have been pretentiously polysyllabic.

Yet, for all his weakness, Morse was a far more experienced performer than PC Carter; and hurriedly taking the Warden to one side, he had swiftly sought directions to the nearest loo. It was not, therefore, into the Thames, but into a lone lavatory-pan in the Riverside Centre, that Chief Inspector Morse vomited, late that Sunday morning.

'Been in the river about a fortnight, they reckon,' ventured Lewis when Morse finally emerged.

'Good! That fits nicely,' replied the pale-faced Morse.

'You OK, sir?'

'Course I'm bloody OK, man!' snapped Morse.

But Lewis was not in the least offended, for he and Morse were long acquainted; and Lewis knew all his ways.

# CHAPTER FIFTY-SIX

He could not be a lighterman or river-carrier;
there was no clue to what he looked for, but he
looked for something with a most intent and
searching gaze

(CHARLES DICKENS, *Our Mutual Friend*)

IF A few minutes earlier it had been his stomach that
was churning over, it was now the turn of Morse's brain;
and somehow he managed, at least for a while, to look
down again at the semi-sealed body. Heavy condensa-
tion between the plastic layers was preventing any close
inspection of the knife stuck into the corpse's back. But
Morse was determined to be patient: better than most,
he knew the value of touching nothing further there;
and to be truthful he had been more than a little
surprised that Morrison had gone as far as he had.

Nothing further, therefore, was touched until the
arrival of the police pathologist, Dr Laura Hobson,
whose bright-red Metro joined the little convoy of
vehicles half an hour later. Briefly she and Morse
conversed. After which, with delicate hands, she performed a few delicate tasks; whilst Morse walked slowly
from the scene, along a track between a line of trees
and the riverbank, up to a building housing the Falcon
Rowing Club, some seventy yards upstream to his right.
Here he stood looking around him, wondering earn-
estly what exactly he should be looking for.

After returning to the slipway, he took the Warden to one side and put to him some of the questions that were exercising his mind. Where perhaps might the corpse have been pushed into the river? How could the corpse have been conveyed to such a spot? In which direction, and how far, could the corpse have been conveyed by the prevailing flow of the waters?

The Warden proved to be intelligent and informative. After stressing the importance, in all such considerations, of time of year, weather conditions, river-temperature, volume of water, and frequency of river-traffic; after giving Morse a clear little lesson on buoyancy and flotation, he suggested a few likely answers. As follows.

The strong probability was that the body had not been shifted all that far by the prevailing flow; indeed, if it had been slightly more weighted down, the body might have rested permanently on the bottom; as things were, the body could well have been put into the river at a point just beside the Falcon Rowing Club; certain it was that the body would not have drifted *against* the north–south movement of the tide. The only objection to such a theory was that it would have been an inordinately long way for anyone to carry such a weighty bundle. With the barrier locked down across the approach road to the slipway, no car (unless authorized) could even have reached the river at that point, let alone turned right there and deposited a body sixty, seventy yards upstream.

Unless . . .

Well, there were just over a hundred members of the Riverside Club who possessed boats, who used the slipway fairly regularly, and who were issued with a key to the barrier. Not infrequently (the Warden confessed) a boat-owner neglected to close the barrier behind him; or deliberately left it open for a colleague known to be sailing up behind. And so . . . if the barrier happened to be left open – well, not much of a problem, was there?

'You know what I'd've done, Mr Holmes, if I'd had to dispose of a body here?' Morse's eyes slowly rose to the top of Donnington Bridge, where public interest was, if anything, increasing, in spite of the makeshift screen which had now been erected around the body.

'You tell me.'

'I'd have driven here, about two o'clock in the morning, and pushed it over the bridge.'

'Helluva splash, you'd make,' said the Warden.

'Nobody around to hear it, though.'

'A few people around then, Inspector. You know who they are?'

Morse shook his head.

'Three lots o' people, really: lovers, thieves, police.'

'Oh!' said Morse.


Twenty minutes later the young pathologist got to her feet – the grim, grisly preliminary examination over.

'Mustn't do much more here,' she reported. 'Been in the river between a week and a fortnight, I'd guess. Difficult to say – he's pretty well preserved. Neat little job of packaging somebody did there. But we'll sort him out later. All right?'

Morse nodded. 'We're in your hands.'

'Not much doubt he's been murdered, though – unless he died, then somebody stuck a knife in him, then wrapped him all up and put him in the river here.'

'Seems unlikely,' conceded Morse.

Dr Hobson was packing up her equipment when Morse spoke again:

'You'll be sure not to touch the knife until—?'

'You've not got much faith in some of your colleagues, have you?'

She was an attractive young woman; and when first she had taken over from the sadly missed Max, Morse had felt he could almost have fallen a little in love with her. But now he dreamed of her no longer.

Morse had taken the sensible (almost unprecedented) precaution of refraining from a few pints of beer on a Sunday lunchtime; and at 3.15 p.m. he and Lewis stood in the path lab beside the prone body of Edward Brooks, the plastic bags in which he had been inserted lying folded neatly at his feet, like the linen wraps at the Resurrection. Apart from Dr Hobson herself, two further forensic assistants and a fingerprint expert stood quite cheerfully around the body, in which the handle of a broad knife stood up straight.

Yet it was not the handle itself, so carefully dusted now with fingerprint-powder, which had riveted Morse's attention. It was the label attached to the side of the handle; a label whose lettering, though washed and smudged by the waters of the Thames, was still partially legible on its right-hand side:

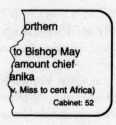

orthern

to Bishop May
amount chief
anika
v. Miss to cent Africa)

Cabinet: 52

'*I just do not believe this,*' whispered Morse slowly.

'Pardon, sir?'

But Morse was not listening. He touched Laura Hobson lightly on the shoulder of her starched white coat, and for the second time that day asked for the quickest way to the nearest Gents.

315

# CHAPTER FIFTY-SEVEN

Karl Popper teaches that knowledge is advanced
by the positing and testing of hypotheses. Count-
less hypotheses, I believe, are being tested at once
in the unconscious mind; only the winning shortlist is handed to our consciousness

(MATTHEW PARRIS, *The Times*, 7 March 1994)

THE FOLLOWING day, Monday, 26 September, both
Morse and Lewis arrived fairly early, just after 7 a.m., at
Thames Valley HQ.

Morse himself had slept poorly, his eyeballs cease-
lessly circling in their sockets throughout the night as
the dramatic new development in the case had gradu-
ally established itself into the pattern of his thinking;
for in truth he had been astonished at the discovery
that Brooks had been murdered *after* the theft of the
Rhodesian knife; murdered in fact *by* the Rhodesian
knife.

As he had hitherto analysed the case, assessing
motive and opportunity and means, Morse had succeeded in convincing himself that two or perhaps three
persons, acting to some degree in concert, had probably been responsible for Brooks's murder. Each of the
three (as Morse saw things) would have regarded the
death of Brooks, though for slightly different reasons,
as of considerable benefit to the human race.

Three suspects.

Three women: the superficially gentle Brenda Brooks, who had suffered sorely in the role of the neglected and maltreated wife; the enigmatic Mrs Stevens, who had developed a strangely strong bond between herself and her cleaning-lady; and the step-daughter, Eleanor Smith, who had left home in her mid-teens, abused (how could Morse know?) mentally, or verbally, or physically, or sexually even . . .

Women set apart from the rest of their kind by the sign of the murderer – by the mark of Cain.

A confusing figuration of 'if's' had permutated itself in Morse's restless brain that previous night, filtering down to exactly the same shortlist as before, since the Final Arbiter had handed to Morse the same three envelopes. In the first, as indeed in the second, the brief verdict was typed out in black letters: 'Not Guilty'; but in the third, Morse had read the even briefer verdict, typed out here in red capitals: 'GUILTY'. And the name on the front of the third envelope was – *Eleanor Smith.*

For almost an hour, Morse and Lewis had spoken together that morning: spoken of thoughts, ideas, hypotheses. And when he returned from the canteen with two cups of coffee at 8 a.m., Lewis stated, starkly and incontrovertibly, the simple truth they both had to face:

'You know, I just don't see – I just *can't* see – how Brenda Brooks, or this Mrs Stevens – how either of them could have done it. We've not exactly had a video-camera on them since the knife was stolen – but not far off. All right, they'd got enough motive. But I just don't see when they had the opportunity.'

'Nor do I,' said Morse quietly. And Lewis was encouraged to continue.

'I know what you mean about Mrs Stevens, sir. And I agree. There's somebody pretty clever behind all this, and she's the only one of the three who's got the brains to have thought it all out. But as I say . . .'

Morse appeared a little pained as Lewis continued:

'. . . she couldn't have done it. And Mrs Brooks couldn't have done it either, could she? She's got the best motive of any of them, and she'd probably have the nerve as well. But she couldn't have *planned* it all, surely, even if somehow she had the opportunity – that night, say, after she got back from Stratford. I just don't see it.'

'Nor do I,' repeated Morse, grimacing as he sipped another mouthful of weak, luke-warm coffee.

'So unless we're looking in completely the wrong direction, sir, that only leaves . . .'

But Morse was only half listening. 'Unless', Lewis had just said . . . the same word the Warden had used the previous day when he'd been talking of the red-and-white striped barrier. In Morse's mind there'd earlier been a *logical* barrier to his hypothesis that Brooks's body must have been taken to the Thames in some sort of vehicle – as well as that *literal* barrier. But the Warden had merely lifted that second barrier, hadn't he? Just physically lifted it out of the way.

So what if he, Morse, were now to lift that earlier barrier too?

'Lewis! Get the car, and nip along and have a word with the headmaster of the Proctor Memorial. Tell him we'd like to see Mrs Stevens again. We can either go round to her house or, if she prefers, she can come here.'

'Important, is it, sir?'

'Oh, yes,' said Morse. 'And while you're at it, you can drop me off at the path lab. I want another quick word with the lovely Laura.'

# CHAPTER FIFTY-EIGHT

Now faith is the substance of things hoped for,
the evidence of things not seen

(*Hebrews*, ch. 11, v. 1)

COMING OUT of her lab to greet Morse, Dr Laura Hobson appeared incongruously contented with her work. She pointed to the door behind her.

'You'd better not go in there, Chief Inspector. Not for the minute. We've nearly finished, though – the main bits, anyway.'

'Anything interesting?'

'Do you call stomach contents interesting?'

'No.'

'Looks as if they've got some vague prints all right, though – on the knife. I'll keep my fingers crossed for you. We're all hoping, you know that.'

'Thank you.' Morse hesitated. 'It may sound a bit far-fetched I know, but . . .'

'Yes?'

'The knife – I'm doing a little bit of hoping myself – the knife used to murder McClure was very similar to' – Morse nodded towards the main lab – 'to the knife that was stolen from the Pitt Rivers.'

'Yes, I knew that.'

'What I was wondering is this. Is there any possibility – any possibility at all – that Brooks was murdered with *another* knife – one of the same type, one with the same sort of blade – *then* for the knife you've got in there – the one with the possible prints on it – to be stuck in him . . . *afterwards*?'

Laura Hobson looked at him curiously.

'Have two knives, you mean? Stick one in him, take it out, then stick the other in?'

Morse looked uneasy, yet there was still some flicker of hope in his face. 'When I said "afterwards", I meant, well, a few *hours* later – a day even?'

With a sad smile, she shook her head. 'No chance. Unless your murderer's got the luck of the devil and the skill of a brain-surgeon—'

'Or a boy with a model-aeroplane kit?'

'—you'd have some clear *external* evidence of the two incisions – and don't forget he was stabbed through his clothes.'

'And there aren't . . . ?'

'No. No signs at all. Besides that, though, you'd have all the *internal* evidence: the two separate termini of the knife-points; two distinct sets of lacerations on either side of—'

'I see, yes,' mumbled Morse.

'I don't know whether you do, though. Look! Let me explain. Whenever you have a knife-wound—'

'Please, not!' said Morse. 'I believe all you say. It's just that I've never been able to follow all these physio-logical labellings. They didn't teach us any of that stuff at school.'

'I know,' said Laura quietly. 'You did Greek instead. You told me once, remember, in our . . . in our earlier days, Chief Inspector?'

Feeling more than a little embarrassed, Morse avoided her eyes.

'How would it have helped, anyway?' continued Laura, in a more business-like tone.

'Well, I've been assuming all along that the theft of the knife from the Pitt Rivers was a blind: a blind to establish an alibi, or alibis; to try to establish the fact that Brooks wasn't murdered until *after* the knife was stolen.'

She nodded, appreciating the point immediately. 'You mean, if he'd been murdered on a particular day with one knife, and then, the day after, a second knife was stolen; and if the first knife was subsequently removed from the body, and the second knife inserted into the wound – people like the police, like you, could well have been misled about the time of death.'

'That's a splendidly constructed sentence,' said Morse.

'Waste of breath, though, really. *I* wouldn't have been misled.'

'You're sure?'

'Ninety-nine per cent sure.'

'Could you just rule out the other one per cent – for me? Please?'

'Waste of time. But I will, yes, if that's what you want.'

'I'm very grateful.'

'Don't you want to see the contents of his pockets? His clothes?'

'I suppose I ought to, yes.'

Again she looked at him curiously. 'It's as if you've

been putting your ... well, your *faith* in something, isn't it? And I feel I've let you down.'

'I lost all my faith a long time ago, I'm afraid.'

'Much better to have *evidence*, in our job.'

Morse nodded; and followed Laura Hobson's shapely legs into a side-room, where she gestured to a table by the window.

'I'll leave you to it, Chief Inspector.'


Morse sat down and first looked through the official 'In Possession Property' form, listing the items found on Brooks's person.

The wallet which had been removed at the river-side to establish identity (and which Morse had already looked through, anyway) was among the items, and he quickly examined its few (now dry) contents once more: one £10 note; one £5 note; a Lloyds Bank plastic card; an ID card for the Pitt Rivers Museum; a card showing official membership of the East Oxford Conservative Club. Nothing else. No photographs; no letters.

Nor were the other items listed and laid out there in small transparent bags of any obvious interest: a black comb; a white handkerchief; £2.74 in assorted coinage; what had once been a half-packet of now melted indigestion tablets; and a bunch of seven keys. It was this latter item only which appeared to Morse worthy of some brief consideration.

The biggest key, some 3 inches in length, was grimy dark-brown in colour, and looked like a door-key; as perhaps did the two Yale keys, one a khaki colour, the other shinily metallic. The other four keys were (possibly?) for things like a garden shed or a bicycle-lock or a briefcase or a box or ... But Morse's brain was suddenly engaged now: the fourth small key, a sturdy, silvery key, had the number 'X10' stamped upon it; and Morse gazed through the window, and wondered. Was it one of a set of keys? A key to what? A key to where? Would it help to spend a few hours sorting out these seven keys and matching them to their locks? Probably not. Probably a waste of time. But he ought to do it, he knew that. So he would do it. Or rather he'd get Lewis to do it.

From the dead man's clothing Morse quickly decided that nothing could be gleaned which could further the investigation one whit; and he was standing up now, preparing to leave, when Laura came back into the small room.

Phone-call for Morse. Sergeant Lewis. In her office.


Lewis was ringing from the Head's office of the Proctor Memorial School. Mrs Julia Stevens had been granted temporary leave from her duties. Well, indefinite leave really – but the terminological inexactitude had avoided any difficult embarrassment all round. She would not be returning to school, ever; she had only a few months to live; and a supply teacher had already taken over her classes. Soon everyone would have to know, of course; but not yet. She wasn't at home, though; she'd gone away on a brief holiday, abroad –

the Head had known that, too. Gone off with a friend, destination unknown.

'Do we know who the friend is?' asked Morse.

'Well, *you* do, don't you?'

'I could make a guess.'

'Makes you wonder if they're guilty after all, doesn't it?'

'Or innocent,' suggested Morse slowly.


The condition of Kevin Costyn was markedly improved. With no surgery now deemed necessary, he had been removed from the ICU the previous lunchtime; and already the police had been given permission to interview him – at least about the accident.

Very soon he would be interviewed about other matters, too. But although he was reluctantly willing to talk about ram-raiding and stolen vehicles, he would say nothing whatsoever about the murder of Edward Brooks. He may have lied and cheated his way through life, but there was one promise, now, that he was never going to break.


Seated in the sunshine outside a small but fairly expensive hotel overlooking La Place de la Concorde, Julia reached out and clinked her friend's glass with her own; and both women smiled.

'How would you like to live here, Brenda?'

'Lordy me! Lovely. Lovely, isn't it, Mrs Stevens?'

'Anywhere you'd rather be?'

'Oh no. This is the very best place in the whole world – apart from Oxford, of course.'

Since she'd arrived, Julia had felt so very tired; but so very happy, too.

# CHAPTER FIFTY-NINE

St Anthony of Egypt (c. 251–356 AD): hermit and founder of Christian monasticism. An ascetic who freely admitted to being sorely beset by virtually every temptation, and most especially by sexual temptation. Tradition has it that he frequently invited a nightly succession of naked women to parade themselves in front of him as he lay, hands manacled behind his back, in appropriately transparent yet not wholly claustrophobic sacking

(SIMON SMALL, *An Irreverent Survey of the Saints*)

AT 9.30 A.M. on Tuesday, 27 September, Morse walked down the High from Carfax. There were several esteemed jewellers' shops there, he knew that; and he looked in their windows. He was somewhat uncertain, however, of what exactly to purchase – and wholly uncertain about whether his present errand was being made easier, or more difficult, by his strong suspicion now that it had been Eleanor Smith who had murdered her step-father (the same Eleanor who had formally identified the body the previous day). Perhaps in a sense it was going to be easier, though, since in all probability he wasn't looking for a wedding present any longer, the prospect of an imminent marriage now seeming increasingly remote. Yet for some reason he still wanted to buy the girl a present: a personal present.

Something like Lewis had suggested.

'How much is that?' he asked a young female assistant in the shop just across from the Covered Market.

'Nice little pendant, isn't it, sir? Delicate, tasteful, and quite inexpensive, really.'

'How much is it?' repeated Morse.

'Only £35, sir.'

Only!

Morse looked down at the representation on the tiny oval pendant of – of somebody? 'St Christopher, is it?'

'St Anthony, sir. A well-known Christian saint.'

'I thought he was the patron saint of Lost Property.'

'Perhaps you're thinking of a later St Anthony?'

But Morse wasn't. He thought there'd only been one St Anthony.

'If . . . if I bought this, I'd need a chain as well, wouldn't I?'

'It would be difficult to wear without a chain, yes.'

She was laughing at him, Morse knew that; but it hadn't been a very bright question. And very soon he was surveying a large selection of chains: chains with varied silver- or gold-content; chains of slightly larger or slightly smaller links; chains of different lengths; chains of differing prices.

So Morse made his purchase: pendant plus chain (the cheapest).

Then, after only a few steps outside the jeweller's up towards Carfax Tower, he performed a sudden U-turn, returning to the shop and asking if he could please exchange the chain (not the pendant) for something a little more expensive. The assistant (still smiling at him?) was happily co-operative; and five minutes later

Morse started walking once again up towards Carfax. With a different chain.

With the most expensive chain there.

He was ready for the interview.

When earlier he had rung Eleanor Smith, she had sounded in no way surprised that the police should wish to take her fingerprints – for 'elimination purposes', as Morse had emphasized. And when he'd explained that it was against the rule-book for anyone who had been at the scene of the river-side discovery (as *he* had been) to go anywhere near the homes of those who might possibly be involved with the, er, the investigation, she'd agreed to go along to Thames Valley HQ. A car would pick her up. At 11.15 a.m.

Morse just had time to call in at Sainsbury's supermarket, on the Kidlington roundabout, where he made his few purchases swiftly, and found himself the only person at the 'small-basket' check-out. Just the four items, in fact: two small tins of baked beans; one small brown loaf; and a bottle of Glenfiddich.

# CHAPTER SIXTY

When the Himalayan peasant meets the he-bear
  in his pride,
He shouts to scare the monster, who will often
  turn aside.
But the she-bear thus accosted rends the peasant
  tooth and nail.
For the female of the species is more deadly than
  the male
    (RUDYARD KIPLING, *The Female of the Species*)

'WHAT LINE are you going to take with her, sir?'

'I'm not at all sure. All I know is that if any of our three ladies actually murdered Brooks – and pretty certainly one of them did – we can forget the other two, wherever they're sunning themselves at the minute. It's odds on that one of them, or both of them, had some part to play in the plot; but I'm sure that neither of them could have murdered Brooks. It's a physical impossibility, knowing what we do about dates and times. But *she* could have done. Ellie Smith could have done – if only just. She went to Birmingham that Wednesday – you've checked on that. But we can't be sure when she came back, can we? You see, if she'd come back an hour, even half an hour earlier . . .'

'*She* could have stolen the knife, you mean?'

'Or she could have got someone to steal it for her.'

'Ashley Davies.'

'Yes. Could well have been. Then he gets his reward: he gets the hand of the increasingly desirable Miss Smith – a young woman he's had his lecherous eyes on even when she was a sleep-around-with-anybody girl.'

'What about the attendant at the Pitt Rivers, though? He says he probably saw this young fellow Costyn there.'

'It's always dodgy though – this identification business. We can't rely on that.'

Lewis nodded. 'He doesn't seem to have any real link with the case, anyway.'

'Except with Mrs Stevens. She taught him, remember. And I suppose if he's on drugs or something – got a regular habit to feed – short of cash – and if she was prepared to pay—'

'You mean she got him to steal the knife – for somebody else? For Ellie Smith, say?'

'Who else?'

'But you've always thought—'

'Give it a bloody rest, Lewis, will you?' snarled Morse. 'Do you think I get any pleasure from all this? Do you think I *want* to get Ellie Smith in here this morning and take her prints and tell her that she's a bloody liar and that she knifed her sod of a step-father?'

He got up and walked to the window.

'No, I don't think that,' said the ill-used Lewis quietly. 'It's just that I'm getting confused, that's all.'

'And you think I'm *not*?'

No, Lewis didn't think that. And he wondered whether his next little item of news was likely to clarify or further to befuddle the irascible Chief Inspector's brain.

'While you were shopping, I went down to Wolsey and had another look in Mrs Ewers' pantry.'

'And?'

'Well, something rang a bit of a bell when we found Brooks's body: those plastic bags. Do you remember when we first went to the Staircase?'

'The pile of them there in the pantry, yes.'

Lewis sought to hide his disappointment. 'You never said anything.'

'There's no end of those around.'

'I just thought that if Brooks used to take a few things home occasionally, unofficially – toilet-rolls, cartons of detergent, that sort of thing . . .'

'We could have a look in Brooks's place, yes. Where do you reckon he'd keep them?'

'Garden shed?'

'We'd need a search warrant . . . unless, Lewis—'

'Oh no! I'm not forcing any more locks, sir. Look what a mess I made of the box in his bedroom.'

'Perhaps you won't need to.' Morse opened a drawer of his desk and took out the bunch of keys. 'I'd like to bet one of these fits the garden shed; but I doubt we're going to find any bags there. They'll have been too careful for that.'

'What are you thinking of exactly?'

'Well, you'd have expected a few prints on the plastic bags, don't you think? But there aren't any, it seems. The water wouldn't have washed them off completely, I'm told. So they wore gloves all the time. And then they took good care to make sure the body wouldn't float, agreed? There's a gash in the bags, through all three layers – I don't think that was caused accidentally in the river. I think it was made deliberately, to let the air out, and get the body to sink ... at least, temporarily. That's what the Warden thought, too.'

Yes, Lewis remembered. Holmes had claimed that unless any body was weighted down it would almost certainly have come up towards the surface sooner or later because of the body's natural gases.

'Why do you think they – somebody – went to all that trouble with the bags, sir? It's almost as if ...'

'Go on, Lewis!'

'As if somebody *wanted* the body to be found.'

'Ye-es.' Morse was gazing across the yard once more. 'You know what's buggering us up the whole time, don't you? It's simply that we're going to have one helluva job making out a case against *anybody*. If somebody like Helena Kennedy, QC, was hired for the defence, she'd make mincemeat of us: we've got all the motive in the world; and all the means – but we just can't find any bloody *opportunity* ... except at about teatime on that Wednesday afternoon. They've been too clever for us. But it's not just cleverness: it's ruthlessness too. Not a blatant ruthlessness, but certainly a latent ruthlessness – latent in all three of them. Something that suddenly hardened into a cold-blooded resolve to get rid of Brooks – not just because they knew, *must* have known, that he was a murderer himself, but for an even better reason. Hatred.'

There was a knock at the door, and a WPC announced that Ms Smith was now seated in Reception.

'Bring her up, please,' said Morse, quickly opening a small, square black box, lined with white satin, and passing it across to Lewis.

'What d'you think?'

Lewis, like Dr Hobson the previous day, looked across at Morse most curiously.

'But if what you say's right, sir, she's going to have to postpone the happy day indefinitely – for quite a few years, perhaps.'

'She can still sit in a cell and twiddle it in her fingers. No law against that, is there?'

But before Lewis could remind Morse of the very strict and very sensible prison regulations regarding necklaces and the like, there was another knock at the door, and Morse swiftly took back the pendant of St Anthony – plus his golden chain.

# CHAPTER SIXTY-ONE

The total amount of undesired sex endured by women is probably greater in marriage than in prostitution

(BERTRAND RUSSELL, *Marriage and Morals*)

AFTER ROLLING the little finger of her left hand across the pad, after pressing it firmly on to the fingerprint-form, Eleanor Smith had finished; and Lewis now asked her to add her signature to the form.

'That didn't take very long, did it?' said Morse patronizingly.

'Does all this mean you've found some fingerprints on the knife?' she asked.

Morse was slightly hesitant. 'We think so, yes. Unidentified prints – unidentified as yet. As I explained, though, it's just a matter of elimination.'

She looked rather weary; gone was the sparkle that had characterized the latter part of that champagne evening at the Old Parsonage.

'You think they could be mine?'

Rather weary too was Morse's smile.

'We've got to have *some* suspects, haven't we? In fact my sergeant here's got a long list of 'em.'

She turned to Lewis. 'Whereabouts am I on the list?'

'We always try to put the most attractive at the top, don't we, sir?'

Morse nodded his agreement, wishing only that he'd thought of such a splendid rejoinder himself.

'And when exactly am I supposed to have murdered that shithouse?'

She looked from one to the other, and Morse in turn looked to Lewis the Interlocutor.

'Perhaps,' said the latter slowly, 'when you got back from Birmingham that Wednesday?'

'I see . . . And did I pinch the knife as well?'

'I – we don't think you could have done that because, as you told us, you didn't get back into Oxford until after the museum had closed. We checked up on the train time: it got into Oxford Station at 16.35 – just three minutes late.'

'You still don't sound as if you believe me.'

'We don't think you took the knife,' said Morse.

The slight but perceptible stress on the 'you' was clearly not lost on Suspect Number One.

'You suggestin' somebody else pinched it – then slipped it to me on the way home from the railway station? Then I just called in to have a chat with him and decided to murder the old bugger there and then – is that what you're thinking?'

'There are more unlikely scenarios than that,' said Morse quietly.

'Oh, not you! How I hate that bloody word "scenario".'

She had touched a raw spot, for Morse hated the word too. Yet he'd not been able to come up with anything better; and he made no protest as Ellie Smith continued, changing down now into her lower-gear register of speech.

'And what am I s'posed to 'ave done with 'im then?'

'Well, we were hoping you could give us a few ideas yourself.'

'Is this turnin' into a bleedin' interview or something?'

'No,' said Morse simply. 'You're under no obligation to answer anything. But sooner or later we're going to have to ask all sorts of questions. Ask you, ask your mother . . . Where is your mother, by the way?'

'Abroad somewhere.'

'How do you know that?'

'She sent me a postcard.'

'Where from?'

'The postmark was smudged – I couldn't read it.'

'Must have had a stamp on it?'

'Yeah. I'm no good at them names of foreign countries, though.'

'Some of them aren't very difficult, you know. "France", for instance?'

She made no reply.

'Have you still got the postcard?'

'No. Threw it away, didn't I?'

'What was the picture on it?'

'A river, I think.'

'Not the Thames?'

'Not the Thames.'

'You're not being much help, you know.'

'That's where you're wrong, though.'

She produced a small pasteboard business card and handed it to Morse.

'You were asking me about that Wednesday, weren't you? Well, I met a fellow on the train, and he got a bit, you know, a bit friendly and flirty, like; said if I ever wanted any, you know, work or anything . . .'

Morse looked at the white card: 'Mike Williamson, Modelling and Photographic Agency', with a Reading address and telephone number.

'He'll remember me – for sure, Inspector. I can promise you that.'

She smiled, her eyes momentarily recapturing the sparkle that Morse could recall so well.

'Better check, Lewis.'

But as Lewis got up and moved towards the phone, Morse held up his hand: 'Office next door, please.'


'Why did you want him out of the way?'

Morse ignored the question, feeling quite irrationally jealous. 'What did this fellow offer you?'

'Oh, Christ, come off it!' Her eyes flashed angrily now. 'What the 'ell d'you think? He just thought I was an intelligent, ill-educated, expensive prostitute – which I am.'

'Which you *were*.'

'Which I *am*, Morse. By the way, you don't mind me calling you "Morse", do you? I did ask you – remember? – if I could call you something more pally and civilized but . . .'

'What about Mr Davies? When you're married—'

'To Ashley? That's all off. He came last night and we stayed up till God knows when, talking about it – going round and round in the same old circles. But I just can't go through with it. I like him – he's nice. But I just . . . I just don't fancy him, that's all; and I could never love him – never. So it's not fair, is it? Not fair on him. Not fair on me, either, really.'

'So you won't be needing me any more – for the wedding,' said Morse slowly.

''Fraid not, no. There wouldn't have been a wedding anyway, though, would there – not if you're going to arrest me?'

For a brief while the two looked at each other across the desk, their eyes locked together with a curiously disturbing intimacy.

The phone rang.

It was Strange; and Ellie got to her feet.

'Please, stay!' whispered Morse, his hand over the mouthpiece. 'Yes, sir. Yes . . . Can you just give me five minutes . . . ? I'll be straight along.'

'Why d'you want me to stay?' she asked, after Morse had put down the receiver.

He took the little black box from the drawer and handed it to her.

'It's not wrapped up, I'm afraid. I'm not much good at that sort of thing.'

'Wha—?' She held the box in her left hand and opened it with her right, taking hold of the gold chain lovingly and gently, and slowly lifting up St Anthony.

'Wha's this for?'

'I bought it for you.'

'But like I say—'

'I want you to have it, that's all. I've never bought anything like that for anybody – and, as I say, I just want you to have it.'

Ellie had been looking down at the pendant and suddenly the tears began. 'Oh God!' she whispered.

'Do you like it?'

'It's ... it's the most wonderful ...' But she could get no further. She stood up and walked round the desk, and kissed Morse fully and softly on the mouth; and Morse felt the wetness of her cheek against his own.

'I must go,' said Morse. 'My boss'll be getting impatient.'

She nodded. 'You know what I just said – about Ashley? That I couldn't marry him because I didn't love him? Well, that wasn't really the reason why I broke it off.'

In his brain Morse had become convinced that Eleanor Smith must be guilty of her step-father's murder; but in his heart he felt grieved as he awaited her words, for he knew exactly what they would be.

Yet he was wrong.

Spectacularly wrong.

'The real reason is I've ... I've fallen in love with somebody else.'

Morse wondered if he'd heard correctly. 'What?'

'You gettin' deaf or something?'

'Not – not with that charlatan from the modelling agency, surely?'

She shook her head crossly, like some unhappy, exasperated little girl who will stamp her foot until she can get her own way, her own selfish way. *Now.*

'Are you going to listen to me, or not? Can't you guess? Can't you see? Can't you *see?*' She was standing beside the door, her head held high, her sludgy-green eyes closed, trying so hard to hold back the brimming tears. 'I've fallen in love with you, you stupid sod!'

# CHAPTER SIXTY-TWO

**dactyloscopy** (n): the examination of fingerprints
(Early Twentieth Century)
                (*The New Shorter Oxford English Dictionary*)


ALWAYS HAD Morse been a reluctant dactyloscopist,
and throughout his police career all the arches and
whorls and loops, all the peaks and the troughs and the
ridges, had ever remained a deep mystery to him – like
electricity, and the Wheatstone Bridge. He was therefore perfectly happy, on Friday, 30 September, to
delegate the fingerprinting of Mesdames Brooks and
Stevens to Sergeant Lewis – for the two overseas travel-
lers had returned to Oxford early that afternoon.
Immigration officials at Heathrow, Gatwick, and
Stansted airports had been alerted about them; and the
phone-call from Heathrow had been received at
Thames Valley HQ just after midday: the two had
boarded the Oxford City Link coach, scheduled to
arrive at its Gloucester Green terminus in Oxford at
2.30 p.m.

Neither had appeared to show any undue surprise
or discomfiture when Lewis, accompanied by a fingerprint officer, had taken them into the manager's office
there, and trotted out the 'purely for elimination' line.

After his colleague had left for the fingerprint
bureau at St Aldate's (where there was now a computerized search facility) Lewis had returned to Kidlington

COLIN DEXTER

HQ, to find Morse dispiritedly scanning some of the documents in the case.

But the Chief Inspector perked up with the return of his sergeant.

'No problems?'

'No problems, sir.'

'You're a betting man, Lewis?'

'Only very occasionally: Derby, Grand National . . .'

'Will you have a bet with *me*?'

'50p?'

'Can't we be devils, and make it a quid?'

'All right. I've got to be careful with the money, though – we've got the decorators in.'

Morse appeared surprised. 'I thought you did all that sort of stuff yourself?'

'I used to, sir, when I had the time and the energy. Before I started working for you.'

'Well, take your pick!'

'Pardon?'

'The fingerprints. Brenda Brooks or Julia Stevens – who do you go for?'

Lewis frowned. 'I can't really see his wife doing it, you know that. I just don't think she'd have the strength for one thing.'

'Really?' Morse seemed almost to be enjoying himself.

'Mrs Stevens, though . . . Well, she's a much stronger person, a much stronger character, isn't she? And she's got the brains—'

'And she's got nothing to lose,' added Morse more sombrely.

'Not much, no.'

'So your money's on her, is it?'

342

Lewis hesitated. 'You know, sir, in detective stories there are only two rules really, aren't there? It's never the butler; and it's never the person you think it is. So – so I'll go for Mrs Brooks.'

'Leaving me with Mrs Stevens.'

'You'd have gone for her anyway, sir.'

'You think so?'

But Lewis didn't know what he was thinking, and changed the subject.

'Did you have any lunch earlier, sir?'

'Not even a pint,' complained Morse, lighting a cigarette.

'You're not hungry?'

'A bit.'

'What about coming back and having a bite with us? The missus'd be only too glad to knock something up for you.'

Morse considered the proposition. 'What do you normally have on Fridays? Fish?'

'No. It's egg and chips on Fridays.'

'I thought that was on Wednesdays.'

Lewis nodded. 'And Mondays.'

'You're on,' decided Morse. 'Give her a ring and tell her to peel another few spuds.'

'Only one thing, sir – as I said. We're in a bit of a pickle at home, I'm afraid – with the decorators in.'

'Have you got the beer in, though? That's more to the point, surely.'

It was Lewis himself who took the call from the finger-print bureau half an hour later. No match. No match

anywhere. Whoever it was who had left some fingerprints on the Rhodesian knife, it had *not* been Mrs
Brenda Brooks or Mrs Julia Stevens; nor, as they'd
already learned, Ms Eleanor Smith. One other piece of
information. Classifying and identifying fingerprints
was an immensely complicated job and they couldn't
be absolutely sure yet; but it was looking almost certain
now that the fingerprints on the knife-handle didn't
match those of any known criminals either – well over
two million of them – in the Scotland Yard library.

'So you see what it means, Sarge? Whoever murdered your fellow doesn't look as if he had any previous
conviction.'

'Or *she*,' added Lewis, after putting down the phone.

There was no need to relay the message, since a
glum-looking Morse had heard it all anyway.

In silence.

A silence that persisted.


The report that Lewis had written on the visit to
Matthew Rodway's mother was on the top of Morse's
pile.

'Hope I didn't make too many spelling mistakes, sir?'
ventured Lewis finally.

'What? No, no. You're improving. Slowly.'

'I don't suppose she gives tuppence really – Mrs
Rodway, I mean – about who killed Brooks. So long as
somebody did.'

Morse grunted inarticulately. His thoughts drifted
back to their meeting with Mrs Rodway. It seemed an
age ago now; but as his eyes skimmed through the

report once again he could clearly visualize that interview, and the room, and the slim and still embittered
Mrs Rodway . . .

'I know it's probably nonsense, sir, but you don't
think that *she* could have murdered Brooks, do you?'

'She had as good a motive as anybody,' admitted
Morse.

'Perhaps we ought to have another little ride out
there and take her fingerprints.'

'Not today, Lewis. I'm out for a meal, if you
remember.'

'I'll see you there, sir, if you don't mind. About six,
is that all right?'

'What are *you* going to do?'

'Lots of little things. Make a bit more progress with
the keys, for a start. I'm expected at the Pitt Rivers in
twenty minutes.'

After Lewis had left, Morse lit yet another cigarette
and leaned back in the black leather chair, looking
purposelessly around his office. He noticed the thin
patina of nicotine on the emulsioned walls. Yes, the
place could do with a good wash-down and redecoration: the corners of the ceiling especially were deeply
stained . . .

Suddenly, he felt a brief frisson of excitement as if
there were something of vital importance in what he'd
just read, or what he'd just thought, or what he'd just
seen. But try as he might, he was unable to isolate the
elusive clue; and soon he knew it was of no use trying
any more.

It had gone.

# CHAPTER SIXTY-THREE

> Fingerprints *do* get left at crime scenes. Even the craftiest of perpetrators sometimes forget to wipe up everywhere
>
> (*Murder Ink, Incriminating Evidence*)

HER FIRST sentence, spoken with an attractive Welsh lilt, was a perfect anapaestic pentameter:

'We shall have to eat here in the kitchen, Inspector, all right?'

'Wherever, Mrs Lewis. Have no fears.'

'We've got the decorators in, see? But just go and sit down in the lounge – where I've put out some beer and a glass.' (Anapaestic hexameter.)

As he passed the dining-room, Morse stopped to look inside. The decorators had finished for the day; almost finished altogether, it seemed, for only around the main window were some paint-stained white sheets still lying across the salmon-pink carpet, with all of the furniture now pushed back into place except for a bookcase, which stood awkwardly in mid-room, a wooden step-ladder propped up against it. Clearly, though, there would be no problem about its own relocation, either, for the site of its former habitation was marked by an oblong of strawberry-red carpet to the left of the window.

Mrs Lewis was suddenly behind him.

'You like the colour?'

'Very professionally painted,' said Morse, a man with no knowledge whatsoever of professionalism in painting and decorating.

'You were looking at the carpet, though, weren't you now?' she said shrewdly. 'Only had it five years – and they told us the colours in all of their carpets would last till eternity.' (Anapaests everywhere.)

'I suppose everything fades,' said Morse. It hardly seemed a profound observation – not at the time.

'It's the sun really, see. That's why you get most of your discolouration. In the cupboards – on the lining for the cupboards – you hardly get fading at all.'

Morse moved on into the lounge where he opened a can of Cask Flow Beamish, sat contentedly back in an armchair, and was watching the *Six o'Clock News* when Lewis came in.

'You look pleased with yourself,' said Morse.

'Well, that's two more of the keys accounted for: that second Yale opens the staff entrance door at the back of the Pitt Rivers, just off South Parks Road; and that little "X 10" key – remember? – that's a Pitt Rivers key, too: it's a key to a wall-safe there that's got rows and rows of little hooks in it, with a key on each of 'em – keys to all the display-cabinets.'

Morse grunted a perfunctory 'Well done!' as he reverted his attention to the news.

Mrs Lewis produced a slightly unladylike whistle a few minutes later: 'On the table, boys!'

Morse himself had acquired one culinary skill only – that of boiling an egg; and he was not infrequently heard to boast that such a skill was not nearly so common as was generally assumed. But granted that

Morse (in his own estimation) was an exemplary *boiler* of eggs, Mrs Lewis (*omnium consensu*) was a first-class *frier*; and the milkily opaque eggs, two on each plate, set beside their mountains of thick golden chips, were a wonderful sight to behold.

As Morse jolted out some tomato sauce, Lewis picked up his knife and fork. 'You know, sir, if they ever find a body with an empty plate of eggs and chips beside it—'

'I think you mean a plate empty of eggs and chips, Lewis.'

'Well, I reckon if the fingerprints on the knife don't match any of those in our criminal library, the odds are they'll probably be mine.'

Morse nodded, picked up his own knife and fork, found (blessedly!) that the plate itself was hot – and then he froze, as if a frame on the family video had suddenly been switched to 'Pause'.

'Everything all right, sir?'

Morse made no reply.

'You – you're feeling all right, sir?' persisted a slightly anxious Lewis.

'Bloody 'ell!' whispered Morse tremulously to himself in a voice just below audial range. Then, louder: 'Bloody 'ell! You've done it again, Lewis. You've done it *again*!'

Unprecedentedly Lewis was moved to lay down both knife and fork.

'You know we had a little bet . . .' Morse's voice was vibrant now.

'When we both lost.'

'No. When to be more accurate neither of us won.

Well, I'd like to bet you something else, Lewis. I'd like to bet you that I know whose fingerprints are on that knife in Brooks's back!'

'That's more than the fingerprint-boys do.'

Morse snorted. 'I'm very tempted to report *them* for professional incompetence.' Then his voice softened. 'But I can forgive them. Yes, I can understand them.'

'I'm lost, sir, I'm afraid.'

'Shall I tell you,' asked Morse, 'whose fingerprints we found on that knife?'

His blue eyes looked so fiercely across the kitchen table that for a few moments Lewis wondered whether he was suffering from some slight stroke or seizure.

'Shall I tell you?' repeated Morse. 'You see, there's a regular procedure which you know all about; which *every* CID man knows all about. A procedure that wasn't – couldn't have been – followed in this case: that when you take fingerprints from the scene of any murder you take everybody's – including the corpse's.'

Lewis felt the blood in his veins growing cold – like the plate in front of him.

'You can't mean . . . ?'

'But I do, Lewis. That's exactly what I do mean. *The prints are those of Edward Brooks himself.*'

# CHAPTER SIXTY-FOUR

> **Gestalt** (n): chiefly *Psychol.* An integrated percep-
> tual structure or unity conceived as functionally
> more than the sum of its parts
> ( *The New Shorter Oxford Dictionary*)

As MORSE well knew, it was difficult enough to
describe to someone else such a comparatively simple
physical action as walking, say – let alone something
considerably more complicated such as serving a ball
in a game of tennis. How much more difficult then,
later that same evening, for him to answer Lewis's
direct question about the cerebral equivalent of such a
process.

'What put you on to it, sir?'

What indeed?

It was perhaps perfectly possible to describe the
mental gymnastics involved in the solving of a cryptic
crossword clue. But how did one explain those virtually
inexplicable convolutions of the mind which occasionally led to some dramatic, some penny-dropping
moment, when the answers to a whole *series* of cryptic
clues – and those not of the cruciverbalist but of the
criminological variety – combined to cast some completely new illumination on the scene? How did one
begin to explain such a sudden, almost irrational,
psychological process?

'With difficulty,' was the obvious answer; but Morse

was trying much harder than that, as he now sought to identify the main constituents which had led him to his quite extraordinary conclusion.

It was all to do with the fortuitous collocation of several memories, several recollections, which although occurring at disparate points in the case – and before – had suddenly come together in his mind, and coalesced.

There had been the report (Lewis's own) on the interview with Mrs Rodway, when he had so easily been able to re-visualize some of the smallest details of the room in which they had spoken with her, and particularly that oblong patch above the radiator where a picture had been hanging.

Then there had been (only that very evening) a second oblong, prompting memory further, when he had looked down at the pristine strawberry-red in the lounge there, and when Mrs Lewis had spoken of the unfading linings in her cupboards.

And then, working backwards (or was it forwards?) there had been the visit to the Pitt Rivers Museum, when the Administrator had pointed with pride to the fine quality of the hessian lining for her cabinet-exhibits, with its optimistic guarantee of Tithonian immortality.

Then again, a much more distant memory from his childhood of a case of cutlery, a family heirloom, where over the years each knife, each fork, each spoon, had left its own imprint, its own silhouette, on the blue plush-lining of the case. Things always left their impressions, did they not?

Or did they?

Perhaps in the Pitt Rivers cabinets, in those slightly

sombre, sunless galleries, the objects displayed there –
the artefacts, the relics from the past – were leaving
only very faint impressions, like the utensils in Mrs
Lewis's kitchen-cupboards.

No impressions at all, possibly . . .

Then, and above all, the discrepancy between the
pathologist's report on the knife used to murder
McClure, and the statement given by the Raysons about
the knife found in their own front garden: the 'blade
not really sharp', in the former; the 'blade in no
immediate need of sharpening', in the latter. Not a big
discrepancy, perhaps; but a hugely significant one – and
one which should never, never have passed unnoticed.

Yes, all the constituents were there: separate, though,
and unsynthesized – waiting for a catalyst.

Lewis!

Lewis the Catalyst.

For it was Lewis who had returned from his p.m.
investigations with the information that one of the
small keys found in Brooks's pocket fitted a wall-safe in
the museum; in which, in turn, were to be found row
upon row of other keys, including the key to Cabinet
52. It was Lewis, too, who so innocently had asserted, as
he picked up a knife with which to eat his meal, that
his own fingerprints would soon be found thereon . . .

And whither had such ratiocination finally led the
Chief Inspector, as, like Abraham, he had made his way
forth from his tent in the desert knowing not whither
he went? To that strangest of all conclusions: that on
Wednesday, 7 September, from Cabinet 52 in the Pitt
Rivers Museum in Oxford – *nothing whatsoever had been
stolen.*

# CHAPTER SIXTY-FIVE

Behold, I shew you a mystery
(ST PAUL, I *Corinthians*, ch. 15, v. 51)

A COUNCIL of war was called in Caesar's tent two days later, on Sunday, 2 October, with three other officers joining Chief Superintendent Strange in the latter's Kidlington HQ office at 10 a.m.: Chief Inspector Morse, Chief Inspector Phillotson, and Sergeant Lewis. Morse, invited to put a case for a dramatic intensification of enquiries, for a series of warrants, and for a small cohort of forensic specialists, did so with complete conviction.

He knew now (or so he claimed) what had been the circumstances of each of the murders, those of McClure and Brooks; and he would, with his colleagues' permission, give an account of those circumstances, not seeking to dwell on motives (not for the present) but on methods – on *modi operandi*.

Strange now listened, occasionally nodding, occasionally lifting his eyebrows in apparent incredulity, to the burden of Morse's reconstructions.

McClure lived on a staircase where Brooks was the scout. The latter had gained access to drugs and became a supplier to several undergraduates, one of whom, Matthew Rodway, had become very friendly with

McClure – probably not a homosexual relationship, though – before committing suicide in tragic and semi-suspicious circumstances. As a result of this, McClure had insisted that Brooks resign from his job; but agreed that he, McClure, would not report the matter to the Dean, and would even provide a job-testimonial, provided that Brooks forswore his dealings in drugs.

Feelings between the two men were bitter.

Things settled down, though.

Then it came to McClure's notice that Brooks had *not* finished with his drug-dealing after all; that some of the junkies were still in touch with him. A furious McClure threatened disclosure to Brooks's new employers and to the police, and a meeting between the two was arranged (or not arranged – how could one know?). Certain it was, however, that Brooks went to visit McClure. And murdered him.

On the way home, on his bicycle, Brooks suddenly became aware that he was seriously ill. He managed to get as far as St Giles', but could get no further. He left his bicycle outside St Mary Mags, without even bothering to lock it, perhaps, and covering himself as best he could, got a taxi from the rank there up to East Oxford – and very soon got an ambulance up to the JR2, minus the bloodstained clothing which his wife disposed of.

One thing above all must have haunted Brooks's mind once he knew he would recover from his heart attack: he was still in possession of the knife he'd used to murder McClure, because whatever happened *he couldn't throw it away*. He ordered his wife to lock it up somewhere, probably in the box in his bedroom, and she did as he asked, surely having enough common sense to handle the knife – both then and later – with the greatest delicacy, pretty certainly wearing the glove she'd taken to using to protect her injured right hand. She was terrified – certainly at that point – of incurring the anger of a fearsomely cruel man who had physically maltreated her on several occasions, and who in earlier years had probably abused his step-daughter – the latter now putting in an appearance after many moons away from home, no doubt after somehow learning of Brooks's illness.

Brenda Brooks had an ally.

Two allies, in fact: because we now become increasingly aware of the unusually strong bond of friendship and affection between her and the woman for whom she cleaned, Mrs Julia Stevens, a schoolma'am who, although this fact has only recently become known to us, was suffering from an inoperable brain-tumour.

A plot was hatched, an extraordinarily clever plot, designed to throw the police on to the wrong track; a plot which succeeded in so doing.

'Let me explain.'

'At last,' mumbled Strange.

Brenda Brooks took Mrs Stevens wholly into her confidence, with both now knowing perfectly well not only who had murdered McClure but also exactly where the knife had come from – and why Brooks was unable to get rid of it.

On the Saturday before McClure's murder, the very last thing in the afternoon, Brooks had taken the knife from Cabinet 52 in the Pitt Rivers Museum, fully intending to replace it the very first thing on the following Monday morning, when he planned to turn up for work half an hour or so early and to restore it to its position amongst the fifty-odd other knives there. Nobody would have missed it; nobody *could* have missed it, since the museum was closed on Sundays.

'Why—?' Strange had begun. But Morse had anticipated the question.

Why Brooks should have acted in such a devious way, or whether he had taken the knife with the deliberate intention of committing murder, it was now only possible to guess. The only slight clue (thus far) was that one of the few books found in the Brooks's virtually illiterate household was a library copy of *The Innocence of Father Brown*, in which Chesterton suggested a battlefield as the safest place to conceal a corpse ... with the possible implication that a cabinet of weapons might be the safest place to conceal a knife.

But Brooks couldn't restore the knife. Not yet.

His great hope was that no one would notice its absence. *And no one did.* Apart from the attendant circumstance of so many other knives, one further factor was greatly in his favour: the cabinet had been recently re-lined, and there was no outwardly physical sign that any object could be missing. The normal routine, when anything was taken out, was for a printed white card – 'Temporarily Removed' – to be inserted over the space left vacant. But there *was* no space left vacant, since Brooks had only to move two or three other knives along a little to effect a balanced row of exhibits. And as day followed day, no one in fact noticed that anything at all was missing.

But, apart from Brooks, two other persons now knew of all this.

One of whom was Julia Stevens.

And the beautifully clever idea was born: if ... if Brooks were to be murdered with the very same knife which he himself had stolen ...

Ah, yes!

Two things only were required.

First, a knife, a different but *wholly* similar knife, *would have to be planted* – somewhere in, or near, Daventry Avenue. For when it was found – as surely sooner or later it would be – the police, with a little luck, would discover that it had been taken from one of the Brooks's kitchen drawers.

Second, the cabinet from which the actual murder weapon had been taken ('Cabinet 52' was clearly marked on the tag) *would have to be broken into* so that its contents would inevitably be checked. For then, and then only, would the pedigree of the missing knife become known.

Someone was therefore delegated to break open that cabinet, to ruffle around a few of the knives there – exactly the *opposite* of what Brooks had done earlier – and the deception was launched. The 'theft' was duly spotted, and reported; the missing knife was fairly quickly identified; and, above all, the crucial alibis were established.

How so?

Because of the wholly incontestable fact that any person found murdered by means of that stolen knife must have been murdered *after that knife was stolen*.

But the truth was that Brooks was murdered *before* the knife was stolen – probably murdered the day before, since the two women lied about seeing him alive on the afternoon when they set off with the school-party for Stratford.

The only thing now calling for some sort of explanation was the curious circumstance of Brooks's body being so elaborately wrapped up in plastic, then wrapped up again in a brown carpet, before being dumped into the Isis, just upstream from Donnington Bridge, almost certainly driven there in the boot of a car. Mrs Stevens' car? Most probably, since she was the only one of them to own such a means of transport.

Well (as Morse saw it) the reason was fairly obvious: if and when (and *when* rather than if) the body was found, such wrapping would ensure one vital thing: that the knife would still be found with the body – still be found *in* the body, it could be hoped. There would be no danger of it being lost; and thereby no danger that the alibis so cunningly, so painstakingly, devised would be discounted or destroyed.

'So you see,' finished Detective Chief Inspector Morse, 'the two women we assumed could never have murdered Brooks have overnight moved up to the top of the list.' He looked up with a fairly self-satisfied smile to Chief Superintendent Strange. 'And with your permission, sir, we shall go ahead immediately, apply for a couple of search warrants—'

'Why only two warrants?' asked Detective Chief Inspector Phillotson.

# CHAPTER SIXTY-SIX

The mind is its own place, and in itself
Can make a heaven of hell, a hell of heaven
(JOHN MILTON, *Paradise Lost*, Book 1)

THE FOLLOWING day, a call was put through to Morse ('Must be Morse') from Mr Basil Shepstone, Senior Neurologist at Oxford's Churchill Hospital; and twenty minutes later the two men were seated together in Shepstone's consulting-room.

Mrs Julia Stevens (Morse learned) had been admitted at midday, having earlier been discovered unconscious at the side of her bed by her cleaning-lady. Some speedy deterioration in her mental condition had been expected; but the dramatic (the literal) collapse in her physical condition had come as some surprise. A recent biopsy (Morse learned) had confirmed *glioblastoma multiforma*, a fast-growing tumour of the neuroglia in the brain: wholly malignant, sadly inoperable, rapidly fatal.

When Julia had been admitted, it was immediately apparent that, somewhere on the brain, pressure had become intolerably severe: she had been painfully sick again in the ambulance; clearly she was experiencing some considerable difficulty with both sight and speech; showing signs too of spatial disorientation. Yet somehow she had managed to make it clear that she wished to speak to the policeman Morse.

Twice during the early afternoon (Shepstone reported), her behaviour had grown disturbingly aggressive, especially towards one of the young nurses trying to administer medication. But that sort of behaviour – often involving some fairly fundamental personality change – was almost inevitable with such a tumour.

'Had you noticed any "personality change" before?' asked Morse.

Shepstone hesitated. 'Yes, perhaps so. I think ... well, let's put it this way. The commonest symptom would be a general loss of inhibition, if you know what I mean.'

'I don't think I do.'

'Well, I mean one obvious thing is she probably wouldn't be over-worried about the reactions and opinions of other people – other professional colleagues, in her case. Let's say she'd be more willing than usual to speak her mind in a staff-meeting, perhaps. I don't think she was ever *too* shy a person; but like most of us she'd probably always felt a bit diffident – a bit insecure – about life and . . . and things.'

'She's an attractive woman, isn't she?'

Shepstone looked across at Morse keenly.

'I know what you're thinking. And the answer's probably "yes". I rather think that if over these past few months someone had asked . . . to go to bed with her . . .'

'When you say "someone" – you mean some *man*?'

'I think I do, yes.'

'And you say she's been a bit violent today.'

'Aggressive, certainly.'

Morse nodded.

'It's really,' continued Shepstone, 'the unexpected-ness rather than the nature of behaviour that always sticks out in these cases. I remember at the Radcliffe Infirmary, for example, a very strait-laced old dear with a similar tumour getting out of her bed one night and dancing naked in the fountain out the front there.'

'But *she* isn't a strait-laced old dear,' said Morse slowly.

'Oh, no,' replied the sad-eyed Consultant. 'Oh, no.'

For a while, when Julia had regained some measure of her senses in the hospital, she knew that she was still at home in her own bed, really. It was just that someone was trying to confuse her, because the walls of her bedroom were no longer that soothing shade of green, but this harsher, crueller white.

Everything was white.

Everyone was wearing white . . .

But Julia felt more relaxed now.

The worry at the beginning had been her complete disorientation: about the time of day, the day, the month – the year, even. And then, just as the white-coated girl was trying to talk to her, she'd felt a terrible sense of panic as she realized that she was unaware of *who she was.*

Things were better now, though; one by one, things were clicking into place; and some knowledge of her-self, of her life, was slowly surfacing, with the wonderful bonus that the dull, debilitating headache she'd lived with for so many months was gone. Completely gone.

She knew the words she wanted to say – about seeing

Morse; or at least her *mind* knew. Yet she was aware that those words had homodyned little, if at all, with the words she'd actually used:

'One thousand and one, one thousand and two . . .'

But she could write.

How could that be?

If she couldn't speak?

No matter.

She could write.


As he looked down at her, Morse realized that even in her terminal illness Julia Stevens would ever be an attractive woman; and he placed a hand lightly on her right arm as she lay in her short-sleeved nightdress, and smiled at her. And she smiled back, but tightly, for she was willing herself to make him understand what so desperately she wished to tell him.

At the scene of the terrible murder that had taken place in Brenda's front room, when she, Julia, had stood there, helpless at first, a spectator of a deed already done, she had vowed, if ever need arose, to take all guilt upon herself. And the words were in her mind: words that were all untrue, but words that were ready to be spoken. She had only to repeat repeat *repeat* them to herself: 'I murdered him I murdered him *I* murdered him . . .' And now she looked up at Morse and forced her mouth to speak those self-same words:

'One thousand and three, one thousand and four, one thousand and five . . .'

Aware, it seemed, even as she spoke, of her calamitous shortcomings, she looked around her with frenzied exasperation as she sought to find the pencil with which earlier she'd managed to write down 'MORSE'. Her right arm flailed about her wildly, knocking over a glass of orange juice on the bedside table, and tears of frustration sprang in her eyes.

Suddenly three nurses, all in white, were at her side, two of them seeking to hold her still as the third administered a further sedative. And Morse, who had intended to plant a tender kiss upon the Titian hair, was hurriedly ushered away.

# CHAPTER SIXTY-SEVEN

We can prove whatever we want to; the only real
difficulty is to know what we want to prove
(EMILE CHARTIER, *Système des beaux arts*)

EVENTS WERE now moving quickly towards their close.
There was much that was wanting to be found – was
found – although Lewis was not alone in wondering
exactly what Morse himself wanted to be found. Certainly one or two minor surprises were still in store; but
in essence it was only the corroborative, substantiating
detail that remained to be gleaned – was gleaned – by
the enquiry team from their painstaking forensic investigations, and from one or two further painful
encounters.

Morse was reading a story when just after 3 p.m. on
Tuesday, 4 October, Lewis returned from the JR2 where
he had interviewed a rapidly improving Costyn – to
whom, as it happened, he had taken an instant dislike,
just as earlier in the case Morse had felt an instinctive
antipathy towards Ms Smith.

Lewis had learned nothing of any substance. About
the ram-raid, Costyn had been perkily co-operative,
partly no doubt because he had little option in the
matter. But about any (surely most probable?) visit to
the Pitt Rivers Museum; about his relations (relationship?) with Mrs Stevens; about any (possible?) knowl-

edge of, implication in, co-operation with, the murder of Edward Brooks, Costyn had been cockily dismissive.

He had nothing to say.

How could he have anything to say?

He knew nothing.

If Lewis was ninety-five per cent convinced that Costyn was lying, he had been one hundred per cent convinced that Ashley Davies, whom he'd interviewed the day before, could never have been responsible for the prising open of Cabinet 52. In fact Davies *had* been in Oxford that afternoon; and for some considerable while, since between 3.45 p.m. and 4.45 p.m. he had been sitting in the chair of Mr J. Balaguer-Morris, a distinguished and unimpeachable dental-surgeon practising in Summertown.

*Quod erat demonstrandum.*

Lewis sensed therefore (as he knew Morse did) that the two young men had probably always been peripheral to the crime in any case. But *someone* had gone along to the Pitt Rivers; *someone's* services could well have been needed for the disposal of the body in the Isis. For although Brooks had not been a heavy man, it would have been quite extraordinarily difficult for one woman to have coped alone; rather easier for two, certainly; and perhaps not all that difficult for three of them. Yet the help of a strong young man would have been a godsend, surely?

With the Magistrates finding no objections, the three search warrants had been immediately authorized, and the spotlight was now refocusing, ever more closely, on the three women in the case:

Brenda Brooks
Julia Stevens
Eleanor Smith . . .

The previous afternoon, great activity at the Brooks's residence had proved dramatically productive. At the back of the house, one of the small keys from Lewis's bunch had provided immediate, unforced access to the garden shed. No transparent plastic bags were found there; nor any damning snippet of dark green garden-twine like that which had secured the bundle of the corpse. Yet something *had* been found there: fibres of a brown material which looked most suspiciously similar – which later proved to be identical – to the carpeting that had covered the body of Edward Brooks.

Brenda Brooks, therefore, had been taken in for questioning the previous evening, on two separate occasions being politely reminded that anything she said might be taken down in writing and used as evidence. But there seemed hardly any valid reason for even one such caution, since from the very start she had appeared too shocked to say anything at all. Later in the evening she had been released on police bail, having been formally charged with conspiracy to murder. As Morse saw things the decision to grant bail had been wholly correct. There was surely little merit in pressing for custody, since it was difficult to envisage that gentle little lady, once freed, indulging in any orgy of murder in the area of the Thames Valley Police Authority.

In any case, Morse liked Mrs Brooks.

Just as he liked Mrs Stevens – in whose garage earlier

that same day a forensic team had made an equally dramatic finding, when they had examined the ancient Volvo, *in situ*, and discovered, in the boot, fibres of a brown material which looked most suspiciously similar – which later proved to be identical – to the carpeting that had covered the body of Edward Brooks . . .

Morse had nodded to himself with satisfaction on receiving each of these reports. So careful, so clever, they'd been – the two women! Yet even the cleverest of criminals couldn't think of everything: they all made that one little mistake, sooner or later; and he should be glad of that.

He *was* glad.

He himself had taken temporary possession of the long-overdue library book found in the Brooks's bedroom, noticing with some self-congratulation that the tops of two pages in the story entitled 'The Broken Sword' had been dog-eared. By Brooks? Were the pages worth testing for fingerprints? No. Far too fanciful a notion. But Morse told himself that he would re-read the story once he got the chance; and indeed his eye had already caught some of the lines he remembered so vividly from his youth:

Where does a man kick a pebble? On the beach.
Where does a wise man hide a leaf? In the forest . . .

Yes. Things were progressing well – and quickly.

There was that third search warrant, of course: one that had been granted, though not yet served.

The one to be served on Ms Smith . . .

Of whom, as it happened, Morse had dreamed the

previous night – most disturbingly. He had watched her closely (how on earth?) as semi-dressed in a plunging Versace creation she had exhibited herself erotically to some lecherous Yuppie in the back of a BMW. And when Morse had awoken, he had felt bitterly angry with her; and sick; and heartachingly jealous.

He had known better nights; known better dreams.

Yet life is a strange affair; and only ten minutes after Lewis had returned that Tuesday afternoon Morse received a call from Reception which quickened his heart-beat considerably.

# CHAPTER SIXTY-EIGHT

She turned away, but with the autumn weather
Compelled my imagination many days,
Many days and many hours
           (T. S. ELIOT, *La Figlia Che Piange*)

SHE CLOSED the passenger-seat door, asking the man to wait there, in the slip-road, for ten minutes – no longer; then to drive in and pick her up.

She walked quite briskly past the blue sign, with its white lettering, 'Thames Valley Police HQ'; then up the longish gradient to the brick-and-concrete building.

At Reception she quickly made her errand clear.

'Is he expecting you, Miss?' asked the man seated there.

'No.'

'Can I ask what it's in connection with?'

'A murder.'

The grey-haired man looked up at her with some curiosity. He thought he might have seen her before; then decided that he hadn't. And rang Morse.

'Let her in, Bill. I'll be down to collect her in a couple of minutes.'

After entering her name neatly in the Visitors' Log, Bill pressed the mechanism that opened the door to the main building. She was carrying a small package, some 5 inches by 3 inches, and he decided to keep a precautionary eye on her. Normally he would not have let her through without some sort of check. But he'd always been encouraged to use his discretion, and in truth she looked more like a potential traveller than a potential terrorist. And Chief Inspector Morse had sounded happy enough.

He pointed the way. 'If you just go and sit and wait there, Miss . . . ?'

So Ellie Smith walked over the darkly marbled floor to a small, square waiting-area, carpeted in blue, with matching chairs set against the walls. She sat down and looked around her. Many notices were displayed there, of the 'Watch Out', 'Burglars Beware' variety; and photographs of a police car splashing through floods, and a friendly bobby talking to a farmer's wife in a local village; and just opposite her a large map . . .

But her observations ceased there.

To her left was a flight of white-marbled stairs, down which the white-haired Morse was coming towards her.

'Good to see you. Come along up.'

'No, I can't stay. I've got a car waiting.'

'But we can take you home. *I* can take you home.'

'No. I'm . . . I'm sorry.'

'Why have you come?' asked Morse quietly, seating himself beside her.

'You've had Mum in. She told me all about it. She's on bail, isn't she? And I just wondered where it all leaves her – and me, for that matter?'

Morse spoke gently. 'Your mother has been charged in connection with the murder of your step-father. Please understand that for the present—'

'She told me you might be bringing *me* in – is that right?'

'Look! We can't really talk here. Please come up—'

She shook her head. 'Not unless you're arresting me. Anyway, I don't trust myself in that office of yours. Remember?'

'Look, about your mother. You'll have to face the fact – just like we have to – that . . . that it seems very likely at the minute that your mother was involved in some way in the murder of your step-father.' Morse had chosen his hesitant words carefully.

'All right. If you're not going to tell me, never mind.'

She stood up; and Morse stood up beside her. She held out the small parcel she had been carrying in her right hand and offered it to him.

'For you,' she said simply.

'What is it?'

'Promise me one thing?'

'If I can.'

'You won't open it till you get home tonight.'

'If you say so.'

Morse suddenly felt very moved; felt very lost, very helpless, very upset.

'Well – that's it then. That's all I came for . . . really.'

'I'll ring you when I've opened it, I promise.'

'Only when you get home.'

'Only when I get home.'

'You've got a note of my number, haven't you?'

'I have it by heart.'

'I have to go. Hope you'll like it.' She managed to speak the words; but only just as she picked up St Anthony and fondled him between the thumb and forefinger of her left hand. And almost, for a moment or two, as they stood there, it was as if they might embrace; but the Assistant Chief Constable suddenly came through Reception, raising his hand to Morse in friendly greeting.

She turned away; and left.

As she stepped out of the building, a red BMW was beside her immediately; and she got in, casting one lingering look behind her as she locked her safety-belt.


'I was rather hoping you'd bring her up, sir. She's getting a bit of a smasher, that one, don't you think?'

But Morse, reclosing the door quietly behind him, made no reply. Suddenly his life seemed joyless and desolate.

'Coffee, sir?' asked Lewis in a low voice, perhaps understanding many things.

Morse nodded.

After Lewis was gone, he didn't wait.

He couldn't wait.

Inside the bluebell-patterned wrapping-paper was a small, silver, delicately curving hip-flask.

Oh God!

The letter enclosed with it bore no salutation:


My mum rung me up and told me everything,
but she never killed him. I know that better than
anybody because I killed him.

I'm not much cop at writing but I wish we
could have gone out for shampers together
again. That was the happiest night of my life,
because for some cockeyed reason I loved you
with all the love I've got. I hope you like the little

present. I wish I could finish this letter in the way
I'd like to but I can't quite think of the right
words, you know I'm trying though. If only you'd
known how much I wanted you to kiss me in the
taxi so some few kisses now from me

xxxx Ellie xxxx


Unmanned with anguish, Morse turned away as
Lewis came back with the coffee, folded the letter
carefully, and put it in a drawer of his desk.

Neither man spoke.

Then Morse opened the drawer, took out the letter,
and passed it over to Lewis.

The silence persisted long after Lewis had read it.

Finally Morse got to his feet. 'If I ever see her again,
Lewis, I shall have to tell her that "rang" is the more
correct form of the past tense of the verb "to ring",
when used transitively.'

'I don't think she'd mind very much what you told
her,' said Lewis very quietly.

Morse said nothing.

'Mind if I have a look at the present, sir?'

Morse passed over the hip-flask.

'Remember that crossword clue, Lewis? "Kick in the
pants?" – three-hyphen-five?'

Lewis nodded and smiled sadly.

Hip-flask.

# CHAPTER SIXTY-NINE

Amongst the tribes of Central Australia, every person has, besides a personal name which is in common use, a secret name which was bestowed upon him or her soon after birth, and which is known to none but the fully initiated

(JAMES FRAZER, *The Golden Bough*)

'YOU MUST admit what a trusting, stupid brain I've got, Lewis. "Don't open it till you get home," she said, and I just thought that . . .'

'*Numquam animus,* sir, as you tell me the ancient Romans used to say.'

'We'd better get along there.'

'You think she's done a bunk?'

'Sure she has.'

'With Davies?'

'Has Davies got a red BMW?'

'Not unless he's changed his car.'

'I wonder if it's that randy sod from Reading. Where's his card?'

'The traffic boys'll be able to tell us in a couple of ticks.'

'Can't wait that long.'

He found the card, the number – and dialled, informing the woman who answered that he was ringing from police HQ about a stolen car, a red BMW, and he was just checking to make sure . . .

Mr Williamson was out, Morse learned. But there was no need to worry. He *did* have a red BMW all right, but it hadn't been stolen. In fact, she'd seen him get into it earlier that afternoon. Going to Oxford, he'd said.

Half an hour later, in Princess Street, it became clear that Ellie Smith had decamped in considerable haste. In her bed-sit-cum-bathroom there had been little enough accommodation for many possessions anyway; yet much had been left behind: the bigger items (perforce) – fridge, TV, record player, microwave; a selection of clothing and shoes, ranging from the sedate to the sensational; pictures and posters by the score, including a life-sized technicolour photograph of Marilyn Monroe, a framed painting by Paul Klee, and (also framed) a fading Diploma from East Oxford Senior School, Prize for Art, awarded to Kay Eleanor Brooks, signed by C. P. Taylor (Head), and dated July 1983.

'Not much here in the drawers, sir. An Appointments' Book, though, stuck at the back.'

'Which I am not particularly anxious to see,' said Morse, sitting himself down on the bed.

'You know – if you don't mind me saying so, sir – it was a bit cruel, wasn't it? Her leaving her mum for all those years and not really getting in touch with her again until—'

He broke off.

'Sir!'

Morse looked up.

'There's a telephone number here for that Tuesday the sixth, with something written after it: "GL" – and what looks like the figure "1".'

Morse got up, and went to look over Lewis's shoulder. 'It could be a lower-case letter "l".'

'Shall I give the number a go?'

Morse shrugged his shoulders disinterestedly. 'Please yourself.'

Lewis dialled the number, and a pleasing, clear Welsh voice answered, with an obviously well-practised formula:

'Gareth Llewellyn-Jones. Can I 'elp you?'

'Sergeant Lewis, Thames Valley Police, sir. We're investigating a murder, and think you might be able to help us confirm one or two things.'

'My goodness me! Well, I can't really, not for the moment, like. I'm in the middle of a tutorial, see?'

'Can you give me a time when you *will* be free, sir?'

'Could be important,' said Lewis, after putting down the phone. 'If she was . . . out all night—'

'Don't you mean "in" all night?' said Morse bitterly. 'In bed with some cock-happy client of hers – that's what you mean, isn't it? So stop being so bloody mealy-mouthed, man.'

Lewis counted up to seven. 'Well, if she *was*, she couldn't have had too much of a hand in things with Brooks.'

'Of course she did!' snapped Morse. 'I don't believe her though when she says she murdered him – she's just trying to shield her mother, that's all – because it was her mother who murdered him.'

'Isn't it usually the other way round, though?'

'What do you mean?'

'Isn't it usually mums who try to shield their kids?'

The word 'kid' did to Morse what 'scenario' did to

Ellie Smith; and he was about to remonstrate – when suddenly he clapped a cupped right hand hard over his forehead.

'What year did the Brooks marry?'

'Can't remember exactly. Twelve years ago, was it? We can soon check.'

'What time are you seeing Armstrong-Jones?'

'Llewellyn-Jones, sir. Half-past eight. After he's had dinner in Hall.'

'Good. I'm glad you're not letting our own enquiries interfere with his college routine.'

'It wasn't like that—'

'Come on, Lewis!' Morse pointed to the Diploma. 'When you said Ellie Smith must have been a bit cruel to run away from her mother, you were right, in a way. But she didn't run away from her mother at all, Lewis. She ran away from her *father*, her natural father.'

'But she could just have changed her name, surely?'

'Nonsense!'

Morse consulted the directory lying beside the phone: only one C. P. Taylor, with an Abingdon Road address. He rang the number, and learned, yes indeed, that he was speaking to the Former Head of East Oxford Senior School, who would willingly help if he could. That same evening? Why not?

After Lewis had dropped Morse ('I'll find my own way home') at a rather elegant semi-detached property in the Abingdon Road, he himself proceeded to Lonsdale

College, where his mission was quietly and quickly productive.

Llewellyn-Jones freely admitted that he'd met the young woman he'd always known as 'Kay' fairly regularly for sexual purposes: never in his college rooms; more often than not in a hotel; and twice in her own little place – as was the case on Tuesday, 6 September, when he'd spent the evening with her, and would have spent longer but for a phone-call – half-past nine? quarter-to ten? – which had galvanized her into panicky activity. *She'd* have to leave: *he'd* have to leave. Obviously some sort of emergency; but he knew no more, except perhaps that he thought the voice on the phone was that of a woman.

Lewis thanked the dark, dapper little Welshman, and assured him that the information given would of course be treated with the utmost confidentiality.

But Gareth Llewellyn-Jones appeared little troubled:

'I'm a bachelor, Sergeant, see? And I just loved being with her, that's all. In fact, I could've ... But I don't think she's the sort of woman who could ever really fall arse-orver-tit for any man – certainly not for me.'

He smiled, shook his head, and bade farewell to Lewis from the Porters' Lodge.

As Lewis drove up to his home in Headington, he realized that Morse had almost certainly been right about Ellie Smith's involvement in the murder.

With a tumbler of most welcome Scotch beside him, Morse sat back to listen.

'Kay Brooks? Oh yes, I remember *her*,' said the ex-headmaster, a thin, mildly drooping man in his early seventies. 'Who wouldn't . . . ?'

Aged eleven, she'd started at his school as a lively, slightly devil-may-care lass, with long dark hair and a sweet if somewhat cheeky sort of smile. Bright – well above average; and very good at sketching, painting, design, that type of thing. But . . . well, something must have gone a bit sour somewhere. By her mid-teens, she'd become a real handful: playing hookey, surly, inattentive, idle, a bit cruel, perhaps. Trouble at home, like as not? But no one knew. Kay's mother had come along to see him a couple of times but—

Morse interrupted:

'That's really what I've come about, sir. It may not be important, but I rather think you probably mean her *step*-mother, don't you?'

'Pardon?' Taylor looked as if he had mis-heard.

'You see, I think Brooks, Edward Brooks, the man fished out of the Isis, could well have been her real father, not her *step*-father.'

'Nonsense!' (The second time the word had been used in the past half-hour.) 'I can understand what you're thinking, Inspector; but you're wrong. She *changed* her name when her mother got remarried; changed it to her mother's new name. You see, I knew her, knew her mother, well before then.'

Morse looked puzzled. 'Is that sort of thing usual?'

Taylor smiled. 'Depends, doesn't it? Some people would give an arm and a leg to change their names. Take me, for instance. My old mum and dad – bless their hearts but . . . you know what they christened me? "Cecil Paul". Would you credit it? I was "Cess-pool" before I'd been at school a fortnight. You know the sort of thing I mean?'

Oh, yes, Morse knew exactly the sort of thing he meant.

'And I'm afraid,' continued Taylor, 'that Kay got teased pretty mercilessly about her name – about her surname, that is. So it was only natural, really, that when the opportunity arose to change it . . .'

'What *was* her surname?' asked Morse.

Taylor told him.

Oh dear!

Poor Ellie!

After gladly becoming Eleanor 'Brooks' on her mother's remarriage, so very soon, it seemed, had she come to detest her newly-adopted name. And when she had left home, she had plumped for 'Smith' – a good, common-stock, unexceptionable sort of name that could cause her pain no more.

Yes, Morse knew all about being teased because of a name – in his own case a Christian name. And he felt so close to Ellie Smith at that moment, so very caring towards her, that he would have sacrificed almost anything in the world to find her there, waiting for him, when he got back home.


'Ellie Morse'?

'*Eleanor* Morse'?

Difficult to decide.

But gladly would Morse have settled for either as he walked slowly up into Cornmarket, where he stood waiting twenty-five minutes for a bus to take him up to his bachelor flat in North Oxford.

# CHAPTER SEVENTY

Then grief forever after; because forever after
nothing less would ever do
(J. G. F. POTTER, *Anything to Declare?*)

THE SUBJECT of each of these last two enquiries, the
young woman who has been known (principally) in
these pages as Ellie Smith, had hurriedly wiped her
eyes and for a considerable time said nothing after
getting into Mike Williamson's car. Her thoughts were
temporarily concentrated not so much on Morse himself as on what she could have told him; or rather on
what she could never have told him . . .

It had been that terrible Tuesday night, when her
mother had phoned, pleading in such deep anguish for
her daughter's help; when she'd got rid of that quite
likable cock-happy little Welshman; and finally reached
the house – a full five minutes before that other woman
had arrived in a car – to find her mother standing like
a zombie in the entrance hall, continuously massaging
a gloved right hand with her left, as if she had inflicted
upon it some recent and agonizing injury; and when,
after going into the kitchen, she'd looked down on her
step-father lying prone on the lino there, a strange-
looking, wooden-handled knife stuck – so accurately it
had seemed to her – halfway between the shoulder-
blades. Strangely enough, there hadn't been too much

blood. Perhaps he'd never had all that much blood in him. Not warm blood, anyway.

Then the red-headed woman had arrived, and taken over – so coolly competent she'd been, so organized. It was as if the plot of the drama had already been written, for clearly the appropriate props had been duly prepared, waiting only to be fetched from the back-garden shed. Just the *timing*, it appeared, had gone wrong, as if a final rehearsal had suddenly turned into a first-night performance. And it was her mother surely who'd been responsible for that: jumping the starting-gate and seizing the reins in her own hands – her own hand, rather (singular).

Then, ten minutes later, following a rapidly spoken telephone conversation, the young man had appeared, to whom the red-headed woman had spoken in hushed tones in the hallway; a young man whom, oddly enough, she knew by sight, since the two of them had attended the same Martial Arts classes together. But she said nothing to him. Nor he to her. Indeed he seemed hardly aware of her presence as he began to manoeuvre the awkward corpse into its polythene winding sheet – sheets, rather (plural).

She'd even found herself remembering his name.

Kevin something . . .


As the car turned right from Park End Street into the railway station, Ellie's mind jerked back to the present, aware that Williamson's left hand had crept above the top of her suspendered right-stocking. But she would always be able to handle people like Williamson, who now reminded her of their proposed agreement as he humped the two large suitcases from the boot.

'You ring me, like you said, OK?'

Ellie nodded, adding a verbal gloss to her unspoken promise as she took his business card from her handbag and mechanically recited the telephone number.

'Right, then. And don't forget we can do real business with a body like yours, kid.'

It would have been a nice gesture if he had offered to carry her cases up the steps to the automatic doors; or even as far as the ticket window. But he didn't; and of that she was glad. Had he done so she would probably have felt obliged to buy a ticket for Paddington, for she had spoken to him vaguely of 'friends in London'. As it was, once he had driven off, she bought a single ticket to Liverpool, and with aching arms crossed over the footbridge to Platform Two – where she stood for twenty-five minutes, forgetting for a while the future plight of her mother; forgetting the minor role she herself had played in the murder of a man she had learned to hate; yet remembering again now, as she fingered the gold pendant, the man who had given it to her, the man for whom she would have sacrificed anything. If only he could have loved her.

# EPILOGUE

Life is a progress from want to want, not from
enjoyment to enjoyment
                    (SAMUEL JOHNSON, in Boswell's *The Life of
                                            Samuel Johnson*)

IT IS now Friday, 28 October 1994, the Feast of St
Simon and St Jude, and this chronicle has to be
concluded, with brief space only remaining to record a
few marginal notes on some of the characters who
played their roles in these pages.

On Thursday, 20 October, Mrs Brenda Brooks was
re-arrested, additionally charged with the murder of
her husband, Mr Edward Brooks, and remanded in
custody at Holloway Prison. From which institution,
four days later, she was granted temporary leave of
(escorted) absence to attend a midday funeral service
at the Oxford Crematorium, where many teachers from
the Proctor Memorial School were squeezed into the
small chapel there, together with a few relatives, and a
few friends – though the couple from California were
unable to make the journey at such short notice.

Two others completed (almost completed) the sad-
dened congregation: the facially scarred Kevin Costyn
and a pale-looking Chief Inspector Morse, neither of
whom participated in (what seemed to the latter) the
banal revision of Archbishop Cranmer's noble words
for the solemn service of the dead.

And one other mourner: a dark-suited, prosperous-looking, middle-aged man, who went last of all into the chapel; and sat down, as it happened, next to Morse, on the back row of the left-hand side of the aisle. A minute earlier, wholly unobserved, he had added his own floral tribute to the many others laid out in the Garden of Remembrance there: a wreath of white lilies. The card attached bore no salutation, no valediction – just the same words that Julia Stevens had read on a birthday card some eighteen months before:

'Don't forget we had some good times too!'

St Giles's (enforced) new home is some little way from Oxford. Yet that aristocratic cat is not displeased with his environment – particularly with the wildlife opportunities offered in the open field just behind Number 22, Kingfisher Way, Bicester; and with the soft, beige leather settee on which he now sleeps for long stretches of the day until his attractive young mistress returns from her duties at the Oxford University Press.

Janis Lawrence, only temporarily she trusts, is now unemployed once more; and her familiar, exasperated 'Stop frowin' them bricks, Jason!' is still often to be heard in the streets of the Cutteslowe Estate.

On the whole, Mrs Lewis is well pleased with the work of the decorators; and extremely pleased with her husband's present to her of a new set of five black-handled knives, including one (Number 4) whose blade, unusually broad at its base, curves to a dangerous looking point.

The former dwelling of Dr Felix McClure has now been on the market for two weeks, its lounge completely re-carpeted. But Mrs (Miss?) Laura Wynne-Wilson, though maintaining a dedicated vigil behind her carefully parted lace curtains, has yet to spot any prospective client arriving to view the property. And Messrs Adkinson, renowned for their meticulous room-measurements, are a little worried that the vicious murder enacted in Number 6 has, quite understandably, postponed the prospect of any immediate purchase.

And what of Morse?

His proposed lunchtime meeting with Strange, with a view to launching a twin assault on the complexities of form-filling, has not yet been arranged; and Morse is not pursuing the matter with any sense of great urgency, since he is undecided about the 'sooner or later' of his own eventual retirement, and curiously unsettled about the immediate months ahead of him . . .

He knew, of course, that it would be utterly hopeless to ring Ellie Smith, and therefore he rang her number only three times in the week following her disappearance; only twice in the second week. After all, as Morse recalled from his believing days, Hope is one of the greatest of all the Christian virtues.

In the third week, his normal routine in life appeared to reassert itself; and at about 9.30 p.m. he was again regularly to be observed walking fairly purposefully down the Banbury Road to one of the local hostelries. He has promised himself most faithfully that he will dramatically curtail his consumption of alcohol wef 1 November; which same day will also mark his permanent renunciation of nicotine.

In the meantime there is much work still to be done in the aftermath of the case – the aftermath of both cases, rather. And above all else in Morse's life there remains the searching out of Ellie Smith, since as a police officer that is his professional duty and, as a man, his necessary purpose.

www.panmacmillan.com